BEHIND CLOSED DOORS

Michael Donovan was born in Yorkshire but brought up in Lancashire where he still lives. A consultant engineer, this is his first work of fiction.

BEHIND CLOSED DOORS

MICHAEL DONOVAN

MOTH
PUBLISHING

First Published 2013 by Moth Publishing an imprint of Business Education Publishers Limited.

Paperback ISBN 978 1 901888 89 8

Ebook ISBN 978 1 901888 93 5

A CIP catalogue record for this book is available from the British Library.

Cover design by **courage**.

Printed and bound in Great Britain by Martins the Printers Ltd.

Moth Publishing
Chase House
Rainton Bridge
Tyne and Wear
DH4 5RA

www.mothpublishing.com

FOR ODETTE

siyempre

CHAPTER ONE

I was sifting paperwork one Monday morning, frozen by the northerly that leaked through my office window along with the racket of Westway traffic and commuter trains slowing into Paddington. My electric 2-bar was toasting my feet but making no impression elsewhere in the room, and the cold conspired with the distractions of a weekend's memories to impede concentration. I'd begun to sense a long day looming. Then my intercom kicked into life with an explosion of static that snapped me back to reality with the more immediate prospect of a cardiac.

The intercom is an eighties-vintage Motorola I'd picked up on Camden Market. It had come with some kind of short-circuit that blasted out static that drowned messages to the untrained ear. The thing was mostly used for coffee and sandwich orders. I'd had coffee and it was early for lunch so I figured that something was up.

Lucy waited a moment then repeated my name.

'Mr Flynn. Are you available?'

As if she hadn't watched me go into my office twenty minutes back with nothing more than a cup of coffee and a hazy expression. I grinned; it wasn't the pointlessness of the question it was the way Lucy could "Mr Flynn" me so you'd never imagine that the two of us had a history steamier than a Chinese laundry. The history was very old history but something still sparked. Lucy hung on to the desire to mother me even after she'd wrecked my life by ditching me. I put it down to guilt.

I had my Herman Miller chair tilted back at an awkward angle for business. I had to strain my abs to get my mouth to the intercom.

'What's up, Lucy?'

'There's a visitor to see you.'

'What visitor?'

'A Miss Bannister.'

'Do we have an appointment?'

'No.'

That tallied with my memory. We usually see clients by appointment only but I sensed an excuse to defer paperwork. 'How are we fixed?' I asked.

You'd barely notice the pause as Lucy offered to check my diary. Behind the static I heard the sound of blank pages turning.

'You're free, Mr Flynn.'

That tallied too. My excuse was on. I told Lucy to show our guest in and tilted myself upright, pushing a mess of paperwork aside.

Our visitor came through and stopped just inside the door. Lucy followed her in and I knew immediately that she was there to see my reaction. But I can be good at not reacting. My smile barely wavered. Lucy finally got the message and backed out, closing the door. My visitor still didn't move. Maybe it was the look that had replaced my smile. I needed to work on that customer-relations thing.

The girl was a kid. Six stones of nervous energy in pink Fred Perry trainers, trying to look adult and failing somewhere around the five-foot mark. Her face, behind a spiderwork of mascara, was something you might call sultry in a few years. Right now it just looked nervous. It was framed in a halo of streaked hair that looked like it had been through a mangler but had probably cost upwards of a hundred quid in Knightsbridge. The agency gets its share of odd callers but this kid was right out there. For a moment the thing threw me.

We could have stood gawping at each other all morning. But then a crackle on my desk distracted me and told me that someone was listening. I held up an apologetic finger and leaned across to kill the intercom. You do this by pulling out the mains lead. Then I looked up to see if I'd been dreaming.

No such luck. The kid was still there.

Her clothes had an agenda. Square-cut jeans slung low enough to give a peek of turquoise panties cinched into puppy fat below her navel. Up top a wash-shrunken red cami sported a logo of shattered letters that made you look where you shouldn't. The letters said *Come to Mamma*.

Mamma was fifteen. Or twelve. I couldn't say. The only certain thing was that she'd come in the wrong door. Eagle Eye was a detective agency. The girl looked like she wanted a nursery. I rebuilt my smile with a discouraging firmness and stood up.

'This is rather a surprise,' I said. 'Are you lost, young lady?'

Apparently she was. For the moment the girl's nerve seemed to have deserted her. Her eyes flicked around the office a couple of times before she drew in a breath and spoke.

'This isn't a detective agency?' she said.

I looked at her and held my smile. Asked what she meant.

Her eyes replied for her. She gave the place another gander. Instinctively I turned and gave the room the once-over myself. My office was not much but if I hadn't known about the dirty windows and the damp ceiling I wouldn't have noticed. When I looked back the girl was watching me. I turned my smile up and answered her question.

'Yes, we are a detective agency. Since you ask.'

Her face stayed dubious. She shrugged her shoulders.

'Yellow Pages said you were...' her eyebrows sought help, 'you know...'

I raised my own eyebrows.

'...a real agency?' she suggested.

'Real?'

'With detectives? Like the police?'

'We are,' I said. 'Ex-Metropolitan.'

Her confidence didn't seem to improve with the information. She was still looking at me like I was kidding her.

I checked the room again. Exaggerated my inspection. When I looked closer I could see that a few things needed fixing. More than a few. But nothing that said I should be listening to a snot-nosed kid critique the place. I turned back and opened my palms.

'This is us, young lady. We're happy with it.'

She still looked at me like I was kidding. Then she started to get bolder.

'Are the other agencies the same?' she asked.

'The same?'

Her eyes took another tour, expressing what it was the other agencies might be the same as. Again my eyes followed. The two of us had an act. I checked more carefully this time. Maybe I'd missed something. Maybe the wallpaper had restuck itself or the ceiling patch had dried. Maybe the dead potted plant had blossomed. But everything was normal. Kind of messy. I turned back.

'Yes, the other agencies are the same.' I grinned: 'But we've got the best detectives. That's why we're successful.'

'Successful?'

Charm was suddenly becoming a chore. I was still trying to guess what the hell had brought the kid in here but my main focus was on trying to figure why I was being suckered into idle chit-chat when I had work to do. I decided to move things along a little.

'What's your first name, young lady?' I asked.

'Sadie.' She stepped forward and held out a hand with phoney boldness.

I took it. It was the size of a doll's with half the grip. I held it gently and gave her my best advice.

'Sadie,' I said, 'you need to leave.'

She dropped my hand like it was greased. Got no resistance.

I stooped for the intercom lead to call Lucy back in. But the girl wasn't finished yet.

'Are you always this rude to clients?' she asked.

I turned. 'Sadie' I said, 'you're not a client. But if you were I'd be very polite indeed.'

She looked at me. Shook her head.

'Jesus Christ!' she said. 'I bet you're not real detectives at all.'

I kept my mouth shut as I reconnected the intercom. If the kid was trying to provoke me it wasn't going to work. Our short discussion was over. Any transient interest I might have had in what had brought her in here had evaporated. All that mattered was getting her back out.

The "real detectives" stuff stung though. I had a nasty idea. I went round to dig one of George Giannetti's business cards from my drawer. Giannetti was a detective in the sense that Jack the Ripper was a consultant surgeon. He operated out of a sub-let basement under an adult shop near Marylebone Station and took anything that fell through the cracks in the floor. Giannetti worked both sides of the line. Good guys, bad guys, he bled them all. I'd picked up a couple of his cards from the phone-boxes where he snared his less salubrious clients. His office was only a dozen blocks away. Sadie could be there in half an hour and it happened that I had an axe to grind with George. The girl wanted a real detective? Let her go mess up Giannetti's day! I dug through the chaos in my roll-top, but the girl wasn't waiting. Apparently she'd moved three laps ahead because suddenly she let me in on her decision.

'Okay,' she said. 'I'll hire you.'

That stopped me. I turned to look at her. Six years of Eagle Eye polishing its reputation, and finally our million-dollar client had arrived. I'd have to get Lucy to pull the champagne.

I didn't ask the girl about the "Jesus Christ" and the "not real detectives" stuff she'd been spouting thirty seconds back. Maybe that was just setting us up for a discount.

What I did was give her my brightest smile and wait for polite words to come. Sadie smiled back. Sultry changed to pretty. Even if her nose was pointy and her lips a little thin I knew that she was her mother's pride and joy. The kid had charm. What could I say?

'Young lady,' I said, 'you're out of your tiny skull.'

The smile vanished. Sultry came back. The girl had a range.

'What do you mean?' she asked.

'Crazy! Loco!' I did an act.

She stayed quiet for a second.

'Is there a problem?'

'A problem? Yes, there is a problem. The problem is that our clients are adults. Commissions are expensive. Like buying a house. We don't work with children. That's the problem.'

Must be something I said. Her mascara locked into a smouldering stare. She spoke slowly so that she didn't lose me.

'I'm not a child,' she said. Her eyes could have shattered diamond. 'And I know I have to pay. But hiring someone to snoop around is not like buying a house. All I want is someone to check on a friend of mine. I can pay. Just...don't try ripping me off.'

That was reasonable. Business acumen I could respect. What I couldn't respect was the snooping bit. Eagle Eye's surveillance methods are the best in the business. Even if we're sometimes sneaky that doesn't mean we snoop. I stayed with the specifics though.

'How are you going to pay?' I said.

She sighed, as if talking to pedantic fools dragged her day down.

'I've got a savings account,' she said. 'I can withdraw anytime.'

I laughed. 'Sadie,' I said, 'you'd better leave now.'

For I moment I though she'd realised that she was wasting her time. I wasn't interested in whatever crazy notion she'd brought up the stairs to Eagle Eye's door. Babysitting kids didn't pay our rent. And this kid was out on her backside. As of now. She was almost turning to go but suddenly she looked around the room again and puffed out a disdainful laugh. 'Fine,' she sneered, 'I guess you're too busy.'

Now we were getting cheeky. I'd have to ask Shaughnessy if we were too busy. I wouldn't mention the snooping bit though. The guy had feelings. But Miss Cutie Pants was still chipping away.

'Are you really a detective or not?' she said.

She looked like she knew the answer but I went ahead anyway.

'Yes,' I said. 'I'm what's called a private detective. A rather busy one, actually. Also – to repeat – our firm only deals with adults.'

'I'm seventeen,' she said. 'I am an adult.'

'Not by law,' I said. 'And you don't look seventeen.'

She rolled her eyes: 'Since when can an old guy tell anyone's age?'

'Old?' I rolled my own eyes. 'I'm thirty-eight, but I guess to you "old" is any boy with his own shaving kit.'

Witty. Not as witty as the way she lifted the side of her mouth. Words don't compete with the disdainful facials these teenaged girls dig out. The face told me everything she wanted to say.

'Thirty-eight,' I repeated, 'is not old. And seventeen is not adult. I'm sorry Sadie, this agency doesn't work for kids.'

My words finally seemed to get through. Her face dropped like the barometer on my office wall. 'That's the way it is,' I said gently. 'If you need investigation services you have to come here with an adult.'

Wrong words again. The barometer rebounded.

'There is an adult!' Her eyes took on a pleading look. 'She'll back me up!'

I knew before I opened my mouth again that this was a conversation I didn't want to have. Whatever was in this kid's mixed-up mind was nothing that could possibly interest Eagle Eye. Despite appearances, the firm actually was busy. I had work to do. Work that didn't include nattering to kids who happened to barge in off the street. I knew all this but I took the bait anyway.

'Back you up about what?' I asked.

'About my friend. She's disappeared.'

I smiled condescendingly. 'Disappeared? Since when?'

'Since a week ago.'

Finally I saw a look in the girl's face that passed for adult. It was fear.

I dropped my smile. Breathed a sigh, aware that I was wasting time on something of no possible interest to Eagle Eye. But there's an instinct all investigators share: the lure of the curious. We're like collectors rummaging through the shadowy corners of a bric-a-brac shop: we just can't resist intrigue when it pops up. I hesitated a moment then swung one of my club chairs around to face the other and told the girl to sit down. What was I? The Ghoul? All she needed was a quick heart-to-heart then I could feel good when I booted her out. She took my invitation and sat but kept most of her weight on her toes like she was watching for a bad move. I sat on the arm of the other chair and tried to look like I wasn't a bad-move kind of guy. Then I got involved in something I should never have touched.

CHAPTER TWO

'Tell me about your friend,' I said.

The girl stayed perched on the edge of the chair. Her fingers worked nervously through her hair.

'Her name's Rebecca Townsend. She's my best friend.'

'And Rebecca's not at home?'

She shrugged. 'I don't know. Her parents won't let me talk to her.'

'Why not?'

'They say she's ill.'

'That's reasonable,' I said. 'You don't want to catch a bug.'

The girl shook her head. Her toes danced on the threadbare carpet. 'They're lying. Becky was fine before she disappeared. We had lunch together. Then in the afternoon she was gone.'

'Gone how?'

'Didn't answer her phone. Didn't text. Didn't show up at college next day.'

'Did you call her house? '

'Yeah. They said she was ill.'

'Bugs strike suddenly.' Dr Reassuring.

'So suddenly that she can't even text me? Becky would text at her own funeral. And she's been gone a week now. It's like she never existed.'

'And her parents say she's ill?'

'They say she's got some kind of virus.'

'When did you last speak to them?'

'Yesterday. Every day. They just give me the same story. When I go round to the house they won't let me in.'

I gave her a grin. 'So you decided to sick a detective on them?'

This girl was cute. If I had a daughter she'd be like this. There were always people needed sicking. I clasped my hands and sat forward, gave her the let's-slow-down sigh that says everything's going to work out. This is your dad talking. Or, rather, your granddad.

'Sadie,' I said, 'if your friend's parents say she's ill then that's probably the case. You can't ask a detective agency to check them out. Why not believe them?'

Sadie closed her eyes like she was teaching a slightly stupid child its multiplication table.

'I told you,' she said. 'They're lying. Becky hasn't texted me in a *week*. Even if she was ill she'd do that.'

Sadie was sticking with this text thing. To teenagers, texting is breathing. If you're not doing it you're dead. The girl pushed her hands through her hopeless hair. The cami stretched to reveal more bare midriff. Mamma did a jig. I noticed that her navel was pierced with three gold rings that glittered above the pants. What were her parents thinking, sending her out like this? That wasn't my problem, though. I felt kind of sorry for the kid but I had reports to pull together, invoices to post. I needed to lead this thing towards an exit.

'Sadie,' I said, 'whatever's happening with your friend there'll be a simple explanation. No reason to hire an investigation agency.'

'So what should I do?' Her eyes were pleading.

'You should leave it to her parents. That's what they're for. Whatever the problem is they'll sort it out.'

'Not her father,' she said. 'Becky hates him.'

'I bet you hate your own parents sometimes.'

Her eyes flashed again. 'Are you listening at all?' she said. 'Something's wrong in Becky's house. Her father is a creep. There's things going on that Becky never even tells me.'

This was getting tackier by the minute. Time to change direction. 'What do your parents say, Sadie?'

'The same as you. That I shouldn't interfere.'

I raised my hands.

The girl's shoulders dropped. I don't know what fantasy had gone through her mind while she searched Yellow Pages, but there was no TV hero waiting to charge in to rescue her friend – who almost certainly didn't need rescuing in the first place. And I could tell Sadie was beginning to get a sense of things. She'd get the same answer at any other agency in town, except maybe George Giannetti's. But I decided that she didn't need Giannetti's card after all. Giannetti was exactly the guy to take her to the cleaners.

'Sometimes it's the families,' she said.

I looked at her.

'You read it in the papers. Kids abused, murdered. All along it's the parents. No one helps until it's too late. Teachers. Social workers. Police. They don't want to know.'

'Yes,' I said. 'But private investigators don't fill the gap.' Simple truth, even if saying it didn't make me feel better. 'You said there was an adult.'

She nodded. 'An old lady. She and Becky are kind of friends. Becky helps her around the house.'

'And this lady's spoken to you?'

'Yeah. She's really mad at Becky's parents. Says they need a good talking to.'

Kind of interesting. We were well into the shadows at the back of the bric-a-brac shop now. Despite knowing better I found myself rummaging.

'What's this lady's name?'

'Gina. Gina Redding.'

'Why exactly is Gina worried?'

'Same as me. Becky hasn't been in touch with her and her mother is giving her the cold shoulder.'

The thing sounded odd. But I knew there'd be an explanation. Eagle Eye wasn't in the social services business. Specifically, we didn't work for kids. We worked for clients with a little capital to back up their concerns. That's why I was going to have to show Sadie the door. Knowing my luck of course she'd be back in a week throwing the newspapers in my face. The ones with her friend's picture under eighty-point headlines. I made a decision. A quick chat with this lady friend would do no harm. I'd persuade the woman to talk to Sadie and maybe even to Sadie's parents. Then it was up to them to sort things out. I asked Sadie if she had a telephone number for Gina Redding.

The girl's eyes brightened. I realised that deep down she'd expected to get the brush-off anywhere she went. She'd just been on a fishing trip and Eagle Eye had been first on the hook. I was going to have to check that Yellow Pages wording again.

'You're taking the case?' she asked.

I sat back and laughed. Couldn't help it. Miss Comedienne. I got hold of myself and pulled my face back to discouraging.

'No,' I said, 'we're not taking the case. It's like I told you, Sadie. The agency only takes commissions from adults. What I'm going to do is talk to Mrs Redding. See if there's some advice we can give. Then the two of you will need to sort it out between you. Without involving detective agencies.'

Sadie didn't argue further. Opted for satisfied. She didn't have a telephone number but gave me an address on the south side of Hampstead Heath. She also gave me her own mobile number which

I wasn't going to need. Finally we were through. I stood up and she followed suit. I gestured and she moved ahead of me towards the door.

'One thing,' I said.

The girl turned.

'Thirties is not old,' I said. 'You'll be thirty yourself one day.'

She gave me her diamond smile.

'Sure,' she grinned. 'It's barely middle-aged.'

I gave her my best shit-eating grin and opened the door. Lucy was behind her desk watching us, desperate to hear what this was all about, but I decided that a little suffering was in order. She was the one who'd set the girl onto me. I asked her to show our guest out and by the time she got back I was locked behind my door, chasing paperwork.

CHAPTER THREE

I hunkered down behind my roll-top and attacked the paperwork again. I had a client-report for a sportswear chain that had hired us to watch one of its outlet managers. A second report for a private client: an airline pilot curious to know why his wife was always out when he called from halfway around the world. The sportswear chain got the evidence they were expecting and the airline pilot got something he wasn't. Another week's bric-a-brac to file away in the back of our shop.

I hit a button and the inkjet spat the reports out on agency proformas. Something tangible to deliver with the always-tangible final invoices. With luck the invoices might induce a transfusion into our bank account. Then we could be friends with our utilities companies, maybe even pay Lucy's wages. I couldn't remember if we were two weeks behind or three. Lucy handled that stuff. She brought her paycheques to sign when she knew they wouldn't bounce.

I filed the case folders, grabbed the reports and went out to find envelopes. Lucy was messing about at her desk. It was already after twelve and normally she'd be gone. Most afternoons we managed without a receptionist or accountant. Just me and Shaughnessy, in and out. I sensed her watching as I rooted in her stationery cupboard.

Lucy's got a way of watching you that gets you on your toes. Eventually you drop something or spill your drink and when you try to blame her she closes up her smart eyes and shrugs, as if fools are better tolerated than reprimanded. Lucy's got a pair of eyes would have any male acting the fool. Without the eyes she'd be just a punk who'd slipped in a dye factory. Her eyes made her a punk you wanted to grab hold of. For us the grabbing days were over but her looks could still trip me like a drunk's shoelaces.

Lucy quit pretending to tidy up and sat up on her desk watching me while I stuck on the address labels and stamped the envelopes. I stayed cool. Only two of the Queen's heads finished upside down.

'What's up?' I said.

'Has your intercom stopped working, Eddie, or am I going deaf?'

I gave her shocked. 'Were you trying to eavesdrop?'

'Someone has to look out for you.'

'What can I say?' I said. 'The intercom's shot. Maybe I'll just bug my office so you can listen whenever you want.' I slammed the stationery cabinet. 'Or did you already do that?'

'That's for you to find out. See how good you are.'

'You know how good I am.'

She looked at me. Her hair was so bright we could have saved on lighting. This month's colour was red.

I went back to switch off my computer. Her voice came after me.

'So what's the story on Miss Belly-Button?'

'Nothing's the story on Miss Belly-Button. She's seventeen. I sent her packing.'

'You took an awful long time to send her packing, Eddie.'

I came back out. 'She took a lot of persuading. I thought I was going to need a crowbar to get her out of the door. That's why I employ you, Lucy. To filter undesirables.'

'Is that what it says in my job description?'

'How do I know? I've never read your job description. Just ad-lib. Do what's needed.'

'Me neither.'

'Neither what?'

'Read a job description. And I was ad-libbing.'

I gave her a severe look.

'You sent her in on purpose? How did you know she wasn't dangerous?'

Lucy's eyes closed up again. 'Actually, Eddie, a hornet was what came to mind.'

I wagged a finger. 'I wonder about you, Lucy. After all these years I still wonder.'

'All these years, Eddie? You make us sound so old.'

I looked at her. Age was a touchy subject today. I gave her worried. 'How old do I look, Luce? No one would say middle-aged, would they? Be honest.'

'Better not,' Lucy said. 'You wouldn't like it.'

I gave her my shit-eating grin. 'Why did we ever split?' I asked.

'Because if we hadn't we'd have killed each other. Or you'd have had a heart attack. At your age.'

I chilled the grin. 'This isn't the way to get the story on little Miss B-B,' I said.

'So what is the way?'

'Come have lunch. I'll treat you to a sandwich and diet-something. Then we can find somewhere quiet to canoodle the rest of the afternoon, see if we can find some more interesting belly-buttons.'

Lucy's eyes stayed closed up. 'And what about your lady-love? What's she going to say about you eloping with the office girl?'

Arabel. Now there was a girl with plenty of belly-button. If I was worried about heart attacks that's where I'd start.

'You're right,' I said. 'We'll need to be finished by three.'

'We'd be pushed for time,' Lucy said. 'Better stick to the sandwich.'

Ever the practical one. But a sandwich sounded good.

Shaughnessy was out so I flipped the door sign as we left. The old-fashioned IN/OUT card behind the glass adds colour, even if the BACK SOMETIME SOON has as much credibility as a plumber's promise. We walked along the street to Connie's.

Connie Papachristou ran an eatery that served kebabs and sandwiches on home-baked bread two doors up. The weather was still too cold for his pavement tables so his customers were all squeezed into eight tables jammed down the side of the counter inside. We got the last table in the back and Connie came over to give the special attention warranted by his biggest tab. Connie always put on a good face but he was getting more uneasy by the month. If Eagle Eye went broke before we'd settled he'd go under. The way I saw it, since the problem was mostly caused by his extortionate prices in the first place, it was a case of what goes around comes around. Connie must have been hoping to even things up a little today because he took away a distinct frown in lieu of cash.

Lucy opted for a baguette and diet Coke whilst I went for a Mediterranean vegetable and feta cheese monster with a coffee, extra cream. When Connie brought the stuff over I filled Lucy in on our precocious visitor. The missing girl intrigued her.

'Are you going to take a look?' she asked.

I shook my head, mouth full of sandwich.

'I'm going to have a chat with this Redding woman,' I said. 'That's it. A kind of mercy thing.'

'For Sadie?'

'For me. The girl might come back. Remind me to write you a list of undesirables to keep out of our door.'

'Then we'd end up with no clients,' Lucy said.

Good point.

'So what's going on?' she asked. 'The thing sounds kind of strange.'

'Sure it's strange,' I said. 'But there's strange with money and strange without. We need the *with*-type. Helps pay your wages.'

'You don't pay my wages. Not for four weeks.'

Always the smart answer. Four already?

I kept quiet, waited for her to get back to the missing girl. Lucy kept quiet longer. I broke first.

'Lots of things are strange,' I said, 'until the blindingly obvious explanation turns up.'

'So what's the blindingly obvious explanation for this missing girl?'

'Haven't a clue. And I doubt if we're going to find out. This Redding woman will think I'm nuts coming to see her on some kid's say-so. She probably won't even talk to me.'

I got Directory Enquiries on my phone. They texted back a number. I hit return and dialled the old lady. If no one answered I'd call it quits.

Life isn't like that. The call was picked up on the first ring. A woman's voice, gravely and querulous at the same time. Not the kind of voice to be reassured by talking to a private investigator. So I identified myself only as a friend of Sadie Bannister and repeated what the girl had told me she had concerns for her friend.

If Gina Redding was surprised by the cold call she hid it well. Waded right in on the topic. In three seconds flat I was hearing what I didn't want to hear. Namely that there really was some kind of problem with this kid Rebecca. Suddenly we were jawing like she'd known me a hundred years. Wanted to know what we should do. We! Bang went my afternoon canoodling with Lucy. I shot Lucy a grin and told the old woman I'd drive over for a chat. Lucy looked smug as I cut the connection but I didn't rise to it. We finished our drinks and split before Connie worked up the nerve to ask for a donation. Lucy told me she'd see me tomorrow and headed home. I headed for my car.

CHAPTER FOUR

Sadie's story about Rebecca's elderly friend threw up a picture of a struggling pensioner misplaced into the millionaires' ghetto bordering Hampstead Heath. When I got to Hampstead I adjusted the picture.

Gina Redding's house was more like a mansion, a faux Lutyens crouched behind high walls on the south side of the Heath. The architecture was borrowed from the Garden Suburb but scaled up by three and with an acre of landscaped grounds thrown in. The place had to be keeping a platoon of gardeners in clover. Whatever way Rebecca was helping the old lady, weed-pulling didn't come into it.

I parked the Frogeye on white gravel and rang the doorbell.

I was half expecting a butler, but the door was opened by a stocky woman in her late seventies with eyeglasses ugly enough to be trendy.

The glasses were throwbacks to the sixties, which was probably where she'd got them. The woman popped a cigarette from her lips and blinked up at me.

I told her my name and handed her a card. She jabbed the fag back into her mouth and read it.

When she took in the *Private Investigator* her eyes opened. She looked up at me again and said she'd be damned if she'd ever met a private-eye. She invited me in whilst her smoke-lined tonsils coughed out a fog that could have derailed a steam locomotive.

We went through a walnut-panelled hallway to a lounge the size of my apartment and sat on a sofa bigger than my car. She was still damning herself and looking me up and down as we sat. I apologised if my call had mislead her about my identity – which had been the aim – but Gina waved it off. She wasn't shocked by me: it was the thought of Sadie hiring me. Proof it wasn't only me who thought the kid was crackers.

Gina's cigarette wagged like a conductor's baton as she took a lead from those forties crime films for private-eye etiquette and offered me a scotch. I gave her my teetotal smile. Said it was a little early. I asked how she knew Rebecca Townsend. My diplomatic way of asking why someone with all the appearance of serious money needed a girl helping about the house. Gina chortled and sucked her cigarette.

'Rebecca doesn't help in that way,' she said. 'That's just how it started. She came here two years ago as part of a voluntary initiative. Helping the needy of the borough.'

I couldn't stop myself from looking around the room and out through the french windows at a landscape that most people would call a park. It had to be some needy list! Gina chortled some more. She'd got the reaction she was after.

'Officially I was needy,' she said. 'I'd slipped and broken my ankle. I had my domestic covering extra hours while I was convalescing, but the local authority fools had put me on their list of vulnerable pensioners.'

'And Rebecca turned up to help?'

'Her school was involved in a volunteer scheme. Rebecca saw how things were the moment she walked in. But she was kind enough to do some little chores and we ended up talking. She was interested in my experiences.'

'Experiences?'

'Travel. I'm a retired doctor. Worked in third-world countries for twenty-three years. I only came back to Britain when I married. Exchanged poverty for affluence. Never really adjusted.'

The old lady looked pretty well adjusted to me, but I didn't argue.

'Rebecca always wants to hear about India and Africa. She's everything I was. More interest in the far side of the world than the far side of London.'

'So Rebecca's been visiting you for two years?'

'We hit it off, Mr Flynn. The home help thing was a sham but I hinted that if she wanted to call again I'd appreciate her doing a little reading for me. My eyesight's my only problem. Rebecca was happy to oblige. She's been coming ever since.'

'Sounds like a nice kid.'

'She is. Always happy to read for me or just to natter. She's here twice a week, hail or shine. The most dependable girl you could imagine.'

'Until now,' I said.

Gina's eyeglasses glinted behind the smog. She took a last suck and stubbed her cigarette.

'I don't know what happened last Wednesday,' she said. 'Rebecca phoned to say she'd be round after classes but she didn't turn up.'

'Did you try to contact her?'

Gina shook her head. 'Not immediately. She doesn't have to explain herself to me. I was just surprised that she hadn't let me know when her plans changed. Very unlike her. I only called two days later when I still hadn't heard from her.'

'No answer?'

'Her phone was off.'

'Did you try her house?'

'Immediately. I had the awful thought that she'd had an accident on her way to see me. I talked to her mother.'

'What did she say?'

'Well that's the strange thing.' Gina leaned forward. 'I couldn't put my finger on it, but Jean was prevaricating. First she said Rebecca was not in. Then when I mentioned about her not turning up two days earlier she became more specific and told me that her daughter was laid up with the flu.'

'She was contradicting herself.'

'Yes. And the flu thing was nonsense. I've worked with tropical diseases half my life and there's very few viruses can lay you out in just an hour or so. Certainly not the flu. It sounded to me like Jean was pulling the story out of thin air.'

The same suspicion as our little Sadie.

She told me the rest: she'd talked to Rebecca's mother three times since that day. Got the same story. No change in Rebecca's condition. Brusque answers bordering on rudeness so that Gina had to suspect there was a problem at the house.

'How well do you know the family?' I asked.

'Hardly at all,' Gina said. 'Rebecca doesn't talk about them. I've suspected that there's a problem there but I've never felt entitled to interfere.'

She gazed out over her gardens. 'What can I tell you? Rebecca's mother remarried five years ago. I don't know the details but it was not a happy change. There seems to be a tension now between Rebecca and her mother. And Rebecca has bad feelings towards her stepfather, Larry. It's nothing she's said outright but I sense hostility. I suspect that's why Rebecca keeps coming to me. She feels safe here. Wanted.'

The thing was going in the direction I'd anticipated. Family troubles. Probably a tear-jerker. But Eagle Eye weren't in the Kleenex business. I kept my eyes dry and asked about the girl's recent state of mind. Gina jabbed another cigarette into her mouth and flicked her lighter.

'Rebecca has been a little down,' she said. 'She split up with her boyfriend a month or so back. I got the impression she wasn't happy about other things too, but nothing she talked about. Oh, I could kick myself for not taking time to understand her better. Now this has happened I feel as if I've let her down.'

I asked Gina about Sadie.

'The Slaters have given Sadie the cold shoulder too,' she said. 'The two girls are the best of friends but I get the impression Jean has never been too keen on her. Wrong class and all that, which makes you wonder, considering Jean's own background. But since Rebecca was taken ill Jean won't let Sadie into the house. Unforgivable.'

I gave it a moment. Gina got to the bottom line.

'What do you think could have happened, Mr Flynn?' she asked.

'That's difficult to say,' I said, 'I guess something's not right.'

Just not the sort of thing Eagle Eye should get involved with. So I trotted out my spiel about how it would be good for Gina and Sadie to call at the Slaters' together. It might carry more weight than the individual approach. More particularly, it was something they could do without Eagle Eye. My suggestion was reasonable but Gina shook her head. She didn't buy it.

'I can't see them coming clean,' she said. 'The Slaters are taking a hard line with anyone poking their nose in. Poor Rebecca. What on earth are they hiding?'

I shook my head sadly. The sadness was mostly at the fact that Gina hadn't bought my suggestion. Even sadder that I had other business to attend to. I repeated my advice that they go to see the Slaters together and maybe talk to Sadie's parents, and that was my good Samaritan act over and done. We were through. I thanked Gina for her time and stood to leave.

Gina nodded and walked with me to the door, sighing heavily as she came along.

'It was good of you to call, Mr Flynn.' Her face was resolute. 'Who'd ever imagine young Sadie hiring a private investigator? I do like initiative in a young person.'

I kept quiet. Initiative is an over-rated virtue in my experience.

Gina was alongside me as we got to the door. 'I hope we haven't wasted too much of your time,' she said.

'Not at all,' I said. What mattered was how little more we could waste.

'I suppose I should ask.' Gina hesitated. 'Has Sadie incurred any charges?'

I kept my face straight.

'None,' I said. 'Initial consultations are free. I told Sadie that she was not old enough to engage our services.'

Gina was reaching for the door handle. She stopped short, thoughtful. 'Would there be anything you could do?' she asked. 'Hypothetically.'

'Hypothetically?'

'To check on Rebecca. Do you do that kind of thing?'

'Not exactly,' I said. 'We do some private surveillance work but it's usually on behalf of a family member. Suspicions of infidelity, that kind of thing. We wouldn't normally be brought in from outside the family.'

'I understand,' said Gina. 'But my nose tells me that the Slaters are hiding something bad. It may be none of my business but it would be a tremendous relief to know that Rebecca was safe.'

I looked at Gina and saw where this was going. She watched me right back until my mouth opened without permission.

'In theory,' I said, 'we could take a look. The fact is, though, that our firm is a little busy right now.'

'Of course,' Gina said. 'But maybe you might manage to squeeze something in. I'd be happy for you to do that on my behalf.'

At least she didn't say "snoop". One-up on Sadie. And Gina Redding had obvious liquidity. Two-up. I thought it through. Figured we could fit in a few hours. In this business many a payday is shored up by the penny-pullers. Jobs low on prospect but fast on cash.

And the thing had an intrigue. Why would a girl vanish with the apparent connivance of her parents? More puzzling, why were the Slaters covering it so clumsily? Why the believe-it-or-get-lost approach?

It was hard to see an explanation that was simultaneously both credible and innocent. When I found the credible and innocent explanation I'd kick myself. But maybe Gina Redding could do the kicking while we banked the cheque. I made a decision.

'We could make a few enquiries, Gina,' I said. 'As long as you understand that we'll probably find something very ordinary. You might wish you'd not put up the fee.'

'I'm sure there will be an innocent explanation,' Gina said. 'Then we'll all laugh about it. That's better than worrying.'

She had a point.

So, without knowing quite why, I agreed to take a quick look. We went back into the house and Gina wrote out a retainer cheque. I told her we'd mail the contract by return. I took five minutes to ask a few more questions about the Slaters. Finally I headed for the door again and promised to be in touch. We shook hands. Gina's grasp was shockingly firm.

'Gina,' I said, 'you're in good hands.'

'I'm entirely confident of that,' she said. 'I feel better already.'

That made one of us.

I drove back to Paddington, thinking over what I had.

Gina's info said that Rebecca's stepfather, Larry Slater, was co-owner of Slater–Kline, a high-street stockbroker in Islington. Business sounded good because even Gina rated the family as well-off. Apparently the Slaters had a nice house, nice cars and took nice holidays. The sort of stuff you get with nice money.

Rebecca's mother Jean was an ex-travel-rep who'd worked with one of the major package tour companies. Nowadays when they weren't holidaying she stayed at home and focused on the more esoteric challenges of the London social scene.

By Gina's account she'd made the transition to the higher stratum of London life a little more comfortably than Rebecca. Rebecca had been shunted into a North London girls' academy in line with her mother's aspirations after she remarried, coasted through three years at the top of her class and promptly transferred back to the West Kilburn College after her sixteenth birthday. Whether the purpose was to team back up with her friend Sadie or to cock a snoot at the pretensions of her mother and stepfather, Gina didn't know. She guessed a mix of both.

All in all, Gina's knowledge didn't amount to much. Hints of family secrets or of nothing at all. If there was something going on maybe I could turn up a few clues. More likely, the girl would turn up herself and we'd be off the case inside twenty-four hours.

If life was so simple I'd be on a beach.

CHAPTER FIVE

'Business is business,' I said.

Shaughnessy was behind his desk washing a late lunch down with mineral water from a cooler he kept in the corner. He gave me a lopsided grin.

'Are we going to end up with this Sadie kid under our feet?' he asked.

'You'll never meet her,' I assured him.

I needed this to be true. My street cred had felt fragile enough when I described the girl's assault on Eagle Eye. There was no way Shaughnessy was ever going to meet the vixen in the flesh.

'A couple of college girls,' Shaughnessy said. 'It's gonna be a tough one.'

'Yeah.'

'You know what these kids are like.'

'No.'

'We're going to have to watch our backs.'

I was watching his wall.

'So is something happening to this family?' Shaughnessy said.

'No,' I said. 'The girl's sick in her room or grounded for bad behaviour. Or packed away in an abortion clinic. Something they're not talking about, but nothing illegal.'

'So tell me again. Why are we taking Gina Redding's money?'

'Because despite my infallible confidence something smells.'

'What kind of smell?'

'A hunch kind of smell.'

'Hunch?' Shaughnessy coughed. 'I'd better write that down.'

'Sure,' I said. 'Like lunch. With an "H".'

I heard his ballpoint tapping on his notepad. There was a quiet moment before he conceded the point.

'The family's lying,' he said.

When Shaughnessy's gut feeling lined up with mine we knew we were on to something. Miss Brassy-Button had tossed us something that fitted mundane like the Mayor of London fitted diplomatic. Teenaged girls don't disappear completely behind their own front doors. Not the modern girl armed with her preloaded Samsung. Jean Slater's flu story had a credibility gap a mile wide. And Gina Redding's retainer gave us the incentive to take a peek.

Shaughnessy snapped his notebook closed with *Hunch* or *Lunch* written down. You sensed the case building.

'How are you going to play it?' he said.

'I'll start at the Slater house. See if anything's out of kilter there. Then we'll try some digging.'

I was meeting a client in West Hendon at four. That would leave me a stone's throw from the Slater home at the top of Hampstead Heath. I'd detour through on the way back. Pick up some first impressions.

'If you need help,' Shaughnessy said, 'just call.'

'I'll do that.'

'These kids...' he repeated.

'If it gets dicey I'll text you,' I said.

'I'll keep the line open.' He pointed to his mobile on his desk so I knew where it was.

I took note. 'Are we through?' I said.

'Guess so,' said Shaughnessy.

I left him and went to meet my West Hendon client.

I was running late but midafternoon traffic was light on the Edgware Road. I put my foot down to catch up.

I got off the North Circular a little before four and followed signs that took me through an industrial park and brought me to a haulage depot with a gate sign that displayed the name HP Logistics. My client was the owner, a guy named Harold Palmer. He'd not given much over the phone other than that he had some urgent work.

The depot was housed in a defunct machine-tool factory, constructed of dirty yellow brick with inset mesh-reinforced windows. The building had been converted to a warehouse, with offices and an HGV maintenance shop at one end. Out beyond the loading bays I could see tractor units parked up.

The depot was secured by twelve-foot mesh topped with razor wire and cameras, but the uniformed pensioner who hobbled out of the gate-house notched the image down to Dad's Army. With twenty thousand square feet of transit warehouse behind the wire I figured they'd use a different crew at night. While the pensioner checked a clip-board I watched a solid guy with a razor cut and dark glasses watching me from inside the office. This one looked more the part. His shirt-sleeved stance and calm observation suggested someone who maybe ran Palmer's security. The pensioner ticked my name and sent me through.

I parked in a visitors' spot at the side of the maintenance shop. A metal door opened onto a flight of stairs that climbed into the upper reaches of the building and summited at a door that swung outwards, threatening to knock you all the way back down. Beyond the door the corridor dog-legged into a reception area fronting a sixty-by-thirty office. A dozen clerks with headsets jabbed at keyboards under spitting fluorescents in a working environment that suggested high staff turnover. The reception desk was manned by a fifteen-stone woman whose main purpose seemed to be to frighten callers back down the stairs. She continued battering her keyboard without noticing me. Either her job description said to ignore visitors or she'd already marked me as a nobody, the way a good waiter knows the lower-class diner.

When she finally looked up it was with the welcoming expression of a boar disturbed at its toilet. The look was enhanced by a fretwork of frown lines that would have made a rhino swoon.

I announced myself and Rhino ran a finger down a desk diary and told me I was six minutes late. I didn't ask if this included the two minutes she'd had me on hold. We just skipped the small talk. She pressed a button and spoke my name, then waved me at a door and I went through to see the boss.

Harold Palmer was a big man behind a bigger desk. The flesh I could see above the surface, combined with my knowledge of icebergs, put him at close to twenty stone, with a face hardened by decades of clawing for market-share in the trucking business. More of the company policy for warm welcomes: Palmer skipped the handshake. He just gestured towards a collection of chairs by the door. I walked back to grab one. The office space would have made a city tycoon agoraphobic, but the bare walls and metal cabinets said that Palmer hired cheap when it came to interior designers. Not a potted plant or sales chart in sight. What did get my attention were the panoramic windows that gave him a god's eye view over the maintenance bays on one angle and the warehouse on the other. The maintenance window showed two Volvo units being serviced down below. The glass was single-glazed to let the din of air tools through. Muzak for the trucking business.

My seating choice was between a couple of wooden chairs that made me wonder if a church hall was missing furniture or a frayed leather swivel that was mostly lumps but had the benefit of castors to save me from lifting. I rolled the swivel out in front of Palmer's desk. The seat was convex and slippery. Balancing took muscle and gave you the body language of Quasimodo. If Palmer found me ridiculous he kept quiet. He seemed to be concentrating on something bad he'd eaten. At least he didn't tell me I was late. He paid his receptionist for that. Palmer looked at me for a moment then opened the discussion.

'I hear that Eagle Eye are discreet,' he told me.

He stressed our name as if it was the known practice of all other agencies to shout their clients' business from the rooftops. But his puzzled look let me know that he wasn't convinced about his information.

I smiled and kept quiet. With that kind of opener it was best for the client to talk.

'I have some business that needs absolute discretion,' Palmer said. 'Can I trust your agency?'

No idle chat about the challenges of the trucking business. No mention of who had put in the good word for Eagle Eye. Not even a polite query about which partner he was talking to. Palmer was sticking to the simple fact that this whole thing was giving him indigestion.

'What can I do for you, Mr Palmer?'

Palmer pulled a pack of kingsize from his jacket and lit up. Apparently he was running the last bastion of pro-smoking policy in London. It was my second dose of the afternoon. The amount of fug I was inhaling today I'd soon need a respirator to work. Palmer took a drag and blew out a cloud.

'I've got a sensitive matter needs attention,' he said.

'How sensitive?' I said.

'Big bucks sensitive. If you do the job right I'll pay.' He watched me from behind the cloud. 'I'll go triple your standard.'

He waited for me to be impressed. Private investigators don't come cheap, and Eagle Eye are not at the bargain-basement end of the market. That's why no one had ever offered us three times our rate. What people usually offer, when we present our commercial rates, is an awed silence.

The same as in a good lawyer's office. Private clients – like Gina Redding – get sixty percent discount. The differentiation lets us cover the market.

Palmer gave me time to go over what we had. So far we had discreet and we had reliable and we had three times the going rate. The ingredients of a perfect deal. So perfect that I knew straight away that it was going to fall apart. It would unravel the second Palmer described the nature of his sensitive issue. I saw it a mile off.

Palmer heaved himself from his desk and dragged a smoke trail over to the panoramic window, did his God bit watching over his warehouse. You could see he was proud of his view the way City types love the strip of river they get with their corner office. He sucked on his weed for thirty seconds like I wasn't there, contemplating his empire.

'We're bidding for a haulage contract,' he said finally. 'The tender closes at the end of next week.' He did a ninety and strolled along the other glass to watch his crew down in the maintenance bays. He was talking to the glass but his voice had an edge that said I'd better be listening.

'The client is a clothing wholesaler relocating from Birmingham. They're opening a warehouse here in Wembley. They run their own logistics but they don't own their fleet. They wet-lease thirty units to cover their European and UK distribution.'

'Wet-lease?' I said. The thing sounded like some kind of rainy-day service.

Palmer left his window and orbited back to his desk. He sat down and stubbed the cigarette in a steel ashtray. He looked at me and decided I really didn't know what wet-leasing was. He leaned forward to educate me.

'We supply the trucks, maintenance, drivers and fuel. The client pays a retainer and a straight mileage charge. He says where we go and when, controls the schedule. It's the most efficient way for some businesses to run their logistics. More flexible than owning a fleet. Cheaper than paying ad hoc haulage.'

He stabbed a finger in the direction of the haulage world beyond the panoramic window. 'For a number of reasons,' he said, 'we need to land that contract.'

'A number of reasons?'

'A number of reasons,' he confirmed.

'How many trucks do you operate?' I asked.

'We run fifty container trailers. A few bulk carriers and vans. Our main business is container.'

'So this contract would cover most of your fleet.'

'For two years,' he said.

'That would be a good contract.'

He gave me a kind of smile. I had it.

'So what's the problem?'

'The problem,' he said, 'is that we have to win the contract.'

He stayed silent, watched me take this in. I was wondering how much of HP Logistics had been built on legitimate operations. I recognised Palmer's type.

'What,' I asked again, 'can we do to help?'

He waited a moment, like he was deciding whether to bring me in or kick me out. Decided to go with the risk.

'There are three firms bidding,' he said, 'including us. The way the client works is they contract to the second-lowest bidder. They don't want to pay high prices but it's essential to avoid the vendor who's under-bidding. He's the one who will let you down when he can't deliver.'

Seemed logical.

'In this particular case,' he said, 'we believe that all three bids will meet the key operating requirements. So the selection will come down to price.'

'The second lowest,' I said.

He nodded. 'The middle of the three gets the job,' he said.

'So,' I said, 'ideally speaking HP Logistics would be the middle bidder.'

Palmer's expression switched to surprise, as if he'd only just though of that one. Then he sat forward and dropped his fist gently on the desk.

The smile came back. I'd got it again.

'We need to be the middle bidder,' he said. 'Funny how simple life is.'

I though about this.

'So what you need,' I extrapolated, 'are your competitors' prices. Before you put in your own bid.'

The smile held. We were moving together on this.

'And you want Eagle Eye to get that information,' I concluded.

Palmer's smile broadened. He raised his palms. Simple as that. 'I need you to get that information,' he said, 'fast. I want those bids on my desk by this weekend.'

'So,' I said, 'we burglarise these competitors and steal the information.'

Palmer's smile chilled. I sensed disillusionment stirring. A creeping suspicion that he'd gone with the wrong risk.

'We don't steal anything,' he said. 'I just want you to copy the key figures and get them to me. So we can finalise our bid.'

I had it. A little break-in at his competitors' offices. Find out what their tender prices are. Quietly. So no one knows that HP Logistics' bid is rigged. And for this discreet operation Palmer was offering three times Eagle Eye's going rates. There was only one fly in the ointment.

'Rigging bids is illegal, Mr Palmer.'

Palmer's face transitioned to certainty. His instinct had been right. He'd gone against his gut feeling and gambled wrong. His expression was granite.

'Sometimes you have to bend the rules a little in this business,' he said quietly.

I gave this some consideration then explained Eagle Eye's policy.

'I'm sorry, Mr Palmer,' I said. 'We don't do illegal stuff.'

Palmer watched me. His expression remained stony but a fuse was lit. Suddenly he leaned forward like he wanted to come over the desk.

'Illegal?' he hissed. 'Am I hearing you right? Are you shitting me?'

We continued to lock stares while he tried to figure out just how big a blunder he'd made.

'Since when did legal come into it? ' he said. 'All you guys play behind the rule book.'

'Not Eagle Eye,' I said.

Palmer watched me a moment then threw out a laugh like a Volvo backfiring. He pointed a fat finger.

'So you're Flynn,' he said. 'The ex-filth. I knew it the moment you walked in. Smelled it a mile off.' He rocked back in his seat and shook his head. 'Half the private dicks in this city are Met failures,' he said, 'but not many of them have the gall to squeal about legalities. Coppers are the most bent people I know.'

'You don't know me,' I pointed out.

I wasn't smiling myself. Maybe the sound of the triple-fee bubble popping had spoiled my mood. I'd known the bubble was going to burst but that didn't make it easier. At least as commissioning interviews went this was short and sweet, because I was through.

I slid off the swivel chair and wheeled it back to the wall. Palmer waited until I reached the door.

'Sure I know you,' he yelled. 'I did my homework. I made sure I knew what kind of a fuck-up I'd be hiring. And I found it was the worst kind. The high flyer who thinks he's God right up to the day they cut his strings. How does it feel, Flynn? King of the rubbish dump.' I heard him getting up from his desk behind me.

'You're as bent as any copper I ever met,' he said. 'But my information said that your agency was the best. Name your price. I'll pay it. Only don't give me pious, Flynn. Pious gives me acid. I never met an ex-filth yet who didn't have his price!'

I had the door open. I should have walked out. I shouldn't have been listening to any of this. Instead I turned back and wheeled the swivel chair out from the wall again.

Palmer laughed and slapped his desk.

I picked the swivel up. The thing weighed an absolute ton. You get hernias that way. I saw Palmer's eyes pop as I heaved my shoulders and launched the chair. It went through the panoramic window as if it was paper, showering glass down onto the bays. Palmer was charging round his desk like a scalded walrus, but his tonnage was against him. By the time he'd got half way across the room I was out of the door and down the stairs.

It looked like Harold's acid tablets were going to take a hit today.

CHAPTER SIX

My business acumen had shaved forty-five minutes off my schedule, which meant that the North Circular was still moving when I exited the depot. I drove north-east and took the Golders Green turn-off.

The Slater home was a two-storey Spanish villa facing woods in a cul-de-sac south of the golf course. Ten-foot hedgerows hemmed the roads in like the avenues of a maze, testifying to the area's premium on privacy. Luckily the Slaters preferred their wealth to be visible. Their house stood open to the road behind a fir-shaded lawn circled by a curving driveway that serviced triple garage doors. There was nothing parked. No sign of life. I spotted an ivy-covered substation set into the trees fifty yards back along the lane. Fibre optics were going down in the area and a ten-foot cable drum on the station parking area gave me cover. I reversed the Frogeye alongside the drum and settled in with a view of the house.

The lane was quiet. Ditto the Slater house. I tuned in to LBC and listened to two hours of regurgitated headlines and traffic nightmares. Sometimes you learn just by waiting and watching. Sometimes you get nothing. In two hours only three vehicles passed me, heading for properties further in. One was a Porsche with a forty-something woman at the wheel. The two others were high spec Mercs that whispered by as the light faded. I glimpsed shirt-sleeved execs behind tinted windscreens.

Around seven o'clock thick cloud drifted over the trees behind me and killed the last of the light. In response, the glass around the Slaters' front door lit up. Someone was home. But the rest of the house stayed dark. I waited another fifteen minutes and decided to call it a day. I'd evaporated two and a half hours of Gina Redding's money without even dipping my toe. Looked like we'd been lumbered with the quietest family in the city.

Just as I reached for the choke another car came up the lane and passed in a silent rush. A light metallic Lexus, its driver invisible. Fifty yards on the Lexus turned into the Slaters' driveway and swung round in front of the garage. When the driver got out the light and distance worked against detail but I got an impression of a tall, casually-dressed man. No business suit. No briefcase.

The man was expected. The house door opened before he reached it and a woman's figure held it while he entered.

No embrace. No welcome home. The man strode past without any sign he'd seen her. The door closed and the show was over. Maybe affection was not the Slater family strong point. Assuming these were the Slaters.

On a hunch I flipped the radio to a music station and waited another thirty minutes.

Bad hunch. The guy didn't reappear. The house looked like it was settled in for the night. The family were probably sat around *EastEnders*, or maybe Father was helping Rebecca with her studies while Mother worked at her embroidery. Blissfully unaware that they had London's hottest detective sitting on their doorstep.

Life is spooky.

At seven thirty I gunned the engine and left them to it.

I reviewed what I'd achieved. Distilled it down to having avoided the rush hour. Not something to trivialise. I headed towards Cricklewood, killed the radio and slotted in a Gil Evans tape. Added my own rendition to the opening of 'Little Wing'. Drops of rain hit the windscreen. Drizzle turned into a downpour. I pulled in for petrol on the Edgware Road. The rain sparkled like crystal beyond the fluorescents as I pumped unleaded and watched the traffic, listened to the breath of the city hissing on wet tarmac. I was back in Battersea by eight twenty and Lady Luck combined with the Frogeye's dimensions to get me a parking space outside my apartment. When I climbed the stairs I detected more luck. An aroma of fried chicken and paprika was emanating from my doorway. I wasn't expecting visitors. Maybe my fairy godmother had dropped in. I hoped she'd cooled the beer.

Instead I found Arabel in the kitchen. I'd known it wasn't my fairy godmother. That old crone had left home when I was six and hadn't shown her sorry backside since. Luckily, Arabel's backside made a spectacular substitute. I walked up behind her and got reacquainted with it to the extent possible when the owner is holding a frying pan that's erupting like Vesuvius.

'Nice surprise,' I stated. Arabel turned her head too quickly and caught my eyes on the pan instead of her. Pushed her rear against me in what was meant as a fend-off but had the opposite effect.

'Hey, babe,' she yelled, 'you're gonna be wearing this chicken.'

I wasn't sure what she was offering but I backed off. She returned the pan to the gas and turned to fend me off some more. When we got our lips unglued she gave me a big 'Wow'. And that smile.

Wow!

'Thought you were working,' I said.

'Someone asked a favour. Swapped for an early next week.' Her skin was golden in the kitchen spots. The gold comes from mixing Anglo-Saxon and West Indian. I don't know what mix had produced her brown-speckled eyes. They were pure Caribbean warmth – the thing I loved most as long as I kept a weather-eye for the tropical storms. Arabel got my arms untangled from her body, changed her mind and tangled them back. Her eyes were closed. Mine stayed on the frying pan. When Arabel realised that the saliva she was drowning in had nothing to do with her she broke the clinch, told me to go freshen up.

'You nearly missed the feast, Flynn,' she said. 'Stir-fry doesn't reheat.'

Flynn.

It's what she calls me. Nothing impersonal - Arabel just comes from a generation that likes their names backwards. I wondered about age again. I'd never considered thirties old until my encounter with Miss Prissy-Pants this morning. But when I thought about it I realised that Arabel was halfway back to Miss P-P's age. Made me wonder why a twenty-seven-year-old was cooking my dinner. Then I looked at Arabel and I knew why she had my front door key. A man has no way of defending himself against a girl like that. I swear I'd tried.

I showered and scurried back to the aroma of paprika and cayenne mixing with hot chilli. Arabel served the chicken on a green salad with a homemade dressing that was heavy on honey. We sat at the table overlooking the street and a basket of wholemeal rolls emptied fast between us.

We talked about things and swigged Grolsch to cool the chilli. I told Arabel about my missing girl. She was all ears – still found private investigation romantic even though her instinct must have been screaming that this was not a good profession in a guy. While she listened she attacked her chicken like she was on the run between shifts. With Arabel meals were a metaphor for life. Take what's offered before the plate gets snatched. She finished ahead of me and sat back with her Grolsch. Came back to the missing girl.

'You think there really is something funny going on?' she asked.

'There's always something funny going on,' I said. 'The longer you do this job the more you realise that there's no one leads a simple life.'

'Some people must.'

'No one I ever met.'

'What about us?'

I gave her incredulous.

'Relatively,' she said.

'Relatively,' I agreed. 'But we're probably the only people we know who aren't trailing skeletons around in their closet.'

Arabel's eyebrows raised. 'How do you know I've got no skelingtons, babe?'

'Your skeletons would have left years ago,' I said, 'to save wear and tear on their bones.'

She threw me a look.

'So how about you, Flynn? How do I know you've no boneyards? Since you never tell me anything.'

I stopped with my fork in mid-air. Looked at her.

Good point.

'You don't know,' I said softly.

She watched me with those eyes, letting the point smoulder.

'I just wonder sometimes,' she said.

I broke the stare first. 'My skeletons are buried,' I told her. 'Six feet under. Better leave them in peace.'

I concentrated on clearing my plate but she was still watching.

'Sometimes it's better to know, Flynn. Even the bad stuff.'

'That's what my clients say. Till they hear the bad stuff.'

I downed the Grolsch to souse the spices. The chillies gave the beer an edge. Brought out the sweetness of the fermentation and sent the liquid down my throat like a spring stream.

'Sometimes,' I said, 'I wouldn't recognise my own skeletons if they came knocking on the door.'

I reached under the table and gave the wood a good loud rap. Arabel jumped a mile and spilled her beer, cursed me. Ended up laughing but her eyes were darting. She cursed me some more and swigged the rest of her Grolsch to steady her nerves.

'What's your guess?' she said. 'Has the girl run away? Is she in danger? Is the family hiding something?'

'Any of those,' I said. 'Or all. Or nothing. Who knows?'

Her eyes opened wide. 'Sounds like you've almost closed the case.'

'The biggest part of closing a case is knowing how to open it,' I said. 'Head off in the right direction and you're as good as home. You just listen and watch, tug a few lines and see which tug back.'

The trouble was that the tugging usually started with inside information. This time I was outside, looking at a family who had declared that there was no problem. Maybe there wasn't. Just Sadie Bannister's overactive imagination and the fears of a lonely pensioner. Leaving us to disprove a negative. Arabel asked the question that I'd been asking.

'How you gonna start?'

'I'll figure something,' I said. 'Tomorrow.'

Tomorrow would bring inspiration. Of that I was sure.

CHAPTER SEVEN

I was up before six and went out in the dark to run three laps of the park. As I pushed myself hard along the river the needles of rain that stabbed my face told me that this must be healthy. In the investigation business it pays to keep ahead of the ageing process – or ahead of the self-destruct process, in my case. If I ever relaxed, I knew that the gremlin that grinned at me from the other end of my lifestyle see-saw would come scampering across and devour me.

Thirty-six minutes was my standard for three circuits. Slower was a sign that the gremlin was sliding my way. Today I managed forty, blamed the weather, and staggered back to my front door with health oozing from every pore. My legs didn't give way until I was half way up the stairs.

I showered and swallowed a pint of orange juice, crammed sliced ham into wholemeal rolls. I dug out my old briefcase and dropped the rolls inside, then went to the bedroom and stooped to kiss the duvet under which I'd last seen Arabel. The duvet didn't move. I picked up my Burberry and headed out.

When I turned the Frogeye onto Battersea Bridge at just before seven the tingle of blood sluicing through clear veins rewarded me for my fortitude. A mid-river burst of sunlight lifted the morning. The wind was still gusting but the rain had stopped.

I cranked the radio up and beat the traffic through Chelsea and Kensington, headed north towards Hampstead. By seven twenty I was parked up in my substation fifty yards from the Slater house, ready for a second look.

The house was quiet and dark. The Lexus hadn't moved. I tuned in Capital and listened to a mixture of rap and news headlines while the clock crept towards eight.

Just after seven thirty the two Mercs from up the lane headed out towards the City. There was a lull until the post van drove by at eight fifteen and dropped mail at the Slaters' and the properties further up. Five minutes later it returned in convoy with a four-by-four driven by a woman with a child perched illegally in the front seat. Next action was eight twenty-three when an elderly woman walked up the lane to domestic duties further in. Then nothing for another half hour. The Slaters' front door stayed shut like it was Sunday morning.

It looked like Larry Slater didn't follow the twelve-hour city routine. Maybe a perk of running your own business. Let someone else open up. Nine o'clock and still no action. No sign of the girl heading for college either. Rebecca Townsend was either indisposed or not there.

At nine fifteen the door finally opened and Larry Slater came out. He wore a leather jacket and an open-collar shirt. He fired up the Lexus and rolled by me without a glance. His casual garb didn't exactly say City stockbroker. I was intrigued but stayed put. The most important information was right here at the house: was Rebecca Townsend home in bed like her parents said?

I tuned in Radio Four and ate my sandwich rolls, allowing Larry Slater forty minutes to fight through traffic. Then I pulled a number from directory enquiries and dialled his company, Slater–Kline. The call routed to a computerised pitch that some delusional had worked up to keep customers entertained while you stalled them. Between bursts of muzak the spiel assured me that my call was deeply valued. After five minutes even the computer was sounding unsure. I was about to hang up when the line was finally picked up. A bright female voice asked how she might help me. The brightness was that of someone who hasn't just endured five minutes of muzak brainwashing. I asked for Larry Slater.

'Mr Slater's out right now,' Brightvoice said. 'May I help?'

'No,' I said, brainwash-brusque. 'I'll catch him when he's back in. Do you know what time that will be?'

Brightvoice told me she didn't know exactly and offered to take a message.

'An hour?' I guessed. 'Shall I try at eleven?'

'I'm sorry,' Brightvoice insisted. 'Mr Slater is out on business. We're not sure when he'll be in. Did you have an appointment? We're rearranging some of his schedules today.'

I told her I didn't have an appointment, said I'd ring back, and cut the line before she could ask questions I didn't want to answer.

So Slater was not in the office. And schedules were being rearranged. A priority business client? Or had Slater just left it till the last minute to tell them he wasn't turning up?

I settled back to watch the house, wondering if I should have tailed the Lexus. But if I'd been tailing Slater I'd have been worrying that I should have stayed at the house to find out whether the girl was home. The endless neuroses of private investigation.

As surveillances went this threatened to be a slow mover. Conventional surveillance (what Smarty-Pants called *snooping*) is typically away from home – tailing rogue husbands and the like. Less often it involved watching for house calls whilst said husband was away. This one was different: I was entirely on the outside. I had to get in.

At ten fifteen I slid out of the car. I donned my Burberry and pulled my briefcase from the Sprite's footwell. Then I walked up the road and rang the Slaters' doorbell.

The chimes brought no response. I tried a second time. Still nothing. I leaned on the button.

The message finally got through.

The woman who opened the door was the one I'd seen the night before. Tall and good-looking, late thirties. Classic high cheeks and ocean-blue eyes. She would have been beautiful without the fatigue. She looked at me with a clamped mouth that showed no sign of starting a dialogue. Her best effort was an indifference that barely papered over her impatience to close the door.

Her lassitude helped gloss over the rudimentary ID I held up. The ID was one of an inkjet stock conjured up by our part-timer Harry Green. The card was designed to look as official as possible whilst remaining sufficiently generic to fit most bills. The trick was the heavy use of acronyms and meaningless titles with words like *authority* and *registered association*, plus a few machine-readable numerals and a generic logo. Add a geeky-looking photo of yourself, encase the lot in plastic and your legitimacy will never be challenged. Most people wouldn't recognise the name of their utilities provider, much less the subcontractor who reads the meter. When police recommend that you check visitors' IDs they don't tell you that the con men have the best of the lot.

Jean Slater was not in a perceptive mood. She glanced at my ID for two seconds then looked at me for the explanation. I gave her the name on the card and made up something about the Local Education Authority.

'Just a routine call,' I said. I checked a clipboard I'd pulled from my briefcase: 'This is Rebecca Townsend's home?' I looked up.

Jean's eyes widened briefly then her expression clouded into a look that said she wanted me gone, whatever my business. She pulled herself together to deal with the situation. Forced herself to frown more convincingly.

'What's this about?' she said.

'Nothing official,' I assured her. 'May I come in?'

She thought about it. Lacked the resolution to refuse me. She stepped back and held the door open. I walked in. Easy.

I held out an official hand. Repeated my false name and apologised for intruding. Jean's hand was clammy. No suggestion of a grip. The handshake is another con man's trick. Confers legitimacy to even the most outrageous of cold calls. If I wasn't in investigation I could have been a top-notch insurance salesman.

I asked Jean how Rebecca was.

Jean stayed puzzled but she answered me. 'Fine,' she said.

I saw that she was close to asking questions I didn't want her to ask. I gave her my most reassuring smile and headed her off.

'It's nothing official,' I repeated. 'We try to follow through on students who are away from college.'

'That's unusual,' she said. Her frown deepened but she didn't have the willpower to disbelieve me. I was there in her house so I must be proof of the Education Authority's concern.

'Perhaps you're familiar with our "Access to Education" policy,' I suggested. 'One if its tenets is that we offer assistance to students who are detained by medical factors for more than five consecutive college days. If I understand,' another glance at my empty clipboard, 'Rebecca has been absent for eight days. That makes her eligible for home assignments prepared by her course tutors.'

The spiel sounded dodgy even to me. I sensed the suspicion wavering behind Jean Slater's eyes and moved quickly on.

'It depends, of course,' I extemporised, 'on the student's condition and inclination. How can I put it?' I used the cover of a thoughtful gaze to get a quick look around the place. The entrance hall was designed to impress visitors whose own lives were dedicated to impressing others. A square two-storey space with green and gold wall fabrics that would have outpriced the carpets in my apartment by a factor of ten. And the carpet here was an Axminster you could have run a combine harvester through. The Axminster ran back towards distant doorways and curved seamlessly up twin oak-banistered staircases to right and left. The stairs came together at the top to feed a gallery that crowned the grand entrance. Everything was Ideal Home perfection. No dropped coats or bags. No shoes in the corner. No domestic appliances. The only item out of place was a half-empty wine glass Jean had dumped on the Italianate telephone stand as she scurried to the door. Maybe the slight thickening in her voice was more than fatigue. It looked like our devoted mother was an early starter.

My pause left the house deadly quiet. When I looked back, Jean Slater's eyes were locked on me. I went back to my spiel.

'If it helps your daughter,' I explained, 'we can authorise home assignments in lieu of regular coursework. Reduces the risk of her falling behind. Everything is her decision, of course.'

My little speech seemed to settle Jean. She smiled a little and hunched up her shoulders with a kind of helpless understanding.

'Of course,' she said. For the first time her eyes opened with something like confidence. The realisation that she would soon have me out of the door. 'Unfortunately Rebecca is convalescing from a rather bad virus. She's sleeping most of the time. There's no way she could take on any academic work.'

I gave her my gravest smile.

'Of course. Perhaps a short chat with her? She could let me know if she'd like anything preparing for when she feels up to it.'

Jean shook her head emphatically. 'That won't be possible,' she told me.

'I would take just five minutes,' I assured her.

'No.' Her eyes were harder now. She looked at the ID I'd clipped onto my Burberry and I sensed that she was drawing herself up to ask questions.

I backed off. 'Fine, Mrs Slater, we'll trust to your judgement. You know your daughter best. If she is not up to it I'll not impose. Perhaps I should call in a couple of days?'

'No.' She shook her head again with wine-assisted vigour. 'Rebecca is staying with my sister in Berkshire. She'll be there another week. And

I'm sure she'll pick up quickly when she gets back to college.' She gave me a smile that didn't quite make it. 'I'll mention your visit. If there's anything she needs then she'll get in touch.'

'Marvellous!' I gave her my most brilliant smile to mark this tremendous achievement. We'd sorted the problem wonderfully. I waxed lyrical as I handed over a generic card and told her to make sure that Rebecca asked for me personally when she called, although it was unlikely she'd get me or anyone else on the card's number. I threw in a few more best wishes for her daughter's recuperation and let Jean shepherd me back out of the door. As she held the door wide, her smile was so bright that you almost missed its insincerity.

She certainly missed mine.

I walked back down the lane in bright sunlight, sweating under the Burberry. At the substation I ditched the coat and pushed it back into the Frogeye's tiny boot. Then folded myself into the tiny seat.

Time for a meeting I didn't relish. My fingers actually hesitated on the keypad. But I needed information. I made the call.

I pushed in a Claire Martin tape and cranked up the volume to fill the Frogeye with her gutsy, smoky flow and drove south, thinking through what I had.

Rebecca Townsend was not at the house. I got that from my senses rather than from faith in Jean Slater's words. And the house screamed of something amiss. I pictured Jean wandering alone around the perfect home with her perfect glass of wine. Husband away, daughter some place unknown. Jean's agitation was almost tangible, something that craved early tranquillising. What stage of marital disharmony had Jean and Larry Slater reached? What sort of home was the Slaters' when you looked behind the gloss? Maybe one that would have a recuperating teenager jump at the chance when an aunt offered her a bed. Assuming that the aunt had made the offer. What if the girl had simply decided to up and leave? Was that what I saw in Jean's face?

But would Rebecca run away from home without informing her

best friend? I doubted it. I just needed to hear it again from the best friend herself.

Winter had switched to spring inside four hours. Micro-seasons breaking up the day. The sun slid in and out of the cloud, turning the wet road alternately grey and blinding white. I cranked the volume up beyond the cassette's limit until Martin's voice rasped like sandpaper over my backing vocals. I let the Frogeye take me at its own pace, slipping gracefully through the traffic at wheel-arch height. I headed through Swiss Cottage then swung west and drove into West Kilburn at just before eleven thirty.

I parked in a convenient Waitrose and walked up towards a nest of fast food shops across the road from the sixth-form college. The shops and kiosks were busy with students. I spotted Sadie sat on the low wall fronting the college, munching something that looked like a health-insurance catastrophe.

Her belly was still taking the air but her upper parts were covered by a cotton jacket today. She'd even found a pair of jeans that reached her hips. Sadie still looked thirteen, but so did most of the youths milling around us. I stopped in front of her and she wrapped her cholesterol-special in a napkin and set it on the wall, pulled the tab on a canned drink. Her eyes were a little friendlier today. Like an affectionate rottweiler's. I sat down next to her.

'Have you found out what's happened to Becky?' she asked.

I raised my eyebrows.

'Yeah, I know.' She took a sip. '"Don't expect miracles." Well at least you're looking. Hey,' her eyes widened, 'have you got a name or anything? You know,' she shrugged, 'to be friendly?'

She made it sound like names were a young-generation thing.

I shrugged back. 'Call me Eddie,' I said.

'Like Eddie Gumshoe? That guy off the old repeats?' She swung her right fist under my nose. If she'd followed through it would have been like a gnat had collided with me but her drink can sloshed threateningly.

I shifted away but kept my tough-guy smile to let her know I wasn't intimidated.

'How are you today, Sadie?' I said.

'I'm okay,' she said. 'What do you think's happened to her?'

Enough small talk.

'I need to ask some questions,' I said. 'Gina Redding gave me some details but I need more background.'

'Sure,' Sadie promised. 'I just don't know what will help.'

'I'm looking for a bit more on Rebecca's parents.'

She shrugged. 'There's not much I know. We never go to her house. Becky doesn't get on with Larry.'

'Any particular reason?'

Again the shrug. Her eyes gave nothing. Whatever Rebecca had said to her friend she didn't see fit to pass on. 'Larry's a dick,' she offered finally. 'I think he bullies her mother.'

'But nothing ever happened between him and Rebecca?'

She looked at me. 'You mean like him coming on to her?'

'It happens,' I said.

'Ugh,' she said. 'Sick. The guy's at least fifty. I'd throw up.'

'Rebecca never mentioned anything?'

'No.'

'What about her mother? Does Rebecca get on with her?'

'So-so,' Sadie said. 'Jean's a control freak. Wants to rule her life, you know? Where Becky goes. Who she sees. When she gets home.'

'Do the two of them argue about it?'

'All the time.'

'Would they argue enough to piss Rebecca off? Enough that she might walk out?'

Sadie shook her head. 'No,' she said. 'Becky's always pissed off with Jean but she's never talked about leaving. And she'd tell me if she was going to do that. She wouldn't be like "see you later" one minute then disappear the next. And she gets her diploma next year. Then she's out of there anyway. We're going to share a flat.' She looked at me again:

'Becky hasn't run away, Mr Gumshoe.'

'Eddie,' I said. 'Does her mother have any problems?' I wondered if the drinking was under wraps.

'Nothing I know about,' Sadie said. 'She's okay. Like any mother.'

Maybe Rebecca saw things but didn't tell. Things you'd not want even your best friend to know. Rebecca was up-front about not liking her stepfather but there was no reason she'd want to shred her mother's name. Rebecca's family sounded as normal or abnormal as the next. It was just the thing with the stepfather that bothered me.

'How's Rebecca been acting lately? Happy? Sad?'

She gave it some thought.

'Just the usual. Rebecca's always up and down. She's a crazy bitch.'

'A crazy bitch?'

'You know what I mean. Life's a big saga with Becky. She should be in a soap opera.'

'What kind of things make her crazy?'

'You know.' She looked at me again. 'Whatever.'

'Whatever?'

'Yeah. You know?' She lifted the can again.

I turned to look squarely at her. 'No, Sadie,' I said. 'I don't know. Detectives never know things until people tell them.'

She stopped swigging and rolled her eyes like I was diverting from the relevant.

'Becky's had some problems,' she said.

'What problems?'

'She's split with her boyfriend. It kind of got to her. Now she's started hanging about with this older guy? He's like, a real creep. Into drugs. I told Becky she should be careful but she says there's nothing going on. Claims she just hangs out with him.'

'The boy she split with,' I asked, 'was that serious?'

'Yeah. They were together for a couple of years. His name's Marcus. He's doing IT.' She tilted her head back towards the college buildings behind us.

'When did they split up?'

'Couple of months ago. I thought they'd get back together but I guess it's not going to happen.'

'Why did you think they'd get back together?'

'They were into each other. Like, real sweet. Marcus is okay. Not my type.'

'What type is he?'

She rolled the question around and took a swig of her can. 'Bookish,' she concluded. 'You wouldn't think he was Becky's type but you couldn't separate them.'

'So why did they split?'

'Some kind of fight? Becky didn't say. One day it was all off.'

'Has Marcus got over her?'

'Dunno. I haven't spoken to him.'

'What about this guy she's taken up with?'

'He's called Russell Cohen. Becky's been keeping it low profile but there's definitely something going on between them. He works up the West End? She's down there every other night.'

'You don't like this guy?'

'Nah. I only met him a couple of times but he was all over me every opportunity. I wouldn't let a creep like that near me.'

'In what way is he a creep?'

'Every way. He's a smarmy bastard. Likes the girls chasing him. Thinks it makes him a celeb. Fancies himself – all muscles and fuzz. He tries to act tough but he's just a loser with no proper job.'

'What does he do?'

'Works on the door up the West End,' Sadie said, 'but I heard he's into dealing. I went to the club with Becky once, saw him and his mates - guys trying to act cool and sluts who think they're something. Pricks, the lot of them. They'd never guess how stupid they all look.'

'You said the guy is old.'

'Yeah. Twenties or something. He just needs to grow up past ten.'
She pulled out a pack of cigarettes.

I gave her my Sly Uncle. 'I hear that smoking is what the girls do to act cool too,' I said. 'They'd never figure how it makes them look either.'

'Right,' she said. 'Sod that.' She lit up.

Kids. You can only advise.

She blew a vapour trail and looked at me. My advice was on-target. The cigarette put ten years on her, lost the cute. Trouble was it would still be putting ten years on in ten years' time. The years would get behind, as the song said.

'What's this got to do with Becky disappearing?' she said.

'We still don't know if Rebecca has disappeared,' I pointed out. 'But if she has, then anything might be relevant. You tell me she's had a rough time splitting with her boyfriend and now she's involved with a guy who's into dealing drugs. That doesn't sound irrelevant to me.'

'So how do you explain the fact,' Sadie countered, 'that Becky was fine that day. No mention of Marcus or Russell or anything. Then she's, like, gone! And what's with her parents?'

Smart one, this. I'd been asking myself the same question. Even if Jean Slater's story about illness was true the family was still acting strange. First thing I needed to do was find the aunt and confirm whether Rebecca was with her.

'Have you got it?' I asked.

Sadie rooted in her bag. Pulled out a four-by-three photo. It was the two of them on a beachfront, Sadie in a mini skirt, Rebecca in jeans, both wearing tops that economised on material. Rebecca was side-on, arms around Sadie's shoulders pulling her in, but her face was turned to the camera and gave a good picture. I recognised Jean Slater's looks, the same well-defined bone structure, the pretty eyes, a face rolled back twenty-five years and unclouded by Jean's problems. Sadie was attractive if you looked beyond the eyeliner and the combative stare but you could see that Rebecca was the beauty in the act.

I slipped the photo into my pocket hoping that no one was watching, maybe wondering why I was taking pictures from a teenaged girl. People might jump to conclusions. Think I was a tutor.

'What do you know about Rebecca's aunt?' I asked.

Sadie took a drag. 'That's her Aunt Kath. I never met her.'

'Do you know where she lives? Any second name?'

She shook her head. 'She lives in Berkshire. Becky never told me where. I can't remember her surname. Something clerical?'

I already had Berkshire from Jean Slater but a clerical-sounding surname narrowed it down. A couple more gems like this and I'd be camped on her doorstep. I changed tack.

'The last time you talked to Rebecca,' I said, 'when exactly was it?'

'That day. At lunch. I was right here and she came and sat with me while we ate.'

'Did she say anything special?'

Sadie though for a moment. 'Only that she wouldn't be seeing me after class. She was going straight round to see Gina.'

'And did she go to class that afternoon?'

Sadie shrugged. 'I guess so.'

'Does she always turn up for class?'

Again a shrug. 'Same as any of us? No one goes all the time.'

A refuse truck pulled up ten yards away and started tipping bins. The noise stopped us talking.

Sadie stubbed her cigarette and picked up her uneaten lunch. She was looking over the road. Maybe she had a guy of her own. Wouldn't want to be seen chatting up a tutor.

I told her to let me know if she remembered anything else. Said I'd be in touch. The refuse truck moved on and she flipped her attention back to me.

'Something has definitely happened to Becky,' she told me. 'I'm scared, Eddie.'

I smiled. 'We're on the case, Sadie.'

Maybe my smile encouraged her. She stood and returned a half-hearted smile then disappeared into the college entrance.

I sat watching the street, trying to figure which way to move.

CHAPTER EIGHT

I was only two minutes from the office so I headed back there.

Eagle Eye have the top floor in an Edwardian house backing onto the Great Western lines a mile out from Paddington Station. The area is mostly residential with a scattering of shops and cafes, but a nest of accountants and solicitors had got into a couple of the buildings part way down Chase Street, a cul-de-sac that curves and dead-ends along the railway. The eventual arrival of a private investigator at Number Twenty Six probably went unnoticed by the wider world.

The lower floors in our building were occupied by Rook and Lye, a law firm that mutated in the nineties from property conveyancing to the more lucrative world of personal-injury litigation. They'd cut loose their estate clients, expanded to full-page ads in Yellow Pages and bought slots on local radio. Then they redesignated their ground floor as a 'clinic' and never looked back.

Six years ago, Eagle Eye took the top floor lease. If Bob Rook and Gerry Lye were still uncomfortable sharing a roost with another image-challenged profession they no longer mentioned it. In terms of image, ambulance-chasers and private investigators sat on the same pot. Where we differed was in client numbers.

I was barely halfway up the stairs when Bob Rook ejected himself from the lawyers' first floor offices and was suddenly rolling down towards me like the runaway boulder in *Indiana Jones*. I flattened myself against the wall to let him pass. It was either that or learn about the personal injury business from the sharp end. If Bob noticed me he made no sign. After six years he was still keeping up the pretence that he didn't have a flock of private investigators in his attic.

When we'd first moved in it was his partner Gerry who'd come up to request that we relocate our nameplate and bell push to the opposite wall of the lobby where it wouldn't clash with their own brasswork. Nameplates are stacked together for the practical reason that a visitor can see them all in one go. Also, the bell wiring was set up that way. Gerry showed neighbourliness by offering to stand the cost of us moving our plate. I talked it over with Shaughnessy and we rejected the offer. The matter was sorted amicably when Rook and Lye moved their own name-plate to the opposite wall where I never though it looked quite right. Bob Rook hadn't spoken to me or Shaughnessy in the six years since. When we met on the stairs Bob's trick was to boost his twenty stones to planetoid mode and roar past in a cloud of incandescent gas. If we wanted to live, we got out of the way. If we got out of the way we never needed to talk.

I let Bob roar past and burst onto the street. When the building stopped shaking I continued up the stairs.

Shaughnessy was behind his desk chewing a stick of celery, and Lucy was packing to leave. She asked about Rebecca. When I hinted that I'd picked up a couple of things she hung around to get the story.

I made her wait while I poured a coffee. The filter machine's light was on but the hot-plate was dead. I'd mentioned this only a week ago but Lucy had countered by asking for money. Always the same solution. I poured a cold cup and shovelled in sugar, took it through to Shaughnessy's office along with a monster baguette from Connie's. Shaughnessy took a look at my lunch and gave me a smirk. I ignored him. Who needs sermons from a guy waving celery?

Lucy perched her backside on Shaughnessy's desk and I crashed in one of the leather and chrome easy chairs that he'd brought in to let clients know which partner had the class. I put my feet up on the other chair to confirm it.

'How's the building trade?' I asked. Shaughnessy and Harry Green had been watching a contract foreman whose company was seeing too many thefts from the building sites he worked.

'Booming.' Shaughnessy said. He watched me push my face into Connie's special and waited until I came up for air.

'Need extra eyes?' I asked.

'None,' he said. 'It's a wrap.'

I sat up and made the best surprised sounds I could with a mouth full of coleslaw.

'You've already got the guy?'

Shaughnessy's mouth slanted in what passed for a smile.

'We watched our man lock up the site yesterday. Locking up included stashing about five grand's worth of electrical gear in the back of a Transit and cutting the locks on the store shed so it would look like a break-in.'

'The ubiquitous inside job,' I said. 'You get his fence?'

'First thing this morning.' Shaughnessy dipped his celery in a tub of hummus, chewed slowly and took a swig of bottled water. 'The guy offloaded the stuff at a dodgy DIY place in Ilford,' he said. 'We snapped the whole deal. Site to store-counter.'

'Any material proof?'

Shaughnessy leaned back and strained his muscles. He tossed something onto his desk. The object landed with a crash that sent

Lucy yelping like a scalded puppy, which was what he'd intended. Shaughnessy's a sucker for the dramatic gesture. The gesture probably raised some blood pressure downstairs too. Lucy swore and looked at the thing as if it might bite.

It was a hundred metre reel of electric cabling. Heavy duty. Had to weigh at least thirty pounds.

'You went right in and bought this from them?'

'Like they say,' said Shaughnessy, 'make hay.'

'You get a receipt?' I said.

'Do I look like a fool?'

'Not you,' I said. 'You don't look like an electrician either.'

'They weren't looking too closely,' Shaughnessy said. 'I walked into the shop while they were still stacking the reels. Told them it was just the gear I was looking for. What could they tell me? Come back when we've advertised the stuff on Crimewatch?'

'A wrap,' I concurred.

'The report will be in tomorrow,' Shaughnessy said. 'Colour photos and all.'

'Anything else?' I said. I was just stalling Lucy, who was only hanging around to hear about the girl. She looked at Shaughnessy.

'We got a call,' Shaughnessy said.

'New business?'

'Ex-business.'

He sat back and waited for Lucy to elaborate. She took the cue and perched herself back on his desk where she could switch to schoolmarm.

'Eddie,' she said, 'you need a diplomacy course.'

I agreed. 'I applied once but the admin clerk threw me out when I mentioned her halitosis.'

'Well someone's pretty pissed at you.' Lucy wiggled her backside on Shaughnessy's desk, happy to be back on the familiar ground of my screw-ups.

Shaughnessy leaned forward. 'I got in just before Lucy's ears burned off,' he said.

'One of those,' I said. We got those calls all the time. Hazard of the trade. The utilities companies were the worst.

'One of those,' Shaughnessy agreed. 'This was the tricky type. The type with stuff about lawsuits.'

'Lawsuits?' I gave him astonished. 'Who've we been dealing with that knows about law? Are we going upmarket?'

'Not unless you consider HP Logistics upmarket.'

I gave that some thought. Palmer and his dirty tricks had slipped my mind. 'HP Logistics is definitely not upmarket,' I said. 'What did they want?'

'Something about damages. Vandalised equipment.'

'A lousy office chair?' I said. 'Let them sue.'

'That and the lousy truck,' Shaughnessy said. 'A Volvo FH tractor. HP were keen to read Lucy the list price. Eighty-six thousand on the road.'

'Including road tax?' I asked.

'Excluding.'

I pursed my lips. 'And the chair on top.'

'And the window.'

'A pane of glass,' I said.

'A thirty-foot pane of toughened plate glass,' Lucy said.

'Yeah,' I conceded, 'it was a big window. But we should challenge the toughened bit. The chair went through it like Perspex.'

'I take it the consultation didn't go well,' Shaughnessy said.

'We didn't land the job,' I admitted.

'Personality clash?' Shaughnessy asked.

I nodded and finished my baguette. Swilled it down with cold coffee. 'The guy wanted us to burglarise a competitor to set up a rigged bid.'

Shaughnessy looked thoughtful. 'Did you give him our rates?'

'He'd already trebled them before I gave him anything.'

'And you threw a chair through his window? What were you pushing for? Share options?'

'I wanted to hit him,' I said.

'Might have been cheaper.'

'Yeah,' I said. 'But thirty foot of glass is a strong temptation.'

'We're going to be bankrupt by the time you've handled all your temptations, Eddie,' Lucy said.

I looked at her. 'You think I should phone him back? Say we'll take the job?'

'On triple fees?' said Shaughnessy. 'Might be worth thinking about.'

I swallowed the last of the coffee and looked pop-eyed at my partner. Shaughnessy grinned.

'Just kidding,' he said.

We decided to let the HP Logistics thing ride itself out. If they sued we'd fight our corner. I gave Shaughnessy and Lucy what I had on the missing girl, which wasn't much. There were six hours remaining of Gina Redding's commission. After that she'd have to decide whether to throw more money the same way or to call it quits. Six hours was tight to find out where Jean Slater's sister lived and confirm or disprove the story about her looking after the girl. But I wanted at least that much before I went back to Gina.

Plan A had been to report that Rebecca was safe at home and to refund the unused hours. The story about the aunt in an unknown Berkshire location expanded things awkwardly.

I needed a brainstorm to figure out how to track this aunt down. Berkshire was a big place. Until the brainstorm hit I had other jobs.

I headed back to my office for some research involving checking numbers on a long telephone list, looking for a name that shouldn't be there. Another commercial contract. Another suspect employee. This time it was a high ranking executive on the board of a mid-size pharmaceutical company, suspected of selling inside knowledge to a party that would gain from trading short.

Lucy went out and Shaughnessy soon after. I settled in behind my roll-top and stared at a computer screen for a couple of hours until the telephone numbers were dancing circles on my retinas. Time to quit. If I left I could still beat the traffic home.

Arabel had left a note on my table. She had a late. I had the evening to myself.

The frustration of not knowing whether the Rebecca Townsend thing was real or not was chasing around in my head and threatening to drive me crazy. The solution was to quit thinking. I showered and changed and went through to the rear attic. My therapy is painting. It's a hobby that actually brings in some small change. The random fads of city culture had worked to turn my stuff into cash in a half-dozen outlets around the markets and tourist spots. I sell occasional cityscapes and a few portraits in half-impressionist style – something like Augustus John but less unkind. Acrylics on canvas, or on hardboard in my cheapskate moments.

My rear attic had the original skylights. These leaked when it rained but gave the room a light that inspired on a summer's evening. The present weather was running more to leak but the light was good enough to give me an hour or so. My current work was a portrait of Arabel. Arabel had the perfect face with just the right blemishes to make what I saw sublime. But my fixation on capturing perfection was cramping my style. Fixate on perfection and you're as likely to bring out the blemishes. It's too easy to make an ogre of an angel. Ask John. I worked for an hour and a half and forgot about lost girls. When the hues began to go flat I called it quits and went out.

I crossed town, ate in Camden, then drove back to Paddington and parked the car behind Eagle Eye and walked the quarter mile to The Podium. The Podium was a spit and sawdust bar that played live jazz every night until two a.m. Weekdays were open house for new talent gigging to supplement day jobs and student loans. There was often more noise than talent but the jazz never lacked energy.

It was early for the live sets. I grabbed a beer and found a quiet corner. My phone rang. Probably Arabel, calling before going on shift. When I punched the button I was disabused. The background music and yelling didn't come from a hospital.

'Hey! Mr Gumshoe!'

'Sadie,' I said. 'Nice to hear from you.'

'I've got something.' Her voice was raised against the hubbub. A little too animated.

'Are you drinking, Sadie?' I said. 'Is seventeen legal now?'

'Yeah,' she said, 'tonight it's legal.' A voice broke through the background, yelling something unintelligible down the phone. Sadie yelled back to shut up. 'Every night's legal,' she shouted. 'It's what students do. Chill out, Mr Detective! You going to arrest me?'

I looked around. The Podium's noise level was barely high enough to cover what was coming from my phone. I remembered what I'd said to Shaughnessy. No kids under our feet. Now it was calls.

'What's up, Sadie?' I said.

'I've got her address!' Sadie yelled.

'Whose address?'

'Becky's aunt!'

That got my attention.

'I found a letter,' Sadie said. 'Becky sent it when she was staying with her aunt last year. The address is right there!'

'Read it out, Sadie.'

'Got your pencil out, Mr Detective?'

'My pencil's always out, Sadie.'

That got a giggle. I let it go. Sadie shouted an address in Hungerford and I wrote it on a beer mat.

'That's great,' I told her. 'What about the aunt's name?'

'Dunno,' she yelled. 'I already told you. Something clerical.'

I must have forgotten. The address was enough though.

'Good girl,' I said. 'That helps me.'

Another burst of laughter came out of my phone. Sadie's voice in there amongst the racket.

'Hey, Mr Detective, how about coming down here? My friends wanna meet you.'

'Some other time, Sadie,' I said. I killed the line.

Not this side of hell, though.

An ensemble was warming up. I grabbed another beer and settled in for the night. My phone rang again. This time it was Arabel. She asked how I was doing. A duel between drums and baritone sax answered her question. Arabel realised that conversation was impractical. Promised to call by tomorrow. I told her to take care and took my drink over to join a table where a crew of regulars had camped out. We touched glasses and relaxed in the flow of the first set. The ensemble lacked balance and swayed unpredictably between funk and down-low dirty and I knew that in another year they'd have broken up and recycled themselves into more subtle groupings but for the moment the raw energy swept us along in the flow. The oldest of the musicians was twenty.

The late set finished at twelve thirty but the diehards stayed at the table and the bar stayed busy. It was two fifteen before I left them to it. I told myself as I always did that I was going to ease up on the Podium. I'd been saying it for ten years.

I trudged towards Paddington, found that my luck was in: I still had the building key. The lower floors were dark. No midnight oils in personal injury. When I opened Eagle Eye's door a freezing draft rushed out and hugged me. Our offices were colder than the stairwell. Maybe we should move our furniture out here in winter. But then our landlord would want a rise.

CHAPTER NINE

At seven thirty next day I unfolded myself from the couch and stood to move my limbs around for a couple of minutes to restore feeling.

The office lease included a heating clause, but the landlord's interpretation stretched only as far as a responsibility to deliver metallic rapping and background thuds from the feed pipes. The radiators themselves never got above freezing.

In cold weather we burned a propane heater in the outer office while Shaughnessy and I toasted our feet on two-bar radiants by our desks. The propane heater produced a sweat-house atmosphere that triggered dizzy spells in susceptible clients and generally acclimatised them for when they got the bill.

I finished my callisthenics and carried the electric heater through from my office. Placed it dangerously close in the tiny bathroom whilst I shaved and freshened up. When I checked the mirror the result was passable.

Back in the office I retrieved the folded beer mat from my jacket and checked the address Sadie had given me. The writing was shaky but legible. I had my lead to Rebecca's aunt.

I fired up the coffee machine and spooned in a 'mountain of Colombian. Then I took the electric heater back to my office and booted up my PC.

I continued with my pharmaceutical company search, looking for the telltale calls that would trap our double-dealing board member. Out in reception the filter machine kept me company with intermittent stutters and coughs that had me almost tasting the coffee.

After twenty minutes the machine had hit a crescendo. I went to see. Found the thing backfiring steam into the water tub, the coffee dry in the filter. I switched the machine off and poured the coffee back into the tin. Then I tipped the hot water out of the reservoir into my mug and spooned in some instant, heaped it with Marvel and a couple of sugars and went back to my desk. The brew was undrinkable. I got up and tipped the liquid into the bathroom sink and rinsed my mug. Ten more productive minutes in the life of a private investigator.

Shaughnessy arrived at eight and poked his head in. He had a steaming cup from Connie's that filled the place with a nostril-flaring aroma. I pretended not to notice. Filled him in on our missing girl and my planned trip to her aunt's. Shaughnessy watched me through steam.

'So we'll either find the girl safe,' he said, 'or we'll know for sure that the family is telling fibs.'

'Yeah,' I said. 'The only problem is that if it's fibs we'll still not know whether it's something we should be involved with.'

'That's Gina Redding's call,' Shaughnessy said.

I agreed. Went back to my pharmaceutical company.

At ten I decided that the traffic would be tolerable and rolled my desk top down. Shaughnessy had already gone out. I called at Connie's and picked up a coffee and a ham roll. Paid cash at the counter without him seeing me. He would have wanted more. I ate the roll on the way round to the back of the building and sipped the coffee while the Frogeye warmed up.

I called in at my apartment for a change of clothes then headed west out of London, chasing heavy jets. I made Hungerford by eleven thirty and got directions on the main street. By eleven forty-five I was parked on a grass verge two and a half miles outside the town looking at a terrace of eight cottages. The address Sadie had given me placed Rebecca's aunt in the second from the end. I didn't have a name and I didn't have a plan but what's life without spontaneity?

An upstairs window was open but there was no other sign of life. I was tempted to bluff my way in to see if I could pick up any sense that the girl was there, but if I failed I'd be blocked out. Better to wait to see if Rebecca's aunt came out. It's easier to bluff someone when you catch them off their doorstep. If nothing came up in a couple of hours I'd take my chance with the direct approach.

You could almost mistake the day for early summer. The gales had died, the sun was out and the grassy bank beside the Frogeye was a carpet of foxglove. I wound the window down and listened to birdsong.

I got lucky. Five minutes after I'd started my watch a woman came out and unlocked a Ford Ka parked by the cottage gate. The woman was in her early thirties and there was no doubt that I was looking at a younger version of Jean Slater. She was a little taller but the high cheeks and attractive eyes were the same. The real difference was in the lack of wear and tear. You saw the two sisters' faces and you saw different lives. The Ka did a three-point and headed down the lane towards Hungerford. I fired up the Frogeye and followed.

The Ka drove into the centre of the town and I played cat and mouse whilst Rebecca's aunt did some errands, in and out of shops. Finally saw my chance when she drove under the railway bridge and swung into a

Tesco store. I followed her in and parked a dozen slots away.

Rebecca's aunt went into the store.

She came out twenty minutes later burdened with bulging carriers. Her unwieldy load meant that she wasn't agile enough to avoid me when I stepped backwards from between two cars and dragged a shopping trolley into her path.

She hit the trolley and staggered back, hanging onto her shopping, while I floundered about with an act I've perfected from the people in airports and railway stations who specialise in looking the other way as they crash into you. Rebecca's aunt gave me an exasperated look while I flustered my apology but before she could step around me I switched to lockjaw, like I didn't believe what I was seeing.

'Jean!' I yelled.

She looked at me in astonishment but I was already making a big 'O' with my mouth, as if I'd just realised my mistake. I shook my head and muttered another apology. This seemed to end the affair for her. She gave me an indulgent smile and moved towards her car, probably saying things inside that I didn't want to hear. I gave her ten yards then pushed my trolley after her.

'Excuse me!'

She turned back. Cautious now. Wondering what kind of nut she'd met.

'You don't have a sister?' I said. 'Jean?'

That got her. Cautious shifted to curious.

I threw in another tantaliser. 'Hampstead?'

Her eyes widened.

'Jean Slater!' I said. 'I know her.'

I finally got a smile. It was mostly astonishment but still a smile.

'Jean's my sister,' she confirmed. She tilted her head. 'Have we met?'

I smiled back. Grin-opolis. Shook my head.

'I'd remember for sure,' I said. 'I'm a friend of Larry and Jean's.' I walked forward and held out my hand, dropped it self-consciously when she struggled to free herself from her shopping. Gave her flustered again.

Her smile got wider. She recognised harmless when she saw it.

'You really had me there,' I grinned. 'I could have sworn you were Jean—'

—The sister who had to be at least eight or ten years older.

It was the kind of gaffe women notice, and helped to confirm my harmlessness. I back-pedalled: 'You must be Jean's young sister,' I said. From gaffe to suave in one easy move. Not *younger* sister. *Young* did it better. Another difference women notice. Jean's sister noticed. Coming from an idiot the compliment had to be sincere.

She laughed and gave me the standard denials about youth, but the flattery had struck home. Right then she'd have invited me home for tea. We both shook our heads at how small the world was. Luckily Jean's sister had never heard the Second Rule of the investigation business which is that the world is very big. If it ever seems small it's because you're being crowded by someone you should be watching. The Second Rule complements the First Rule, which says that there's no such thing as coincidence. Where a layman sees coincidence the investigator sees connections. Where a layman sees a small world the investigator sees trouble closing in.

We got over our small-world chuckles and I threw in my pitch.

'So,' I said, 'how are Larry and Jean?'

Rebecca's aunt tilted her head and gave me a that's-life grin. 'They're just fine,' she said.

I looked thoughtful for a second like I was squeezing my memory.

'Kathy!' I said. 'You must be Kathy.'

The power of my recall stunned her. She nodded. 'Kathy Pope,' she said.

Pope. Something clerical!

That Sadie.

'I'm going to ring them,' I promised. 'They'll never believe we've met.'

'Yes,' Kathy smiled in her Rule Two ignorance, 'it's an incredibly small world!'

'Well it's great to have met you,' I said. 'Wait till I tell Jean!' I was nodding like a car-window dog. Then I gave her just-another-thought: asked how Rebecca was. I watched her face. Her smile strengthened. On this subject she was effusive.

'Rebecca's fine,' she said. 'She's coming to stay at Easter. I just wish I had her more often.' Her face was a vision of warmth. Not the look of someone nursing a sick girl. If Rebecca was recuperating in Kathy Pope's house it was news to this woman.

We wrapped it up and said we'd see each other at the Slaters' some time. I yelled again that Jean would be knocked out when I told her whom I'd met.

She'd be knocked out all right.

If I told her.

I took the M4 back to London, chewing over what I had. What I had was a quick solution that had just popped. Someone was telling porkies about Rebecca Townsend.

If the girl was not at her aunt's then where was she? What was happening to her?

Time to take a closer look at the family.

CHAPTER TEN

The Eagle Eye office was closed up. Lucy was out somewhere attending to our six-monthly purchase of stationery and supplies. Maybe I'd find a new intercom on my desk tomorrow. Maybe a cup of hot coffee.

She'd done some sifting before she went. A post-it on my roll-top gave me Slater–Kline's address. I sat down and called their number again. This time I was answered by a human. Probably their computer's day off. A different female from yesterday. Less bright and breezy. I asked for Larry Slater and was told that he was tied up at the moment. The woman took a few false details and my real mobile number. She couldn't tell me when Slater would be free to call back but assured me it would be soon. Her assurance had the sincerity of a car dealer's Christmas card. I rang off.

Slater–Kline. The name had a big-city ring but Lucy's address was high street Islington. The City shadow-land where money is made on a more personal scale but with equal dependability. Slater's luxury home testified to the efficient sluicing of money through the fibre optics that burrowed their way up to Islington. They say the streets of London are paved with gold, but your best bet nowadays is in the tunnels beneath.

I wanted something to take back to Gina Redding. So far all I had were negatives: proof that the Slaters were telling fairy stories, a near-cert that the girl was not at their home. Nothing to help Gina decide whether to continue the search. I needed a quick look at Larry Slater to complete the family snapshot. My best bet would be to pick him up as he left the office, get some first impressions, even if I only followed him home.

I filled a couple of hours with my ongoing telephone search for the straying executive. My call list included the dial-out record from the guy's office, supplied by his company, and the record from his mobile, supplied by Eagle Eye. Eighty-plus contacts. I'd tracked twenty-seven through company books and reverse directories, working in order of call frequency. Sixty-six to go.

Time rushes when you're doing that kind of stuff. At only the twentieth time of looking I saw that the clock had reached four fifteen and I could legitimately pack in on the pretext that Larry Slater might soon leave the office.

The weather had turned bad again. The rain was holding off but a looming storm dimmed the afternoon. I swung the Frogeye up onto the Euston Road and into the rush-hour flow. Thirty minutes of red lights got me to Islington. I drove past the Slater–Kline business, a sixty-foot window just up from the Angel. Got an impression of industry behind the glass. I found an alley a couple of blocks away whose double yellows were mostly concealed under rubbish sacks. I backed in, blocking the alley. If a service truck needed access it would have to drive over the Frogeye.

A steady drizzle chilled me as I walked back down the main street

72

and looked into the Slater–Kline window. The business was thriving, judging by their street frontage and brightly-lit office. A dozen desks were scattered informally, each equipped with the latest in low footprint plasma monitors and ergonomic wireless keyboards. Two or three clients were seated at the agents' desks. Bigger clients with juicy portfolios would probably be taken through to private rooms at the back. I walked around the block and discovered an alley running behind the buildings. Larry Slater's Lexus was nosed up against the rear wall in a chained-off parking area. The angle of the parking bays prohibited turning, so Slater would exit at the far end.

I retrieved the Frogeye and parked it closer to the alley under a loading gate with two clamping signs posted. My observation spot at the end of the alley was only ten seconds away. If anyone tried to clamp me I'd be driving away before they'd got the collar on. I stood for half an hour as the rain came on, watching the slots behind Slater–Kline free up one by one as they shut up shop. Eventually only the Lexus was left. Slater had got home at seven the other evening, so I might have a long wait. I wondered at a guy putting in the hours despite the family problem waiting at home.

The rain intensified. The alley behind Slater–Kline faded into a mist of spray. In those old films the private eyes stand under lamps, kept dry by lined trilbys and macs down to their ankles. The old-timers would have rolled their eyes at my leather jacket and bare head. But what choice was there? How invisible would I be in a trilby? I did the modern thing. Stood and got wet.

Luckily the patron saint of detectives was watching over me. I'd expected another hour's wait but I'd been there barely five minutes when Slater came out. I was sprinting towards the Frogeye before he'd unlocked the Lexus and by the time he nosed out onto the street I was rolling, the Frogeye's fan blowing cold air around my soaked slacks. The Lexus pulled into the traffic and I followed.

The car headed south and turned onto Pentonville. Looked like Slater wasn't going home. I got trapped three cars back, nearly lost him at the lights as the Lexus crossed the junction. Luckily two of the three cars in front of me jumped the amber so I only had one to pass. I put my foot down and skidded across a wall of oncoming traffic. When I straightened up I saw the Lexus four ahead, heading west. I kept my distance, still trying to clear the fogged windscreen.

We continued along Euston in stop-starts. Slater stayed on the Euston Road at Eversholt and accelerated into the underpass and out onto Marylebone, heading towards where the A40 ran west out of town. At the Edgware Road Slater took the flyover and we got up to fifty, streaming out along the Westway behind Eagle Eye's offices as if we were heading for the open road. Everyone knew different. The open road didn't exist. Our speed was rushing us towards the tail end of the Hanger Lane log jam.

The rain slackened and the city rippled in a multicoloured blaze below us, poised on the edge of night. Then the rain kicked back in and made a crazy kaleidoscope of the whole thing. The Frogeye's wipers began to struggle. I'd started to wonder if Slater was set for a long journey when the Lexus edged onto an off-ramp and braked hard for the West Cross roundabout. There were no cars between us on the slip road. I thanked God for my rebuild discs and braked hard to open up the distance, kept my indicator off. Then I turned after the Lexus and followed it down into Holland Park.

Slater drove into the residential streets behind the park. A hundred and fifty yards in his indicator signalled and he turned into a street of white-stuccoed Victorian mansions converted into luxury apartments with luxury cars parked nose-to-tail outside. Half way down, Slater found a spot and pulled the Lexus in. I braked and squeezed into a tiny space behind a Bentley fifty yards back. My lights were off before I'd stopped rolling.

Nothing happened for a couple of minutes. I wondered if Slater was waiting for someone to come out. Then the Lexus' door opened and he stepped out and walked back along the pavement. He climbed the steps to a door whose number was displayed in flowery white script on

74

a black base. No. 93. He pressed the top floor bell and waited for thirty seconds. No response. He pressed again, turning to stare up and down the street while he counted off the time. Then a final attempt – a good, long push. Still no result. Someone was out or didn't want to see him. He came back down the steps and walked to his car. I started the engine.

But the Lexus didn't move. I switched the ignition back off. The rain eased and the street stayed quiet. I pushed in a Roy Eldridge tape and set the volume to low to give me background without distraction and waited for Slater to make his move. Ten minutes turned to twenty, then half an hour. The Lexus stayed silent and dark. I pictured Slater watching No. 93 in his mirror.

Forty-five minutes went by and the only life in the street was a handful of cars arriving and departing. Lights burned in all the front windows. On the hour the rain came back and blurred the windscreen. A couple of times I switched on the ignition and gave the wipers a sweep.

Whatever I'd been expecting this was not it. I was supposed to be looking at something happening inside the Slater house. Instead I was watching a vigil miles away. I tried to guess how this street might be connected to Rebecca. Was Slater looking for the girl here? What would a college kid be doing in this area? Plenty of things came to mind, all of them wild speculation and all of them hanging on the assumption that this had anything to do with her in the first place.

The last of Gina Redding's hours ran out. We were in the free-bonus phase and the risk was that all I'd get would be more fog.

The Eldridge tape ended. I slotted in another, a crackly Gasser to counterpoint the slow-moving minutes. It was getting cold. Did Lexuses have electric heaters? I checked my watch and saw that we'd been there an hour and twenty. When I looked up Slater was out of his car and walking back up the street. He climbed the steps once more and put his thumb on the same bell push. Same routine: three tries, swinging his head to search up and down the street while he waited. Same result as last time. I saw him give a frustrated shake of his head and walk back to his car. This time he fired up the Lexus and drove off.

I let him go. My guess was that he was headed home. Whatever this detour had been about it started and ended here. The droop in Slater's shoulders as he came down the steps had told me that. I hoisted myself out of the Frogeye and crossed the road. The bell plate at No. 93 said that the top apartment was inhabited by someone called Brown. No initial. No title. The name narrowed things down nicely. Whatever I was narrowing down. Which might be something entirely unconnected with the missing – or not-missing – girl.

But whoever Brown was, he or she was significant enough to keep Slater sat around in the cold for an hour and twenty minutes like a felon casing a target, when a simple phone call could have done the job.

My gut feeling said that there was a connection to the missing girl. Her stepfather needed to talk to someone. Badly.

I didn't have much more to take to Gina Redding but I would put money on one thing.

Brown was a woman.

CHAPTER ELEVEN

My first house call was Gina Redding's.

I gave her what we had, which was mainly that we'd confirmed that Jean Slater was lying about her daughter's supposed illness. The girl had dropped out of sight for some other reason.

I described Larry Slater's mysterious stakeout of the previous evening. I'd no evidence to say it was related but I gave Gina my experience which was that in the investigation business there's no such thing as coincidence. When you're looking at one funny going-on and stumble across another there tends to be a correlation between the two.

'Larry may be searching for Rebecca,' I postulated. 'Maybe she's eloped with some rich guy.'

Gina shook her head. 'Rebecca didn't run off, Mr Flynn,' she said. 'She wouldn't mislead her friends like that.'

'Intentions change,' I suggested.

Another emphatic shake. 'She'd have called Sadie at least.' Gina thought of something else. 'If she'd run off, why are the Slaters keeping it a secret?'

I gave her a grim smile. That was my own question, the one which made me doubt the elopement theory. Would a family hide the fact that their daughter has run away out of sheer embarrassment? Sure they would. But there was a factor that argued against it.

'If Rebecca had run off,' I said, 'the Slaters would be talking to Sadie. She's the one person who might know something.'

Gina nodded. We were on the same track. 'They've done the opposite,' she said. 'They've cut Sadie out, just like me.'

'Which means that they know Sadie knows nothing,' I said. 'Therefore they know that Rebecca hasn't run away.'

The old lady unsealed a new pack and lit up. 'So someone really has taken her?' She looked at me like I'd let her down.

'It's beginning to look that way,' I said. 'We just need to figure a reason that would explain why the Slaters haven't gone to the police. Kidnap for ransom might keep them quiet, but the Slaters don't stand out from the crowd as an obvious target. There are far richer pickings around town. Unless financial extortion wasn't the purpose.'

Gina sucked at her cigarette and watched a couple of swifts squabbling in the garden.

'The Slaters may have something the abductors need,' I said. 'Slater's line of work suggests possibilities. But we may be wide of the mark with abduction. It's still possible that the thing is to do with the family itself.'

'You think Larry and Jean might have harmed her?' Gina was right back with her first supposition.

I held up my hands. 'The question is,' I said, 'do we take this further? If we dig then we'll find out what's going on. But my feeling is that we'll be fighting the family all the way. I'll need to put in the hours, ask my partner to help, maybe grease a few palms. It's going to be expensive, Gina.'

Gina shook her head, blew smoke.

'Do whatever you need,' she said. 'Let's get Rebecca back safe. I'll handle the bill.'

'Fine,' I said. 'We'll step things up a gear. Give us three or four days. We'll find her.'

Gina nodded but her expression told me that she was thinking the same as me. Three or four days was a long time if the girl was in trouble; something bad may already have happened. I was confident we could find her, but that didn't mean she'd be okay.

I headed to the Slater house. If Larry was out then I wanted to take a look at Jean Slater's day.

The early morning drink I'd spotted yesterday didn't point to anything particularly productive in her schedule. If Jean just stayed cooped up inside the house I'd waste another half day. But it was the best shot I had before bringing Shaughnessy in and starting the heavy digging.

In the event Lady Luck presented a better option. As I turned into the lane I had to pull the Frogeye hard into the verge to avoid becoming roadkill under the wheels of a four-by-four coming out. My mind was on avoiding the agricultural-size Michelins, but I caught a peripheral glance of Jean Slater's face up behind the windscreen. Going somewhere fast. Looked like she'd not started so early on the lubrication today. Unless I was luckier than I knew.

Decision time. It would be good to see where Jean was going but the opportunity of an empty house was too good to pass. Empty if Larry Slater or Rebecca were not there, of course. I got back onto the tarmac and continued up the lane. I turned into the Slaters' driveway and parked outside their front door. Slater's Lexus was missing and Jean hadn't looked like she was popping out for the paper. I might have an hour or two.

I rang the door bell. Better safe, et cetera.

No answer.

I reached into the Frogeye's boot and grabbed a couple of tools that help with house calls. I slipped them under my jacket and walked along the front of the building. The villa was abutted by white stuccoed walls hiding the gardens but I found an access gate unlocked beside the garage and went through.

The grounds were a half acre of impeccable gardens that suggested regular staff. I hoped that today was their day off. I went round the back and found a conservatory that added nothing to the Spanish architecture. An add-on at the stage of needing either major refurbishment or demolition. Its main feature was a door that didn't need any tools other than hand pressure to ease the lock's tongue out of the frame. I went inside and walked along the back of the main house. Three doors opened into the building. Two were secure. The third was the kitchen door and was unlocked. If they'd put an ENTRANCE sign up they'd save a burglar's time. The house was alarmed but something told me that Jean Slater hadn't stopped to set the panel. I took a chance and stepped into the kitchen.

The place stayed silent. I walked through to an alcove at the back of the hall and confirmed that the alarm was disabled. I listened again. Still silence. I took the nearer staircase onto the gallery. The gallery served two doors on each side of the house. I started clockwise from the east. The first two doors opened onto lifeless guest rooms. I moved on to the front of the house. Both front rooms had been knocked into one master bedroom the size of a tennis court with walk-in dressers and a double-sized ensuite. Jean and Larry's room. The room was just-vacated untidy. Bed unmade. Walk-in closets open. Lid askew on a laundry basket. It looked like Jean was not a neat freak. I guessed that she had a domestic, although there had been no sign of work going on when I was here on Tuesday. I did a skim search, pulled drawers on the off chance that there might be something significant. Found nothing. If the Slaters had anything to hide it would not be here. I continued my walk, checked two more guest rooms on the west side and finally arrived at the rear of the house. The first door opened into a bright and untidy bedroom crowded with soft furnishings and wall posters. Rebecca's room.

Two rooms knocked into one again. The ultimate teenage den. Six full-height windows looked out over the gardens and illuminated walls decorated in cheerful pastels that matched the curtains and bedspread. The bed was made up but in a half-hearted way. Clothes and shoes were scattered about the room but I didn't get the impression that the girl had been around in the last few days. If Rebecca had been gone a week then the domestic was moving slow.

A teak desk had a clutter of student stuff: notebooks, scrap paper, card files with work assignments. No computer – Rebecca probably carried her laptop around. I looked through the loose stuff and found nothing.

I checked out shelves loaded with more clutter – books, boxes of tissues, cuddly toys, a rack of CDs already made obsolescent by the iPod on the desk. I sifted through a teak chest of drawers full of girl's designer stuff, turned everything, corner to corner, in forty-five minutes. Nothing amongst her paperwork or clothes, nothing under the mattress, no love-letters hidden in her underwear. I went through the clothes in a walk-in closet and found what mattered by chance when my foot caught a piece of loose flooring while I was riffling jacket pockets. I coaxed up a short floorboard that had been fitted around heating pipes. Saw things hidden beneath it. Three slim exercise books, spiral bound. I pulled out Rebecca's diaries.

I sat in a chair and opened the books. The pages held a mass of tiny handwriting packaged into short cryptic entries going back three years. I started with the current year. The entries were a teenaged girl's standard concoction of drama and daydreams but it didn't take long to get to something that seemed significant.

What caught my attention was Rebecca's reaction to the split with the boyfriend, Marcus. The separation looked to have cut deep. Deep enough to explain what might have triggered her association with

Sadie's "creepy guy" Russell Cohen.

Three months back things were fine. Rebecca and her boyfriend were solid. The diary entries were a mixture of one-liners and short paragraphs scattered cryptically with Marcus' name. Sweetheart stuff. Rebecca's shorthand might have protected her secrets a generation back but nowadays everyone texts the same code a dozen times a day.

I turned the pages, found the moment eight weeks back where the entries changed in tone and length. Rebecca and Marcus had had a fall-out. The storm had closed in fast. The diary skipped specifics, went blank for a couple of days. Avoiding stuff that was too painful. When it took up again there was a page and a half of barely-coded pain that skittered between guilt and blame. Rebecca got it all into three short sentences:

> *He dsnt lv me.*
> *Hate him. All my fault!!*

The subsequent pages counted Marcus' phone calls. Rebecca recorded the number of times he called her without saying whether the two of them ever talked but I got a feeling she wasn't answering. Preferred to wallow in the misery of logging the missed calls. The importance of Marcus trying was clear in her counting fixation, but I got the sense that reconciliation was locked in a bear hug with something destructive inside Rebecca. I turned a page and two halves of a photo dropped out. I held the pieces together. A chest and head view of a good-looking boy in a black t-shirt, college buildings behind him, squinting into the sun with a loopy grin. Marcus, I guessed.

The photo was large enough to be shreddable twenty ways. The single rip screamed restraint. Said that Rebecca's heart wasn't in it. I slipped the photo back and read another week's worth of half-pagers, Rebecca pouring out her misery in a mixture of self-castigation and stubbornness. I sensed the two of them entrenched behind their defences. Did Rebecca show any of these emotions outside her room?

Something told me this wasn't a house for sharing problems.

A couple of weeks later the entries reverted to one-liners. It looked like the split was permanent. Then the first hint of Rebecca's new attachment. The code would have been tricky if I didn't already know the characters:

Kiks club. Rsl got me in. Pssd. Nyt @ his.
and
Skipped class. Pm w Rsl, smoked, let him.

Smoked what? Let Russell what?

Whatever it was it seemed that Rebecca was doing more than just hanging out with the guy. The entries stayed short and cryptic, but what was there was clear enough. Stuff like *2e's* and

R + J + me!! – crazy -- J's sxe but shes a bij
and another day
R on stuff, wntd me – no wy – got nasty, ran out –
Bstd. Calld me latr, 4gottn!!
Pikn me up 2mor. Bstd!

I was getting the picture.

R stayed in the picture right till the end. If you were looking for signs of a slide it was there. But nothing that pointed to the reason Rebecca had vanished that afternoon. Unless she simply didn't come back from one of *R*'s little parties. Ten days ago the diary just stopped.

I skipped back a couple of years for anything that might give me a picture of how things were inside the Slater household. Spotted stuff that didn't look good. In amongst Marcus and teenaged angst Rebecca poured out her feelings about her mother and Larry. The stuff on her mother was just odd cryptic comments, complaints about her interferences, her indecisiveness. Her unwillingness to stand up for her daughter. But Rebecca's hostility towards Larry Slater needed no interpretation. Things were not good between the two of them. The girl's thoughts on her step father didn't take much decoding.

What did Jean ever c in this prik?
(Money!)
and
I just want 2 get out. Bstd yelled @me ryt in front of Jean & she said nothin. So I said it 4 her!! Letch almst hit me. But he knows thers a line. He only has 2 cross it once & his littl secrets out – then its goodbye Happy Familys

Happy families. How do they get like that?

The diaries took me an hour. I kept an ear open for the sound of anyone returning. Finally decided that I was living on borrowed time.

I slotted the books back under the floorboard and made a fast search of Rebecca's bathroom, digging through the clutter of cosmetics and girl stuff for anything that shouldn't be there – maybe an indiscreet cache of "e" or "stuff" brought back from one of her evenings with Russell. Nothing. The place was clean.

The phone rang downstairs.

I froze like a guilty schoolboy. Heard voicemail kick in. I closed Rebecca's door and went down.

I had what I'd been looking for. The picture was pretty much what Sadie and Gina had hinted – the unhappy home, Rebecca's break-up with her boyfriend, the thing with the new guy Russell. The diaries gave me an explanation for the tension at home. And it didn't take much to figure what the thing was between Rebecca and her stepfather. It looked like Rebecca had been holding the guy at bay for a long time. Despite my previous assumptions the thing made me wonder again whether her disappearance might not be self-imposed. A home where you're not safe is no home at all.

If the situation in this house was part of what had happened then that still left a wide range of possibilities. Explanations that might be found with Rebecca's friend Russell Cohen or be solely inside the Slater family. Or maybe the unhappy house wasn't related.

I took one last instalment on my borrowed time to give the ground floor a once-over. Covered four rooms lightning-fast, hoping for a break – maybe a ransom note saying *Leave one million pounds in a locker at Paddington Station* – but the only extortion I found was a stack of utilities bills in amongst the unopened mail in the lounge. The mail dated from nine days back. It looked like the Slaters had had other priorities since then.

I picked up the phone and listened to the voicemail. A woman named Meg wanted Jean to get back to her, let her know when she should start again. She offered to fit in extra hours to get the place straight. It looked like the Slaters had put their domestic on hold. That explained the unmade beds. So the Slaters didn't want anyone around the house right now. I picked up Meg's number and let myself out of the front door.

As I drove the Sprite down the lane the menacing shape of Jean's four-by-four appeared right on cue, tearing back up from the main road. Five minutes earlier and I'd have had an interesting improvisation to serve up. Mr Education Authority, back without his coat or briefcase. As it was our vehicles flashed by each other. I doubt if Jean Slater even saw me. Her eyes were staring straight ahead like she was fleeing from a nightmare and losing ground.

CHAPTER TWELVE

I pulled over at the main road and phoned a number Sadie had given me. Marcus Moxham, Rebecca's ex, picked up through a hubbub that sounded like a college cafeteria. Or maybe classes were livelier nowadays.

The voice was deep for a youth under twenty, difficult to match to the nerdy photo in Rebecca's diary. Sadie had warned Marcus that I'd be talking to him. He sounded bemused at the thought of her calling in the detectives, but I heard concern in his voice. He told me he was at the West Kilburn college, taking early lunch. We agreed to talk outside in fifteen.

I spotted him, a lanky kid in crisp denim and suede ankle boots, seated on a bollard outside the college. He stood when I arrived. People don't meet private detectives every day. It makes them uneasy, like with a trainee dentist. Detectives – police and private – are evidence of a world that people prefer not to know about. The detective is tainted by association. Marcus strained a grin and we shook hands. I asked him when he'd last seen Rebecca.

'A couple of weeks ago,' he said. 'I see her here at college off and on.' His voice was matter of fact but the way he was watching the street and not me told me this was a heavy subject for him.

'Did Rebecca mention anything that might suggest a problem?'

'We didn't talk.' He grimaced at his feet. 'We just pass by. Nothing much to say.'

'The two of you are finished?' I watched him, still waiting for him to look at me but he continued to watch the street as he gave the world an aw-shucks grin.

'Yeah, we're finished,' he said. 'It was kinda sad, but that's life.'

'Sad?'

He finally looked at me. 'For me.'

'I heard you were serious.'

'That's what I thought. It fell apart. Things got in the way.'

'What things?'

'Rebecca had problems. She could be hard to take when she was in her moods.'

'Is that why you split? Her moodiness?' I though of the diary: Rebecca blaming herself. But Marcus shook his head.

'No,' he said. 'I could put up with the difficult side.'

'So why did you break up? Did Rebecca walk away?'

This time he stayed silent. Went back to watching the street. He thought it through and finally decided it was none of my business. He changed the subject to the more immediate matter.

'What's going on?' he asked. 'Sadie's hysterical about Rebecca disappearing.' He forced another grin. 'I can't believe she called in a private eye.'

'Neither can I,' I said. 'I guess Sadie told you that Rebecca has dropped out of sight. She's not been able to get her for a week.'

Marcus nodded. 'She told me,' he said. 'I don't know if I'd go calling in the cops though.'

'Why's that?'

Marcus shrugged again. 'You never know with Rebecca. She's unpredictable. Maybe she's just lying low. Problems at home. Late with her coursework. I wouldn't automatically assume that anything had happened.'

'Has this happened before?'

'Not like this,' Marcus admitted. 'But there's been times she's laid low for a few days when she's been pissed with me. Hit the town, stayed out nights, slept over at friends of friends. Her mother always got mad at me because she assumed she was with me. And I had to let her think it was true. But Rebecca's never dropped right out.' He looked at me again. 'Is she in some kind of trouble? '

My turn to watch the street. My grave look was meant to scare him a little so he'd open up some more. 'From what I've seen,' I told him, 'it's possible that she's in trouble, yes.'

Maybe the words coming from me and not from Sadie made the thing real. The boy's face dropped. Split up or not, Rebecca still meant a lot to Marcus.

'I'm trying to understand what state of mind Rebecca has been in the last few weeks,' I said. 'Did you pick up anything, Marcus?'

He shook his head. 'Like I said, we've not spoken. I've seen her a dozen times but if there was a problem she didn't tell me. We've pretty much gone our own ways.'

'She showed no sign that she might have wanted to get back together?' I asked.

'None,' he said. 'I called after we split but she'd cut herself off. Didn't call back. Whenever I bump into her she doesn't have time, just rushes by. She's been kinda cold, actually, after what we'd had. I guess she's made up her mind that I'm history.'

Kind of cold. Mind made up. Marcus' account contrasted with the emotion I'd read in Rebecca's diary. I wondered what drove a girl to bury her feelings and let a bad act play out until something that mattered was trashed. Marcus seemed like a good guy.

Sadie's information was that Marcus knew about this new guy Russell Cohen, but he hadn't brought it up. I guess the idea of his ex-girlfriend looking to a lowlife as replacement company must have cut deep. And who's going to pour their heart out to some private detective they meet on the street? Somewhere in Marcus' head, though, was a better picture of Rebecca than he was giving me.

I asked him what he knew about Cohen.

Marcus switched his gaze smartly back to the street. He paused while he tried to find something neutral.

'I heard stuff,' he said. 'Don't know the guy.'

'What did you hear?'

He shrugged. 'Nothing good. Rebecca's a fool, getting involved with someone like that but I don't know if there's anything between them.' He spoke the words but his eyes told a different story. Marcus saw Russell as Rebecca's new boyfriend. He still hadn't told me anything about the guy.

'What do you know about him?' I repeated.

'Just stuff. Cohen's a shithead. He works the door down the West End. Deals drugs. Small time but he thinks he's a mobster. It's hard to understand Rebecca. The dropout scene isn't hers.'

'And she's been seeing this guy for a few weeks?'

'I heard she's been hanging out with him, yeah.'

Another discrepancy with Rebecca's diary. The diary didn't sound like just hanging out. To me it looked like Rebecca was dipping her toe deep into the doggie-doo.

An antique Beetle swerved into the kerb and a scruffy youth wearing aviator shades yelled out of the window and hit the horn. Marcus held his hand up to hold the car. He shrugged his jacket, ready to go, but stayed put.

'You need to understand something,' he said. 'Rebecca's a great girl.

She's just a little mixed up. Everyone talks about her moods, how crazy she can be, but do you know what I think of?' His guard was down. I kept my mouth clamped.

'I think of what Rebecca loves most in the world: peace.'

'Peace?'

This didn't sound quite the same girl.

'We used to meet in Regents Park,' Marcus said. 'It's halfway between us. There's a café by the colleges. Whoever got there first was supposed to buy the drinks. If it was Rebecca she'd usually sit outside, feeding the squirrels. Other times she'd be in with the oldies, watching the world go by. I used to watch her there. You'd think she was seeing the most wonderful thing in the world. The old people talking, the squirrels chasing around. You see someone that way and you know what's important to them.'

He suddenly realised he was giving a speech. Shut his mouth. Turned to walk across to the Beetle.

'Just find her,' he called back. 'Make sure she's safe. It's something I could never do.'

He jumped into the car and it roared away.

I sat in the Frogeye and dialled the number I'd picked up from the Slaters' voicemail. Recognised the voice above the drone of a hoover. A lilt of Caribbean ancestry. I asked to speak to Meg.

'This is me, hon,' the voice said.

I introduced myself as an acquaintance of the Slaters. Said I was looking for part-time domestic help. The hoover quit.

'That's nice of Jean to give me a recommendation,' she told me. 'I'm busy but I can always fit you in.'

I stayed vague. Details about moving house and possible future dates. Nothing specific to mess up her diary with false bookings. Meg told me she'd be available whenever I was ready. I flicked her some bait.

'Jean says you do a great job,' I said.

That got a yelp from the other end.

'Here's me wishing,' she said. 'But I ain't touched their house in nearly a fortnight. Ever since Jean said they were getting some work done and she didn't want me in. Left a hole in my schedule. I just wish she'd tell me when they're gonna be through.'

'Yeah,' I said, 'those plumbers are unpredictable.'

'Plumbers? You sure your hearing's right, hon? It's the electricity they's repairin'.'

'Sure,' I said. 'But you know how they need to earth the electrical supply to the water pipes. Means resetting the pipes the right depth in the ground.' Mr Know-It-All. Sometimes known as Mr BS. But the BS usually works.

'Lord,' Meg yelled, 'I bet the whole house is topsy-turvy. I hope they ain't expectin' me to get it all tidy in a half-day! Honey, you just give me a call when you're ready for me.'

'Yeah. And if I need some cleaning too.'

Meg laughed and cut the line.

I fired up the Frogeye.

So the Slaters didn't want a domestic inside the house right now. Maybe whatever was happening with Rebecca had complications that might be difficult to hide from someone inside their front door. I just needed to get a line on what the complications were.

Time to try Slater's office door.

CHAPTER THIRTEEN

I detoured back to Paddington and caught Shaughnessy in the office. Brought him up to date on what I had on my missing girl, which was basically a jumble. But along with the confusion I had lines to tug. With the girl missing a week I had some urgency too. Shaughnessy agreed to come into the thing for a few days.

Shaughnessy's view coincided with mine. The Slaters were not in control. Someone had taken their daughter. The question was what to make of the peripheral stuff – Rebecca's bust-up with her boyfriend, the Cohen character, the thing with her stepfather, and Larry Slater's fixation with Holland Park.

Shaughnessy said he'd talk to someone we knew in the DPP's office and see if they'd heard of this Cohen guy. Then he'd take a closer look at

Jean Slater. I'd take Larry Slater.

Shaughnessy sat down to work his phone and I headed out to Islington.

I parked on a meter a hundred yards from the Slater–Kline premises and walked down. Waiting for Slater's call-back wasn't going to work. Besides, I wanted to meet the man face to face, get a feeling for him, look for any sign of something gnawing at him.

I went into the shop and walked to the nearest desk where a thirty-something woman in Day-Glo ovoid spectacles and a pinstripe suit sharp enough to raise legal action from Gillette was packing a bag. She asked how she could help. Her smile made it clear that it had better be the kind she could deliver in two minutes because it was closing time and she was revving for a quick getaway. I asked to see Larry Slater.

She asked if I had an appointment. I said I hadn't. She told me that in that case she didn't think it would be possible.

I assured her I only needed a couple of minutes, hinting that Larry and I were old business buddies, used to operating on the fly. Fly operations didn't work for Ms Gillette. She turned her smile to full wattage and explained that she was personally authorised to assist all Larry's investment clients. I declined her offer, said I needed to see Slater face to face. She locked smiles and repeated her offer. Slater was not available.

We could have gone on all evening. Gillette probably got overtime. I apologised again, slowly, and said that I really wanted to see Larry Slater. Personally and right now. While I was talking I was sneaking a look around the place. The office was modern – pine floor and pine furniture and pine wall cladding. The open plan room went back thirty feet to an array of pine filing cabinets and pine fire doors off to each side. The door to the left was propped open. A clerk came through it, closing up a bag, and walked back to her desk. The door on the right was closed. Probably gave access to private meeting rooms and the bosses' offices upstairs. When I looked back, Ms Gillette's smile was set so hard it was cracking her makeup. She put finality into her voice and repeated that I couldn't see Slater today.

I looked at her desk nameplate.

'Ms Mellor,' I said. 'I guess you don't know who I am.'

If she did I was in trouble. Unsurprisingly, she didn't. Which explained the uncertainty that replaced her fend-off smile. She threw a glance at a male colleague a couple of desks away and shook her head.

'I'm sorry Mr…?'

'…Pine,' I said. 'Just tell Larry that Jerry Pine is here.'

My officious tone kept her off-balance. Ms Gillette's voice took on something that might have been genuine regret. 'I'm very sorry, Mr Pine, but Larry is totally tied up this week. Some unexpected business. He's cancelled his appointments through to next Tuesday. But I'll let him know you called. I know he'll want to speak to you at the earliest opportunity.'

Appointments cancelled. Unexpected business. My bet said that the unexpected stuff had nothing to do with stocks and shares. Ms Gillette's face told me that she'd been turning clients away all week and was up to her eyebrows with it. She just wanted to pack and leave.

I gave her tight-lipped while I thought it through.

Ms Gillette's spectacles glinted under the fluorescents. She was going to be late getting out. She came to a decision. 'Let me call his partner – Mr Stevens. I'm sure you know him.' She reached for her phone.

'Stop!' I held up my hand. 'I know Mr Stevens very well. And Mr Stevens knows that when I come here I talk to Larry. At least I used to talk to him. I hope Larry will be able to explain why he doesn't have time for his oldest clients any more. Just tell him I was here, Ms Mellor. Tell him I'd like him to call me sometime when he's not tied down with too much unexpected business. Tell him I may be reviewing where I do my own business.'

I gave her Eddie-Vindictive and walked out before she could reply.

I'd not got my face-to-face with Slater but I had something I needed.

I walked back by way of the rear of the Slater–Kline block. Slater's parking slot was empty, which explained why he was not available to see his old pal Piney. It didn't explain why Ms Gillette hadn't just told me that he was out in the first place and saved our confrontation. Unless she hadn't been sure. It looked like the guy was sowing chaos this week.

I got back to the Frogeye and called Shaughnessy. He'd finished his telephone research and was outside the Slater house watching for anything interesting. Slater's Lexus wasn't there. He gave me what he'd found on Russell Cohen.

'This boy's a bad apple,' Shaughnessy said. 'List of convictions as long as your arm. Twenty-eight years old and he's spent nine of those inside. Young offender plus two stints in adult, both GBH. Out the first time after eighteen months, the second after three and a half years. The second was a lucky break. Cohen got into a fight and apparently his opponent took a half-dozen slashes across the face with a Stanley knife. The story is that one cut came within a quarter inch of the guy's carotid. That's a quarter inch away from our boy going down for life. Some people are just lucky.'

'Who? Cohen or the guy who got slashed?'

'With Cohen's take on life I guess the other guy's luck doesn't come into it,' Shaughnessy said.

'Figures. So who did he slash?'

'Officially the incident was a random scrap,' said Shaughnessy. 'Unofficially the victim appears to be a punter who got behind in his debts. The word is that Cohen has had a sideline supplying drugs since before his juvie. Nothing they've pinned on him. He's just a name that crops up regularly. The guy's strictly small time but nasty with it. According to the DPP the two GBHs are the tip of the iceberg. They cover a whole list of incidents that didn't get to court. Victims who changed their mind and so on.'

'What did he go down for the first time?'

Shaughnessy laughed cheerlessly. 'You'll love this one, Eddie. He beat up his girlfriend and threw her out of a window. She fell two storeys and spent eighteen months in rehab. Still wouldn't shop him. Cohen only went down because a witness disputed the girl's claim that she'd fallen accidentally. The witness lived in the flat below. Claimed that the girl was screaming long before her acrobatics. In the end the jury went for the word of an independent witness against that of a victim with a shattered pelvis who remembered slipping on a banana skin.'

I heard Shaughnessy's sigh down the line. 'How much punishment do these women have to take,' he said, 'before they realise that whatever they're afraid of can't be any worse than what's actually happening?'

'Psychology,' I said. 'Better the devil you know than a really pissed-off devil you know.'

'This violence against girls,' Shaughnessy said, 'it's not a good thing to be hearing.'

'Nothing sounds good about Rebecca being involved with this guy. Did you pick up anything on what Cohen is up to right now?'

'I talked to Steve at Hammersmith Magistrates' Court,' Shaughnessy said. 'Cohen's probation office is Balham. They have him officially on the dole. Waiting for the headhunters to offer him a City job. Word is he's ticking over nicely with the drugs thing. Work's a few casual door jobs.'

'Did you get an address?'

Shaughnessy gave me an address in Streatham. A council flat in a working class area. Whatever deals Cohen was into weren't getting him rich.

Shaughnessy said he would stay at the Slaters' house for a while, see who came and went. Tomorrow we'd go for the direct approach. Confront the Slaters and suggest that they bring us in on what was happening or have it go public. If Rebecca was involved with someone like Cohen it might need sorting fast. I dialled Sadie to see if she had anything on Cohen's door jobs. Her voice screamed into my ear over the top of another racket. I held the phone at a safe distance.

'I knew it would be that creep!' she yelled, 'I knew he'd got her!'

It's impressive the way people are always ahead of us. What can they see that detectives can't? Maybe the agency should recruit a few doorstep gossips and teenagers. Save a whole lot of legwork. I repeated my question about Cohen's place of work.

'Up the West End,' Sadie said. 'A place called Kicks?'

'Is he there every night?'

'Most. He starts around eight. That's the time Becky's always gone up there.'

'Okay,' I said. 'I'll go talk to him.'

'Tell him that if he's hurt her you're going to tear him apart.'

'Sure,' I said, 'unless he's bigger than me.'

'He's not so big,' Sadie said, 'just a mean prick.'

'Watch your language, young lady,' I said.

'Forget my language,' she said. 'You just get that bastard. I hate guys like that.'

'So do I,' I said.

'Hey, Eddie?'

'What?' I said.

'It's a jacket and tie place? You might want to know.'

The racket went dead. I held up the phone wondering whether service providers could be held responsible for the stuff that came through. The phone stayed silent for about five seconds before it bust into life again and nearly gave me a heart attack. I picked up and Arabel's husky voice came over the airwaves.

'How's it going, babe? Thought you were never getting off the line.'

'Just client stuff,' I said.

'I'm just checking that you've not forgotten that your girl has an appetite.'

My girl had lots of appetites. I deduced that this one was a reference to our dinner-date. We were eating out before she went on shift.

'I'm on my way, Bel,' I said.

She made me an offer: 'If you got here early we could have a little hors d'oeuvre.'

The invitation was tempting but if we started down that road we'd never eat. Didn't seem fair to send the girl to work hungry. I turned down the offer and said I'd see her in an hour. The happy way she accepted told me that she knew her priorities too.

'Bel?' I said.

'Yeah?'

'Do you remember if I have a suit and tie?'

'Are we going somewhere posh or are you getting kinky?'

'Answer the question.'

'A suit? Yeah. I saw something once. You'll have to fight the moths though.'

'That's what I thought.'

'So what's with the dressing-up?'

'Nothing's with the dressing up. Just a passing thought. We're eating Italian.'

'Suits me. Gives me my carbs for eleven hours' slog.'

I put incredulous into my voice. 'You telling me night shift is a slog?'

'Babe,' she said, 'don't fall ill and come to my hospital.' She cut the line. It was a day for cut lines.

CHAPTER FOURTEEN

I decided against the suit. Arrived at Arabel's flat off Roman Road at ten past seven. The Italian restaurant was a five minute walk, a small place, not yet trendy but with the right buzz and food you couldn't better in Rome. We ordered seafood platters and played footsie under the table while we waited. The fooling about was instigated by Arabel, to make sure I regretted her being on night shift as much as she did. In the verbal part of the conversation she asked about my missing girl. I gave her the latest. She picked up on the Cohen character. The image of a vulnerable girl tripping on the wild side had a particular resonance for her.

'You think Cohen has got her into trouble?' she asked.

'I don't know. I need to talk to him. The problem is that we've come into this hunt a week late.'

'You think Rebecca may have been hurt already?'

'It's possible. But it doesn't fit with the Slaters keeping quiet. If they thought Rebecca had been harmed they'd not be hiding anything. So either Rebecca has got herself into a fix or the Slaters are being coerced. The girl may be okay for the moment.'

'Maybe she's run away with this Cohen guy.'

The seafood platters arrived. Each the size of a small table. Our allowance for a trip back to Arabel's for her to change began to look marginal. We attacked our plates for a couple of minutes before I came up for air.

'I don't think Rebecca has run away,' I told her.

'Okay, so the Cohen guy is holding her. Perhaps he's extorting the family.'

'Dodgy boyfriend turns predator,' I mused. 'It's a possibility.'

'You need to be careful with him, babe,' said Arabel. I'd given her Shaughnessy's unflattering bio.

'I'm always careful.'

We left food on the plates. Clearing them would have put us both in A&E. We settled for a double espresso apiece that would keep Arabel on adrenaline for the shift and me hovering above my bed till morning. Then we walked back to her digs and six minutes later I escorted a lady of the medical profession out to my car. Frogeyes don't have central locking. I opened the door for her to squeeze in. The operation takes dexterity if you're over five feet. In the case of females the squeezing in is incompatible with keeping hemlines where they should be. Even NHS hemlines. It paid to play the gentleman. Something about the awkwardness of the legs and the particular curves that formed as Arabel folded herself in could fairly distract a man. A girl might even suspect that you drive a car like a Frogeye to achieve that exact result. But Arabel was used to the car. She'd got slick at getting in and out and I knew that any difficulties were deliberate. She messed about until she figured I was truly regretting her being on shift then flapped her hand for the door.

'Come on, babe. Are we staying here all night?'

I took the question as rhetorical.

I slammed the door and folded myself into the other seat. Dropped her at the hospital and got a last showing of her limbs as she climbed out.

Then I turned the Frogeye and headed back onto the Mile End Road and followed the traffic towards the West End.

Kicks nightclub had a smoked-glass entrance in a narrow street north of Chinatown. It was Thursday night and still early for the club scene. I watched the place from down the street. Saw one couple go in and a group of girls stop to chat with the doorman before deciding to get drunk somewhere cheaper. The doorman was a gorilla in a mid-calf trench coat and dickey-bow. He watched the street with his hands at his sides, looking for signs of enemy action. I wondered if the guy was Cohen.

Only one way to find out.

I walked down. When I stopped in front of him the guy gave me the doorman's universal expression of boredom that lets you know that you're looking at a shark behind the respectable veneer. The genie is corked but it's your call. The guy was white, six-three, eighteen-plus stone.

'I'm looking for Russell,' I said.

'What's up?' the guy asked.

I didn't ask him if he was Cohen. If he was then he already knew I didn't know him.

'Tell him I want a word,' I said.

He looked me over and decided that I wasn't worth Cohen's time. He shook his head.

'He's busy,' he said. 'See him tomorrow.'

He focused his attention back on the street. I could either stand there or piss off.

Instead I said; 'I need to see Russell tonight. Okay if I drop inside?'

I stepped forward but Dickey-Bow shifted casually and the door was suddenly blocked. It didn't look like it was going to get un-blocked unless I called a tow truck.

'Ties only, mate,' he said. He was still watching the street, ignoring me the way a rhino ignores a flea. I wondered what it would take to shift him out of the doorway. I didn't have a tow truck.

I looked down the street myself. Gave it a few moments for him to register that I hadn't disappeared. Then I turned back and gave him a stare I practice sometimes in the mirror. My Marginally-Sane. It got his attention. Probably he was petrified but he didn't show it. He just stared right back like this was a very boring night. I carried on the act and jabbed my finger at the doors.

'Why don't you ask your friend to step out,' I said. 'Tell him Mr E wants a word. Unless he'd prefer us to call back later.'

That's E for Eddie. Lucky I wasn't called Xavier. Hard to get someone to take you seriously when you tell them Mr X is waiting.

I watched Dickey-Bow trying to work out whether Mr E was someone Cohen should be worried about or not. But the hint that the club might be visited later struck a chord. A visit didn't sound good, even to someone who likes a rumble. He gave me a stare that let me know how hard he was working to hold it in, but he didn't repeat his suggestion that I leave. I stayed watching the street.

'Are you the rozzers?' he said.

I turned back. Gave him Stand-Up-Comedian. Looked round for the audience.

'The rozzers?' I said. 'Who's your optician, mate?' I shook my head and pursed my lips like I was deciding whether it was simpler just to walk away and call back later with the boys. Dickey-Bow finally opted for caution.

'Stay there,' he said. He went in through the smoked glass. I turned to face the street again so that Cohen couldn't ID me – or rather not ID me – without coming out onto the pavement. The ruse worked. When I turned back there were three of them on the steps. A bad publicity shot for *The Blues Brothers*.

Next to Dickey-Bow was a black guy in shades. He was the same height but three feet wider. He'd either had his trench coat cut at a carpet factory or had mugged Demis Roussos. Rebecca's dodgy boyfriend was white, which made him the last of the line-up. Russell Cohen was half the size of the others but his attitude made up for the missing body mass. Cohen was five-ten and fourteen stone max but my guess was that it all counted. His hair was a white fuzz capping a puffy, mean face. He sported shades that perfectly matched Carpet Man's. Dickey-Bow was probably cursing that he'd left his own back home.

Cohen's expression was a contrived blandness. With this guy, the first you would know about trouble was when you connected with his ten-pound fist. His body stance though told me that the visit from Mr E had got him on edge. He was trying to figure if he'd brought trouble to the club.

The three of them stared at me the way they'd watch a punter with holes in his jeans.

'What's your game?' Cohen asked. 'Who the hell's Mr E?'

I gave him straight-faced.

'I'm Mr E,' I said. 'Eddie Flynn. You must be Russell.'

'Who wants to know?'

You'd think that would have been obvious. I guess they keep the questions simple at the doormen's examination boards. I let the query go. I had questions of my own.

'I'm looking for Rebecca Townsend,' I said. 'I hear she's pally with you.'

'Never heard of her.'

His answer slipped out so fast that I knew he wanted it to sound false. He wanted me to contradict.

Detectives are the contradicting type. 'We can do this the easy way,' I said, 'or the hard way.' I wasn't sure if it was Willis or De Niro had said that. If Cohen was a film buff he'd know. 'Either way,' I said, 'I want to know where the girl is.'

Dickey-Bow and Carpet Man flashed each other glances. Cohen just stared at me with the focus he'd apply to watching a fly on a turd.

'I think,' he said finally, 'that you should piss off.'

His voice was calm. Still waters.

Despite the cool act I could see something tugging inside him. Maybe he still didn't know what this was about, but he didn't sense anything good brewing. What I sensed was the beginnings of movement from the two stooges at his side.

Cohen decided that he had enough backup. He stuck with his proposal.

'Sod off now, mate,' he repeated, 'before you get a smack.'

'Russell,' I told him, 'it would take more than you.'

Russell gave me incredulous and looked sideways to see if his buddies had dematerialised. They hadn't. That must have boosted his confidence. He didn't run for cover.

'I'm looking for Rebecca Townsend,' I repeated, 'and I'm going to find her. Very soon. If she's with you it's better we talk now.'

Cohen shook his head a little more emphatically, playing to his buddies. 'What would be better,' he said, 'is for your plates to start shuffling down that old pavement. Before me and my friends get annoyed.'

The sight of Cohen getting annoyed would be interesting. The sight of Dickey-Bow and Carpet-Man getting annoyed would probably be fatal. Dickey-Bow's face had a look that said I might not need to wait too long for the experience. It looked like I'd exhausted my novelty value. Dickey-Bow leaned forward to explain the deal.

'You've got five seconds,' he said. 'If I come off these steps Russell's gonna be the least of your worries.'

I still didn't move. Russell and I had a thing going. Messages passing between us. Before I knew it the five seconds were up and Dickey-Bow and Carpet Man were coming down the steps in a deceptively casual way. Just business as usual. Cohen watched and smirked. Some people you just can't frighten. The two hulks rolling towards me were definitely frightening and looked about as stoppable as road rollers. There's only one way to beat road rollers. Speed.

I nodded a signal at Cohen and turned away. The gorillas could still have jumped me but I was backing off and top rule in the door business is don't get blood on your suit before the punters are all in. I walked away in one piece.

I headed back to where I'd left the Sprite parked on double yellows, musing at how detection is ninety percent frustration and ten percent results. That would be fine if the results weren't so often negative.

I'd got nothing for my detour except the certainty that if Rebecca was mixed up with Cohen she was in big trouble.

The question was whether Cohen was involved in this thing at all, or whether I should be looking somewhere else.

A real puzzle for Mr E.

CHAPTER FIFTEEN

At seven next morning I was parked up by my substation outside the Slater home. The house was quiet. Larry Slater's Lexus was still in front of the garage.

There was a tap on the Frogeye's window and Shaughnessy folded himself in with the sigh of someone trying a boot three sizes too small.

Shaughnessy had parked his Yamaha somewhere down the lane. No one notices a bike. A bike is easier to get around on, too, but who wants his backside out in the rain every day? The Frogeye suited me fine and gave Shaughnessy something to complain about whenever I gave him a ride.

'One day, Eddie,' he said, 'you'll buy a car that doesn't put my back out.'

I'd listened to his complaints for six years. It was part of the routine.

'If I want to drive a tank I'll join the army,' I told him.

Shaughnessy gave me leery. 'Just a normal car would be fine, Eddie! One where you don't need to consult a yoga manual.'

'It's all just a matter of technique,' I told him.

'Sure, like with a straightjacket.'

'Houdini could get out of a jacket in under sixty seconds with his hands chained,' I pointed out.

'Yeah, and look what happened to him. Dead in a fishtank! And I bet the bastard couldn't have got out of this tin can if you greased him with warm lard.'

Shaughnessy had watched all the movies. History, Hollywood-style. I didn't correct him on the Houdini thing.

'Are you taking the first one out?' Shaughnessy asked.

I said I would. 'My guess is it will be Larry. I'll leave Jean to you. If she stays home you can follow her up and down the hallway with the Yamaha.'

'Got it. And if Larry drives past us before I can escape from this sardine tin you can just drop me off at the nearest motorway services.'

Shaughnessy and I had opened the agency when I came out of the Mets six years before. Shaughnessy was twenty years older than me and had seen a different side of life by way of the special services. He never talked about his old job and I never talked about mine. Shaughnessy also stayed fit. I knew he could beat me in and out of the Frogeye any day. It just made him feel good to gripe about it.

I flicked on the news and we listened in on the world for forty-five minutes. Just on eight Larry Slater came out of the house and climbed into the Lexus. Despite Shaughnessy's words he was out of the Frogeye and had vanished before Slater had even pulled out of his drive.

I followed the Lexus towards the main road and into the rush hour. One detail Shaughnessy had forgotten to mention about the Sprite was how it eluded rear-view mirrors better than any motorcycle. When we merged into the traffic in Hampstead I was only three cars back and invisible. If Slater had been a professional the short tail wouldn't have worked, but Slater was just a guy in the street. I could have sat in his back seat and he wouldn't have noticed.

Slater drove down through Camden and we crawled through the log jam on the Euston Road. Looked like he was headed for the office. Maybe he'd put in a regular nine-to-five, but if he came out early I'd see where he went.

I was right about the destination. I parked on a meter a hundred yards from the Slater–Kline business and went to stand on my corner. I was there for three hours. I'd just reloaded the parking meter at noon and was walking back with a cup of coffee when Slater's Lexus rolled out onto the main street. I poured the coffee down a drain and sprinted back to the car. I abandoned a two-hour load on the meter and turned across the traffic to catch up. Stayed on Slater's tail and followed him home to Hampstead. By twelve thirty I was parked up by the substation, right back where I'd started. I swore and flicked the radio to Kiss, turned up the volume.

Two minutes later Shaughnessy slid into the car and asked what was happening. I told him. Gave him exact details of the wasted coffee and the two-hour load running in the meter. Petty stuff, but it helped. Shaughnessy confirmed that Jean Slater hadn't budged.

Decision time. I told Shaughnessy to hang in a while longer and call me if anything happened. There was a call I had to make.

I crossed the river and worked over to Streatham, watching for street names. I found the one I was looking for in a run-down area wedged between converging railway lines. The address was a fifties council development, a flaking four-storey bunker with a facade of french windows and false balconies weeping rust stains. It was an architectural graffito, standing shoulder to shoulder with a Victorian terrace like a shady character in a bus queue. I squeezed the Frogeye into an empty slot and tried to ignore a queasy feeling as I locked it up.

The bunker's communal door was open. Apparently security doors and house phones hadn't reached this far down the council list. I went in. The stairwell inside smelt of something unpleasant. I trotted up to the third floor before my nose could figure out what it was and found a door with a number but no name. A couple of bare wires protruded from where the bell push should have been. Maybe you grabbed the wires and made your own noise. I played safe and knocked. Gave it an official crispness.

Nothing. I made a fist and beat on the wood in a way that suggested I was not going away.

I heard a voice inside. The inflexion said I'd better have a good reason to be there when the door opened. When the door did open, Russell Cohen appeared like a nightmare on dress-down day.

The suit and shades had gone. Black Levis crimped a Guns 'n Roses t-shirt over a belly that was beginning to show curvature. Without the suit you could see he weighed twelve or thirteen stones max, but his demeanour was the one I'd seen the night before. He had the kind of stare to make people look the other way. Without the shades I could see the lifetime's bad attitude that drove him. Cohen was twenty-six but he looked forty.

He clocked who I was and turned around to play out a little pantomime he'd perfected for dealing with idiots outside club doors. The act comprised staring at his own front door as if it shouldered the blame for whoever appeared outside it. The door kept quiet. Cohen turned back to me.

'What's your friggin' game?' he said. He pulled a face like he was looking at some kind of bad dream. He could have saved his act. If I'd wanted nightmare I'd have sent Shaughnessy.

There was a racing channel playing inside the flat and a bad smell that was a distant cousin of the one on the stairs. A cocktail of unwashed laundry, booze and TV dinners. A little spliff thrown in.

'Remember me, Russell?'

'Yeah. I remember you. Mr Friggin' E.'

Memory Man. I gave him my Shit-Eater.

'What are you?' he asked. 'Some kind of fruit?'

'Just a guy needing some answers,' I said.

Cohen stared at me. 'I think,' he said, 'that you're a guy who needs to piss off.'

I dropped the grin. 'Russell,' I said, 'stay cool. I just need two minutes.'

Cohen gave me a couple of seconds then moved up close. The movement was slow, easy. One moment he was in his doorway, the next moment he was in my face. His eyes opened wide to emphasise a proposition.

'I'll count to ten, matey,' Cohen said. 'You need to be gone before I get there.'

This was bluff. There was no way Cohen could count to ten. 'I need some answers about Rebecca Townsend. When I get them I'm out of your face.'

'One,' Cohen said.

Still bluff. Who can't count to one?

'Two.'

We were eyeball to eyeball while Cohen continued to show off. So maybe he could count to ten. While I marvelled at his mathematical skills the clock continued to tick. We got to six, then seven. The thing took me right back to the schoolyard. Cohen hit the eight mark and his head tilted back a fraction, just enough to tell me where this was going. A light came on in his eyes. He wanted me to still be there at ten.

The count didn't make it that far.

At nine, his head moved back like a spring-loaded wrecking ball. He was focusing a headbutt on my nose whilst trying to figure the next number, which explained why he wasn't paying attention. Before he hit double digits I'd stepped back and kicked his knee hard. His headbutt flailed thin air as the shock of the knee doubled him over. I palmed his neck, two-handed, and put my weight on it. Cohen's head went down and his face met my own knee with a painful smack. He bounced up like he was on springs and I lifted my foot, sole out, and slammed him backwards into his flat. He crashed over a phone table down the hallway. The table collapsed. Glass shattered. Cohen sat down in the mess. He was up and ready to go in an instant but my foot caught him between his legs and finally something got through. He doubled over and yelled blue murder but he stopped coming at me. I took advantage of his momentary abeyance and closed the front door. When I turned back Cohen was leaning against the wall, gripping his thighs.

I walked through to his lounge. The room was sparsely furnished but what was there was expensive. A sixty-inch plasma screen on the wall showed a bunch of horses going neck and neck. A leather sofa was half covered by an open copy of the Racing Post and a WAP-enabled phone flickered atop it. Cohen busy investing his ill-earned dough. I picked up the remote and muted the TV, wondering how many month's wages at Eagle Eye would buy me that kind of wall decoration.

Cohen came in cursing and I turned to face him.

I waited for his words to dry up then asked my questions.

'You've been seeing Rebecca Townsend,' I said. 'The story is that you've been showing her the good life. Or what passes for you as the good life.'

Cohen was dripping blood onto his carpet. He gave me a look that said I'd better not turn my back anytime soon but he stayed his distance.

'We've got a situation,' I told him. 'Rebecca has disappeared. No one knows where or why. We assume she's in trouble. What I need to know is whether you're involved.'

I tossed the TV remote between my hands to remind Cohen that there was more furniture to break. Intimidation was the only thing people like Cohen understood. 'I need to know what's going on between the two of you.'

'Nonna your business,' Cohen gasped.

I sighed.

Something inside Cohen's skull held him back for the moment, but with his type enlightenment is a long way from fear. Retreads like Cohen don't come with fear built in. They rely on stupidity. You could pound a nutter like that all day and all you'd get would be complaints from the neighbours.

I bent down and tipped the mess of empty cans and takeout cartons off his coffee table and lifted it. The thing weighed a ton, although it wasn't in the same league as HP Logistics' swivel chairs. I approached the plasma screen and hefted the table.

'Stop,' he yelled. 'Calm down you shithead!'

Finally I had his attention. I lowered the table to the floor.

'Fine, Russell,' I said. 'Let's start again. How long have you been seeing Rebecca?'

Cohen shook his head. His face was crimped like he was sucking a lemon. 'How should I know,' he said. 'Four or five weeks.'

'That's precise,' I said. 'Sounds like a meaningful relationship.'

'Meaningful, shit,' Cohen said. 'She's a stupid kid hanging around looking for action. She wants it she gets it. It's all the same to me.'

'What kind of action? Drugs? Sex? Or are we talking philosophy discussions.'

'None of your business. If she comes to play we play. So what's your gripe? I've not even seen the bitch for a couple of weeks.'

'I'm trying to find out what's going on with her,' I said. 'Starting with what's happening between you and her.'

The head shake again, like an itching bull. 'I told you,' Cohen said, 'we hang out. She likes a bit of rough. Know what I mean?'

'No, Russell,' I said. 'I don't know what you mean. Rough like tramping a little? Or rough like getting slapped around? Or do you just mean rough like hanging out with a turd?'

Cohen didn't take the bait. 'Rebecca never got a single smack off me,' he said. 'And she didn't do nothing she didn't want. The best thing you can do with that kind is grab what's offered. Give it what it wants.'

It.

Cohen was going to have a problem if he decided to settle down. Getting those "it"s into the marriage vows would take finesse.

'How often have you been seeing Rebecca?'

'This day and that,' he said. 'Whenever she cuts class.'

'Is she on anything?'

Cohen sneered.

'That uptight bitch would be scared shitless if you showed her the real stuff,' he said. 'So maybe we have a little smoke sometimes. Maybe we don't. What's all this about? Why's everyone pissing their pants?'

'When did you last see her?'

Another head shake. An annoyed kind of shake, but he answered my question: 'Dunno. Coupla weeks back,' he decided.

'Not since?'

'Nah.'

'Are you shitting me, Russell?'

Cohen let his sneer answer.

'Have you done something to Rebecca?'

He continued staring me out, maybe getting brave again.

'Have you or your slimy pals hurt her?' I clarified. 'Because if you have I'm going to find out and come after you.'

'What are you going to find out?' Cohen said. 'You're full of shit.'

Braver by the minute. I could understand Cohen forgetting the threat to his plasma screen but I had to wonder about a guy who could forget the ache between his legs.

I kept my voice even. 'When precisely did you see Rebecca last?'

He stayed quiet. For a moment I thought he was not going to answer, but he eventually worked it out.

'Middle of the week. Week last Tuesday.'

The day before Rebecca went missing.

'Where?' I asked.

'At the club,' he said. 'She was in for a couple of hours. Went off around ten.'

'With anyone?'

He strengthened the sneer. 'She was with me,' he said. 'I thought you'd got it. The bitch was on heat for me. She comes round the club to get herself tipsy-topsy and thinks she's living the wild life.'

'Being with you doesn't stop her walking out of there with some other guy,' I said.

'Yes it does,' he said.

Possessive. For a guy who couldn't care less.

'So you've not seen her since that night?'

'Nah.'

Whatever little credibility I gave to Cohen's words I got the sense that he didn't know anything. He was sticking to his story like chewing gum on angora.

'Did Rebecca talk to you? Anything about trouble at home? Plans to leave town?'

'Nah.'

'Anything you hear about her? People talking?'

'Nah.'

Cohen's disinterest was getting emphatic. The shock had worn off and he was getting courage. Working himself up for a second round. It was time to quit. If the Slaters pointed at Cohen I'd be right back. Right now my stomach had absorbed as much of the atmosphere as was healthy.

I left Cohen to it and scuttled back down the stairs to get to breathable air. The Frogeye was still in one piece on the street. The sun was out and the day seemed momentarily good. I'd just got the engine fired up when my phone rang.

Shaughnessy.

Things were happening.

CHAPTER SIXTEEN

Slater had left the house. Shaughnessy was following his Lexus south through the city. I drove west across London to intercept them. If Slater was headed out of town I'd take over.

Shaughnessy's hands-free commentary guided me towards Hammersmith as he and Slater moved south-west onto the A402. We got a break when the Lexus got snarled in roadworks coming into Hammersmith. I closed the gap and by the time Shaughnessy reported Slater turning at the roundabout beneath the flyover I was already moving up the eastern ramp. I put my foot down across the flyover and spotted Slater merging into the traffic a couple of hundred yards ahead. Heading out towards the M4.

I called the hit and Shaughnessy broke off to resume his stakeout at the Slater house. I pushed an Eartha Kitt tape in and cranked the volume. I had a full tank and good music. Wherever Slater was headed I was with him.

The Lexus passed Heathrow and took the M25 south. I followed into roadworks, taking the same lane between the cones. Five minutes later we were out of it and the Lexus moved into the slip for the M3. I didn't see out-of-town trips being the norm in a stockbroker's day. So maybe this excursion was part of whatever was shredding Slater's diary.

The Lexus cruised south-west for forty minutes then continued onto the M27 towards Bournemouth. The sun flared bright in the Frogeye's worn windscreen. Keeping Slater in sight took concentration. When the M27 quit we continued on the A-road in heavier traffic. A half-hour later Slater took the roundabout towards Bournemouth, skirted the town and drove into Poole. We went through the town and crossed the harbour bridge.

On the far side the Lexus turned inland again through residential streets and finally pulled into a marina called Cobb's Quay. I held back in the parking area and watched Slater pull up nose to tail with a bright red Toyota SUV out on the jetties. I tucked in behind a beached cruiser fifty yards back and walked down. Enough hardware was bobbing out on the water to start a navy. Motor cruisers and yachts in all directions. This wasn't billionaires' row – there was nothing over fifty feet in sight – but it was serious hobby.

I watched from behind a skip as a man in a flannel sports jacket climbed out of the SUV to meet Slater. The two of them shook hands briefly as if this was routine business then walked down a jetty and skipped up onto the bow of a motor cruiser. They prowled the deck for a couple of minutes then disappeared below. I walked down the jetty, ready to about-turn if they came back up on deck. The vessel was named the *Lode Star*. A sleek forty-footer in brilliant white with a fully enclosed wheelhouse topped by a radar transmitter and a raked VHF. Just the place to do a little discreet business.

I went back to dry land and found a bollard with a view. The sun was warm on my face. A breeze off the Channel ruffled the water, setting masts dancing. As stakeouts went it beat lurking in the bushes outside the Slater house. As stakeouts went it was brief: ten minutes later the two men came out. They quit the boat and moved back up the jetty. I walked back to the Frogeye. By the time I got there they were at their cars. Another brief handshake and the meeting was over.

I started the car. My choice was to stay with Slater or to follow the Toyota. Opted for the Toyota. The chances were that Slater would head straight back home. I was already prepping Shaughnessy as the Lexus passed me on its way out. Ten seconds later the SUV passed and turned towards the sea. I allowed another car to get between us, then followed. Apart from the vehicle between me and the Toyota traffic was nil.

We crossed back over the bridge and got into an area of narrow streets and tourist shops. The SUV turned and squeezed down a side street between an antique shop and a mountain bike outlet. I indicated but took my time making the turn to make sure the SUV had got clear. Saw it parked with its wheels on the kerb just fifty yards down. The driver was opening the door. I waited for non-existent traffic and watched the guy walk into a doorway. Then I cancelled my indicator and found a slot on the main street.

I walked back round. The buildings were mostly residential, terraced cottages with front doors right on the street. A handful of small businesses was mixed in – a grocery store, a bedroom furniture store and a run-down cafe. The Toyota was parked outside a door adjoining the cafe. Side stairs ran up to first floor offices and a plate read DK MARINE. I walked past and crossed the street to a ginnel thirty yards away. Loitered to see if the guy came back out. After thirty minutes he was still there. I walked around the block to avoid passing in front of the building again and got back to the Frogeye. I had a boat name, a licence plate and a business address in addition to all the fresh air.

I cranked up the Frogeye and drove back to London.

I reached Battersea at seven. Arabel had left a message before going on shift. The message reminded me that we were shopping tomorrow morning. She'd be off duty at seven thirty, ready to hit Covent Garden by nine. No mention of anything as mundane as sleep. I started to call, tell her I might not make it. Cancelled before the line connected. I had a busy weekend but I figured I shouldn't let the girl down more than three times in a month. In my line of work you could grow a habit of letting people down. Arabel put up with it mostly but I'd cancelled a few things lately. Building credits this weekend seemed like a good idea.

I freshened up. Grilled a tuna steak that Arabel had sneaked into my fridge. Ate it with a jacket potato and steamed veg and washed it down with a cup of Buckaroo coffee laced with single cream. Then I called Shaughnessy and headed out.

I crossed the river in early-evening traffic and headed for the Podium. There was a live set at nine thirty so entry was a fiver. I told Barney I'd not be staying and he waved me through gratis. The place was mostly empty. I got a seat and relaxed with a pint of Pride and piped jazz. At eight thirty Shaughnessy came in. He brought another beer and a mineral water over. He pushed the beer across the table. Shaughnessy's own tipple never varied much. Sometimes it was plain mineral water, sometimes carbonated. I tried to see what he had today but the light wasn't good.

He gave me the run-down on Jean Slater. She'd not shown her face outside the house all day. Shaughnessy had sneaked around the rear of the property a couple of times out of boredom. The first time he'd spotted her taking out the rubbish, the next she was just a shadow behind a window. The trip tailing Larry Slater to the M4 had been the highlight of his day.

I gave him the details of Slater's nautical excursion. Maybe the meeting on the yacht had nothing to do with whatever was happening to his stepdaughter. But I was staying with the First Rule of the Detective Game. No coincidences.

Shaughnessy agreed. 'Something's thrown a spanner into Slater's routine,' he said. 'I don't see rushing home for lunch or chasing to the coast for a ten-minute business chat being routine.'

'Me neither. You catch him later?'

Shaughnessy took a swig and planted his bottle. Bubbles rose through the water.

Carbonated.

'Yeah,' he said.

Shaughnessy had picked Slater up as he crossed the M25 and tailed him back into London through the rush-hour traffic. By six o'clock the Lexus was parked outside the house in Holland Park. Same routine as two nights ago. Slater had rung the doorbell and got nothing. Then he'd sat in his car for an hour and a half before heading home. It seemed that our mysterious Brown was still out.

'Whatever is going on with the Slaters,' Shaughnessy said, 'this Brown person is part of it.'

I agreed. 'The Holland Park thing has me wondering whether Rebecca has got involved with someone there. Someone linked to her disappearance.'

'So maybe not an extortion racket,' Shaughnessy said. 'If the girl has been kidnapped for money it's hard to see how Slater's fixation with Holland Park fits in. He'd know the girl wasn't findable. So what's the guy looking for?'

He came back to another alternative. 'How did Cohen pan out?'

'I don't think he's part of it,' I said. 'The guy could be good for anything dirty but he didn't seem to know or care. As far as he's concerned, Rebecca is history until the next time she pops up in his sights.'

I detailed my plans to take a quick look at a couple of things over the weekend then we'd go and talk to the Slaters, put pressure on them to bring us in on their problem. We agreed arrangements and Shaughnessy went home to take care of responsibilities I didn't have. I gave him a fiver to pass to Barney on the way out. Might as well stay for the set. If I went home I'd brood about the missing girl. Imagining the worst case.

CHAPTER SEVENTEEN

Arabel and I breakfasted in Covent Garden then spent a morning in the boutiques. Arabel has a figure that carries expensive clothes frighteningly well. Shopping with her could leave the car in hock. Mercifully, even Arabel had to sleep sometime. We called it quits shortly before my bank went into liquidation. I left her to crash out early afternoon and drove back to Battersea.

On the way I made a hands-free to Shaughnessy to see if anything was happening at the Slater house. Shaughnessy wasn't at the house. An hour back Larry Slater had taken a drive and Shaughnessy had tailed him to Holland Park and yet another vigil outside the apartment. Shaughnessy had pulled Harry Green in to take over at the house rather than call me in. Figured he was doing me a kindness. It was his soft spot for Arabel. Shaughnessy had decided that the girl was good for me. I could have told him that already, but he had also figured that the best chance of me keeping Arabel was to shield her from the chronic unreliability that goes with the private investigator's lifestyle, mine in particular. He seemed to think that the occasional morning draining my bank account would show Arabel that I was reliable. Arabel knew better.

'You want me to take over at Holland Park?' I offered.

'No,' Shaughnessy said. 'I'm comfy here. Just clocking variable.'

Shaughnessy and I took a fixed and a variable pay packet. The fixed was a basic wage, sufficient to support a life of penury in the city. We boosted this with the variable, which was a bonus based on the hours we clocked and the cash coming in. In slack months the cash was a figment of our imaginations and the variable simply accrued as credits. Shaughnessy's extra hours were unlikely to bring hard cash in the near future but he could always get off on counting his credits.

'Let me know if anything breaks,' I said. 'Otherwise we'll talk tonight.'

'Tonight.'

I called Harry Green who sounded even happier than Shaughnessy about accruing hours since we paid him cash. Harry reported that Jean was sitting tight inside the Slater house.

'You want me to walk round, take a look?' he asked.

'No,' I said. 'Stay put. Just call me if she moves.'

'I'll do that, Eddie.'

'We may need you this evening,' I said. 'Have you got engagements?'

'None I can't break,' Harry said. 'Anything special?'

'Just some digging,' I said

'Sean tells me this girl's been gone ten days,' Harry said. 'That doesn't sound good.'

'Not to me either. But if she's still in one piece we'll get her.'

Harry said nothing.

I killed a couple of hours in the attic until the light started to go. The sky was clouding over fast. A storm on its way. It would be dark in another hour.

I called Shaughnessy and Harry Green for updates. Slater had quit his vigil and returned home and so had Shaughnessy. Harry was still watching the Slater house. I asked him to hang on for another two hours and warn me urgently if Slater moved.

I changed into dark clothes and a shooting jacket with a modified vest that was useful for holding P.I. stuff and went out to the car.

It was raining hard when I crossed the river. I drove up to Islington and pulled into the alleyway behind the Slater–Kline business. The parking slots were all empty. I drove through and left the Frogeye a couple of streets away then hurried back through the rain to a coffee bar opposite the shop. Carried a drink over to a window seat and watched the place. The main office was brightly lit but nothing moved inside. The only candidates for weekend working would be the firm's partners, but the empty parking spaces behind the building told me that no one was in.

I finished my drink and walked round to the back of the building. A fire escape climbed the rear wall. Yesterday's visit had shown me that the main office was well protected, but my guess was that the upper floors would have minimal security. I climbed the fire escape and gently jemmied a washroom window by the first-floor platform. I was inside in thirty seconds. I went through into the corridor. No security sensors in sight. I walked downstairs and looked through the fire doors into the office. An array of motion detectors and mini-CCTVs protected the area but what I was looking for was on this side of the doors. Back upstairs I located Slater's office at the front of the building.

The door was locked but the lock was meant to deter casual wandering, not a professional assault. I released the lock and went in. The room was bright from the street lights but I needed more. I flipped on Slater's desk lamp. Anyone watching would see a business partner putting in the hours counting his dough Saturday evening.

Shelves around Slater's walls were stacked with company reports and trading magazines. A locked filing cabinet beside the door probably held stuff that Slater was working personally – trading analyses, reports, client correspondence. I was looking for something that didn't belong, something that might give a clue about what was going on at home. Notes, telephone numbers, maybe a ransom demand. It was a long shot but Slater was spending time here in this office despite the thing at home. There was a chance he had stashed something here.

Slater's desk backed onto the window. The inlaid leather work-top was bare except for a low-footprint PC, a telephone and thinly populated in- and out-trays. The desk was built of solid mahogany, had the kind of old-world feel that solicitors go for. Slater's attempt at a status symbol. I sat down. Three pull-out drawers on the left and a file drawer and stationery tray to the right. The drawers were locked; I opened the left drawers inside five seconds with sixteen-gauge wire.

The top drawer was sweep-up from when the desktop was cleared at night. Customer portfolios with graphics tracking gains and losses. I skimmed Slater's cryptic market assessments and action lists, saw nothing unusual. The printouts were dated within the last few days so something like normal business had been going on.

The next drawer down held writing pads and a couple of market weeklies. Nothing of interest. The bottom drawer was twice the depth of the others and Slater used it to stack old material he hadn't got round to throwing out. The dump was near capacity. I pulled the contents out in blocks and set them in order on the desk top, although I wasn't sure there was any order. Last year's company reports, market summaries going back two or three years, torn-out magazine pages with marked-up articles, similarly outdated. A couple more A4 writing pads. Then I found something interesting.

Pushed beneath the bottom layer of market magazines were some sheets that didn't belong: two Amex statements and two bills for Slater's mobile. The statements were recent; February and March. Odd stuff to keep at the office. Even odder under a weight of junk in your bottom drawer.

I cleared some desk space to see what Slater was hiding.

Slater used his mobile freely. The statements were three pages each. All voice calls, no text. Slater wasn't a hot-finger. Most calls were timed during office hours. A few outside that, typically thirty seconds, the calls you make to tell your wife you're on your way home or to make a restaurant reservation. The daytime calls were longer – up to fifty minutes. Nothing stood out but there had to be something in the list that Slater wanted to keep private. The fact that he'd chosen the office to hide the bills suggested that the person he might be hiding stuff from was his wife. I took out my pocket scan and ran it over the pages to capture the info.

Then I looked at the Amex sheets.

The sheets spilt the beans.

Slater used the card sparingly, so what was there stood out. And what was there was stuff he probably didn't want showing on his normal bank statements.

The bill for February had a clear opening balance then a single transaction: Slater had paid a company called Blueglades fifteen hundred pounds. The rest of the sheet was blank.

The March statement showed Slater clearing the fifteen hundred and then adding six transactions. Two more were payments to Blueglades in mid- and late-March, fifteen hundred and three thousand respectively. The dates coincided with two hefty payments made to the Royal Trafalgar Hotel in Brighton where Slater had settled an eight hundred and then sixteen hundred pound bill. A final couple of charges were for restaurants in the Brighton area around the same dates. From the size of the bills Slater had either been feeding a football team or the restaurants were outrageously expensive. I went for the latter.

Interesting.

The payments had a resonance. Hinted at Slater being engaged in some kind of extracurricular activity that he wanted hidden from eyes at home. An affair? What was Blueglades?

I checked the mobile bill again, looking at dates that correlated with the Amex payments. Picked up a cluster of calls to a single mobile number matching the February and March Blueglades dates. Maybe the number of whomever Slater was extracurricularising with.

It was the kind of thing we dug out all the time. The information would be hot if I was here to investigate Slater and not his stepdaughter.

I pocket-scanned the Amex payments then reinterred the stuff in the bottom of the drawer and locked up.

I moved to the right hand side. The file drawer held ten card files of open business. I went through them one by one. Client files circulating from the main office. Nothing unusual.

After an hour I had nothing more. I decided to pass on the main filing cabinet. It would take me ten minutes to open it and I doubted that I'd get anything new. The stuff Slater wanted to hide had been there at the bottom of that desk drawer. I sat back in his chair and tried to see the picture. Nothing obvious came through.

It was nine p.m. I relocked the office and let myself out of the washroom window. The jemmied window could not be relocked but no one would notice for a month or two. No one would be looking.

I recovered the Frogeye and called Shaughnessy. He said he was ready to roll.

CHAPTER EIGHTEEN

We watched the place for fifteen minutes while I filled Shaughnessy in on Slater–Kline.

Shaughnessy thought about it. 'So we're looking at a mistress or a hooker,' he said. 'But it's hard to see the connection with Rebecca's disappearance.'

'Maybe it's coincidence,' I said.

Shaughnessy looked at me like I'd abandoned religion.

'On the other hand,' I jabbed a thumb across the street, 'Slater watching this place just now day and night is stretching coincidence.'

The lower floors of the house were lit. The top apartment was dark, as always. It looked like Brown didn't stay home much.

'Unless Brown is hiding out up there,' Shaughnessy said.

Only one way to find out.

We crossed the street. The outer door was open and let us into a vestibule with three post boxes. Junk mail was bursting from the top one. The vestibule's inner door was locked, with a keypad and electric release. Shaughnessy went to work whilst I pressed the bell push for the top apartment. No point breaking in if someone was home. I gave it a single brief push. Nothing to stir up the apartment below. We didn't want an audience when we went up. The bell brought no response.

Shaughnessy beat the lock in under two minutes and we went in. A light came on automatically to illuminate hallway décor that matched the affluence of the street. Plush carpeting and varnished woodwork, framed prints. Not bad for a communal space. The stair carpet muffled our footsteps and we walked up in silence, wary of nosy neighbours with fisheye peepholes.

At the top Shaughnessy started on the apartment door without knocking. If anyone was home we'd soon find out, but I was betting against it. If someone was home there would probably be deadbolts drawn across which would stop us. I'd not packed my sledgehammer.

No deadbolts. Shaughnessy released the door and held it open to reach inside for the light switch. We went in and closed the door.

The air was hot, with a taste that said that the windows had not been opened in a while. Maybe it was just my overactive imagination but the place had an abandoned feel. I didn't get a sense of someone away on vacation.

And what owner leaves houseplants to die? Shaughnessy and I both spotted the dracaena on an ornamental table under a skylight. The plant's leaves had yellowed on collapsed stems. I looked at Shaughnessy for comment. Dead plants were too commonplace in my life for reliable judgement. My house plants died like they had a suicide pact unless Arabel was around to resuscitate them.

'The heating's accelerated the drying,' Shaughnessy said. 'These things wilt after three days without water. I'd say someone was in here a week ago.'

Shaughnessy and I looked at each other. A week had a particular resonance in relation to our missing girl. Made me wonder if we had another unaccounted-for person.

We split up and walked through the apartment. I took the front. Opened a door onto a lounge. Found a dimmer that brought wall-lamps to life. Gold tessellated shades. Italian furniture. Matching table lamps. Pearl, gold, green everywhere. Expensive wall fabrics. An ornate fireplace. And a sixty-by-forty gilded mirror that might have graced the original drawing room downstairs. I drew the curtains, turned the dimmer up and went through to the adjacent room.

A modern kitchen, also facing the street. Venetian blinds that wouldn't hide the light. I'd have to take the risk. I threw the switch. The kitchen was compact but expensively kitted out. High-tech appliances. Marble worktops. All clear and clean. Just a few dishes stacked on the draining board. A small corkboard beside the door held half a dozen Post-It stickers.

I left them and went back into the hallway and opened the next door. Sensed soft furnishings as I walked over to close the curtains. I hit the light switch. A woman's bedroom, as lavishly kitted out as the lounge. Lots of free-standing teak furniture and a queen-size bed. Bright colours splashing over browns and creams. A dresser spread with girl things, and a bedside table topped by an ornate lamp featuring an entwined couple each holding aloft one arm to support the fixture. Under the lamp were two framed photographs. One was a faded shot of a middle-aged couple posing in a garden. The woman had short-cropped hair framing an attractive face that watched the camera with an affectionate smile. The man was tall, dark-complexioned. Similar smile, slightly strained. The second photo featured two girls in t-shirts and shorts. One was standing behind the other with her arms wrapped around her companion's stomach. The background was a hotel swimming pool, a hint of ocean and palm fronds. The girls had a beauty that stole the breath. Sisters, maybe twins. Carefree smiles and crescent eyes. Identical long black hair and natural long lashes. The faces suggested that they were the daughters of the older couple. Instinct told me that one of these girls was Brown.

When I got back to the hallway Shaughnessy had finished scouting the back.

'A woman's stuff in the bathroom,' he said. 'One bedroom used for an office and a small room for ironing and airing.'

We started at the front and worked back. Shaughnessy took the kitchen. I worked through the lounge.

It didn't take long to come up with an identity for Brown. A display cabinet held pull-out drawers cluttered with photo albums and old letters, postcards, foreign travel memorabilia. The albums had more pictures of the middle-aged couple, a decade or two younger with two young girls beside them. The girls' beauty blossomed in the later albums, or at least one of theirs did. After mid- or late-teens there were no pictures of the two together. Was the photo in the bedroom the last? The sister who featured in the later albums was snapped in a variety of desirable locations, sometimes in a group, a couple of times with a male companion. The girl looked to be in her late teens, maybe early twenties. The guys with her were three decades older. A final album captured the girl as a fully-bloomed beauty in her mid-twenties, mixing with different crowds at different locations but always looking somehow alone. Every photo captured the same breathtaking beauty. In amongst the albums was a scattering of loose photos, including passport shots and head and shoulders. I slipped one of them into my pocket.

The last of the pull-out drawers revealed a Minolta digital SLR. I flipped it on and scanned for stored images. None. Who leaves their camera behind when they go on vacation?

I moved on. Brown's music taste was soul and reggae, two CD stacks brimming with Motown and Marley. A stack of hip hop albums in suspiciously generic covers. Pirated versions bought up Camden or on Petticoat Lane. Brown's home entertainment was a top flight Yamaha system with four-foot Ikon speakers.

Shaughnessy came out of the kitchen.

'Someone left in a hurry,' he said. 'There's stuff in the fridge that should have been thrown. The sell-by dates on the milk and salad packs say the owner was shopping about a week ago.'

I asked about the corkboard.

'Nothing,' Shaughnessy said, 'unless we're looking at a dry cleaning conspiracy.'

I handed him the last photo album, opened at a set of pictures of the dark-haired beauty. He looked at me.

'Our absentee tenant,' I deduced. Shaughnessy pursed his lips.

'She's not someone you'd easily lose,' he suggested.

'All we need is a name,' I said.

Shaughnessy headed off to the back and I sat on the couch and picked up the phone. There were six recorded messages. I played them, expecting to hear Larry Slater's voice, but the first five messages were from two females. One identified herself as Julie and had left a breezy greeting a week ago, asking for someone she called "Sis" to call her back. No return number. The other caller left four messages, starting a week back and ending two days ago. In the first message the caller identified herself only as "me" and asked someone called Tina to ring. A mobile number was logged.

The second and third messages were more urgent.

'It's Sammy,' the caller said, 'What's happening, Tina? I need to sort out with the agent's. Call me.'

Sammy's final message was more assertive.

'Tina, where are you? Bloody well ring me, girl.'

I noted Sammy's number then played the last of the six messages.

Bingo! Larry Slater's mobile number and the most urgent voice of all.

'Tina! It's Larry! For God's sake talk to me.' A short pause and a final plea: 'For pity's sake, Tina, what are you doing? Call me!' The message clicked off.

The desperation was clear in his voice. Mirrored the long vigils in the street outside. I sensed things shifting, centring. The silence of the apartment thickened around me.

I replaced the phone and went to take a look at the bedroom.

I felt like a sneak going through the woman's private things, just like when I'd rooted through Rebecca Townsend's room. But you've got to be resolute in this business. Tina's wardrobe matched her looks. Sexy stuff – short skirts by the inch-load, low-cut dresses, designer jeans that looked like Tom Thumb's sister wouldn't squeeze into them but probably looked just right packaging Tina Brown's curves.

Her lingerie drawer would have made a sergeant major blush, might even gain Arabel's respect. A riot of silk and lace, thongs cut so tiny the labels stood out like banners. Underwear designed to kill, or at least disable. I kept my mind on the task. I wasn't looking for lingerie. I was looking for the stuff Ms Brown might have hidden beneath it, mislead by the woman's universal misconception that the lingerie drawer is a safe place to hide secrets.

I found nothing apart from several packs of condoms shoved amongst the stuff in a top drawer – assorted styles and colours. Not so much hidden as pushed away where they could be conveniently retrieved.

Her dressing table was covered in a couple of thousand pound's worth of cosmetics. I wondered how many of them were gifts. If this woman didn't get expensive gifts then there was no hope for the rest of the female species. Nothing of interest, though, amongst all the extravagance.

The bed was tidily made and patted over. Decorated with half a dozen throw-cushions. I searched in and under the bed and in some less likely spots – on top of the wardrobe, underneath the wardrobe, underneath rugs – but nothing turned up.

Shaughnessy was having fun in the office room. That was where Tina stashed her bills and that's where he found the documents that confirmed her ID.

He gestured to the top of an old desk he'd been emptying.

'Driver's licence and birth certificate,' he said. 'Tina Brown. Date of birth seventeenth of August, nineteen eighty. Driver's licence seven years old. Same face as the photo album.'

'Any sign of who's paying the bills?' I asked. The oldest connection.

'The bills are all in her name,' Shaughnessy said. 'The lady is self-sufficient. Rents this place at two-five a month. Shorthold contract signed four years back. The girl's a high earner.'

'She's not your average sales girl,' I agreed. 'Makes you wonder what her line of business is.'

'Take a look at this,' Shaughnessy said. He picked up a biro from the back of the desk.

The pen was a click-top with a slender, solid feel. Black with a gold band. The sort presented as promotional giveaways. This one had a name in gold lettering along its length.

The Royal Trafalgar, Brighton.

The same as Larry Slater's Amex bill.

Bingo again.

Beautiful woman. Rich guy. Mysterious hotel bills. Slater staking out the place. Something was going on between them that Jean Slater for sure didn't know about. Was the woman Slater's mistress?

If so, what had taken her out of town right now? Had she ditched Slater for a bigger fish? I hadn't noticed any holes in her wardrobe to suggest she'd packed a suitcase.

More importantly, why was this woman top of Slater's agenda the week his stepdaughter was missing? Why the desperation in Larry Slater's voice? My First Law was screaming the obvious: Tina Brown was connected. Maybe central to it all.

We had everything we were going to get without asking Tina or Slater.

We tidied things and switched off the lights, drew back the curtains. The street light washed back into the front lounge and restored the apartment's deathly stillness. As we walked out, a sense of oppression tingled at the nape of my neck, like a ghost was looking over my shoulder. We closed the door quietly and went back down to the street.

We'd got what we came for. Brown was ID'd. But now we'd got something else: another missing person.

What was the connection with Rebecca?

CHAPTER NINETEEN

At eight a.m. I ate two rounds of wholemeal toast and washed them down with a cup of Buckaroo loaded with cream. Then I headed out.

The city was buzzing with rumours of spring. I drove through Sunday traffic, slowing for cagouled tourists crossing the roads. I played Wyn Marsalis loud with the Frogeye's windows down, let his Levee stuff swirl around me as I skimmed in and out of lanes. I hit greens and made Hampstead in under twenty minutes.

I drove up to the Slater home and turned into the driveway, circled behind the lawn and parked by the front porch. The Lexus was absent. A bonus. I rang the bell.

It took a couple more attempts but eventually Jean Slater opened the door. The five days since I'd last seen her hadn't improved Jean. Today she looked too weary even to question the appearance of an education official on a Sunday morning.

I greeted her with my most harmless smile, which must have worked because she stepped back instinctively. I took it as an invitation. By the time her senses caught up I was in the house. I wondered where Larry was.

'Can we sit down for a moment?' I said. 'Your husband should join us if he's here.'

Despite my request Jean made no move to invite me further in.

'I'm sorry, I don't understand,' she said. Something was finally getting through her cloudy mind. Something about education officials and Sunday mornings not mixing.

'We need to talk about Rebecca,' I said.

'What about her?'

'Why don't you tell me?' I suggested.

Jean Slater looked like I'd spat on her shoes. She shook her head emphatically.

'Mr Anderton,' she said, 'why are you calling on a weekend?'

For a moment the name threw me. Then I remembered the card I'd left.

'I'm not Mr Anderton,' I said, 'and I'm not with the Education Authority.' I gave her my real name and one of my real cards. Her eyes glanced over the card and she jumped like she'd touched a bare wire. Suddenly she was fully alert.

'What is this?' she said. 'Who the hell are you?'

'Like it says, I'm a private investigator.'

'Who sent you here?'

I gestured into the house. 'Let's sit down,' I said. 'I'll explain.'

'No!' Jean Slater's voice gained strength. Anger breaking through her lassitude. 'How dare you come into my house under false pretences? I asked who sent you here!'

'Jean, I'm here to help.'

'Leave!' She swung the door wide. 'My husband will be back any moment. Please go!'

Private investigation. It's like being a Jehovah's Witness. Everyone wants a piece of you. I took a chance and stood my ground.

'I'm working for a friend of Rebecca's,' I said. 'She's concerned for your daughter's safety. My agency has taken a look and it's pretty clear to us that your daughter is in some kind of trouble.'

Jean's anger didn't diminish but I could see distress gaining the upper hand.

'Five minutes,' I repeated, 'that's all I need.'

Jean hesitated then eased the door closed. She turned and walked stiffly into the lounge. I followed. The unopened post from four days ago was still unopened, the pile bigger. Jean sat down but didn't invite me. I perched myself on a convenient chair.

She waited for me to speak.

'Someone's taken Rebecca.' I said it for her.

She opened her mouth, on the verge of denial. Then she thought better. She shook her head.

'Maybe we can help,' I suggested.

'Who sent you,' Jean asked again.

'Two of Rebecca's friends,' I said. 'Sadie and Gina Redding. You know them.'

Jean's eyes widened. She struggled for composure.

'Mr Flynn,' she said, 'Rebecca's friends are well intentioned but they are not helping. This is a private matter. You could help us by telling them that.'

I raised my eyebrows. Waited. She stared back.

'Eight days is a long time,' I said.

Jean flinched as if I'd lashed her with a whip. Her eyes flared but then the beaten look came back. I saw fatigue, helplessness. The woman was terrified.

'Eight days!' I said. 'I don't know what's happened but I do know that your daughter needs help.'

Jean Slater shook her head again. 'You don't know anything,' she said.

'Tell me,' I said.

She was still hesitating, wanting to hope, but afraid to believe.

'Start at the beginning,' I suggested. 'Tell me when it started.'

I heard a footstep.

'When what started?' A man's voice. Authoritative. No hint of trepidation in this one. Jean Slater looked over my shoulder and drew herself in.

I stood and turned to face Larry Slater. He was looking at me with the expression of someone who's eaten a cheeseburger too fast.

He glared at his wife then glared at me again. I took the initiative and held out my hand.

'Larry,' I said, 'I'm Eddie Flynn.'

Slater left my hand hanging. I dropped it with what I hoped was a semblance of dignity. Slater's rebuff brought my count in kiss-off handshakes to forty-nine since primary school. Private detectives attract kiss-off handshakes the way double-glazing reps attract closed doors. Familiarity made them no easier to take. If my face showed anything Slater didn't notice. He was too busy scowling at his wife.

'Who the hell is this?' he asked. He saw that Jean wasn't capable of explaining so he redirected his interrogation.

I repeated my name.

'Who sent you here? What the hell are you doing in my house?'

'I'm a private investigator,' I said. 'I've already explained to your wife that I'm acting for two of Rebecca's friends.'

'Which friends? What the hell's going on?'

'What's going on is that I'm trying to find out what has happened to your daughter,' I said.

Slater did an idiot act. Open-mouthed. Phoney right through. When he'd impressed me with his acting skills he switched back to business.

'Whatever might have happened or not happened to our daughter,' he said, 'is none of your damned business. That's all you need to understand.'

'I was explaining to your wife,' I continued, 'that in my professional experience your daughter may be at risk, whatever has happened.'

'But whatever you think may have happened,' Slater repeated, 'is none of your damned business. Your business is to get the hell out of my house.'

I looked back at Jean Slater. She looked at her husband. 'Larry–' she began.

'Stop!' Slater barked at her. She fell silent. 'Have you said anything to this person?'

'Of course not.' Her face hardened.

But in another minute she would have. One lousy minute. That's the investigation business. All the minutes you never get.

And right now Larry Slater wasn't giving me any more minutes.

He jabbed his thumb over his shoulder. 'Mr Flynn, I want you out of my house.'

'Larry,' I said. 'It's essential we talk. Just be reasonable for one minute.'

'Reasonable, hell,' he said. 'You've got ten seconds then I'm calling the police.'

I stayed put. Figured he was bluffing. I said: 'You don't want the police here any more than you want me. But with me there's less paperwork.'

Slater walked out into the hallway and showed me his bluff by picking up the phone. Gave me a good view as he punched three numbers. All nines, I wouldn't be surprised. Next he was going to bluff a report of an intruder in his house and a squad car was going to turn up and bluff my arrest. I had important business waiting. Business that would be tricky from the holding cell at the local station. I turned to walk towards the door.

'Don't bother,' I said. 'We'll call them ourselves tomorrow. We'll have enough by then.'

I nodded to Jean Slater, pointed to the card in her hand. 'Any time you want to talk,' I said.

I walked out. Neither of them followed me through. See yourself out, Eddie. Another tradition of the investigation trade.

I jumped into the Frogeye and headed back to town.

CHAPTER TWENTY

I had thirty minutes to kill. I detoured through Paddington and parked on Chase Street right outside the office. It felt good to do these things sometimes, even if you had to work Sundays to do them.

Connie's was doing roaring business. Connie himself was behind the counter the same as every other day. He gave me a yell that said he was more than pleased to see his planet-size debt staying close. I guess he thought I'd just walk in one day and pay it off.

The day was brightening by the hour. The sounds of spring echoed along the street. I sat at the bar and ordered brunch. A salad-and-bacon baguette and a coffee. Then paid homage to the perfection of the moment by handing over cash. The surprise on Connie's face made it all worthwhile. He rewarded me with a radiant smile that he interrupted only to hold my twenty up to the light. Connie brought my sandwich personally and set it down like he was Egon Ronay. Ronay would have wanted the tab paid before I ate, though.

'Why you go to work today, Eddie?' he said. 'Such a beautiful day.'

'Same as you,' I said. 'Money.'

He let out a laugh that would have tripped the Frogeye's alarm if it had had one.

'My work is my love,' he agreed. 'What else I'm going to do Sunday morning? Stay home, fight the wife?'

'Don't kid me, Connie. You're crazy about your wife.'

He tried to throw it back but as always the noisier Connie got the less I believed him. Connie's wife was a Latina with looks that had grown men howling at the moon.

I chewed my baguette and sipped coffee. Wonderful, as always. The half-hour killed I drove down into Holland Park and found an empty space opposite the apartment. I parked and wound the window down.

The street had come to life in the sun. Cars, bicycles, couples walking to bistros, oldies taking miniature dogs to the park. Five minutes after I arrived there was movement at No. 93. An old guy came out of the front door and walked away up the street. I assumed he was one of the lower-floor residents. I watched him disappear towards the main road. After that nothing happened for an hour. I was beginning to worry that the arrangement had flopped. But you learn patience in this game. I'd been on stakeouts in worse places and for far longer. I listened to a tape and tapped the beat on the metal of the door.

It got past two and the old guy rolled back. Disappeared inside and the door was closed again. I watched pricey cars glide past. Couples returning from lunch. I checked my watch. The hand had crawled past two thirty. Then a red Porsche Boxster backed into a spot five cars behind me and a woman got out. I watched her in my rear-view as she walked up the street. When she got to No. 93 she climbed the steps and pressed the top bell. By the time she pressed it a second time I was on the steps beside her.

She sensed me coming and turned to stand aside but I stopped in front of her.

'Sammy?' I asked.

The woman's eyes focused on me, trying to recall from where she knew me. She was in her late twenties, slim and lithe with astonishing green eyes and gold-blonde gossamer hair. Tina Brown's friend from her voicemail.

I told Sammy my name and apologised for my sudden appearance. 'I'm here about Tina,' I said. 'Do you mind if we talk?'

The introduction didn't clarify much. She backed away, puzzled.

'Are you a friend of Julie's?' This was Julie, Tina Brown's sister, the other person who'd left voicemail messages on Tina's phone.

'In a business sense,' I extemporised, 'related to Tina.'

'I don't understand.' She'd continued backing away until the railing was pressing into her backside. 'Julie didn't mention you. She just told me she was worried about Tina.' She looked nervously up the street. 'Is something wrong?'

Three hours ago Sammy had received a call from Tina's sister saying she was concerned about her. It seemed she hadn't been able to contact Tina in a week and was looking for someone nearby to check her out. The convenient "someone" was Tina's friend Sammy. Whether Tina's sister had actually been trying to get in touch, bar the single message we'd picked up on the voicemail, I didn't know. The call Sammy had received was from Lucy May – receptionist, secretary, accountant and impersonator.

Sammy's call-back number on Tina Brown's voicemail had been an unlisted pay-as-you-go. Difficult to trace. One way to chase down a PAYG caller is to get them to come to you. Hence the bogus call. Playing on the concern I'd heard in Sammy's messages.

'I'm sorry to surprise you this way,' I said. I held out an Eagle Eye card. 'I believe Tina's sister explained her concerns. We've been asked to take a look, make sure that Tina is okay.'

Sammy stared at the card.

'Julie didn't mention a detective agency,' she said.

Neither did Lucy May. That was so we didn't scare Sammy off.

'We're trying to find out where Tina is,' I said.

'Is something wrong?' Sammy asked again.

I nodded. 'According to her sister there is. Tina has disappeared, dropped completely out of sight. Nothing like this has happened before.' Which was what I hoped Sammy had also been thinking. We needed to get on the same side. Sammy nodded back, not sure she wanted to be on anyone's side, but she couldn't deny her concern.

'Yeah, I am a little worried,' she admitted. 'I've been trying to get hold of Tina all week.'

'I understand that you and she are close,' I said. Information squeezed from my undisclosed source, namely Tina's voicemail.

'Yes,' Sammy said, 'we're good friends. I'm not quite sure what's happening with her. She's just seems to have dropped out of sight. Hasn't returned a single call all week.'

Rule One triumphant! If there had been half a chance that Holland Park and Rebecca Townsend were unrelated, that chance had just evaporated like spit on a stovetop, unless I was imagining the spooky similarity between Sammy's words and those of Sadie Bannister when she first ambushed me at my office.

'They didn't give me your full name, Sammy.'

'Samantha Vincent,' Sammy said. 'Are you saying that something's happened to Tina?'

'We're concerned,' I said. 'Nothing more than that. But we do need to locate her. Maybe you can help.'

'In what way?'

'We need to know about Tina's lifestyle,' I said. 'The one she's reluctant for her sister to know. I assume you can help us.'

Sammy shook her head. 'I can't pass Tina's private affairs on to her sister, Mr Flynn.'

'Eddie,' I said. 'We don't need to be formal, Sammy. But if Tina is in trouble it may be more important to help her than to keep her secrets. Her sister's priority is to make sure she's safe. Anything you know might help us.'

'I'm just not sure what Tina would want me to tell you.'

Sammy was still in denial, still wanting Tina's disappearance to be routine. She may even have been right but Tina Brown was connected to Rebecca's disappearance for certain, which meant that I needed everything Sammy had about her.

'Let me buy you a coffee,' I offered.

I had a hunch about Tina and I needed Sammy Vincent to confirm it.

Sammy looked up at the house, giving Tina a last chance to show her face. I didn't look up. I knew Tina wasn't there. Sammy finally reached the same conclusion.

'Let's have the coffee,' she said. 'Perhaps you can explain what's going on, Mr Flynn.'

'My name's Eddie,' I repeated. 'And I think I can put you in the picture.'

I figured at least one of those statements was true.

CHAPTER TWENTY-ONE

We walked up to a Coffee Republic on the main road. The front seats were busy with people being seen. We found a couple of loungers in the back away from prying ears, and ordered lattes.

'I guess this is a sensitive question,' I said when the coffees came. 'But are you and Tina in the same line of business?'

When I looked up from dunking my biscotto Sammy was staring at me.

'I'm not here to intrude,' I said, 'but my information is that escorting is Tina's main occupation.'

Sammy's hesitation had already confirmed my guess. Beautiful girl, single lifestyle, expensive tastes, no sign of regular payslips, no sign of regular relationship, given to trysts at high-class hotels. The description could have fitted a millionaire's mistress but Slater wasn't in that league. The explanation that worked was that Tina made her money as a top-of-the-line escort, servicing serious wealth, which would account for Slater quite nicely.

My hunch that Sammy was also in the business occurred when I saw the Boxster and the same stratospheric looks, the haughtiness that only years-long reinforcement of beauty-as-divine-provider brings. The Boxster didn't come from working at Boots. Call me male chauvinist. Sure I am. It's a tool of the trade.

'I think you'd better tell me exactly who you are,' Sammy said. 'And why you're prying into Tina's life.'

'It's like it says on the card, Sammy. I'm a private investigator. I'm looking into Tina's disappearance. She's been missing for a week now. And I'm wondering if her line of work is a factor.'

Sammy's mouth opened at the same time as her head shook to deny the possibility. In her line of business I guess there's a tendency to hang on to denial.

'Tina may have become involved with someone she can't handle,' I suggested. 'I don't need to tell you how critical time might be if that's the case. I need to know about her recent activities. Look for a pointer as to where she may have gone.'

Sammy hadn't touched her coffee. I saw her turning things over, figuring out whether there was any option but to trust me. Seeing that there wasn't.

'I've been leaving messages all week,' she admitted finally. 'On her home and mobile.'

'She has a mobile?'

'It's her main number.'

'How long since she's answered any calls?'

'A week,' she said. 'Just like you say.'

'How often do you usually talk to her?'

'Most days. We're close. We'd arranged a night on the town last weekend but when I didn't hear from her I assumed a job had come up, a weekend client.'

'Could she be spending the whole week with a client?'

She shook her head. 'She would have let me know,' she said. 'We keep each other informed if we're going out of town. Security.'

'How does she contact her clients?' I asked. 'Is it through an agency? Blueglades?'

Sammy shook her head. 'Most of her fees are paid by card. Blueglades is her card merchant name. Tina works for herself. Places ads and takes her own bookings. Most of the time she works off repeat custom.'

'When she takes bookings does anyone else know?'

'No,' Sammy said, 'but she takes precautions. Limits herself to a few top hotels for first-time clients. Locations where she knows she's safe and where the clients are reputable.'

Sammy was confusing rich with reputable but I didn't correct her. And you don't have to be rich to stay at the Grosvenor. If you're lashing out fifteen hundred for the girl then an extra five for the room won't break the bank. The only difference with the rich guy is that he can do it all the time. Meeting at high-tariff hotels took out ninety percent of Tina's risk, but like disease and rats, crime breeds in the forgotten ten percent.

'Does Tina visit clients away from hotels?'

'Yes. Like I said, most of her work is repeat. She's more flexible about location for people she knows.'

'Does she have many regulars?'

Sammy shrugged. 'Probably the same as me. Eight or ten. Guys we see once or twice a month. But we make sure we know them well before we take trips. Some clients you see fifty times and you still want a safe location. Something about them. You don't want to get closer.'

'Judgement,' I said.

'Yes. We develop good judgement.'

We. Sammy and Tina exchanging notes – thinking they know each other's work, thinking that makes them safe. But working alone in that profession leaves a girl exposed no matter how good her judgement. I did the sums. Twenty escorts a month at a thousand pounds plus per night and no middle man. The earning potential for top lookers like Tina and Sammy was awesome. The risk probably seemed worth it.

'How long have you known Tina?'

'Six years. We worked for the same agency once.'

'And how long has Tina been in the business?'

Sammy laughed. A touch of bitterness. 'The same as all of us,' she said. 'Since we were kids. Since we first got preferential treatment at home or in the street. I had a twenty-eight-year-old boyfriend and a five carat diamond ring on my finger when I was fourteen. Got picked up from school in a Porsche. You tell me when it starts. I only know when it ends. I'm retiring at thirty, going to see the world. Tina too.'

Maybe.

Shaughnessy and I had found nothing that looked like a client list in Tina's apartment. My guess was that she kept all her client details on her phone. I asked Sammy if she knew anything about the men Tina saw.

'Just two or three we've shared,' she said. 'None in the past couple of years.'

'You must talk about clients sometimes,' I said.

'A few first names. Nothing else.'

'Any recent names stick out? Anyone she was uneasy with?'

Sammy gave me a look of disdain. The same one she'd used as a fourteen-year-old. Some things never change. Her coffee had gone cold. Another fiver down the drain.

'You think that's what we gossip about?' she said.

I shook my head. 'What you gossip about is of no interest to me, Sammy,' I said. 'But I need any names Tina may have mentioned. Any places. Any clients who stand out.'

'Are you looking for dirt, Mr Flynn?' she asked. 'Are you sure you're not working for one of the papers?'

I shook my head again. 'I'm working to find out what's happening to Tina. On the off chance we can get her back safe.'

The melodrama had its effect. Sammy switched back to the business in hand. She closed her eyes for a couple of seconds.

'You know something you're not telling me,' she said.

'I've told you everything I can,' I said. 'Including the possibility that Tina may be in danger. More than that I don't know.'

'Why hasn't her sister called the police?'

'Without evidence that someone has harmed Tina there's nothing for the police to act on,' I said. 'By the time that evidence comes up it might be too late. I want to find Tina while she's still okay.'

Sammy blinked.

'If anything's happened to Tina...' she said.

I came back to the subject.

'Which clients of Tina's you do know?'

She closed her eyes again briefly.

'There's a couple, plus a few first names. Not much. One of Tina's used to be David Lancaster.'

'The MP?' I raised my eyebrows.

'Yeah. The one screaming last year for the Home Secretary to resign when it came out about him hiding a gay affair. Tina told me he used to like it up against the car window with the world passing outside.'

'Is she still seeing him?'

'She hasn't mentioned him in a while. So probably not. Another one is Sir Alec somebody, ex-chairman of the CBI, big donor to the Conservative party. He likes her to spend weekends with him – they travel around Europe. He taught her to ski.'

I knew which Sir Alec she meant. It wasn't going to be hard to memorise this list.

'The others are just names, a couple of details. There's a Middle Eastern guy she's been seeing. Amir. She visits him at the Grosvenor when he's in London. He takes the penthouse and pays her twenty thousand for the weekend.' She smiled sweetly at me. 'He likes to hurt her. Nothing that leaves evidence, but she's always down for a couple of days afterwards. Tina talks about giving him the boot but she still goes back.' She looked at me. 'They say money isn't everything but in our line of work the first thing we ditch is deceit. There's another client, the opposite type. A nice guy she's been seeing for a couple of years up in Buckinghamshire. Divorced. Very rich but no inclination to get attached. I hear other names from time to time but they don't mean anything to me.'

'You ever hear of a guy called Slater?' I said.

She looked blank.

'Did Tina mention a guy who lives up in Hampstead? Behind the golf course. Married. Runs a stockbrokers.'

She shook her head. It had been a long shot. If the two of them talked it would be the bigger fish they hung up for show. Unlikely that Slater would warrant a mention in the circle that included MPs and captains of industry. I kept fishing.

'Did Tina mention a trip to Brighton?' I asked. 'The Royal Trafalgar Hotel.'

Sammy's eyes opened. 'Yes,' she said, 'she did mention the Royal Trafalgar.'

'Any particular reason?'

Sammy nodded. 'She had to cancel a night out. My birthday bash. She got a late booking and had to call me to reschedule.'

'Was there anything special about that job? Anything about her client?'

She shook her head. 'All I know is the hotel. They took the top-floor suite with personal valet. Champagne and strawberries at breakfast. I don't know who the client was.'

'But travelling to Brighton would mean that she already knew him?'

'Yes,' Sammy said.

'Did she tell you anything else about that trip?'

She shook her head. 'The only special thing was cancelling my birthday thing. Otherwise she wouldn't have mentioned it at all.'

'Your birthday is in March,' I said. 'Am I right?'

It's these kind of insights that had Sherlock Holmes impressing Watson.

Sammy stayed unimpressed. 'October,' she said. 'That's when Tina went to the Royal Trafalgar.'

Elementary, my dear Watson. How come Holmes' hunches never bombed? I gave her surprised.

'That's when my birthday is,' Sammy insisted. Even more elementary; you can't beat birthdays as memory joggers. I shook my head. Slater's Amex had him at the Royal Trafalgar twice in March. Sammy's date was five months earlier.

'I'm looking at something more recent,' I said. 'Did Tina visit the Royal Trafalgar again?'

'I don't know. She only mentioned that one time.'

'But she would tell you if she went away for the weekend?'

Sammy shrugged. 'Usually. But not every time. If we're both busy we may not mention it.'

I swallowed the last of my latte.

'I need Tina's mobile number,' I said.

She recited a number from memory. I didn't write it down because I didn't need to. I already recognised it from Slater's bill. The number confirmed the link between Slater and Tina, even if Slater's Brighton stay didn't line up with the date Sammy had Tina there.

'Mr Flynn,' Sammy said, 'who is this Slater?'

'He's someone Tina may be involved with.'

'Is she with him now?'

'No.'

'Might he harm her?'

'I don't think so. But the two of them may be involved in something together. Something that's got her into trouble.'

'What sort of trouble?'

I held up my hands. 'Give me time, Sammy. I'm trying to find out.'

'Sweet Jesus.' Sammy looked somewhere beyond the two of us. A place of shadows. Something happening to Tina could certainly force a rethink of this woman's lifestyle. Maybe consideration of early retirement.

'Mr Flynn—'

'Eddie.'

'Eddie: when will you know something?'

'Soon,' I promised.

'How soon?'

'A couple of days,' I told her. 'We'll know what's happened to Tina by then.'

'Two days,' Sammy said. She pulled the Eagle Eye card from her pocket and looked it over, paying more attention this time. Then she slipped the card into her purse and got up from the table.

'Call me on Tuesday, Eddie. If I've heard nothing from you by the end of the day I'm going to the police.'

She turned and walked out. A dozen heads turned.

I sat in my comfy seat and jotted some notes. Threw in a couple of questions. The confirmation of Tina Brown's line of work had opened up a wide range of explanations as to why she was missing from her apartment. In normal circumstances, I'd put Slater's stalking her down to the action of an infatuated guy let down by his fantasy girl's elopement with another client. But stalking his playmate at the very time his stepdaughter has disappeared does not constitute normal circumstances.

I walked back to the Frogeye and called Gina Redding.

I filled her in on Slater's liaison with Tina Brown, and on the fact that we now seemed to have two missing persons. I also warned Gina that I'd poked a stick around at the Slater house. If she received calls from the family she should be ready. I warned her too that the next step might be costly and might lead only to dead ends. Gina wasn't deterred.

'Just do what it takes, Eddie,' she told me. 'I'll pay the bill. Just find Rebecca.'

That's my kind of client.

I told Gina I'd be in touch in a couple of days. By then we'd have the thing wrapped up. We'd better have. Two days was all we had before Sammy blew the whistle and the situation became much more complicated.

I headed back to Battersea and got busy in the kitchen. When Arabel arrived I had a leg of lamb roasting and by the time she was through teaching me some new yoga moves with her lips it was a race against time to salvage the meat before it carbonised. We ate it with sweet potatoes and sour cream, roasted vegetables. Not even a nod in the direction of healthy eating. The lamb disappeared, fat and all. Cooking unhealthy is a cheat but I find it gets results. Arabel knew exactly what I was up to but it gave her an excuse to pig out once in a while. She knew she could humour me once a month without risk of a coronary.

She made her appreciation known by grabbing me as I cleared the table and pushing me back onto the sofa with some dirty suggestions, but both our stomachs protested so painfully that there was no chance of following through. So much for results. We got ready to go out.

While I was changing I caught Arabel in my loft, trying to sneak a look at her portrait. I drove her off with threats that the picture would turn into an ogre if the sitter uncovered it before it was ready. The real reason was that I didn't want her to spot imperfections before I worked them out. Pride. I liked her to think that painting came natural to me. Like cooking. My reputation for both would crumble if my techniques were known.

'When are you going to have it finished, babe?' she said. 'At the rate you're going you'll need to add wrinkles.'

'Art determines its own time,' I said. 'You can't hurry. Ask Picasso how long it took to create his masterpieces.'

'Picasso could finish stuff in three days,' she informed me. 'I heard he did that Reclining Nude in one.'

Education can be a pain. My fault for introducing Arabel to the Tate.

'The guy was all rush,' I said. 'Do you want to end up looking like his Weeping Woman?'

'Not if you want to live, Flynn.'

'Then keep your nose out until I'm through. I'm not ready to die for my art.'

We climbed into the Frogeye and headed over to the Royal Festival

Hall. I had tickets for the London Philharmonic performing Elgar. Next to jazz I went for the classical composers. Next to soul, blues, reggae, hip hop and half a dozen other things so did Arabel. She would never admit to having an ear for the classics, but the only time I saw her listening to music with tears in her eyes was when I took her to a Dvorak symphony. Somewhere amongst those curves was a cultured soul, savouring what she'd denied herself in her squandered youth.

The evening was almost balmy. I put the top down for the ten-minute trip.

'Have you been working all day?' Arabel asked.

'Justice never sleeps,' I said.

She laid her hand on my neck. 'Not even a nap at the weekend? This detective stuff draws you too tight, Flynn. You take the burden with the case.'

'That's how it is sometimes,' I said. 'Divorce, petty crime, that kind of thing we get the weekend off. But sometimes we're involved with something more serious.'

'Like when you worked for Scotland Yard?'

'Not like that. With the Mets I didn't need miracles – my clients were all dead.'

'What about Rebecca?' Arabel asked. 'Is she dead?'

I took a moment to answer. I'd mostly got away from that side of crime since I'd quit the Mets.

Eventually I said: 'I don't think so. But she may be mixed up in something that's going bad. It's hard to take weekends off when you might be someone's only hope.'

'Poor babe,' Arabel said. 'And who's going to save you?'

I had no answer for that.

CHAPTER TWENTY-TWO

The Mitsubishi Warrior had been sat for an hour and a half on a meter across from Eagle Eye. So far they'd avoided inserting cash but time was running out. The parking Gestapo was moving up on the far side of the junction and the guy would reach them inside two minutes. Sod's law said that the second they slotted coins into the meter their quarry would break but it was the lesser of two evils – the risk of wasting a few quid against the certainty of a fixed penalty notice. Roker went with the probabilities.

'Feed it,' he said.

Mitch broke off from feeding Pringles into his face and swore. The vehicle rocked on its springs as he climbed out. He stood on the pavement with the coins in his fist but dispensing with them was like giving blood. Mitch preferred to psych the warden out. Induce him to cross the street and ignore the Warrior. What Roker preferred was to stay low-profile. He leaned across and smacked his palm on the dash. Mitch gave him a dirty look and slotted the coins home. When he climbed back into the vehicle Roker was tempted to slug him. Resisted. Going with the odds again: Mitch could be unpredictable.

Mitch grabbed the wheel like he was going to wrench it off.

'I hate these uniformed little gits,' he said.

'Just stay focused,' Roker told him.

They watched the warden as he walked up. He passed the Warrior without turning his head but he'd spotted their game, gave them a sideways evil eye. Mitch turned to glare after him then attacked his Pringles again. 'When's this clown going to move,' he said.

'Soon,' Roker said. He went back to watching the building. Now that they'd fed the meter the guy would be out double-quick.

He was. Their quarry came out of the front entrance exactly three minutes later and disappeared round the back of the building.

Mitch stashed the Pringles and started the engine. Roker watched the street.

'Go,' he said.

Mitch rolled. The quarry had pulled out of an access road up ahead and was already crossing the junction. Mitch put his foot down.

'What the hell's that?' he asked.

'Stay back,' Roker said.

Mitch growled. He didn't need Roker's advice. He could tail a guy all day and they'd never know he was there.

'It's a friggin' Tonka Toy,' Mitch said. 'I had a bigger pedal car when I was two years old.'

Roker sneered. Mitch was shut in a room getting smacked around his head when he was two years old. Pedal cars didn't figure in it.

'Is it a vintage?' Mitch asked.

'Yeah,' Roker said. 'Forty years. Probably ninety percent rust.'

The car was the size of a shoebox. Racing green, black soft top. The

Warrior would run right over it if their brakes failed.

'No way you'd get me in something like that,' Mitch said, 'unless they were burying me.'

'Not even then,' Roker said. 'You'd need a Transit.'

Mitch held back then floored the pedal when the Tonka turned at the main road. They hit the junction five seconds behind. He swung the wheel but the traffic closed up, blocking them. The Frogeye was disappearing towards Bayswater. If the midget car got into the heavy flow they'd lose it. Mitch slammed his foot down and skidded out in front of a van. The van fishtailed and missed them by inches and the driver stayed on his horn long after he needed to. Any other time Mitch would have been happy to climb out and discuss the situation. Horn-jockeys pissed him off. It was White Van Man's lucky day.

Mitch accelerated to within four cars of the Tonka. It turned east towards Paddington Station then took a left and drove ahead of them across the bridge onto the A40 ramp. Mitch hung back and let the vehicle get up into the Westway traffic. No risk of losing it there.

They settled two hundred yards back on the carriageway. The Warrior's high vantage point gave them distance without risk of losing the Tonka. Secure tails took a minimum of three vehicles but when you wanted the best single-vehicle job you put Mitch behind the wheel.

For the moment Mitch's skills were redundant. The Tonka stayed with the A40 and drifted towards the M25 in the mid-morning flow. Easy. At the junction the car took the long slip and split left into the south link onto the Orbital. The variable limits were on and they cruised in the second lane at a stately fifty-five, holding well back. Heathrow came and went. The Tonka was in no hurry. They were past Reigate before the vehicle indicated and took the slip road for the M23.

Mitch had substituted the Pringles with a ball of gum. He chewed furiously, focused on their quarry. Roker stayed silent, puzzling over where their target was headed. The M23 had opened up possibilities.

'Gatwick,' Mitch guessed.

Roker said nothing.

'Are they saying this guy's a player?'

'Maybe,' Roker said. 'He'd just better know the rules.'

'What do they want us to do?' Mitch asked.

'They want us to watch and learn,' Roker said. 'We're on a fishing trip, that's all.'

The M23 was busy. The Tonka's diminutive size made it easy to lose but Mitch stayed cool. Fifteen minutes on they passed Gatwick. Continued south. Roker stared ahead and felt something beginning to gnaw in his gut. When the M23 petered out the Tonka continued towards the coast and Roker knew they were headed for Brighton.

As they got onto the roundabout north of the town Mitch closed up the distance. There was too big a risk that the Tonka might make a sudden turn amongst the town traffic. But the car kept to its southerly course and in a couple of minutes they were in the centre. The Frogeye swung around the park and continued towards the sea. A minute later they came out at the pier.

The Tonka crossed the roundabout three cars ahead and took a right along the seafront. Mitch jumped the queue and forced his way across, ignoring the horns. He accelerated past a truck and got his quarry back. The Tonka was moving steadily between the hotels and the beach. They rolled west for sixty seconds before the quarry indicated and turned across oncoming traffic into the walled-off parking lane fronting a five-star hotel. Mitch continued a hundred yards further then swung the Warrior in a U-turn to get back to the hotel. He stopped short just as the guy was extracting himself from the midget vehicle. They watched him go in through the hotel entrance.

The hotel's name was marked in fifteen-foot letters across its white façade: ROYAL TRAFALGAR.

Mitch killed the engine and chewed noisily. The place meant nothing to him.

Roker's face told a different story. 'Shit,' he said.

Mitch turned.

'We got a problem?'

Roker's face stayed neutral but his eyes were locked on the hotel entrance. He was wondering what the hell was going on. Whatever it was, it wasn't good.

'Yes,' he said finally, 'we've got a problem.'

CHAPTER TWENTY-THREE

Revolving doors spat me out into a marble and glass foyer that echoed with the muted reverence of a cathedral. Five-star perfection gleamed in every polished surface, and the shine on the floor was enough to have you watching your balance.

The foyer was busy with big-hotel Brownian motion, people endlessly going somewhere else. Reception held centre stage with the extravagance of a high altar. Baggage and Concierge stood back either side like lady chapels. Mahogany doors behind the desks led through to the admin area, where the people would be who could tell me what I wanted to know and who would sooner have teeth pulled. I needed a way in.

A sweeping staircase encircled a roped-off bistro opposite the check-in desks. I went over and flopped into a leather armchair. A waiter walked across and bowed from the neck when I ordered coffee. The Royal Trafalgar was old fashioned that way: you didn't need to say *latte*. They understood. The coffee was excellent, spoiled only by the bill which merited a saucer of its own. The bill was discreetly folded so as not to upset you while you drank. I'm the kind of guy who can never resist peeking. Nearly spat out my coffee. I'd have to work the thing into our expenses. Maybe if I skipped my next meal I could claim the charge as an extravagant lunch.

Larry Slater had an impressive taste in playgrounds. If the lobby was any guide then the accommodation upstairs would be truly worth seeing. A stunning nest to spend a weekend with a stunning girl. A stunning bill at the end of it, too. It looked like Slater had cash to throw away. Slater's Amex recorded him here twice, and my bet said that he had Tina Brown as company both times.

It took me twenty minutes to see a way in. I waited until the far end of the reception desk was clear, then I finished my coffee and hid a tenner discreetly within the folded bill. I signalled to the waiter and walked across to the desk.

The reception staff were bright and attentive in the way that big money demands. Selected and trained to the hotel's traditional standards, even if the tradition said that they should be paid a pittance.

The clerk at the end was a little different. When I approached the desk he was busy at his keyboard. Took a few moments too long to notice that I was there. I'd been watching him. He could do the bright and attentive stuff, but there was a phoniness he couldn't hide. His head had been up when I'd started my walk but was buried in his computer by the time I reached him. He knew I didn't fit here. Good hotel staff have these instincts. I gave him thirty seconds and then leaned over the counter to invade his space. He looked up and smiled and when he asked if he could help me I recognised a fellow actor.

He was in his mid-forties with slicked-back hair. His badge

identified him as Gerald. Gerald wore black frame spectacles that hid the disappointment lines from two decades of missed promotions. He'd probably worked at another hotel in his younger years before he realised that his prospects were nil. Joined the Royal Trafalgar on the strength of a gladly-given reference. He was the oldest of the check-in clerks by a decade. Seniority: the perk of never being promoted. I leaned closer. Gave him Embarrassed to let him know he was in charge. Lowered my voice.

'This is going to seem a little irregular...' I said.

The word cut him like I'd said something dirty. To Gerald, "irregular" was something that stayed outside the revolving doors, like a dog turd on the pavement. He threw me a frown but restrained himself with the realisation that whatever I was after, he was going to get the opportunity to trash me.

'I'm here in confidence,' I explained, 'on behalf of a lady.'

I looked into Gerald's eyes. His face remained polite but the expression was one of someone expecting me to vomit over his desk as he let the rope play out.

'The lady believes that her husband has visited the Royal Trafalgar under circumstances that were...' I searched for the word: '... unsalubrious.'

I had a feeling it should have been "insalubrious". So did Gerald, but he wasn't sure. And grammar wasn't the point. He was going to dish me whether I could speak English or not. I paused, worked the word in again for effect. 'The lady believes that her husband may have visited this hotel for entirely unsalubrious purposes. She believes, in short, that he may have been unfaithful to her.'

Gerald's face gave nothing. He was calculating the best moment to come in. He knew I was bowling him a spinner and he knew he was going to smack the ball for six. The main thing was not to swing early. His face was a mask of patience.

'I'm looking for some help,' I told him. 'My client assumes that the Royal Trafalgar will have records of past reservations...' I let the thought hang between us.

Gerald let it dangle right there. The only sign he was listening was the glitter of the foyer spots in his spectacles.

'The lady,' I whispered, 'would be deeply obliged to the Royal Trafalgar if it was possible to make a discreet enquiry about certain reservations in the last few months.'

I gave Gerald my deeply obliged look. He gave me deeply patient. He still wanted more.

'If necessary,' I said, 'my client would be happy to come to an arrangement to secure the information.'

Finally we had it. The spinner was angling towards Gerald's raised bat. Now that I'd soiled myself with straight bribery he was ready. Gerald leaned forward so I wouldn't miss anything.

'Sir,' he whispered, 'I don't know what kind of establishment you take us for, but the Royal Trafalgar is not in the habit of divulging client information. If you'd like to leave your name and details,' – he was in agony, trying to keep his face straight – 'I'll pass your enquiry to the manager. Together,' he said, 'with your offer of a financial arrangement.'

I held up my hand. 'Please,' I said, 'that won't be necessary. My client was thinking more about a private agreement.'

Gerald looked blank.

'She's willing to pay you,' I clarified.

Gerald smiled in the way of the devout when someone farts in the front pew.

'Perhaps,' he said, 'if you tried the Metropole. The lady's husband may have stayed there. It sounds more his kind of establishment. They'll be pleased to help, I'm sure. The Royal Trafalgar is not that kind of establishment however, Mr...?'

'Marble,' I told him. 'Private investigator.'

Gerald's smile reverted to smug.

'Mr Marble,' he said, 'may I ask you to step away from the desk?'

He looked for the concierge and raised his hand to bring the guy over. I shifted myself quick to block the view.

'Wait,' I said.

He looked at me. I pulled an envelope from my jacket and opened it on the desk. Made a fan of the notes inside.

'Five hundred,' I whispered. 'This is yours for absolutely nothing.' I turned and nodded towards the bistro. 'I'll be waiting over there. Give me just two minutes of your time when you take a break, and you walk away with this envelope, no strings attached. You can throw me out on my backside and the cash is still yours. With my client's compliments.'

If I was expecting a shout of joy I was disappointed. The expression on Gerald's face had more pucker than a chimp chewing lemons. His contempt had racked up to the sublime at the sight of the dirties themselves. But I recognised something behind the look. The surprise of a fish caught on the hook. For a moment Gerald was lost for words. I slipped the envelope back into my jacket and went to order another coffee. I took a table in the back this time, well under the stairs.

I was sipping the dregs when Gerald slipped into the seat across from me. He tried to combine businesslike with stealth, the act of a schoolboy with his hand in the treacle tin. He gave me a spiteful look as down payment for when this thing blew up in his face. To his credit, he remained cool when I slipped the envelope across the table.

'My client's compliments,' I said. He didn't pick it up. He knew something was off. I nodded encouragement. 'Five hundred,' I said. 'It's all there.'

He worked a sneer onto his face while he waited for the flipside. Now it was my turn to stay poker-faced. Gerald broke first.

'What's the catch?' he said.

'None,' I said. 'The money's yours.'

That's when he realised what the catch was: more money. I saw the cogs turn. Switched back to Sly Uncle.

'If you help me, there's plenty more of those,' I promised.

'What kind of help?'

I held my grin. Somewhere between the reception desk and our cosy table we'd lost the Royal Trafalgar's high ideals. Gerald knew exactly what kind of help I wanted.

I slid a piece of notepaper across the table with Slater's name on it. 'I've listed the dates this guy stayed here. I want them confirmed plus any other dates in the last year when he registered. There's another five hundred if you get me that information.'

'That's not so easy,' Gerald said. 'Searching the invoices takes time.' But I knew he was just playing for more.

'I'll give you thirty minutes,' I said. 'I'll come to the desk. I want a paper copy. It's worth five hundred quid.'

I watched him doing the sums. My guess was that five hundred was a couple of week's net take-home. He gave the matter five seconds' sour consideration for the sake of self-respect then snatched up the envelope and the notepaper and headed back to the desk with as much dignity as he could muster whilst trying not to sprint.

I picked up a copy of the *Observer* and killed time until the waiter came and fingered my second saucer in a subtle hint to hand over more dosh. Places like this they don't do refills. At this rate it was going to be a contest between Gerald and the bistro to get my money.

Spending Gina's money like small change was a gamble. There was a risk that Larry Slater's trip here was innocent. Or at least unrelated to the missing girl. But I was going with the odds. Slater's Amex statement seemed to have put him here with Tina in March. Her friend Sammy remembered Tina being here the previous October also. The odds were that Slater and the girl were here a few times. If my hunch panned out I'd have not only a clearer picture of what was going on between them but also some interesting evidence to wave under Slater's nose next time I visited him. Time was running on. I needed Slater to let me in on what was happening with his step-daughter, and I figured that nothing would lubricate Larry's vocal chords like a little blackmail.

Gerald was in the back office for twenty minutes. When he came out I wandered across to the desk.

This time we didn't need words. Just a fake smile and three sheets of paper pushed across desk. It could have been any old guest checking his bill. I scanned the sheets. Standard database prints of three invoices showing the guest's charge details. Something was off though: the two March dates from Slater's Amex were there, plus another one in January, but nothing for the previous October when Tina's friend remembered her staying here. I raised my eyebrows.

'That's it,' Gerald said. 'The last twelve months.'

So what happened to October?

I slid Gerald's extra five hundred across the desk.

The missing October date puzzled me. That one should have been a cert. Was Tina Brown here with another client? Maybe she'd been so impressed with the place that she'd talked Slater into bringing her back. But without a record of Slater at the hotel in October I had no concrete evidence that he was ever here with Tina. All I had were his calls to her number in March. An interesting coincidence but still circumstantial. I'd needed the October date to tie the two positively. Without that, turning up the heat on Slater might be tricky.

Then something caught my eye. Gerald's paperwork said that Slater's first visit – the January one – was charged to someone called Alpha Security. The room was prepaid, with follow-up bar charges of two hundred and eighty-seven pounds, also settled by Alpha Security. More interestingly, the January booking was for three nights but Slater's name was registered for only the second. I pushed the paper back across the desk.

'What do you make of this?'

Gerald took a discreet glance. Discretion was the thing of the moment. His voice stayed low.

'Mr Slater appears to have stayed a single night,' he told me. 'The suite was reserved for three.'

Slater throwing money away? Or Alpha Security?

I scribbled the Alpha Security name on another piece of notepaper and pushed it across the desk.

'I need all reservations or payments under this name,' I said.

Gerald was about to give me the no-no but my words stopped him.

'Two hundred for each date you find.'

I promised to return in thirty minutes and wandered back to read my *Observer*. This time I resisted the coffee: the two-hundred-per-booking deal with Gerald might be affordable but more coffees were not. And if Alpha Security had a regular thing going at the Royal Trafalgar I'd be bankrupted when I went back to the desk. I wouldn't actually be bankrupt, of course. My remaining cash only ran to five hundred, which limited my exposure. If Gerald turned up more than two bookings he was going to get shafted. But what's corruption without occasional setbacks? What could Gerald do? Call the Fraud Squad?

After ten minutes he reappeared at his place, trying not to be obvious as he scanned the lobby for me. I dropped the newspaper and ambled back over. More discretion and paper pushing. He had two Alpha Security bookings for me. I folded four hundred into another envelope. A professional conjurer couldn't have slid the envelope out of my fingers with greater skill than Gerald.

I took a quick look at what he'd given me. Two more Alpha Security bookings. Each for three nights in the Royal Trafalgar's outrageously expensive Millennium Suite.

One booking was in June. The other was October, the date Tina's friend Sammy had given me. Bingo! Alpha Security, whoever they were, were linked to Tina.

On both occasions Alpha had a guest checking in for the middle night. Neither was Slater. The October guest was someone named John McCabe with an address in Wimbledon. The June man was a David Hanlon. Address in Chevening, Surrey.

I wondered how far back this pattern went. I scribbled again. Pushed a note over the desk saying *Alpha Security. Last five years????* *£200 each*. Gerald's expression was a combination of fear and boggle-eyed greed. There might be dozens of these bookings. He looked to see if I was serious. Were my pockets stuffed with cash? They weren't, but Gerald didn't know it. I left him hurdling towards the admin office and went back to my bistro. Adrenaline fired me to order one more coffee, and Gerald's last hundred took another hit.

Gerald came out fifteen minutes later but he was interrupted by the necessity of dealing with an arriving guest. I stayed seated and watched the fastest checking-in since Anne Boleyn arrived at the Tower. Gerald had the guy through in sixty seconds flat.

Then I wandered across, leaned on the desk. Gerald looked up at me with the expression of a rottweiler whose sausages have been snatched. A single shake of the head. Alpha Security had nothing prior to the reservation last June. It was lucky, in a way. The sausage string wasn't as long as the rottweiler had thought.

I touched my forelock in a manner I judged way out of line with Royal Trafalgar behaviour and headed for the door.

The coffee had been expensive but I'd got something that was going to jump-start this case.

I just had to figure what it meant.

CHAPTER TWENTY-FOUR

'About time!'

Mitch watched the guy come down the steps. He'd been sitting in the Warrior for two hours and his arse was aching. They had a real fast mover here.

As the guy reached his Tonka, Roker came out of the hotel behind him. Mitch had the engine running before he was halfway over.

'Go.'

They got out onto Kingsway fifty yards behind the Tonka and followed it back to the pier. Mitch concentrated on keeping it in sight as it crossed the roundabout. 'Thought you'd checked in for the night,' he said. 'How much longer are we tailing this joker?'

Roker kept his eyes on the quarry. 'As long as it takes,' he said.

Mitch said nothing but his belly was talking. They'd been on the guy since eight thirty this morning and they might still have all afternoon to run. Apart from the Pringles Mitch had gone without. The guy had probably eaten in the hotel. Roker too. Mitch was almost minded to ask. Snarled at the road instead as the quarry headed north, back out of town.

'Did he meet someone?' Mitch asked.

'He talked to a receptionist,' Roker confirmed. 'Greasy little guy. Had him running errands.'

'He get anything?'

Roker watched the tail showing intermittently up ahead. 'Yeah,' he said. 'Two hours tête-à-tête with Grease Jockey tells me he got something.'

'Did he spot you?' Mitch said.

'Jesus,' Roker said. 'Watch the road. Don't let the bastard lose us.'

The moves the guy was making had sandpapered Roker's nerves. They were looking at a leak. And leaks tended to grow. First a little drip. Next thing you're swimming. This they didn't need. Whatever the guy was up to, his digging around at the Royal Trafalgar did not smell good. Roker's instinct said that they were going to have to do some plumbing.

Eddie Flynn. Private Investigator. Ex-cop. That was all Roker had but it was enough. The "ex-cop" in particular he didn't like. It meant the guy was no amateur. Flynn had been putting something together back there at the Trafalgar.

The thing Roker couldn't figure out was whom Flynn was working for. Roker held it all ways to the light but nothing came through. There was no one could have sent Flynn to Brighton. Unknowns scraped Roker's nerves.

They stayed with the Tonka as it picked up the A23 north, then the M23. Heading back to town, Roker decided. The car held the inside lane, skipping between trucks from time to time. They passed Gatwick and it was beginning to look good until the Tonka turned east instead of west at the Orbital.

Mitch cursed noisily. The frigging mystery tour was still on.

They followed east on the M25 until the Tonka took the Sevenoaks slip road. Mitch kicked in the turbo and closed the distance with a brief sprint to a hundred and ten, braking late enough on the slip to have Roker hissing between his teeth. But they needed the speed. Mitch was barely in time to spot the quarry disappearing onto the A21 amongst the afternoon traffic. Mitch cut across a car and got out onto the road. Half a mile further on, the Tonka overtook an artic and was out of sight in front of it. Mitch changed down and pulled out to pass the truck just as Roker spotted the quarry swinging off onto the A25. He yelled out. Mitch killed the manoeuvre and swerved back behind the truck to get the Warrior onto the turnoff. Roker gripped the door handle and gritted his teeth again. The Warrior leaned on its springs and skidded round the curve. They picked the Tonka up, heading west. Then the road narrowed and they hit traffic lights and the quarry turned just as the amber came on, four cars ahead of them. Mitch floored the pedal and passed the line of cars in time to skid through on red. The turn took them north, back over the M25 and on towards Chevening. In the middle of the village the Tonka pulled over and Mitch saw the guy ask directions. He held back then followed the car out into the country. A couple of minutes later the quarry slowed alongside an estate wall and turned into a driveway between brick gateposts. Mitch pulled up on the verge fifty yards back.

'What's the bastard doing now?' he said.

Roker jabbed his thumb towards a track that ran off from the road behind them.

'Pull us in,' he said. 'He may come back this way.'

Mitch backed the SUV twenty yards down the track and stopped against a five-bar gate. Roker jumped out and walked up the road to get a view. He found cover behind bushes thirty yards from the entrance. He was curious about where Flynn had gone, but if he walked right up to the gates there was a risk he'd not reach the Warrior in time when Flynn came back out.

Roker wondered what this place was. Had to be somewhere significant, judging by Flynn's bee line from Brighton. The more Roker saw the less he liked. He sensed the leak expanding minute by minute.

The way things were shaping up, they were going to have to take action.

Soon.

CHAPTER TWENTY-FIVE

I passed a stone gatehouse and followed the driveway as it curved between twelve-foot rhododendrons. An old guy was digging in the gatehouse garden but he didn't glance up.

The Royal Trafalgar records gave David Hanlon's address as Sedgeworth Rise. I'd anticipated a detached house with a pretentious nameplate back in the village but I doubted if this driveway was leading me to anywhere that depended on nameplates. Hanlon, whoever he was, was another wealthy party. He'd probably drunk all the coffees he wanted in Brighton. I followed the rhododendrons, knowing I wasn't going to find a two-up-two-down.

Detective's instincts: I didn't find anything. I'd barely got out of sight of the gate-house when the estate's walls sprang afresh out of the foliage in a pincer movement. The way ahead was blocked by ornate gates featuring more ironwork than the Titanic. A call panel was set up at a height appropriate for visiting SUVs, which made it way out of reach when you're at the wheel of a Frogeye. I extracted myself and pressed the button. Nothing. I tried again with the same result. It looked like David Hanlon and his butler were both out.

You win some, you lose some. The diversion had been a whim, an off chance that I'd find the guy home. It would have been good to catch him cold, watch his reaction when I dropped a few names. I gave the bell one last try, held it for ten seconds. Maybe the butler was deaf. Maybe the sound didn't carry to the pool.

Nowt.

One for tomorrow. I turned the Frogeye around and headed back out. I stopped at the gatehouse. The old man looked up and scrutinised the car with interest as I hopped out.

The guy nodded at the Frogeye. 'Long time since I saw one of those,' he declared.

The Frogeye is a great conversation piece if you meet anyone over sixty. The younger generation think I'm driving a kit car.

I spieled a few facts and figures, waxed lyrical on how sweet she ran. Didn't tell him about the defective heater or the oil change every three thousand miles. I asked whether he knew when David Hanlon was expected back.

The old guy shook his head and apologised. 'Considering I live right here you'd think I'd know whether they were in or out. But I don't really notice, to tell the truth. I just see them coming and going from time to time.'

I clicked my tongue and looked at my watch like I was deciding whether to hang around for Hanlon to arrive. I dug a little further.

'Any chance you'll be speaking to the Hanlons today?' I asked. 'Maybe you could mention I was here.'

The guy shook his head again.

'I don't know them past nodding, to be honest,' he said. 'We've not been here long. I've met Faye a couple of times when she's been out with the dogs but that's about it. I've never spoken to David Hanlon.'

I thanked the guy, nodded farewell and went back around the car. 'Obliged anyway,' I told him. 'I'll call back.'

'If I do see them I'd be happy to say you were here,' he offered. 'Mr...?'

'Coffee.' I smiled my gratitude. 'Gerald Coffee.'

'I'll tell them you were here, Mr Coffee,' he promised, and went back to his digging. If he did tell them he was going to get some funny looks.

I drove out through the gateposts and headed back to town. I'd pay another visit tomorrow. The Hanlons might turn out to be peripheral to whatever was happening with Rebecca Townsend but I was betting otherwise. David Hanlon's involvement with Alpha Security and the Royal Trafalgar linked him squarely to Larry Slater, and right now I was interested in anyone with funny connections to Larry.

Brighton had been a fishing trip. I'd half expected nothing. Picked up a hefty bite instead. A few new names to check out and something much bigger. Along the way the line had taken a tug like a marlin wanted to play.

Time to start reeling in.

CHAPTER TWENTY-SIX

They followed the Tonka back towards Heathrow. The car slipped away from them a couple of times in the congealing traffic.

'Stay on him,' Roker growled. 'I want to know everything this bird is doing.'

'He's headed back to town,' Mitch enlightened him. He chewed gum, skipping lanes to keep the Tonka in range. Two minutes later another prediction bit the dust. The Tonka pulled into the Lodge Clacket services. Mitch cursed and followed it in, swung into a parking slot opposite the pumps as the quarry stopped in front of the unleaded. Mitch killed the engine and watched in his rear-view. Tonka-Man was out filling the car. No idea he was being watched.

'How are we for diesel?' Roker asked.

'Half a tank,' Mitch said. 'We can stay on him.'

Roker looked unconvinced. 'We can until the half tank is out,' he said. 'After that we lose him, unless you push.'

Mitch shook his head. 'We've got the range,' he said. 'I can't see the Tonka holding more than a couple of gallons.'

Roker looked at him. 'You ever see how far a motorbike goes on a couple of gallons?' he said.

'Then it's our unlucky day,' Mitch said. What would be unlucky was if they were still following this joker by the time they ran dry. Mitch's stomach had been on residuals for hours.

'How about I grab a sandwich?' he suggested.

'Make it quick,' Roker said.

Mitch skipped out and hurried across to the shop. He was in ahead of the guy but he needed to take a leak and that lost him time. As he queued for the sandwiches Tonka-Man was nowhere in sight. Outside, Roker was gesturing frantically. Mitch spotted the Tonka tailing out through the far side of the pumps, heading back to the motorway. He cursed and fired up the engine.

He worked the Warrior as hard as the traffic would allow, bullying his way across lanes until they got back within shouting distance. After that he stayed close. Ready in case the target did something sudden.

At the next junction the Frogeye did something sudden. It swerved across the lanes and took the filter for the A22. Mitch's hopes lifted. The guy was finally headed back into town.

Inbound traffic was moving freely. Mitch drove one-handed, savaging his sandwiches as they followed the Tonka up through Croydon and Streatham. They got clear of the Common and headed towards the river. Then the Tonka cut off and turned towards Battersea Park. It pulled into a residential street lined with parked cars, then turned again, looking for a place. Mitch let the Warrior coast past the turn and they watched the Tonka backing into a parking spot. The guy was through. Hallelujah!

'Pull over,' Roker said. He leapt out and jogged back to the corner. So fast that he nearly bumped into Flynn coming back round it. It was one of those moments, but Flynn went right past without noticing. Roker turned and watched him disappear into one of the houses.

The guy's pad, Roker guessed. Home for the night. He waited fifteen minutes but nothing happened. Then he made a call and walked back to the Warrior.

He got Mitch to stop off at the office as they passed. The place was empty except for Vicky who was finishing up ready to go. She had nothing for him so he went back out and had Mitch take him up the road to the Algarve Club which was located just off Fulham Palace Road. He told Mitch to wait and went in. It took a minute to adjust to the dim lighting before he spotted his man leaning at the bar. It was early. Just a half-dozen in for what the club jokingly termed happy hour. At most places happy hour meant half price. At the Algarve you got a normal-price drink and a discount token for your next. Happy hour finished at six on the dot when the floor show started and your tokens were good for nothing.

The man didn't offer a drink.

'What's happening,' he said.

Roker was uneasy around the guy. He'd learned to play it straight. Say his stuff and get out. The Algarve's dim lighting did nothing for the man's appearance, which was grim in any light, something the guy seemed happy about. When you've been through the mangler it's good for people to see it. Saved misunderstandings.

Roker signalled the bar and ordered a scotch. When he turned back the man was still waiting.

'He's on to something,' Roker said.

'What's he onto?'

'Brighton.'

'How come?'

'I don't know.'

Roker gave him details of Flynn's head-to-head with the Royal Trafalgar's reception clerk.

'Why would reception tell him anything?'

'Cash,' said Roker. 'Stuff was going back and forth. There had to be readies.'

'So he's on to us.'

Roker's drink arrived. He slid a tenner across the bar and lifted the glass.

'He's on to something,' he said. 'I figure he knows that Slater was there. Maybe he picked up some other names.' He thought of something. 'How did you know this guy was chasing Slater?'

The man studied the display behind the bar. 'Little bird,' he said.

'Sure,' said Roker. He sipped the scotch, let it slide down his throat and picked up the change from his tenner. The change was bugger all, plastic token to boot. Happy hour! There were more important things on his mind, though.

'This looks like a bit of a problem,' Roker said.

'Yes,' the man agreed. 'It's definitely a problem.'

They stayed silent while Roker drained his glass in a couple of sips. The fastest tenner he'd lost since he put his money on Frenchman's Creek in the National.

'Who's Flynn working for?' Roker asked.

'Haven't a clue,' the man said.

'Slater?'

'Nah.'

'One of the others?'

'That's what I'm thinking,' the man said. 'We're going to have to find out. Did Flynn poke his nose anywhere else?'

'Chevening,' Roker said.

The man's eyebrows lifted. 'He went to Chevening?'

'Yeah. Big place. Estate. High walls. He was in there ten minutes. Is there a connection to Brighton?'

The other man was still watching the bar.

'That's bad,' he said to himself.

'I thought it might be,' Roker said.

The man slid his glass across the bar and the girl refilled it. A double. No tokens needed. One rule for some, etc.

'You want me to stay on him?' Roker asked.

'I'll let you know tomorrow,' the man said.

'And if he's onto us?' said Roker.

'Then we'll stop him,' said the man.

'What's the man say?' Mitch asked when Roker got back into the Warrior.

'He's not happy,' Roker said.

Mitch grinned. 'Is Tonka messing in one of Mac's little schemes?'

Roker didn't smile back. 'The bastard has no idea,' he said.

He got Mitch to drop him back at the office. The place was above a bookmaker's on Fulham Road. A plate by the door gave the name Alpha Security. Roker walked up to shut up shop.

Upstairs the lights were still on. One of the crew must have come back in. But when he went in he saw it was Vicky, still behind her desk and looking like she'd lost a fiver. It had to be something serious to keep her in past five-thirty.

'What's up, darlin'?' Roker said.

Then he saw that his office door was open. The lights were on in there too.

He looked at Vicky.

'Jesus, Jimmy,' she hissed. 'There's some guy waiting for you. Said you'd want to talk to him. I didn't know what to do.'

'Some guy? In my frigging office?'

Vicky fluttered her hands. 'What the hell could I do? Jesus, I've been peeing myself. Why don't you keep your phone on?'

Roker did keep his phone on, but the battery had quit after he'd made his last call. He felt another stirring of unease. Alpha Security was the kind of business that got visits from time to time. Went with the territory. Nothing he couldn't handle but this he really didn't need right now.

'Okay, Vicky,' Roker said. 'Go home.'

Vicky didn't need telling twice. She grabbed her stuff and ran out of the door.

Roker strode into his office. He'd had a hard day. Whoever had barged in here had picked the wrong time.

When he got inside the day got worse. The visitor slid his feet off Roker's desk and waved him through.

'Glad you're back, Jimmy,' said Flynn. 'How was Brighton?'

CHAPTER TWENTY-SEVEN

Roker was uglier, close up. He had one of those faces that's off-balance in a way you can't quite pin down. Something about the nose. The nearest I'd got to him at the Royal Trafalgar was when I'd ordered my second coffee. He was three tables away reading a newspaper that he thought made him invisible. Maybe it would have but I was keen to see who'd been following me down the M23. I only got a peripheral glimpse but it was enough. A face like Roker's doesn't need a photographic memory.

'When you tail someone,' I said, 'choose a smaller car. Wait for cover before you change lanes. Don't rush to catch up when the target makes a move. And never use your indicator.'

I could have gone on. Blah-di-blah. I'm a fountain of advice. Just shop talk between me and Roker, of course. When I paused for breath Roker joined in.

'You!' He jabbed a finger. 'Get the fuck out of my office.'

Moi? I gave him perplexed and looked around the place. As offices went it was unimpressive. Better than Eagle Eye's, of course, but that didn't say much. Roker had all the right computers and telephones and combination cabinets, but something was lacking. The place had a serious style deficiency. Style is what we did have at Eagle Eye. Style is what tells you about the outfit you're hiring – or in this case about the outfit that has been hired to follow you. I turned my attention back to Roker.

'I've got a few questions,' I said. 'Sit down, Jimmy.'

Jimmy didn't sit. 'I'll say it again,' he said. 'Walk out while you can.'

'Number one: who are you working for?'

Roker came around the desk. His ugly beak hovered over me like a constipated hawk's. His fists were bunched.

'Two: what's your connection with Rebecca Townsend?'

Roker's fist made a grab for my shirt collar. I snatched the wrist and his knuckles hit the top of his desk with a crack they must have heard down the street. Then I grabbed Roker's own collar and pulled until his lopsided face hung in front of me, looking surprised in its birdie kind of way. I squeezed until I had his attention then eased him away.

'Sit down, Jimmy,' I repeated.

Roker backed off a little but didn't sit. Too much nervous energy. And he was still close enough to me to make me nervous. For a couple of moments we stared at each other then Roker jabbed another finger.

'Flynn, you've just made the biggest mistake of your private-dick life.'

This wasn't true. The biggest mistake I made was when I'd helped un-hijack a truckload of Welsh sheep on the M4 and accidentally dropped the tailboard at Leigh Delamere. That's when I found out that rounding up eighty-seven sheep is not as easy as those border collies make out. The Leigh Delamere thing was by far my worst screw-up. I guess Roker hadn't heard about that one.

'Three,' I said. 'What's the connection between Alpha Security, Larry Slater and the Royal Trafalgar?'

'Flynn,' Roker said, 'the two of us have nothing to talk about.'

'For a man who's been on my tail all day this is a come-down,' I said. 'I thought you'd be happy we'd finally got together.'

'No,' Roker said. 'I'm not happy. And forget Brighton. You wasted your time chasing down there in that pedal-car.'

'I disagree,' I said. 'Today hasn't felt like a waste. Look at what I've got since I ate my cornflakes. I've confirmed that what's happening to Rebecca Townsend is not just inside the family. I found out that Alpha Security is connected to it. And I've learned that the people Alpha Security are working for hang out at the Algarve Club right here in Fulham. Tell me, Jimmy: what else is going to pop out before I stir my cocoa?'

'Whatever you heard, you heard wrong,' Roker said. 'Go bark up another tree, Sherlock.'

I shook my head. 'I think I'll give this tree a few more shakes,' I said. 'See what falls out.'

'Shake this tree any more and you're not going to like what you get,' Roker growled.

'Occupational hazard,' I said. 'So what's going to come out, Jimmy?'

Roker stooped back into collar-grabbing territory. I sat back.

'Your guts will come out, Flynn, if you poke your nose in any further.'

'All this,' I grinned, 'from a guy who knows nothing. I think you're stalling me, Jimmy.'

'So sue me,' Roker said.

I sighed. Lifted my feet back up onto his desk and opened my arms. 'Why make it hard?' I said. 'You know that I know you're involved with the Slaters. You therefore know that I know you're in on Rebecca Townsend's disappearance.'

'Think again,' Roker said. 'You're digging in piss, Flynn. I've never heard of any Rebecca Townsend.'

I looked at him.

'Someone has heard of her,' I said. 'You say it's not you so maybe I need to go chat with your chums at the Algarve Club.'

'Go ahead,' Roker said. 'I look forward to the result.'

'So what is the Royal Trafalgar thing?' I asked. 'At least you're in on that. Those suite bookings must have cost Alpha Security a bob or two.'

'Hospitality,' Roker said. 'Business clients.'

'What sort of business?'

'You've got to be shitting me!'

'No, Jimmy,' I said, 'I really want to know what sort of business involves hiring a high-class hooker and the best suite at a five star hotel that sets you back three grand before you've even opened the minibar.'

'Confidential sort of business,' Roker said, 'which means you've just hit a dead end.'

'Detective one-oh-one,' I said. 'Dead ends are never dead. You look at what's blocking the road and learn a lot.'

'Not this time,' Roker said, 'because if you carry on with this you're going to find yourself in a very dead end indeed.'

'Is that a threat, Jimmy?'

'Take it how you like.'

I changed the subject.

'What's the deal with Tina Brown?' I asked him. 'Was she just bait to hook Larry Slater? Are we looking at blackmail?'

'Flynn, you're getting tedious.'

'And where is the delightful Ms Brown?' I asked. 'She seems to be awfully hard to find at the moment.'

'This discussion is through,' Roker said. He pulled his phone out, jabbed buttons.

'It's dead,' I reminded him. 'You should keep it charged. Your receptionist was pretty clear on that point.'

Roker snapped the phone shut and grabbed the desk phone. That one wasn't dead. I looked around his office while he made the call. The place got worse the closer you looked. The sort of office a VAT accountant might have. You'd never imagine a private investigation firm was holed up here. Maybe it was just brilliant cover. Roker finished the call and smacked the phone down.

'Hang around for five minutes,' he said. 'We can have your little chat.'

Any chinwag organised by Roker I could do without. I pulled my feet off his desk. Paperwork fell to the floor.

'The guy I need to chat with,' I said, 'is the one who had you chasing me to Brighton. He'll know all about the Royal Trafalgar. And my guess is that he knows about Rebecca.' I stood and straightened my jacket.

'That's a shame,' Roker said. 'Because I won't be introducing him to you.'

I gave him a grin and headed for the door.

'You already did,' I said.

I left the door open on my way out.

CHAPTER TWENTY-EIGHT

I crossed the street, dodging early evening traffic, musing on how the Brighton trip had turned from a long shot into a jackpot. Suddenly I was pushing a loaded trolley through checkout.

My phone rang. I strained to hear Arabel's voice through the street din.

'Where you at, babe? You said you'd be home.'

I kicked myself. When I'd set off for Brighton I'd had no idea that this thing would snowball. Arabel was cooking at my place then I was taking her out.

'Bel,' I said, 'I'm a disgrace. Got carried with the flow. But I'll be there. Promise.'

'Sometime tonight? Or do you want your dinner in the freezer?' Her tone made it clear that dinner wouldn't be the only thing in there.

'Bel, give me an hour. Then I'm all yours.'

'Sure. Whenever you get a minute.'

'Hey, I've always got a minute for you. I just got tied up with this thing. I should have called.'

'Are you looking for the girl?'

'Yes. And things are creeping out of the woodwork.'

'Things that couldn't have crept tomorrow?'

'Things that couldn't wait,' I assured her. 'I'm worried about this girl, Bel.' I was playing the sympathy vote. Arabel understood that I could have turned up for dinner on time as long as she didn't mind about a poor girl huddled in a dark cellar somewhere. The sympathy line used to work but Arabel had grown wiser.

'Flynn,' she cut in, 'I'd walk out right now if the casserole hadn't got me salivating. But I ain't salivating much longer. Come home or I'm gonna eat and go.'

'I'll be there, Bel,' I repeated. 'But don't walk out and make me drive up to Roman Road. You wouldn't do that to a tired guy would you? Hang in, Bel.'

'I am,' she said. 'One hour, then I'm eating. And I'm gonna be planning some suffering while I'm waiting.'

'Are we talking dirty now?'

The phone cut dead.

Not dirty.

I turned down a narrow street and stopped outside a door topped by badly-illuminated lettering. The seedy effect might have been deliberate but I figured it was more likely cheapskate owners. The lettering spelled out ALGARVE CLUB. The street windows were bricked up and the door was steel with a one-way glass. I pressed the button and the door opened.

Behind the door twenty stone of muscle in a tux stood beside the pay-window in case you forgot to hand in your donation. Admission was a tenner, which was cheek for Fulham, but a private investigator's life is nothing if not a charitable enterprise. I handed over the cash and went through. The rhythmic thump of dirty music beckoned.

Bad lighting hinted at teak veneer and fake red leather. Twenty or so tables encircled a postage-stamp stage where coloured spots picked out the gymnastics of a lithe blonde whose skimpy clothing was dissolving by the second. The tables were mostly empty, just a few early customers getting an eyeful before heading off for an Indian.

The place was a monument to wannabe respectability. The teak and leather decor couldn't disguise the fact that the place was a strip joint. The broom closets the girls made up in would have flaking plaster and mesh over the windows just like any in Soho. I sensed an investor with ideas of running a classy bar but unable to resist putting the girls in, the distorted looking-glass of the criminal trying to build a respectable image on dirty cash. When my eyes adjusted I spotted a shady character sitting in the back with two glasses on his table. One glass was half empty and looked like carbonated water. The other was full and looked like beer but I knew this was just the light. I went over and sat down.

'Just in time,' Shaughnessy said. 'The urge to filch your drink was growing by the minute.' He was studying the gymnastics of the blonde with either fascination or despair.

I picked up the beer and took a sip.

'You weren't in danger,' I said. 'This beer would cure any alcoholic urge like wimples check fornication in a nunnery.'

'I've never been in a nunnery,' Shaughnessy said. 'How was your chat with Alpha?'

'Tense,' I said. 'I spoke with a guy named James Roker. He knows nothing about nothing.'

'That figures.'

'But apparently he knows a man who does.'

Shaughnessy nodded. He indicated a table at the far end of the bar. Two men were sat talking. One was big, trussed up in a sports jacket with shoulder seams popping over an open-collar shirt. The spots highlighted a face like a granite sculpture after the chiseller's drinking has taken a turn. His close-shaved head left him ageless. The man could have been thirty or sixty. The guy with him went for expensive suits, and shirts with ties. He was lean but with a charisma that was worth muscle. I put him in his late fifties. A deep-lined face, bushy brows, girlish lips. A natural sneer pulled his lips up when he wasn't speaking. The light reflected off golden hair dropping to his collar. He was the kind of guy that would still have a full mane at ninety. Half dandy, half thug.

Shaughnessy gestured at Granite. 'Your Alpha guy chatted to him for thirty minutes. Looked like he was passing on bad news. Goldilocks came in ten minutes ago. He's getting the replay.'

'Brighton news,' I guessed.

Shaughnessy had picked up the Warrior at the Lodge Clacket services and tailed it as they followed me back into town. He stayed with the vehicle after I bailed out at Battersea and watched it stop off at the Alpha Security offices before moving on to the Algarve Club. Shaughnessy had walked into the club right behind Roker and called me with the location of Alpha Security. When Roker left the club Shaughnessy stayed on to see if anything else went down. He was probably on his third mineral water by now.

'Who's Goldilocks?' I said.

'My guess? The boss,' said Shaughnessy. 'And he's not a happy guy.'

Maybe he'd been drinking the beer.

A waitress in a skimpy outfit passed by, giving Shaughnessy the look that girls on commission reserve for teetotals. She'd given him up as a lost cause but I flagged her over. She came across looking wary. Eighteen or nineteen years old. Nice-looking. Would probably graduate to the tiny stage at some point.

I gave her Harmless Charmer and got a smile in return. When she smiled she was beautiful. Her smile faded when she realised I was asking questions instead of ordering drinks.

'I know that guy,' I said. I jabbed at the Granite-Goldilocks table. 'Can't recall his name. Is he one of your regulars?'

'You could say that.' She brought her smile back gamely. 'That's Paul McAllister. He owns the club.'

Club owner. That had to be Goldilocks. I didn't see Granite as the business type.

I extemporised, wagged my finger. 'I don't mean Paul.'

'Oh,' she said, 'you mean Ray. He's in all the time with Paul.'

'Ray!' I slapped my forehead, 'I know him from somewhere.'

I waited.

'Ray Child,' she prompted.

'Got him!' I broadened my smile to full wattage and pulled a tenner out of my pocket. Ordered a single malt. Told her to keep the change. Her smile broadened but not by much. The change in this place wasn't going to make her rich. Still, commission was the name of the game. She walked off to the bar.

Paul McAllister. Ray Child. Goldilocks and Granite.

The names didn't ring any bells but then London's a big town.

'So where are we at?' Shaughnessy asked.

I filled him in on what I'd found in Brighton. Larry Slater's connection to Alpha Security through his stays at the Royal Trafalgar. Alpha Security's other hospitality bookings: guests Hanlon and McCabe. Maybe it was just business, like Roker insisted. Funny business, was my guess.

Now we were looking at the guys who had set Roker on my tail. And I figured I knew who'd tipped these guys off about Eagle Eye.

'Slater,' Shaughnessy said. 'He called them after your visit.'

I nodded. One little house call and suddenly there's a posse on our heels. So who were these guys? Why had Slater tipped them off after I'd talked to him?

'He's either in it or afraid of it,' said Shaughnessy.

Whatever "it" was.

'Have they got Rebecca?' he wondered.

It was the question that had occurred to me. If someone had taken the Slaters' daughter then this pair would certainly fit. And these people would have no trouble intimidating a family into keeping quiet. Did they frighten Larry enough to have him tip them off when someone started interfering?

A link between the Slaters and these two didn't explain Alpha Security's expensive weekends in Brighton, though. Nor why Slater was chasing Tina Brown. We had jigsaw pieces all around us. I just didn't know how many jigsaws we had. Our cute waitress came back and put down my Scotch. Gave me a cute smile. Maybe there was more left from the tenner than I'd estimated. Shaughnessy handed his glass back to her and waved off the offer of another.

'Gotta go, Eddie,' he told me. 'Promises to keep. Are you going to stay with these guys?'

'Just till I'm through with my Scotch.' I had thirty minutes to make good on my promise to Arabel. She was an easy-going girl but she liked her promises kept. That's why I rarely made any.

'How about we take a look at these guys?' I said.

Shaughnessy nodded. 'First thing tomorrow,' he promised. He slid out of the seat and walked out, still steady on his feet.

I sipped my whiskey and pondered on what to do next. We needed to close this thing before Tina Brown's friend Sammy called in the authorities. I doubted if the authorities could do anything to help, but the waters would get well and truly muddied. I couldn't help wondering if Tina might not want the water muddying. I was seeing her as a part of this.

The stick in the hornet's nest. Why ditch a good idea? I caught our young waitress' eye again and signalled her over. I pulled out a twenty this time. Turned Harmless Charmer right up. 'Keep the change,' I grinned. I nodded over to our conspirators in the shadows. 'A drink each for Paul and Ray. Ask them if they've been to Brighton lately.'

Her smile was genuine this time. We were establishing a pattern. With people like Shaughnessy you could just give up hostessing as a bad job. Party Animal Flynn was a different story. Flynn meant tips. Flynn meant commission.

She went back to the bar and a couple of minutes later delivered the drinks to their table. The men's heads turned in unison. I raised my glass and toasted them across the floor. The music came on again and I sat back to watch the next girl limber up on the stage.

The girl hardly had time to get the audience's circulation moving before she was hidden from view by two silhouettes. The silhouettes sat down opposite me. Granite up close was worse than Granite far away. Close up I could see that someone had once taken a knife to Ray Child's face. A scar ran from his left ear right down to the jaw line and he still seemed pissed about it. I gave him an innocent grin, wondering what had happened to the other guy. All the while Paul McAllister – Goldilocks – was looking at me like he'd spilled his smarties on the toilet floor. He leaned forward.

'You get this once,' he said. 'Pull your nose out and keep it out. If you don't, I will cut it off.' His bushy brows lifted to see if I'd got his message. Child watched me from the other side. His eyebrows didn't move but his stare spoke for him. Child had the kind of stare that had been intimidating people since the school playground. Myself, I'd been to a better class of school. I turned to McAllister.

'Hello Paul,' I said. 'Sorry your boys had such a long trip. If I'd known they were going to Brighton we could have shared a ride.'

McAllister said nothing. His face stayed motionless.

'One comment,' I said: 'I think you're hiring cheap. There are firms who can tail someone all day without being caught. They charge more but you know how it is. You get what you pay for.'

Child's head turned towards McAllister. McAllister's hand came up, a warning.

'Stop!' he said. His eyes hadn't left me.

I stopped.

'Clearly, you didn't hear,' he said. The music was a little loud, I had to admit.

'Either that,' McAllister said, 'or you're stupid.'

He waited a moment to see which one it was.

'If you push your nose any further into our business,' he said, 'I will bury you. You hear this once only.'

I'd heard it twice already but who was counting?

His stare stayed locked onto my face and his soft lips were turned down with the assurance of a hanging judge. I stared back.

'I'm looking for the girl,' I said. 'And I'm finding all these connections. The Slaters. Roker. Brighton. Tina Brown. Hanlon. McCabe. And you guys right at the centre. The thing is falling apart, McAllister. And I'm going to sledgehammer away until I get to Rebecca Townsend.'

I held up my own finger before McAllister could get back. 'Here's the message for you,' I said. 'If anything happens to the girl I'm going to hand so many threads to the police that they're going to form a knitting circle. They'll unravel your whole operation inside twenty-four hours. And you'll go down for anything you do to her.'

I was exaggerating with the twenty-four hours bit. It would take even Eagle Eye longer than that. But the two of them got my drift.

They stayed quiet for a moment. These guys are good with smart comments but they've no answer when you bat something back. Eventually, Ray Child saved the day.

'You're a dead man, Flynn,' he said. He raised his hand and snapped his fingers in my face. 'Lights out! Easy as that!' He turned to McAllister. 'I think this joker's too stupid to back off.'

But not stupid enough to keep buying their drinks.

I stood and squeezed past them, stopped to lower my mouth to McAllister's ear.

'Go for the makeover,' I said. 'Real leather. Neutral colours. Discreet lighting. Hire some classy girls. Lose the Costa del Crime atmosphere. And put less water in the beer. You'll make a killing.'

Not in Fulham, he wouldn't.

I walked out, footsteps as straight as Shaughnessy's.

CHAPTER TWENTY-NINE

I got to Battersea with nothing to spare on Arabel's deadline. She'd held off on eating but it was a close call. It took a little sweet talking - I only needed to say sorry thirty-eight times.

'You're not sorry, Flynn,' she said. 'You're like a little boy with his tadpole jar. The rest of the world is forgotten. Are you telling me I can't depend on you any more?'

I hadn't realised I'd ever been dependable. Maybe Arabel just hadn't noticed at one time.

'Bel, you can always depend on me,' I said. 'But sometimes things just happen in my line of work. They tie me.'

'Letting me know would have helped,' she told me.

'I'm distractible,' I admitted. 'But that's different from undependable.'

'Different how?' She gave me a look. 'Both of them mean you don't turn up.'

Argumentative, this one.

'Bel, it doesn't mean I don't care,' I said. 'A guy who's not dependable doesn't care. A guy who just gets distracted always cares. He hates himself for forgetting.'

'You hate yourself?'

'Whenever I let you down.'

'Oh, babe!'

Oh boy!

My shame might have be hard to swallow if I thought Arabel believed this stuff. That was what I loved about her. She could go along with the fantasy that she had a sincere guy instead of a smooth-talking rogue. Maybe deep down she did understand that I was sincere. More likely, she was just a saint.

I got busy and uncorked a white wine and pushed a few things around on a table that had already been laid for two hours. The aroma of casserole expanded through the room and Arabel served the meal up in a steaming pot with creamed potatoes and vegetables. My diet so far that day had comprised a single overpriced sandwich at the motorway services. The casserole tripped a switch.

Arabel let me gorge for twenty minutes before she interrupted to ask about the girl.

The thought cut into my hog heaven. Funny how easily I'd forgotten. But a man has to take a break. Sometimes you've got to stop saving the world. I told Arabel about the characters we'd unearthed. Didn't tell her about the risk to my nose or the death-threat stuff. The thought that I might not turn up at all one day wasn't going to help convince Arabel she was investing in the right guy. Distractible or undependable she could cope with. Expendable would give her the jitters. And I was pretty clear that Expendable was the category Paul McAllister had assigned for me. I was going to have to watch my back.

'Do you think you'll find Rebecca?' Arabel asked.

I stopped thinking of myself for a moment. Thought it through.

'Sure,' I said, 'we'll get to her.'

We just needed to do it before someone got to me.

CHAPTER THIRTY

The London spring was living up to its reputation. Gales were on the way in. I coaxed myself out of bed and did three laps of the park, battling a stiff westerly on the upriver legs. Then I drove to Chase Street and went up to the office.

The lights were on and the sign said we were open. Shaughnessy was in his office, busy at his PC. I fired up the filter machine and spooned in eight measures of Buckaroo I'd brought from home. If the machine worked we'd get caffeine enough to fly to the moon. I went through and dropped into one of Shaughnessy's easy chairs.

Shaughnessy was watching his screen. 'Did the entertainment warm up last night?' he said.

'Sure,' I said. 'The full cabaret.' I described my chat with McAllister and Child.

'You need to be careful,' Shaughnessy said. 'These guys play hard.'

I noted the *you*. Let it go. So far it was only me in these people's gunsights. If things hotted up I'd have to fax McAllister our full staff list so there'd be no misunderstanding. There was silence from the outer office. I went back and confirmed that the water was still cold in the reservoir and the coffee still dry in the filter. I flipped the switch a couple of times, pulled the plug out and banged it back in. Got a flash and a spark. Something was connecting. There was still a chance we could get the water and coffee together. Then the outer door opened and Lucy came in in an explosion of red. She feigned shock.

'Do you guys never sleep?' she said.

'The forces of law and order are ever vigilant,' I said.

'What's law and order got to do with it?'

Always the comeback.

'It's an analogy,' I said. 'The forces of private investigation are a little like the forces of law and order. Private investigators don't get much sleep either.'

Lucy gave me smarmy. 'So how is Arabel?' she asked.

'Arabel is fine,' I told her. 'It's me you should worry about.'

'No longer,' Lucy said.

Not that I ever recalled her worrying.

'What's with Rebecca Townsend?' Lucy asked.

'We're moving,' I told her. 'If you can voodoo up some coffee bring it through and I'll fill you in.'

I went into my office. The wind had chilled the back of the building and the place was like a bank holiday morgue. I switched on the two-bar radiant by my desk and picked up the phone to call Philippa Scott.

Philippa was the sales director for a media firm that ran a half-dozen regional newspapers and two south-east society magazines. The week Eagle Eye opened for business Philippa had hired us to locate her estranged husband who'd done a disappearing act. Turned out the guy was lying low, avoiding people who wanted to talk to him about gambling debts. Just as we got to him they moved on to the stage of threatening Philippa and her kids. Small time but nasty with it. Eagle Eye helped out.

Philippa's gratitude ran to a little help now and again whenever research in her social files was called for. I played on it without shame. A good investigator values shamelessness right up there with godliness and cleanliness.

'Long time no hear, Eddie,' Philippa said. 'Are things quiet or have you been on holiday?'

'A little of both,' I said. 'I'm back.'

'Looking for some digging?'

'You know me, Philippa. Just tell me when we're out of credit. You paid your dues.'

'I could never pay the dues for what you did, Eddie. My family got their lives back thanks to you.'

'I still feel guilty calling you up.'

Lucy had come in with what looked like coffee. She gave me a look when she heard the guilty bit. Lucy didn't know who I was talking to but the word told her I was shining them on. I gestured for her to drop the coffee off but she stayed put so I hit the speaker phone.

'What's happening?' Philippa asked.

'Something you might relate to,' I said. 'We've got a family in some kind of trouble. A girl's missing. Suspected involvement of professional criminals.'

The speaker amplified an intake of breath.

'It never ends, does it?' she said. 'This stuff sells my papers – kids missing, assaulted, killed – it's what we feed people over their cornflakes. Other people's nightmares. But you don't know anything until it's happened to you.'

'Yeah,' I said. 'We see plenty of nightmares in this game. Though I'm not much of a newspaper reader myself.'

She chuckled. 'I can't see our rags cluttering your coffee table, Eddie,' she agreed.

'I don't have a coffee table.'

She laughed again. 'A man who stays with the basics. Lucky everyone isn't like you. I'd be out of business.'

'So would I,' I said.

'You still seeing that cute girl?'

The last time I'd seen Philippa I'd had a new girlfriend just off shift and all starched up in her nurse's uniform.

'Yeah,' I said. 'We're still together. Looks promising.'

'She's a good girl,' Philippa said. 'Hang on to her.'

'I do.'

'So what do you need?'

'Background on a couple of well-to-do families. Maybe they're in your area.'

'London?'

'One of them's Wimbledon. The other's a little out of town.'

I gave her what I had on the McCabe and Hanlon families. If they were in Philippa's area the Hanlons were sure-fire fodder for her society monthlies. Maybe the McCabes too – their Wimbledon address was in the right property area for the society pages.

'How soon do you need it?' Philippa asked.

'The very soonest,' I said. 'We're worried about this girl.'

She told me she'd get onto it. 'I've got a meeting now but I'll kick something off in the meantime. Let's say an hour or so.'

'Appreciated, Philippa.'

I reached for my coffee. The coffee cup came complete with saucer and spoon and Lucy's backside perched on my roll-top. I keep my desk cluttered to discourage sitting but Lucy always seemed to find parking space. Private investigation runs on discretion. We operated on a need-to-know basis. Lucy needed to know everything. Maybe she figured she had a vested interest this time since she'd set Sadie Bannister onto me in the first place.

'Sounds like you're getting busy,' Lucy said.

I gave her a summary of where we were. Included McAllister's threats to my nose. The threat barely raised an eyebrow. Lucy was here for the important stuff. You had to love her.

'You want extra hands?' she offered. 'I've got the morning.'

I told her to call me with anything that Philippa phoned through. Meantime she could do some independent digging, see what turned up on the two families. Lastly, she could call Sadie Bannister, ostensibly to let her know we were hot on the trail, but actually to dig for anything new that Sadie might have remembered or picked up in the last few days. Including any snippets on Russell Cohen she might have forgotten to mention.

'You still think Cohen might be involved?' Lucy asked.

'Gut feeling says no. This is between the Slaters and McAllister. But we need to cover all the possibilities. I'm not ruling the guy out. Rebecca could be in serious trouble if it *is* Cohen.'

Lucy slid off my desk and went out.

I wasn't ruling Cohen out but you've got to follow the main smell. And it wasn't perfume that hit my nostrils at the Algarve Club. My bet put Rebecca in McAllister's hands. Leverage against the Slaters, even if it wasn't a simple ransom scheme. Nothing was in focus yet, but what I'd picked up yesterday had given me a hunch. I adjusted the angle on my Herman Miller and sipped scalding coffee while I chased the hunch. Punched a Poole number.

'DK Marine.' A man's voice.

'I understand you sell pre-owned boats,' I said.

'Indeed we do. Mr...?'

'Bligh,' I said.

'Mr Bligh,' DK said, 'we've an extensive portfolio. Would you like our listings or do you have something specific in mind?'

'We're looking at a motor cruiser,' I said. 'Six berths. Good level of equipment. My wife and I mostly stay inshore. South and west coast. But we do Jersey too.' I wasn't sure if the cruising fraternity "did" Jersey or anywhere else. In fact I wasn't sure if there was such as thing as a cruising fraternity, outside Soho. My amateur spiel passed muster at DK Marine though. Salesmen handle the whole range of competencies. They'll sell a Porsche to a blind man.

'We've a range of cruisers in our listing,' said DK. 'Any particular specification?'

'We're still weighing things up,' I stalled. 'I was at the marina yesterday and someone told me the Lode Star was on your list.'

'My goodness, news travels fast! We haven't put it out yet.'

'But she's on your books?'

'Just this week,' DK said. 'And you might be lucky. The owner wanted a fast sale so we've financed it ourselves. We're ready to offer if for a knockdown price.'

'Financed it yourself? You mean you own the vessel?'

'It's a little unusual,' DK said, 'but the owner made us an offer we couldn't refuse. We completed yesterday. Effectively the Lode Star is on sale now and I think you'd be very happy with the asking price.'

'She's a nice-looking vessel,' I concurred. 'But I suspect she'd stretch us, even at a good price. We're selling a fifteen metre, a few years older.'

'Mr Bligh...may I ask your first name?'

'Call me Bill.'

'Bill, you might find that the Lode Star doesn't stretch you as much as you assume. We're talking only seventy-five percent of market.'

'Seventy-five?' I put surprise into my voice. 'Did I hear you right?'

'A straight seventy-five of the list price, Bill. And the survey's thrown in for free. You'd see everything before you spent a penny.'

'That's very interesting,' I declared. 'That might almost bring it within reach. What figure were you thinking?'

'I'd prefer to discuss that here,' DK said. 'Maybe we can take a look at your existing vessel. But this is definitely a once-in-a-lifetime, Bill. You'll never see a discount like this again.'

'And you're making a profit at seventy-five percent of market?'

A chuckle. 'We're quite happy with the margin, Bill. The owner needed a fast sale. He gave us a deal that was right on the rocks.'

'I bumped into the chap a while ago,' I said. 'Larry Something. Don't recall his last name. He never mentioned selling.'

'We never discuss client details, Bill,' DK said, 'but I gather that the need to sell came up suddenly. Lode Star won't be on our list until next week so this is your opportunity to get in first.'

'Well, I'd have to say I'm very interested,' I said.

'Could I trouble you for your details Bill?'

'How about I call in later?' I said. 'I'll give you everything then.'

'Fine. I look forward to seeing you.'

'Me too.' I killed the line.

Aye-aye.

I sat back and lifted my heels onto the desk. So Slater was the Lode Star's seller. If DK Marine were making a profit selling at seventy-five percent of market then Slater must have offloaded the boat somewhere around the fifty to sixty level. What would fifty percent of the Lode Star pull in? Four or five hundred thousand? Boats weren't my thing but I knew a guy who'd splashed out half a million on a less impressive boat a couple of years back. That had to put the Lode Star's price somewhere in the seven-fifty thou' region. Suggesting that Slater had just thrown away two or three hundred grand to get his hands on fast cash. What kind of hurry are you in where you chuck away that amount? The kind of hurry that brought us right back to the kidnap-for-ransom scenario. It just didn't explain what was going on though.

I slid my feet back off the desk and went through to Shaughnessy's office. He'd just put his phone down and was working at his computer.

'We hooked our Algarve guys yet?'

Shaughnessy looked up. 'Pretty much,' he said. 'I'm waiting for a call back in half an hour. Then we'll have the picture.'

I left him to it and headed out.

CHAPTER THIRTY-ONE

The first drops of rain hit the Frogeye's windscreen as I was crossing Putney Bridge. A minute later, just as it came on heavy, Lucy rang through with Philippa's information on the McCabe family.

'The guy's a builder turned property developer,' she reported. 'Made his first million at thirty-two. Took an award for a restored Georgian on the top end of Blackheath. The house has been in *Ideal Home* twice. He has a wife and two kids. The family are in the society pages a couple of times a year. Philippa has a whole library on them.'

I struggled to catch the words against the noise of the rain on the soft-top.

'Tell me about the wife and kids,' I yelled.

'Wendy is forty-five, the same age as John. She's a housewife. Supports local causes. They've two girls, fourteen and seven. Both at the Mayfield School on the Common. They sound like the ideal family.'

I wondered how McCabe's trips to Brighton fitted "ideal". Be interesting to find out. I swung right at the top end of the Common and headed towards the McCabes' Wimbledon address.

'Anything on the Hanlons?'

Lucy's words were almost drowned in the din of the rain. 'They're out of Philippa's area. But she promised to keep trying. I'm searching from my end.'

'Anything you can get,' I said. 'The picture's coming into focus. If the families both fit what I'm looking at then we're nearly there.'

I killed the line and focused on the road. The rain turned torrential and made it hard work spotting the turning. I finally located it – a tree-lined lane at the south end of the Park. The McCabe house stood behind brick walls that sported a gateway not so different from the one that had blocked me at the Hanlons', except that these gates were open. I parked on a forecourt in front of a redbrick Victorian mansion that promised *Ideal Home* perfection behind its ten-foot sash windows. A single car was parked in front of the house. A Fiat Panda. I guessed they'd shift that before the photographer arrived.

I sprinted to the porch and pressed the bell. I heard a hoover quit inside and a woman in her middle fifties wearing green work overalls came out. I asked if Wendy was in.

She invited me through and took me to the back of the house. A too-thin woman came out of a sun lounge to meet us. The lounge would be idyllic on a warm summer's day. Today the rain was like machine-gun fire and the place was cold. Wendy McCabe was pretty in a mousy kind of way. Glittery eyes and pointed nose. Kind of cute. But her smile when she saw me was doubtful. After I'd left she'd tell her domestic to have strangers wait at the door in future.

I gave her my best Caring Salesman smile along with my card, one of the genuine ones. I apologised for calling out of the blue and told her that there was an urgent matter she and her husband might help me with.

She didn't rise to the bait and tell me that her husband was not at home. Smarter than that.

'You say you're a private investigator?'

'Security and research services.' I left our job description at that. No need to mention of what kind of research we usually did. 'We're acting for a family who have been approached by some unlawful individuals. Our investigations suggest that other families might be at risk too.'

Wendy McCabe's look switched to concern.

'You mean our family? What kind of risk?'

'Nothing specific,' I said. 'Maybe nothing at all. But we felt we ought to talk to anyone who might have been approached by these people. As a precaution.'

'Precaution? You're frightening me more every minute, Mr Flynn.'

'Perhaps we could sit down a moment.'

Wendy shook her head, didn't offer a seat. No pushover, this one. 'I can't imagine what this is about,' she said. 'Could you be more specific?'

I smiled my most reassuring smile. Backpedalled.

'We may be off-track, Mrs McCabe. But my clients felt an obligation to pass on the information we have.'

There's a limit on how many times you can circle the wagons. At some point you've got to move in. I pulled Sadie's photo from my wallet. Pointed to Rebecca. I didn't see the McCabes knowing the Slaters so the picture should mean nothing. If it did, we'd have a new situation.

Sure enough, Wendy McCabe's face stayed blank.

'Who is she?'

'I've been asked not to provide names,' I said. 'But the girl's family have been threatened. More specifically, a threat against the girl.'

'What kind of threat?'

'I can't give you the details,' I said – Truth was my middle name this morning – 'but the threat involved abduction.'

Wendy McCabe's expression turned to fear. 'Are you saying that our children might be at risk?'

'Almost certainly not,' I said, 'but we're trying to cover all possibilities. The people behind this are targeting wealthy families with children. One of the conspirators may be involved in the London property market. Hence the possible connection with your husband. '

'Do the police know about this?'

I shook my head. 'We're still trying to understand the threat,' I told her. 'It would be difficult to prove risk to any other families. But if we see clear evidence of a threat we'll call the police in.'

'But if you think someone is planning to abduct a child you need to call them in now.'

'We just don't have enough,' I said. 'Nothing that the police could act on . And the chance of your family being involved is a million-to-one.'

A number a little different to my real estimate of fifty-fifty. Don't ask me for racing tips.

'So what do you want from us, Mr Flynn?'

'I need to know whether you or your husband know the men involved.'

So far, Wendy McCabe was coming up blank. She'd shown no reaction to my talk of abduction, at least nothing beyond the obvious – nothing to suggest that one of their own children had already been taken. My theory of what was happening to Rebecca Townsend pointed to the McCabes having already gone through the same thing: if the Royal Trafalgar was part of it then John McCabe was running six months ahead of Larry Slater. But either Wendy McCabe was an impeccable actress or my hunch was wrong. If my hunch was wrong then it was possible that the Royal Trafalgar might not be relevant. Worst case scenario - McAllister had nothing to do with Rebecca Townsend and we were back to square one.

'Has your family ever been threatened?' I asked.

'Absolutely not.' No hesitation. Just annoyance. The thought of her children in danger had Wendy McCabe ready to blame the messenger.

'You heard of a guy named Paul McAllister?'

She looked blank.

'James Roker?'

'No.'

'Maybe your husband might know them through his business contacts?'

'Why don't you ask him?' Wendy McCabe said. She walked over and picked up the phone.

'Sure,' I said, 'I'd like to speak with you husband.' In for a penny. John McCabe might or might not know McAllister and Roker but he could certainly answer some questions about Brighton.

Wendy hit speed dial and passed a curt message. A few seconds later her husband came on the line. She told him what was happening, asked if he knew what it was about. She repeated my name twice then listened.

I could hear McCabe's voice crackling on the other end. It didn't sound like endearments. His wife turned to me: 'Can you go to Kingston right now?'

I said I could be there in thirty minutes. She passed on the message and replaced the phone. Handed me a business card with McCabe's address, a location in the centre of Kingston. I thanked her and repeated my assurances that all was well, but she kept her face set as she walked me to the door. Messenger or not, Wendy McCabe never wanted to see me again. Mothers are like that when their family is threatened. I'd begun to wonder if her torn peace of mind had been worth it.

Maybe her husband would tell me.

CHAPTER THIRTY-TWO

John McCabe was a surprise. Partly because his refined manner didn't shout ex-builder. But mostly because he didn't leap up from behind his desk to get his hands around my throat.

He ran his business from a modest office in a three-storey block a stone's throw from the river. McCabe Enterprises comprised a reception and a few small rooms on the top floor. It looked like McCabe concentrated on the nuts and bolts of money-making rather than the prestige side. His office was unpretentious. The only thing it boasted was a view of the Thames if you looked at an angle.

He shook my hand and sat me down. I repeated my spiel about the threatened clients, possible connections between known criminals and wealthy families. Got no sign of recognition. John McCabe heard me out then asked for my ID.

I handed him my card. He scrutinised it.

'I appreciate that you're acting with the best intentions,' he said, 'but you should know that my wife was somewhat upset by your visit.'

I opened my hands.

'Frightening your wife was the last thing I wanted. But I need to know if these people are targeting anyone other than our clients.'

'Is that not for the police to decide?'

'As I told you wife, we don't have enough evidence to take to them.'

'And what evidence do you expect to get from my family?'

'Any information you may have about these people. Any suspicious approaches by them.'

'Do you believe that my family may have been targeted?'

'Has it?'

McCabe's eyes locked onto mine. His mouth set. 'Of course not,' he said. 'Otherwise we would have informed the police.'

'The people involved appear to exert pressure to keep the police out.'

'What kind of pressure?'

'If they're snatching children then that would be pretty clear.'

McCabe continued to look at me.

'Mr Flynn, I'm happy to say that there has been no abduction in my family. We've had no contact with any criminal parties. I'm afraid you're at a dead end in our case. Unless,' he said, 'you're keeping something back. Have you some specific evidence that my family is at risk?'

I told him we had none. I was still watching him for signs.

McCabe shook his head and turned to look out of the window.

'I don't know what to believe here,' he said. 'Someone walks into my house and suggests that we may be under threat from a criminal group, asks if any of my kids have been abducted. Then remains vague on just what evidence is behind this. I understand why my wife is scared. I'm thinking maybe I should call the police myself.' He held up my business card between thumb and index finger. 'Do you mind if I keep this?'

'Go ahead,' I said. 'We're a legitimate agency. The Metropolitan Police know us.'

They knew us, all right.

'Have you anything else?' He was looking at his watch.

'A couple of the men involved,' I said. 'Maybe you've come across them.'

I gave him their names. His stare didn't waver. Just a curt shake of the head. Either McCabe and his wife were good enough to be on the stage or they'd never come across McAllister, Child or Roker. Time to throw up a stronger candidate.

'How about the Royal Trafalgar Hotel?' I said. 'In Brighton.'

That got a hit but not exactly a bullseye. McCabe looked surprised for a couple of seconds but that was it. He pursed his lips and gave me a noncommittal nod. So he knew the place. I asked what the connection was but he shrugged it off as business and refused to say more.

I wasn't getting even a hint of being warm with McCabe. Persisted anyway.

'May I ask whom you met in Brighton?' I said.

McCabe shook his head. 'I'm sorry, no,' he said. He still looked puzzled though. I pulled out a photo.

'Was this woman one of them?'

I watched his face as he looked at Tina Brown's photo.

Another hit. McCabe's eyebrows raised and he looked at me. But it was still a look of mild puzzlement, not much else. Nothing you'd mistake for guilt or fear. He handed the photo back.

'Do you mind telling me exactly,' he said, 'what this is all about?'

'You do recognise the woman?'

'That's still none of your business, Mr Flynn,' he said. 'Please answer my question.'

I thought for a moment. Decided that answering McCabe's questions would not be productive. I'd got the spark of recognition over both hotel and woman but there was something off. I'd expected a firecracker. Got a damp squib. Another piece of the jig-saw that didn't connect. If I told McCabe that Tina Brown was linked to my criminals that might push him the last step towards the police. A complication I could do without.

I tucked the photo away. Thanked McCabe for his time and stood to leave.

McCabe stood himself and started to say something but I gave him a cheery nod and was already out of the door.

Quick exits were becoming my speciality.

I'd just taken another soaking sprinting back to the Frogeye when my mobile rang.

'What's the news?' Samantha Vincent's voice. 'I've called Tina ten times since we spoke. And I sent a text saying you were looking for her. But she's just not answering.'

'Just hang in there,' I said. 'We're getting some good leads. I think we're close to finding out what's happening.'

'You told me you'd find her in two days,' Sammy said. 'What have you got?'

'Nothing I can give you,' I said, 'but trust me, Sammy. Just hold off a while longer. I'll call you the moment there's news.'

'Mr Flynn,' she said, 'cut the bullshit. I know nothing about you or what you're doing to find Tina. And I'm going to the police right now unless you give me something.'

'Sammy,' I said, 'I won't lie to you. We've not got near to Tina yet.' I considered how to phase my next words: 'But there's a chance that Tina might not want the police involved.'

It took a moment for that to sink in.

'What do you mean?' Sammy asked, but I knew she'd got it.

'It's possible she's involved in something that requires her to stay low for a while,' I said. 'Something she might not want the police to know about.'

'You're saying that Tina's involved in something criminal? I don't believe it.'

'Sammy, it's a possibility,' I repeated. 'I can't explain, but we need a little more time.'

'Mr Flynn,' Sammy said, 'I'm more worried about Tina's safety than the possibility that she's mixed up in something she wants kept quiet.'

'I understand, Sammy. But believe me, my agency is the fastest route to Tina. Give us another day. We'll know what has happened to Tina within twenty-four hours. That's a promise.'

The line was silent while Sammy turned it over. Then she made up her mind. 'Tomorrow,' she said.

The phone went dead.

CHAPTER THIRTY-THREE

As I drove back to Paddington the rain turned torrential again, threatened to punch right through the soft top. The wipers were working but I couldn't see them. Springtime in London.

I parked on a meter outside the building and sprinted inside. I was risking a ticket but what kind of attendant would be out in this storm? The dedicated kind, that's what. If I parked round the back of the building I'd get a soaking. If I paid Westminster's parking rates I'd be bled dry. Life's extremes.

Shaughnessy was in his office eating a smoked salmon baguette. A bottle of mineral water stood next to it. Next to the mineral water, Lucy's bum was cluttering his desk. She was attacking something less low-calorie. I flopped into one of Shaughnessy's chairs and dripped water on his carpet.

Shaughnessy looked at me.

'The McCabes know nothing,' I told him.

Shaughnessy's eyebrows lifted. He'd been betting on the same horse as me: that whatever was going on with the Slaters had already happened to the McCabes.

'Nothing,' I repeated. 'No threats, no funny goings-on, no missing kids.' I was eyeing Lucy's sandwich. I'd skipped breakfast and the rain had nixed the prospect of hopping up the road to Connie's. I'd have to catch up later.

I gave them the details of McCabe's lacklustre responses on the subjects of the Royal Trafalgar and Tina Brown. The guy had stayed at the hotel and he recognised Tina, but none of it seemed to mean much to him. And he'd never heard of anyone called McAllister.

'A photo of McAllister would have been a good memory jogger,' I said. 'Maybe I should have asked him to pose for a couple of snaps at the Algarve.' I asked Shaughnessy what he'd picked up on the two guys.

'Plenty,' Shaughnessy said. He placed the baguette back on its paper and popped the top on his fizzy water.

'We're looking at career criminals. McAllister has a record going back to his eighteenth birthday. He celebrated the occasion by getting nicked for armed robbery on a convenience store. Sent down for eighteen months. Should have done it the day before and avoided the adult record. He was fingered again a few years later for armed robbery but the case fell through when a couple of witnesses changed their stories. Nothing since, but the Mets have him pegged for at least ten capers ranging from robbery and extortion to rigging horses.'

'The sport of kings,' I said. 'Should be an Olympic event.'

'McAllister learned his lesson early and got smart,' Shaughnessy concluded. 'The Mets haven't come near to anything they could take to the CPS in thirty years. He runs a body shop in Brixton but the shop would have to be the busiest on the planet to make the dough he flashes.'

'The guy's a big spender?' I asked.

'Very big,' Shaughnessy said. 'He lives in a House in Bayswater valued at six-point-five million. Owns a three hundred acre farm in Kent. Rumoured to have three commercial properties on the Costa del Sol. Then there's his hobby-horse.'

'The Algarve Club,' I said. 'The way he dilutes the drinks must be costing him a fortune in water rates.'

'My drinks were fine,' Shaughnessy said. 'I guess it's hard to water down water.'

I gave him Sam Sneer. 'Where do you think the Algarve sourced your Buxton Mineral Water at four-fifty a shot?'

'The tap,' Shaughnessy said. 'Where else?'

Shaughnessy had talked to Zach Finch, our man at the Mets. Zach and I went back a long way. Zach had come within a whisker of taking early retirement himself when I got the boot but I talked him out of it. Painted a picture of him sat at home all day under the wife's whip. He reconsidered and put the retirement on hold. We stayed in touch and helped each other out now and then.

Zach's ears had pricked up when Shaughnessy dropped McAllister's name. I'd not come across the man myself but then the Mets' Christmas card list is longer than their proverbial arm. Zach knew the guy well: McAllister had been one of the top dogs on his patch back in Zach's uniform days and he'd stayed on the Mets' untouchable list since then. Anything we could do to throw a banana skin under his feet, Zach was happy. Zach also had some info on Ray Child.

'A.k.a. Merlin the Magician,' Shaughnessy said. 'Only you wouldn't want to get invited to one of his parties. His speciality is disappearing tricks. The way Zach tells it Child is McAllister's sanitation man. He's the reason McAllister has stayed out of jail. No one ever comes forward with anything that could take McAllister down. When the Mets get halfway close any informants or witnesses clam up or disappear.'

'Merlin the Magician,' I said. 'So we're looking at career professionals.' I looked at Shaughnessy. 'These people look perfect for a kidnapping racket.'

Shaughnessy slanted his lips. 'They've got Rebecca.'

That was my feeling too. It didn't explain why McAllister had put Larry Slater up in five-star luxury though. The golden rule in ransom schemes is minimum contact. Strike fast, stay out of sight, grab the dosh, get out. The family never meets you, never sees you. No trail to lead back to you. The thing with the Slater family was all off-kilter. I thought it over. Couldn't make things fit.

'Anything on Alpha?' I asked Lucy.

'I checked the grapevine,' she said. 'Roker is the kind of private investigator that gives the profession a bad smell.'

'A true rarity,' I said.

'He runs the firm,' said Shaughnessy. 'Alpha covers the full spectrum: investigation, notice serving, debt collecting, minders. Specialise in the latter two. High turnover, low skill stuff. They've a reputation,' he said, 'for operating on the wrong side of the law. Basically they're hired hands for anyone who doesn't want his own fingers dirtied.'

'So Alpha Security organises the Brighton thing for McAllister,' I said. 'The room and the hooker. The question is, what kind of business deal needs that sort of sweetener?'

'A dirty deal,' Lucy chipped in. She shoved the last of her baguette in her face.

'What we're missing is the tie in with Rebecca and her supposed abduction,' I said. 'This thing's going round and round. Let's stick with the certs and work from there. Rebecca is missing. Her stepfather is raising money fast and he's involved with McAllister. Putting two and two together the money is going to McAllister.'

'So why is Larry Slater chasing Tina Brown?' Lucy asked. 'I don't see a connection between Slater's dirty weekends and his stepdaughter's abduction.'

'Tina is the oddity,' I agreed. 'But Slater's fixation on her right now says that there is a connection. Maybe Tina is involved in Rebecca's disappearance. I'm wondering if Slater sees her as his route to Rebecca.'

'Except that the lady is AWOL too,' Shaughnessy said.

'Just like Rebecca.'

'Maybe even with Rebecca.'

I nodded. 'That's where I'm finishing up. If they've got Rebecca hidden away then someone must be with her. We know where McAllister and Child were last night. So who was with the girl?'

'If they've got Rebecca,' Shaughnessy said, 'we just need to figure where.' He looked at me and raised his eyebrows.

'McAllister's farm,' I said. 'You want to take a gander?'

Shaughnessy nodded and started back on his sandwich.

'I want to take another drive down to Chevening,' I said. 'See if I can catch the Hanlons this time. The McCabe blank might be the exception.' I looked at Lucy. 'Anything else?'

Lucy wiped coleslaw off her lips and gave me a smirk.

'Thought you'd never ask, Eddie,' she said. 'Do I get a bonus for detective work?'

'Are we paying you nowadays?'

'Not usually.'

'Then double it,' I said. 'Only if you're a detective you'll have to come with me on stakeouts. There's gonna be those long nights parked outside some guy's secret love nest.'

'It wouldn't work out,' Lucy said. 'There'd be detectives staking you out if Arabel heard we were night-shifting together.'

'Yeah,' I said, 'we'd have to wear shades. So what did your detective skills dig up?'

'The Hanlons fit what you're looking for. David Hanlon owns a computer wholesale firm. His wife's an interior designer with a practice in Sevenoaks. The family's worth around twenty million. Two kids - a daughter, sixteen and a son, six. Hanlon is active on the local council. Ran for Parliament for the Conservatives. Came second to the Lib-Dems. He has a seat on the CBI executive. The family's well to do,' she concluded.

The Hanlons fit the pattern perfectly.

'I made your other calls,' Lucy said. 'Gina Redding is confident you're about to crack the case. Sadie Bannister was frantic. She's decided that Rebecca has been murdered. She's coming to see you again.'

I let that pass. 'Did she have anything more on Rebecca's friend Russell?' I asked.

'Nothing. She's changed her mind on Russell, says he's not involved.'

'Well that saves us some legwork. When is Miss Precocious coming to call?'

'She didn't say. She wants to surprise you.'

I gave her my Shit-Eater. 'The girl's a fox,' I said. 'She should be working for us.'

'Then you'd have to pay her.'

'No problem,' I said. 'The two of you could form a queue. If she turns up call me. I'll hide under the desk.'

'She'd probably track you down anyway,' said Lucy.

'Yeah,' I agreed. 'Maybe I should just shoot myself now. Be on the safe side.

CHAPTER THIRTY-FOUR

I made Chevening by two thirty and drove up a waterlogged driveway. The Hanlons' gate was still barred. No answer when I pressed the bell. I pushed an envelope into their post box and turned the Frogeye around. The gatehouse was closed up against the weather but the owner's red Nissan was parked at the side. I knocked on the door.

An elderly woman answered. I put her in her late sixties, but she had a glow a forty-year-old might envy. Her ginger hair hinted at former flame and her girlish face still held echoes of youth. The woman had turned heads in her time. I told her I'd spoken to her husband yesterday.

She invited me in. The cottage was furnished in dark oak that felt aged without seeming worn. A museum's worth of bric-a-brac covered every surface and wall. The woman introduced herself as Lottie and called her husband through. While we waited she launched into the story of how they'd spent their working life abroad. Her husband William had worked in the diplomatic service, toured four South American countries and Malaysia. They travelled the rest of the world in their vacation time. Then two years back William had retired and they'd not set foot outside the UK since. Catching up.

William came through and nodded a greeting.

'Mr Coffee,' he said. 'Still no luck with the Hanlons?'

I shrugged amicably. 'I should have telephoned,' I said. 'But I was passing by again, thought I'd try my luck.'

'They're out most days,' his wife said. 'Both working. Children at school. I think you'll need to phone to catch them.'

'I'll do that,' I said. 'There's no way I want to miss them. I don't get here so often.'

'Welcome to the club,' William said. 'Longest period we ever went without setting foot in Blighty was eight years. Would have been longer but for Lottie's father dying. But now that we're here for good it's hard to believe we ever lived anywhere else.'

'I guess it's quite an adjustment,' I said. 'It's funny we didn't meet last time I was here.'

'Not if it's more than seven months ago,' William said. 'That's when we arrived. We've barely got this place in order.'

Seven months.

Interesting.

'It's a funny thing,' I said. 'David and Faye were never keen to part with this cottage.' A believable spiel if the Hanlons had actually owned the cottage seven months back. Sheer guesswork.

But I was on the button. William laughed. 'Lucky for us they finally changed their minds,' he said. 'A place like this is one in a million. We though we'd spend a year at least finding somewhere when we moved back. Spotted this cottage in an agents in Sevenoaks just by chance. Fresh on the market and at a price that was downright crazy.'

'David and Faye sold it cheap?'

Lottie chuckled. 'William and I had a blazing row over it. The agent assured us that the property was a bargain but the price was so low that William was convinced that something was wrong. William didn't want to waste money on a survey.'

'The price was too low by far,' her husband said. 'Sometimes you have to be cautious.'

'Cautious?' his wife said. 'We nearly walked away from a bargain! Thank God I managed to squeeze the fee out of you. The survey came up clean and we got a once-in-a-lifetime deal.'

'Strange that David was in such a hurry,' I said. 'They never mentioned it to me.'

'Apparently they'd had their eye on a place in France,' William said. 'Got an offer they couldn't refuse and needed to raise the full capital within the week. The cottage was the simplest thing to offload.'

I raised my eyebrows. 'I've never thought of selling property as a fast way to get cash.'

'That's why the low price. The agent took the house off their hands overnight for a knockdown price. Expedited the whole thing. Must have made a killing when he sold it to us a couple of weeks later.'

I shook my head. 'It's amazing how an estate agent can get his hands on that kind of free capital.'

William batted it away. 'These agents can get hold of millions if they need to,' he said. 'But they must have only taken the place off the Hanlons for around four hundred thousand. That's my guess, assuming they made twenty-five percent when they sold to us.'

Four hundred thousand. Seven months back. Three months after Hanlon's date with Paul McAllister in Brighton. This was Larry Slater all over again - first you're feted as McAllister's guest then a couple of months later you're offloading property at a discount to get fast cash. The McCabes had been a dud but my chat with David Hanlon was going to be interesting.

Lottie offered me tea but I made excuses about a schedule. Said I'd be back tomorrow to see the Hanlons.

'If you can catch them,' William said.

'No problem there,' I told him. 'I'm definitely expecting David and Faye to be at home tomorrow.'

On this I was confident. Wild horses wouldn't drag the Hanlons out of the house tomorrow once they'd read the note in their post box.

I drove back into town and went up to the office. Shaughnessy was out looking at McAllister's farm. I called him to see if he needed backup. Shaughnessy didn't need help. He gave me the executive summary on what was happening at the farm, which was nothing.

The place was deserted. Just some stored farm machinery. No one living or working there. No one in the attic or in the cellar. He'd spent over an hour checking the house and walking the land. No suspicious outbuildings where you might stash a girl. The place appeared to be a weekend home. No sign of recent occupancy. The rubbish bins were empty. The larder was bare.

You win some, you lose some. The farm hadn't been a cert. Just an obvious place to look. I'd have given it one in four. In the investigation business those are the best odds you get.

Shaughnessy said he'd give the farm another hour, let me know if anything did turn up. Otherwise we'd talk tomorrow.

Tomorrow was D-Day. Time to end this thing, as I'd promised Sammy, although I wasn't sure it was going to end the way her friend Tina would want. I just needed my chat with the Hanlons first then we were taking whatever we had to the Slaters. As a minimum, what we had was the circumstantial triangle between Slater, McAllister and fast cash. Those links were clear enough to interest the authorities if Slater refused to talk. As a minimum, too, we had the interesting paperwork that pointed to another kind of triangle, the one involving Slater and Tina Brown. Either Slater talked to us tomorrow or the police would be in the house by evening and the divorce lawyers right after.

I drove to Fulham. The Algarve was already open. Another tenner chalked to Eagle Eye's expenses and I was in, nursing another weak lager at a table in the back. Only three other customers. The stage was dark. I didn't chat with the girl who served me and she moved quickly away. I was looking for our hostess from last night.

I was in luck. My girl came out thirty minutes later, wearing something so skimpy you had to use your imagination to picture her clothed. I toasted her, got a smile of recognition. No mean old Shaughnessy and his mineral water today. I passed her a tenner but didn't name a drink. Just turned Harmless Charmer to full strength.

'I've got a question,' I said. The smile diluted a little but the girl kept a game face. I handed her the photograph of Tina Brown.

'Do you know her?' I asked.

'Sure,' she said. 'She comes in sometimes.'

'Recently?'

She thought a moment then shook her head. 'Maybe not for a couple of weeks,' she said. 'Any reason you're asking?'

I shrugged. Kept up the Harmless Charmer. 'Tina's an old friend,' I said. 'She doesn't know I'm in town. Just thought I'd catch up with her.'

Her face relaxed. She shrugged. 'I'm not sure she'll be in anytime soon,' she said.

'Does she usually come in with anyone special?'

Her eyes opened. She glanced around. I guess people didn't ask too many questions at the Algarve. It was that kind of place.

'Mostly with Paul,' she said finally.

'Paul McAllister?'

'Yeah. I think they have something going. I've seen her with him a few times. She's only in when he's here.'

'Is Tina a friend of yours?'

She shook her head. 'I've never spoken to her. Just brought drinks across. I only remember her because of her looks. I see her and think, "If only..."'

'Does she ever perform here?' I nodded at the stage.

She gave me a sad laugh. 'No way! Not her scene.' She looked round again. 'The Algarve is a little low-class for someone like Tina,' she said.

223

'I often wish I was somewhere else, too.'

'I know what you mean,' I told her.

'Can I get you a drink? I really should be working.'

'No,' I said. 'I'm fine with what I've got. Just get one yourself.'

She smiled and turned away with her tenner. When she'd gone I abandoned my drink and walked out.

Tuesday night loomed. I had a bare larder and Arabel was out with her girlfriends. I put it all together and came up with only one solution. I freshened up and drove up to Paddington and parked behind the office. Hit a Chinese up the road and pigged out on Crispy Duck and three bottles of beer. I wouldn't be driving home.

The weather was foul. I walked the quarter-mile to the Podium in gusting winds and intermittent drizzle. Settled down in the warmth and smoke near the stage. Jack brought over a London Pride. No added water. An ensemble called Black and Blue was warming up. I relaxed and let the discord wash over me. Half recognised a face in the smoke across the stage and wondered whether to go over, but I couldn't quite say if we'd met. Decided on isolation. Jack brought another beer and when the lead started up with a squeal of trumpet I was floating. D-Day tomorrow. Tonight my brain could pickle.

The jazz was mellow, post-fusion. Not my kind of stuff but the music soothed my ears and a couple more Prides did the pickling. The Podium filled up. A couple of punks came and sat at my table and I raised my glass but we didn't talk. The first ensemble quit and a five-piece came on for the late-night set. They were fronted by a black singer in her late teens with a voice that took you back to Eartha Kitt. I succumbed to the hypnotic lullabies and floated through the haze. When Barney came to roust me at two thirty the stage was dark and the Podium was emptying. Time to hit the office couch.

The rain was steady, turned to needles by the wind. I moved fast but the wet penetrated. If I was lucky I'd get back to the office before my clothes were too soaked to sleep in. The Eagle Eye couch was not conducive to the best night's rest even in dry clothes. I could have stashed a sleeping bag in my cupboard but that would have been admitting that I used the place as a crash. My sense of style rejected the notion. I was averaging a night a week but it was always unplanned so it didn't count.

Two forty-five. I covered the empty streets in ten minutes.

I turned into Chase Street and saw blue lights by the access road to the rear of the buildings. Two fire engines. One patrol car. Somewhere in the shadows behind the buildings a light was dancing. Something burning. I walked past the police vehicle. A uniformed cop yelled after me and hopped out of his car when I didn't stop.

He yelled at me again, but I was way ahead. Sprinted to where the fire hoses snaked into the alley. When I got to the corner I saw the Frogeye burning merrily, lighting up the back of the buildings. The copper caught up and grabbed me by the shoulder.

'Are you frigging deaf, mate?' he said. I shook him off but didn't go any further in. Watched the firemen playing their hoses over the skeleton of my car.

'You think this is a bleeding show?' the cop said. Being pulled out into the rain had drained his official manners. He grabbed my shoulder again. 'Come out now before I get annoyed.'

'It's mine,' I said. I nodded at the Frogeye.

He let go of my shoulder. Looked at the burning car. The flames were dying, white smoke rising through the dark like an evil genie.

'Well, I hope your insurance is up to date. I don't think you'll be driving those wheels out of there.'

The last flickers died. The show was over. I talked to the firemen while they damped the wreck down, then the cop sat me in his car to answer questions. His partner watched through his rear-view, bored by the action. I narrated my details as the firemen reeled in their hoses. The cop finally snapped his notebook and pushed it into his pocket.

'What's a Frogeye Sprite anyway?' his buddy asked. 'You get it at Hamleys?' I saw his grin in the rear-view.

I smiled back and wagged a finger at his little joke. Then I got out and walked down the street and let myself into the building.

The office was colder than usual and my clothes were soaked. I pulled off the outer stuff and carried the two-bar electric through to reception. Set it a foot from the couch. I lay down and told myself that tomorrow would be better. Maybe when I woke up I'd find that the whole thing was a dream. Maybe I'd find the Frogeye out back, green and shining. That's what I told myself. More realistically, the two-bar would burn the building down while I snored.

I looked on the bright side. A dead Frogeye was better than my nose.

I pushed my nose into the back of the couch and let the electric fire warm my back. Tried to sleep.

CHAPTER THIRTY-FIVE

'We've got some unhappy people downstairs,' Shaughnessy said. He came in at eight fifteen and stood in my doorway.

I'd migrated from the couch to my office via the washroom and was sorting out a plan for the day which now included organising a set of wheels. The stink of burnt rubber seeping through the back window gave the place a truly special aroma. I saw Shaughnessy's nose twitch.

I should have warned him. We shared the rear parking area with Rook and Lye and the fire had damaged Gerry Lye's spot. Worse, we now had a blackened skeleton and the smell of burnt rubber to greet the lawyers when they parked their Mercs. I'd never figured a firm of ambulance-chasers for sensitivity.

'Have you taken up smoking while you drive or is the Frogeye just due for a wash and polish?' Shaughnessy asked.

'It got all the wash it needed last night,' I said, 'but I won't bother with the polish.'

'Lye wants to know when we're going to clear it,' Shaughnessy said. 'It's only the second time he's ever talked to me.'

I gave him a grin. 'A glimmer of good from every misfortune. We're finally getting chatty with our neighbours.'

'Don't be so sure. Gerry wants a response today. I think they're in conference now figuring a strategy to sue us off the street.'

'What are they going to sue us for?' I said. 'Is the parking area part of their company image? If that's what they claim then I'm going to charge for keeping the wreck there.'

'I guess Bob and Gerry are thinking more of the financial side.'

Shaughnessy had a point. Gerry's Merc, parked on a meter while we kept him off his slot, would run at fifteen quid a day. Add expenses and my guess was that they'd bill us at a couple of hundred a week.

'Let them sue,' I said. 'We'll counter with a claim for access rights. How many times a week do we have to run for cover when Bob Rook blocks the stairs?'

'That's not the same,' Shaughnessy said.

'Not the same?'

'They're solicitors,' he explained. 'We're private investigators. They do what they want.'

'Not everything,' I said. 'We're still here.'

'The crazy relative in the attic,' Shaughnessy leered. 'That's the bit we've got over them. They don't know what you're likely to do next. Keeps them on their toes.'

He stayed put in the door.

'So, was your car struck by lightning? Or is someone trying to tell you something?'

'Off the record, the fire brigade say it was torched.'

'Someone is giving you a message.'

'A rag in the petrol filler. I guess that's a kind of message.'

'Let's hear it for the modern car,' Shaughnessy said. 'Locking petrol caps.'

'If the cap was locked they'd just have broken a window and started the fire inside.'

'There's that,' Shaughnessy agreed. 'You saved on glass.'

I looked at him. 'The windows all blew.'

Shaughnessy grimaced. 'Not even a crumb of comfort. You make too many enemies, Eddie.'

'That's business,' I said. 'Only I've got a pretty good idea who's business we're talking about.'

'McAllister.'

'Him or someone near and dear.'

'He must think you didn't hear him the other day.'

'That's what I'm sensing,' I said.

I went through to make coffee. I fed the filter machine and threw the switch. The light stayed off but that didn't mean it wasn't working. Sometimes you got lucky.

Shaughnessy unlocked his office, sorted some stuff then came back out and dropped himself onto the sofa. The coffee machine let out a couple of coughs and spat hot water into the filter. The aroma of Buckaroo filled the place. We looked at each other. The day was picking up already.

'Are we moving like we planned?' Shaughnessy asked.

I told him that we were. 'I just want to hear what the Hanlons have to say,' I said, 'then we'll hit the Slaters.'

'What we have is still circumstantial,' Shaughnessy pointed out. 'The Slaters may still say the girl's not missing.'

'Sure,' I said. 'But this time we spook Larry with his misdemeanours. That should loosen his tongue.'

'So what do we have for certain?'

'What we have for certain,' I said, 'are too many connections.'

The coffee was drizzling steadily into the pot. I pulled out the mugs and opened a tin of Marvel.

'Three families,' I said, 'three husbands connected to Alpha Security, to Brighton and to a classy hooker. Alpha Security operating on behalf of a known criminal, Paul McAllister. The hooker Tina Brown, a crony of his, currently lying low. Two of the three families known to have freed up capital in a hurry – a half-million plus each time. One of those families currently missing a daughter. The connections look solid.'

'The puzzle,' said Shaughnessy, 'is what the connections mean. It looks like we've got two things going on. A blackmail scam with the dirty photos. And a kidnap racket.'

'I don't see how they fit either,' I agreed, 'but they're part of the same thing.'

'How about the Hanlons for simple blackmail?' Shaughnessy asked. 'The Slaters too, but for some reason the stakes were upped and they took the girl.'

I shook my head. 'The Hanlons' estate cottage raised too much cash for a simple sex-blackmail. I'd put blackmail down for twenty grand, not half a million. I want to find out what the house sale was for.'

'You think the Hanlons will tell you?'

I poured coffee. 'I'm not holding my breath,' I told him. 'Something's kept them quiet for a long time. But if I can just get a sense that something did happen to one of their kids then it will show we're on the right track.'

I handed Shaughnessy his coffee. Treacle-thick. Black. His first and last of the day. I spooned Marvel and three sugars into mine.

'That's my plan,' I said. 'How does it sound?'

Shaughnessy smiled his lop-sided smile.

'It sounds like the only one we've got.'

My motor insurance didn't run to courtesy cars so it was either rent cheap or walk. I looked up the local rent-a-wreck in Yellow Pages. They agreed to have something within my tenner-a-day budget by nine thirty.

I found ValuDrive in a portacabin behind a body shop off Camden High Street. I reached them by squeezing between a couple of cars that were going to be a challenge to even the most skilled of the body shop's mechanics. The portacabin's office was the size of a broom closet, floored in cracked linoleum and smelling of Calor gas and mould. At nine thirty in the morning the place was dank. A woman wrapped in an anorak fit for Annapurna stood behind a counter littered with grease-stained contracts. She asked for my licence and credit card. I waited whilst she transcribed the details onto a contract form with a biro that kept smearing. She filled out a million details in triplicate then mashed my card twice through her machine. Once for the rental. Once for the deposit. Wrote the charges and asked me to sign. The rental was cheap but the deposit stung. If I wrecked their vehicle my card was going to finance a new City office for ValuDrive.

I signed a contract that had text too small to read but would have significance if something went wrong. The woman gave me my copy with a scribbled telephone number for the breakdown service. The number was also unreadable. She lifted the flap and came out. The whole time I'd been there she'd said nothing other than the essential. Rent-a-wreck, with service to match.

Outside, she took me to check a damage sheet against a lime green Citroen ZX that turned out to be one of the cars I'd pushed past on the way in. The checks went over my head while I made an adjustment to my understanding of the term *rent-a-wreck*. The wreck might actually be wrecked. Valu's offerings were everything you could wish for in this respect. The Citroen looked like the runner-up in a nursery school drawing competition. It had an engine barely bigger than the Frogeye's to haul a car twice the weight, and the bodywork had enough things bent or hanging off to make the damage report sheet an insane doodle. The rear suspension was so far down it looked like the car was parked on a slope. All this for seven ninety-nine a day. Maybe I got air miles. I was suddenly regretting not getting the woman to write the breakdown number more clearly.

I signed the damage report on the basis that it covered the car so comprehensively that if I had a smash they'd never be able to prove it. Then the woman handed me the keys and walked away. The Citroen started on the seventh attempt. Either the petrol gauge wasn't working or they'd run it so low that even the vapour wasn't registering. A more talkative clerk might have told me to push the thing to the nearest filling station. Zero style, zero fuel. The private investigator on the road.

I coasted on fumes to a BP station, keeping my foot light to conserve petrol and minimise the racket of the blowing exhaust. I pumped fifty-six litres of unleaded but the needle stayed on empty. The car was telling me something. I fired up again and headed south across the river and out towards Chevening.

The Hanlons' driveway was still barred by the electric gates but today when I pressed the bell the metalwork swung silently open. Easy!

A hundred yards brought me to an oval forecourt fronting a three-storey Queen Anne. Converted stables to one side provided garage space for a fleet of vehicles but two cars were parked side by side up against the entrance steps. One was a silver Bentley Continental Coupe and the other a Merc sports. The guy in the expensive suit waiting at the top of the steps was David Hanlon.

He watched as I swung the Citroen round to park by his Bentley, said nothing as I climbed the steps. When I held out my hand he held his own up to stop me. Kiss-off number fifty. I'd batted my half century.

Hanlon was a fit fifty-something. Lean, with streaked silver hair and a bespoke wool suit. The no-nonsense stance of a company MD.

He watched me with cold eyes and asked for ID.

I gave him Eagle Eye's card and held up my driver's licence for good measure. He scrutinised them. Held on to the card.

'You've got five minutes, Mr Flynn,' he told me.

He tilted his head and we went in. I heard dogs barking in the back. Hanlon directed me into a lounge overlooking the forecourt. There was no sign of his wife but my senses told me that she was close by. It looked like both of them had taken the morning off to see me. Hanlon didn't ask me to sit.

'If I get the gist of your note,' he said, 'then I conclude that you are interfering in our private affairs. Would you care to tell me what this is about?'

I scanned the walls, impressed. The room had more expensive artwork than the Tate.

'We're investigating a professional criminal,' I told him, 'and we've picked up a connection with your family. I mentioned the guy's name in my note.' That was the note I'd dropped into their post box yesterday. Either it was third time lucky or the note had produced the desired effect. Hanlon might be playing uppity but he and his wife had both stayed home to see me.

Hanlon shook his head.

'I'm afraid the name means nothing to either of us,' he said. 'Your note said that you had information related to the safety of my family. Is this some kind of game, Mr Flynn.?'

I quit my tour round his artwork and looked at Hanlon again. 'It's no game, Mr Hanlon,' I said. 'We're looking into a serious criminal operation. And we do have a very clear link to you.'

Hanlon shook his head again. 'You're mistaken,' he said. 'I've already told you that I don't know this person McAllister. Why don't you stop running in circles, Mr Flynn. Just tell me what you actually have.'

Hanlon's bluster seemed forced but it was possible that he really didn't know McAllister's name. The McCabes hadn't. If the name meant nothing then it must have been the mention of the Brighton Royal Trafalgar in my note that had given Hanlon the incentive to stay home. I switched to this track and asked him about his stay at the hotel.

'I run a company,' Hanlon said. 'I stay in hotels all over the country.'

I lifted my eyebrows. 'And that includes eight-hundred-a-night hospitality?' I asked. 'I must be in the wrong job.'

Hanlon looked out of the window at the Citroen.

'You are,' he said.

Good point. If the shit-heap was sold it wouldn't buy a set of wiper blades for Hanlon's Bentley. But I wasn't swallowing his line about eight-hundred-quid suites being normal business in the IT trade. When you see that kind of extravagance proffered for free you know that business is not normal.

'Those must have been very generous business associates,' I suggested.

'None of your business, Mr Flynn.'

I looked at him. 'Mr Hanlon, it's become my business. Maybe you didn't know it but your Brighton holiday was financed by a professional criminal. These people do things for a reason. Especially five-star hospitality.'

'I've already told you – I don't know this man McAllister.'

'So bear with me. What business took you to Brighton?'

'Nothing I'd talk to you about,' Hanlon said. 'Understand this, Mr Flynn, I've stayed home to find out what your note was about, not to be interrogated.' He looked at his watch. 'Your five minutes is almost up.'

'Just a couple more questions,' I said. 'From what you say you wouldn't be concerned if the Brighton thing came under the scrutiny of the authorities? You'd stick to your line about normal business?'

'Whatever I did, it would have nothing to do with you.'

I changed track. 'I understand that you sold the gatehouse last year. How much did you lose on the deal? Would I be right saying half a million? What I've been asking myself is why a wealthy guy has to rush into a loss-making deal when he can probably raise the same kind of money economically if he waits a few weeks. Unless he's looking to raise cash in a very short time with minimum visibility. What else did you sell? Is your garage emptier than it was?'

Hanlon shook his head. 'You're talking nonsense, Flynn.'

That had never stopped me before.

'The thing has been puzzling me,' I said. 'Why does someone need to raise cash so fast? To be honest I can't help thinking about dodgy business deals. Payoffs. Has your company been getting into something it shouldn't?'

Hanlon shook his head like a mastiff shaking fleas. 'Let's stop messing around, Mr Flynn,' he said. 'If you have something to tell me then spit it out. Otherwise I'm going to end our discussion. I'm a busy man.'

'Okay,' I said. 'The option I'm actually looking at is that someone was threatening your family. You've got a girl and a boy. Was one of them a target? Was either of them taken?'

Hanlon forced a laugh. 'So that's it,' he said. 'Wild guesses. Illegal business deals. Kidnappings! I don't know what the hell your Mr McAllister is up to but you're barking up the wrong tree. The man has absolutely no connection with my family. Never has had. And now we're through.'

'What did you say about children being taken?'

Faye Hanlon had walked into the room a few seconds before. Her husband turned rapidly.

'Mr Flynn has nothing,' he said. 'He's on a fishing trip, looking for connections to some criminal he's chasing. The whole thing is ridiculous.'

Faye Hanlon was in her early forties but worry lines added a decade. Maybe the lines came with her job. Like her husband, she didn't look like she took nonsense from anyone.

'Why do you ask about children being taken?' she demanded again. She tried to back up her husband's bluster but there was a shakiness in her voice.

'We've found a connection between your family and one we're working with,' I explained. 'Ours has been targeted by a criminal gang in the kidnapping business.'

Faye Hanlon's eyes widened.

'Has someone been abducted?' she asked.

I nodded. 'A young girl. Her name is Rebecca Townsend. She's been missing for over a week.' I watched Faye's face. 'Right now we're trying to find the people who have her.'

Faye's hand went to her mouth. David Hanlon moved to her side. He spoke softly.

'The man is scaring us gratuitously,' he said. 'He's absolutely no proof for anything he's saying. Our children are under no threat.' He gripped his wife's shoulder. 'Remember that!'

He turned to me.

'Mr Flynn, we're through.'

I smiled. Scaring people gratuitously. We should add it to our Yellow Pages listing. But Hanlon was right. I was through. I thanked them for their time and turned to walk out.

At the door I turned back to Faye Hanlon. 'Whom did they take?' I asked. 'Clarissa or Harry? Am I right thinking it was your daughter?'

Faye's hand shot to her mouth and Hanlon stepped between us, his face colouring.

'That's it, Flynn!' he said. 'I want you off my property right now!'

I let him manhandle me to the door. I had what I'd come for. The McCabes' denials yesterday had been puzzling because they smacked of truth. They had threatened to demolish my theory. The Hanlons' denials smacked of desperation. Put me right on the mark. It was time to take this thing to the Slaters and force their hand.

Hanlon opened the front door with an extravagant firmness but I stopped and held up a photo. A final shot.

The picture poleaxed him like garlic bread on Dracula's dinner plate. Hanlon's jaw had dropped before he could control it. He knew Tina Brown all right.

'You probably don't know her real name,' I said, 'but you remember the face. We have her at the Royal Trafalgar that night with you. She's missing too. Any ideas?'

Hanlon got himself back under control. Apart from his too-straight face you'd never know he was coming up for air.

'Stir up trouble with me, Flynn,' he growled, 'and I'll sue you for everything you've got.'

I nodded: 'Sure. But if there's something I should know sooner, rather than later, you have my card.'

Hanlon said nothing as I trotted down the steps. I flicked him a salute as I climbed into the car. We'd be meeting again. We both knew it. I jabbed the key into the ignition. The engine clanked over but refused to start. I tried again, cranked it for twenty seconds while the battery drained to a dying chunter. I watched Hanlon through the chipped windscreen and kept my face straight. I relaxed the key and held off for a moment then pressed my foot delicately all the way to the floor. If the carb flooded that was it. I turned the key again. One last shot. The engine chuntered as woefully as before but then it caught and spluttered to life on three cylinders. The vehicle shook like a spin dryer with a brick inside but it was going. I found reverse and tried to look cool as I backed out, careful not to damage the Citroen's bodywork on Hanlon's Bentley.

As I drove away I watched Hanlon in my rear-view crumpling Eagle Eye's card in his fist and tossing it aside.

I drove back to Paddington and parked in Gerry Lye's unused spot next to the Frogeye. Gerry had a point about his space. The tarmac had bubbled alongside the burned out vehicle and the broken glass didn't feel too good under the ZX's wheels. Shaughnessy's Yamaha stood on the far side of the Frogeye, clear of the debris.

Lucy gave me a sympathetic look when I went in. I'd had the Frogeye when the two of us were together. The car had memories for her. I poured coffee and stirred in powder and sugar.

'I couldn't believe it when I saw it,' Lucy said. 'It looks like you've upset the wrong people again, Eddie.'

'All part of the job,' I said.

'That was a good car,' she said.

'Yeah,' I said, 'but you should see the replacement.' I sipped the coffee. The hot-plate light was on but the coffee was stone cold. The machine was back to normal.

'You've got new wheels already?' Lucy asked.

'Wait till you see, Luce. You'll be begging for a ride.'

'You know I'm a girl who likes fancy wheels,' Lucy said. She grinned her heartbreaker. Flirting already. I wondered if she was serious. Wait till she saw the colour.

'Anything new?' I asked.

'Utilities-final-demand stuff or detective stuff?'

'Detective. I'll save the tough business till next week.'

'Next week we'll have no electricity.'

'Is that what they say?'

'And there's a reconnection charge.'

'Bloodsuckers! Pay them.'

'What with?'

'Don't get technical, Lucy,' I said.

'That's what you always say.'

'And you always find a way.'

'I don't know how you guys would stay in business if I wasn't here.'

'We wouldn't, Luce. You're invaluable.'

'So are you going to give me an invaluable salary to match?'

'One day, Lucy, I'll dress you in diamonds.'

'Wow, Eddie! You sure know how to treat a girl!'

'I'll even take you for a ride in my new car. Just promise not to touch anything.'

'I won't. But don't expect any funny business.'

Not in the ZX I wouldn't.

Shaughnessy came out of his office and I told him what I'd got. The Hanlons had had a child taken, despite their denial. And David Hanlon recognised Tina Brown.

It was time to give the Slaters a choice. Tell us everything, let us help, or have the police in the house within the day. We had enough to convince the Mets that a major felony was under way, with Rebecca Townsend at its centre. The only way the Slaters could keep the police out was to bring us in. And if we decided that the police were needed anyway then we'd call them in, with or without the Slaters' permission. Simply blocking us out was no longer an option.

'I'll call Slater,' Shaughnessy said.

I nodded. 'I'll let Gina know what we're doing.' I slid behind Lucy's desk to make the call while Shaughnessy went to prod Larry Slater out from his Islington office.

Before I could pick up the phone my mobile rang.

I looked at the screen. Sadie Bannister. I almost let it go but then wondered if it might be better to know what she was up to rather than have her jump me. I hit the pick-up against my better judgement.

I'd expected frantic. Heard it.

'Eddie,' she screamed, 'is that you? Did you hear?'

Did I hear? My blood frosted. We'd been chasing around in circles since yesterday, convinced that we were finally spiralling towards the girl. But there was also the chance we'd hear bad news at any moment.

'Calm down, Sadie,' I said. 'What happened.'

'She's back!'

'Rebecca?'

'Yeah! She's okay!' Sadie's volume rose past my pain threshold. I held the phone six inches away. 'I can't believe it,' she screamed.

Lucy watched me. Sadie's voice was loud enough for her to get the conversation even without her paranormal powers. 'Becky's okay!' Sadie yelled. 'She really was ill! All that time! Do you believe it? I just want to kill her!'

I looked at Lucy and switched on my Shit-Eater. Did I believe it? Sure I believed it. It was crazy but I believed it.

'When did you hear this?' I said.

'Right now. I'm just off the phone.'

'Rebecca called you?'

'Yeah!'

'She confirmed that she's been ill?'

'Yeah! I went like totally mad that she'd not been in touch, but Becky said her load had run out and she'd been too ill to top up. She only got out of bed yesterday.'

'Out of bed at home?'

'At her aunt's. But not her Aunt Kathryn. I didn't know she had another.'

Neither did I.

'How did she sound?'

'Down. Like when you've been ill? But she's okay, I guess.'

'Well, that's great,' I said. 'I'm glad you told me, Sadie.'

Sadie's voice dropped. 'Maybe this just got out of hand, Eddie,' she said. 'It seems kind of stupid now. Becky was gobsmacked that I'd had a bunch of private detectives after her.'

'Don't worry about it, Sadie,' I said. 'You weren't the only one fooled. The family didn't help anyone.'

'Are they going to be mad at me?'

I thought about this.

'We'll talk to them,' I said. 'They've no reason to be mad.'

'Thank God it's over,' Sadie said.

'All's well that ends well,' I quipped. Original to the last. I told her we'd speak soon and cut the line.

Shaughnessy had come back out.

'Slater's not answering,' he said. He looked at me. 'Was I hearing that right?'

I nodded. 'The girl's back. Apparently she's never been missing.'

Shaughnessy looked at me.

I flipped the Citroen's keys and he followed me out onto the stairs. Shaughnessy had always hated the Frogeye. Today he was in for a treat.

CHAPTER THIRTY-SIX

Shaughnessy made out that he was cool with the ride but I saw his eyebrows lift as we came round the back of the building. He slid himself into the car like he might catch something off the upholstery. I went through the start-up ritual and we pulled out onto the street.

The weather had switched again, and the sun shone out of a blue sky. I wound the window down but the staccato of the blowing exhaust hurt my ears. I wound it back up and turned on the fan. The fan didn't work but a wash of warm air slid from under the dashboard. I killed the control. I almost flicked the radio on to hide the rumble of the big end bearings but the thought of what might come through the speakers dissuaded me. We rode along in silence, jounced by the engine alternating between three and four cylinders. Shaughnessy was looking around the interior as if I'd bought a turd from the dogs' home.

'What are we going to say?' he said finally.

'I'm more interested in what the Slaters have to say to us,' I told him.

'I don't see them saying anything.'

I'd been chewing the thing over. Our plan had been flawless. March into the Slaters' and hit them with all we had. It would be their choice: let us in or have us throw a spanner in the works. A good plan whilst their daughter was missing. Not so attractive now that the girl was there to prove that we'd been dreaming the whole thing. We'd just got warmed up and the final whistle had blown. Game over. Another case solves itself under the threat of Eagle Eye's attention. We'd feel good if we knew what had happened. The real riddle was what to say in Gina Redding's billing report.

'Let's see what gives,' I said. 'I want to see some evidence that the girl actually is safe. I want to know if there's still a threat to other families. I also want to know who torched my car, why we're riding around in this shit-heap. That's the thing I don't understand. If this really is a kidnap–ransom thing and McAllister was about to send the girl home then why stir things up by attacking me?'

Shaughnessy shrugged. 'He probably assumed you wouldn't follow up. At the end of the day it was just a car.'

I turned to look at him. He was staring ahead through the chipped windscreen, sitting ramrod straight to keep his clothes off the upholstery. Maybe the Sprite didn't seem so bad to him any more.

'The Frogeye means nothing,' I said. 'I'm going to bring the house down over whatever's happened to Rebecca. And to the Hanlons. And whatever McAllister has got lined up for some other family. Not to mention the dent this thing has made in Gina Redding's bank balance.'

'You think Gina will pay us?'

'Maybe not. We might have to kidnap the girl again.'

We reached the Slater house. Larry's Lexus was parked askew by the steps, as if he'd arrived in a hurry.

I parked the Citroen under cover of the vehicle to protect our street cred. When I killed the engine the thing backfired to clarify the issue. We got out and walked over.

The front door was opened with the speed reserved for unwelcome visitors. Larry Slater's face backed up the impression. I had a nice opening line ready but Slater got his in first.

'Holy shit,' he said, 'you guys take the biscuit.'

I gave him a friendly nod. 'Good afternoon, Larry. Meet my partner Sean Shaughnessy. Do you have a few minutes for us?'

Slater ignored Shaughnessy.

'You've got ten seconds to get off my property,' he said, 'then I'm calling the police.'

Ten seconds isn't very long. A ten second spiel must be good.

'Larry,' I said, 'if we leave here without answers I'm going to come back tomorrow morning and see if your wife can help us figure out why your Lexus spends half its time parked in Holland Park. See if she knows anyone by the name of Tina Brown.'

Slater took it in then shook his head like he was shaking off something too stupid to comment on.

'Go ahead,' he sneered. 'Tell Jean about Holland Park.' He sounded confident that he could bluff his way through.

'And while I'm at it,' I said, 'there's some stuff I'll bring along. Copies of your Amex account – the ones with the Blueglades payments and the Royal Trafalgar bills. Will your wife explain those too?'

Cheap but to the point.

The phoney indignation dropped right off Slater's face. 'You've been through my Amex bills?' he gasped. 'You broke into my office? Holy Christ, I'll have your balls!' He pulled a mobile out of his pocket. 'I'm on the phone right now, Flynn!'

His response was disappointing but at least we were through the ten second barrier. We just needed to find a way past Slater's defensiveness so we could talk about the things that mattered. We needed some way to persuade him not to make the call.

'If you touch that phone,' Shaughnessy said, 'I'll break your fingers.'

Slater stopped with his finger poised over the keypad. He gave Shaughnessy the goldfish look.

I looked at Shaughnessy too. Why hadn't I thought of that?

Shaughnessy followed up with a stare that told Larry he meant what he said. I switched back to reason.

'Larry, we need to talk,' I said. 'If we know what has been happening then maybe we can help. This isn't just your family. There are others.'

'Other families?'

The voice was a whisper from behind Slater. He turned and made shooing motions. 'Leave this to me,' he said.

She came forward into the light. A slender teenager with her mother's face. The same high cheeks and pretty eyes but pale, her hair a mess. Right then the illness thing looked credible. But there was something in the girl's face that wasn't caused by the flu. This wasn't someone bouncing back. Rebecca Townsend just looked sad.

Slater made to shoo her again but she swiped his hand away. She looked at me and her face softened into a sad grin.

'You're the gumshoe,' she said.

I grinned back. 'Yeah,' I said. 'We're the detectives. I guess Sadie told you she had us out looking for you?'

Slater moved to get back in control. He made a grab and pulled Rebecca back and tried to close the door. But the door wouldn't close on account of Shaughnessy's foot. Behind Slater, Rebecca was saying some unladylike things. Slater snarled back at her then suddenly something snapped. He yanked the door open again and was out. His finger jabbed in my face.

'Stay right there, Flynn. The cops are on their way.' He keyed his phone, broken fingers forgotten. Shaughnessy sighed and stepped forwards. He shouldered Slater out of the way and took the phone from his hand and we followed the girl into the house. Slater strode after us, yelling, but Rebecca was yelling right back, and finally the girl's anger got through to him. Slater's shoulders dropped as he stood facing his stepdaughter. A puppet with its strings cut.

'Let them talk to me,' Rebecca said, 'or I'll go right out and talk to them. And I swear I'll tell them everything.'

Before Slater could reply Jean appeared from the back of the house. She put her arm around Rebecca's shoulder, pulled her gently away. Her voice was weary. 'No, Rebecca,' she said, 'we don't want you to talk to anyone.' She looked at me and Shaughnessy. 'Why don't we sit down for a moment?'

Larry Slater swore again but no one was listening. We followed Jean through to the lounge. She sat down with Rebecca beside her. Shaughnessy, Slater and I all stood.

'Whatever you're looking for,' Slater said, 'there's nothing here. Whatever misinformation has had you stalking us the last week has been a waste of your time and somebody else's money.'

'Gina's,' Rebecca said. 'She hired them.' She looked at me. I nodded and raised my eyebrows, tried to take some of the tension out of the moment. 'Your friend Sadie was rather insistent,' I said. 'And Mrs Redding was kind enough to retain our services.'

'And all for nothing,' Larry Slater snapped. 'We told everyone that Rebecca was ill. We explained that she needed time to recuperate. But some people just don't listen.'

I was watching the quiet smile that played on the girl's face while Larry talked. The smile was for Sadie and Gina. It must feel good to know that someone cared.

Jean Slater came in to back up her husband. 'Mr Flynn, we're sorry for the mix-up. The wires just got crossed. Rebecca has already explained everything to Sadie.'

Talked to her. Explained nothing.

'Mix-up or not,' Larry Slater said, 'this investigation thing needs to stop. We're asking you again to respect our privacy. And now that you can see our daughter is safe maybe you'll tell Mrs Redding to stop wasting her money.' He stared at me. 'End of investigation.'

'The investigation ends,' I said, 'when we decide.'

Slater's mouth set hard. 'Then you're fools,' he said. 'And I won't hesitate to call the police.'

I turned to Rebecca.

'Are you okay, Rebecca?'

She looked at me but said nothing. Jean answered for her. 'She's still tired,' she said, 'but she's fine.'

I kept watching Rebecca.

'It's okay,' I said. 'We know the people who took you. You don't need to be afraid of them. They won't touch you again.'

'Stop!' Larry Slater said. He stepped between me and the girl. His anger had boiled back up. Jean Slater's eyes were closed.

'How many times must I repeat myself,' Slater said. 'Get off our backs. There is nothing here for you, Flynn. I won't tolerate any more of this harassment.'

He would have said more but his rant was broken by an exaggerated gasp from Rebecca. She stood up behind him. He turned to face her and the two of them locked stares until Jean Slater opened her eyes and clenched her fists.

'Stop it!' she commanded. 'You're tearing us apart with all of this.'

I didn't know if she was speaking to Rebecca or to her husband. Or to me. I still watched Rebecca. She finally unlocked stares with Larry and turned to us. The half-smile was there again.

'Private detectives,' she said. She shook her head. 'That Sadie is one crazy bitch.' The smile stayed on her face as she walked out.

'Okay,' Larry Slater said. 'That's it. Please pass on the message to Gina Redding.'

'First we've got to write a report,' I said. 'It would help if we could clarify a few things with you.'

'Report?' Slater said. 'What the hell can you report? You still don't get it. There is nothing to report.'

'I was hoping,' I said, 'I could get some pointers from you. To clear up loose ends.'

'Jesus.' Slater looked at his wife, but she returned a stare that could have cut steel.

'Your daughter was abducted by a man named Paul McAllister,' I said. 'Now she is back. Therefore we assume that you've recently handed over a large sum of money.'

Slater shook his head but said nothing.

'I also assume that it was you who tipped Paul McAllister off after I came to see you.'

Slater shook his head again. 'You're flying blind, Flynn. No one has abducted our daughter. And I don't know anyone called Paul McAllister.'

McAllister was a guy a lot of people didn't know.

Shaughnessy had strolled across the room and was inspecting a Rothko print on the far wall.

'Don't lie to us, Larry,' he said. 'We have evidence that you've been in contact with the man.'

'We've also got similarities between your family and another one,' I said. 'A family who also had links to McAllister and who also raised some fast cash a few months back.'

'I don't know what you're talking about.' Slater's eyes were wide in phoney confusion.

When I spoke it was to Jean Slater. 'The other family has a teenage daughter too,' I said.

Jean's face stayed expressionless but I sensed the turmoil behind the mask.

'What was the cash for, Larry?' Shaughnessy asked.

Slater let out a laugh that broke even as he forced it out. 'You're way off centre,' he answered. 'Are you two never going to quit?'

'The *Lode Star*,' I said. 'Is that off centre?'

Slater's lips curled. He shook his head.

'What I do with my money or belongings is none of your damn business. Is that all you've got?'

I thought about it.

'There's the Amex thing,' I said. 'We could discuss that in more detail.'

'Amex?' Jean looked at her husband.

Slater gave it the best he had. His indignation was worth an Oscar.

'It's nothing,' he hissed. 'These two idiots are chasing shadows. And I can't believe I'm in my own house listening to this! Okay. Time for the boys in blue. Or are you still going to break my fingers?' he sneered at Shaughnessy.

Shaughnessy said nothing.

Slater stalked out of the room and went for the hall phone. His mobile was on the coffee table in front of us, but maybe he thought that picking that up would provoke Shaughnessy.

It looked like we were through. No point waiting for the coffee and cakes. Most jobs have better perks. I turned for a last word with Jean Slater.

'We've not finished with this,' I said. 'Whoever is still threatening you, we're going to run them down.'

Explaining to Jean about the Amex charges was not going to help. We walked back out to the front door. As he passed, Shaughnessy took the phone out of Slater's hands and set the receiver back in its place. Slater said nothing.

I dropped Shaughnessy back at the office so he could pick up his Yamaha. He came up to get his stuff. Lucy was waiting and I gave her the gist of things. Out next step was to talk to Gina Redding so that she knew that her own commitment was over.

The investigation would go on, though.

Shaughnessy and I had agreed that on the ride back. We had three facts. One: we had an extortion racket involving at least two kidnappings to date. Two: McAllister was behind the racket. Three: there was no reason to think that McAllister was about to wind up his scheme. We also had a few doubts. We still didn't know if the escort Tina Brown was part of the plot or a victim.

I needed to get back to Tina's friend Sammy. If she still insisted on bringing in the police we couldn't stop her. We'd tidy up what we had and hand it over.

Our grand plan to coerce the Slaters into spilling the beans was shot. Plan B was to go after McAllister directly. We had enough material to interest the police. Maybe they'd disrupt his games for a while by looking into his connections with the three families. It would have been better if we'd had enough to blow the thing open but you sometimes have to go with what you've got.

Shaughnessy came out as Lucy considered the question of whether we had enough to close McAllister down. Decided not. 'The thing stinks,' she concluded, 'but I don't think you've enough fertiliser yet to sow your oats.'

Shaughnessy and I looked at each other. When Lucy tosses metaphors you need to duck.

'Lucy, you're a poet,' said Shaughnessy.

I shook my head in wonderment. 'Lucy, we should pay you more.'

'You should pay me,' she said.

Shaughnessy went out and Lucy busied herself closing up. I figured I'd call it quits myself after I'd made a couple of calls. Arabel was free tonight. We'd already arranged to get together, although when she saw my new wheels the chances were high that she'd suddenly remember a prior engagement.

I decided to start on writing up something creative for Gina Redding's report. The thing that interested Gina was over. Her commission was finished. But first I'd call Sammy and see if she was about to blow the whistle. Or whether we still had a little time to go after McAllister. I was also wondering whether I might find Tina Brown at home tonight if I drove by Holland Park.

It turned out to be open season for telepaths. My phone rang while I was scrolling for Sammy Vincent's number.

'Eddie?'

'Sammy, I was about to call,' I said. 'See how you want to go with things.' I was about to give her a summary but she cut me off.

'Tina sent a text,' she said. Her voice was scared. 'Something has happened.'

'What sort of thing?'

'She says someone's got her. I have to go to the police now, Eddie.'

'Hold it a moment,' I said. 'Does Tina say where she is?'

'No – only that she's on a farm.'

Her voice was breaking. I told her to slow down. Asked when she'd received the text.

'Ten minutes ago,' she said. 'Jesus, what's happening? Who's got her, Eddie?'

Questions, questions. I had a few of my own but the main issue was what else was in the text. There are a lot of farms in the UK.

'Is there any more detail?' I said.

'Just a name,' Sammy said. 'Addingford.'

Addingford.

McAllister's farm.

CHAPTER THIRTY-SEVEN

I drove across the city through rush-hour traffic. The Citroen's three-cylinder act had the car bucking and jumping as I worked my feet to keep the engine alive at each stop. Either the distributor was shot or the HT leads were cracked through. Something that tended to get worse rapidly. The unreadable emergency number on my rental contract was playing on my mind but I consoled myself with the though that it was unlikely anyone would turn out to tow me even if the number had been embossed in gold leaf.

Sammy had agreed to hold off whilst I took a look at McAllister's farm. The place had been deserted when Shaughnessy checked it yesterday which suggested that the text was a ruse. Ruse or not, it was a lead I couldn't ignore. Answers of some kind were waiting there.

I crossed the river at Westminster and took another hour to reach the M25 at Swanley. I eased onto the motorway and rolled south in the inside lane at the fifty-five limit the engine could handle. The intermittent misfire settled into a regular beat that promised trouble soon. Traffic was heavy but it was all faster than me.

Shaughnessy had located McAllister's farm a mile off the A21 south of Lamberhurst. If I got a clear run I could be there by seven. I pulled into the middle lane to pass a battered Transit and crawled past it with an artic coming up fast in my rear-view with no indication that it was about to slow. The truck's radiator grille expanded until it filled my mirrors and the roar of its engine shook the Citroen enough to set the oil light flickering but not enough to move the petrol gauge out of red. I got past the Transit and pulled back to the slow lane. The artic batted me with a side-gust and horn blast and roared past. When the truck got clear, I read the logo. Tailgate letters six feet high: HP LOGISTICS.

I felt a shiver down my spine. Even with my new wheels the bastards had spotted me.

I hit the A21 and drove down to Lamberhurst. It took me ten minutes to find the farm. The place was as Shaughnessy described, a shale track dropping down to a cluster of buildings five hundred yards from the road. Spring cereal was profuse in the surrounding fields. They were either someone else's fields or McAllister rented them out. I didn't see him driving a John Deere.

I found a copse five hundred yards past the track and backed the Citroen into a stub road against a barred gate. The engine stalled as I was manoeuvring it in and I left the car where it died.

The copse was separated from the farm by a field of spring barley. I climbed a gate and walked along the edge beside the woods which took me down to a meadow below the farm. I struggled over some barbed wire and walked back up the meadow that curved towards the house. The buildings were losing definition in the dusk, as were the cowpats scattered all around me. You had to tread carefully in this game.

A gate opened into a farmyard. The sight of concrete rather than mud was a relief. I cut down between a rotting corrugated metal storage barn and a modern concrete and brick structure. Reached the house. There were no lights inside. No cars parked. If someone was home they were hiding.

I walked around the barns. The rust holes in the older building showed glimpses of farm machinery. McAllister probably rented out the building along with his fields. I walked to the new structure to check that there were no vehicles parked there before I went to look inside the house. Maybe Tina Brown's text was genuine. Maybe she was here and needed help. Maybe her abductors had been considerate enough to leave her mobile phone in her hands. But maybe not. My guess was that someone was waiting for me in the house.

The barn was open at the end. I walked in. Spotted two vehicles inside. One was a tractor. The other was a Merc S Class, so out of place that I knew something was up. Then someone stepped from the shadows behind the tractor. He didn't look much like a farmer. Not unless farmers were in the habit of pointing shotguns at visitors. When the figure came into the light I recognised Ray Child.

I barely had time to sneer at my own incompetence when a second figure emerged. Paul McAllister was also pointing a gun. I'd expected them to be inside the house. Hiding in the cowshed was more in character. I would have left but McAllister told me not to move and waved his gun at my face. It was a Mossberg 500. He literally waved it, like a smart-alec with a blade. I'd never seen that done with a big gun. I wondered how heavy McAllister's trigger finger was.

The two of them came over. I didn't know who was more scary. Ray Child, who held his gun as casually as a kid with a stick, or McAllister who wanted me to know that this was all good fun.

'Mr Flynn,' he said, 'my advice failed.' He lifted his eyebrows to jog my memory. I waited while I tried to think of a smart reply. With a Mossie pointing at you the smartest thing to say is nothing. I went for that option.

'The advice,' McAllister clarified, 'about keeping your nose out.'

I gave him the evil eye. It was the only weapon I had.

'I guess you didn't hear either,' I said. 'I told you it's coming undone.

Even before I talked to the Hanlons. Before we went back to the Slaters. We've got your scheme, McAllister, and we've got the evidence filed and indexed.'

McAllister made a mouth. 'I'm weeing in my pants, Flynn,' he said. 'Truly I am.'

He didn't actually seem scared but then the Mossberg wasn't pointing at him.

'Is Tina Brown here,' I asked, 'or have you learned to text by yourself?'

McAllister's brows stayed high, surprised I was even asking. The eyebrows suggested that I had more to worry about right now. But you can't keep a detective's curiosity down.

'Is Tina part of your operation or just a victim?' I asked him.

McAllister gestured with the Mossberg. Child came round to my side and suddenly his gun swung and the stock hit me like a sledgehammer just below my ear. I didn't go down but I danced a little. The side of my face opened like a ripe tomato and warm blood trickled onto my collar. I swore with gusto and turned to face Child. Just a little further round and he'd be in McAllister's line of fire. But Child wasn't quite so stupid. He stayed clear, watching me with his casual air. On some kind of whim he pulled the gun up and pointed it at my head like he was considering things. He didn't have orders to open fire but I knew I was on a tightrope.

'People know I'm here,' I told McAllister. 'It's going to be hard to clean up if your gorilla does something stupid.'

McAllister's eyes stayed on mine. 'I'll give you ten out of ten for bullshit, Flynn,' he said, 'but only one for brains. You had the chance to walk away from this. But now here we are.'

'Call me persistent,' I said.

'Yes,' McAllister said, 'I'll do that. Where's your car?'

'Behind the office,' I said. 'Standing in a pool of rubber.'

McAllister gave this some thought then tried again.

'You came by car. Where is it?'

I described the stub-track. If it was the Citroen he wanted it was his.

He should have just told me.

'Key.'

I reached into my jacket and flipped him the ZX's key. He caught it. The Mossberg never lost track of my abdomen.

McAllister flicked his head in the Merc's direction.

'Pop her.'

Child pulled out a remote. The Merc flashed like a Christmas tree and the boot hissed open. McAllister tilted his head. 'Get in,' he said.

I looked at the shadows inside the open boot and suddenly some very bad outcomes were flashing through my mind. I breathed against a sudden tension clamping my chest.

'I don't ride in car boots,' I said.

McAllister dropped the barrel of the gun. It was pointed at my feet. 'Flynn,' he said, 'walk over or we'll carry you.'

Child stayed clear of McAllister's line of fire and watched me with interest to see if I would be stupid enough to call his bluff. I wasn't so stupid. The odds were clear.

I went over and climbed into the Merc's boot. It wasn't actually bad inside but then again I'd arrived in the Citroen.

The two of them stood over me. I expected the boot lid to slam down but they waited. Child held out his hand.

'Mobile,' he said.

Some you lose. I handed it over.

'People know where I am,' I repeated. 'If you're thinking of doing something stupid it's not going to work.'

'Unfortunately,' said McAllister, 'I don't believe you. You're here on your tod, Flynn. I can smell it. And we've a place where no one is going to be looking for you. You're a liability we can't afford, my son.'

The boot lid slammed down.

Blackness.

The Merc's engine whispered to life.

I hadn't really expected to find Tina Brown.

CHAPTER THIRTY-EIGHT

I felt the Merc climb up onto the road and turn down towards where I'd ditched the Citroen. Thirty seconds later we stopped and someone got out. Child, I figured, taking the booby prize of driving the wreck. The Merc turned and left him to it.

I'd seen it in the movies but this was my first time in the boot of a car. The combination of suffocation and blackness played hell with the senses. Whenever the car turned it felt like I was spinning through space and my stomach floated with every dip in the road. In a situation like that it's useful to have something to distract the mind. Fear works well. All kinds of things were dancing through my mind in the dark, and uppermost amongst them was that I had just disappeared from the world as far as McAllister was concerned. He just needed to complete the arrangements to make it permanent. When we got to wherever we were going I'd be lucky for a single shot at getting out of this thing. I said a few choice words into the dark.

The Merc cruised for twenty minutes then turned onto a side road whose surface had me bouncing off the boot lid as if McAllister was trying to write the car off. Maybe it just seemed worse in the dark. Probably we were crawling. Blood was dripping from the side of my face onto McAllister's carpet. The guy needed to sharpen up on the incriminating-evidence side of crime.

Finally we stopped. It was quiet for a few minutes before I heard the Citroen's exhaust in the distance. The din got louder until it was like machine-gun fire outside the boot. Then the Citroen's engine died and the Merc's boot clicked open. I squinted up at McAllister's gun. He was still waggling it in that funny way of his. I climbed out.

We were in a narrow lane. Fading daylight showed me a thatched cottage backing onto trees. The lane continued but didn't look like it went anywhere. We weren't going to be bothered by traffic tonight.

Child pushed open a wooden gate and walked through the cottage garden. He disappeared around the back of the building.

I watched McAllister but he'd read my mind. He stayed out of reach.

'Go ahead, Flynn,' he said. 'I'll put you down right here. I pay Ray to clean up so it's not any bother.' He jerked the gun provocatively like that would make me rush it. I wasn't about to do anything so stupid. But I was going to have to do something soon. I didn't need McAllister's mind-reading skills to know that his plans for me were about to reach their conclusion.

Child came back round. I thought he was carrying a second gun. Then saw it was a spade. He held it casually alongside his shotgun down by his right leg. He had a couple of flashlights too, handed one to McAllister. McAllister waggled the Mossberg again and indicated a path that ran down the side of the cottage into the trees. He flicked on his light. We set off. Me first. McAllister three paces behind. Child further back. When we got into the trees I was looking for an opening in the undergrowth where I could do a head-dive and scarper before

McAllister pulled the trigger but a jab in my spine gave me the benefit of a second opinion.

The path climbed inside the trees. A hundred yards up it branched and McAllister told me to stop. I turned round. McAllister kept the torch in my face and told me to turn right back.

'Hands on the tree,' he said.

I walked over and placed my hands on the rough bark of the tree trunk in front of me. McAllister kept his distance. Not even the hint of carelessness. We were only ten or fifteen miles from his farm but I hadn't a clue which direction we'd taken. Suddenly these woods were a lonely place.

Even lonelier when Child stepped off the path and picked out a shallow mound of earth with his flashlight. He propped his shotgun against a tree while I speculated on what might be under the mound.

Child put his foot to his spade and started digging at fresh undergrowth. Maybe I'd seen too many movies but I was putting two and two together, and the tension was sitting firmly across my chest to tell me that I'd screwed up badly. I'd been looking for an opportunity to dive out of these guys' gunsights since Child had first slammed me back at the farm and I knew now that they weren't going to give me any such chance. McAllister was holding his attention on me like a snake eyeing a mouse. So now I knew it: I had one last ruse, and if that didn't work I was truly in shitsville. I heard McAllister light a cigarette behind me and tried to keep my voice even.

'You're making a mistake,' I said. 'I've left information on where I was going tonight. It'll point right to your farm, McAllister.'

The words sounded desperate even to me.

McAllister didn't reply. Child kept digging. It was like I'd ceased to interest them.

'You aren't going to cover it,' I insisted. 'Two people missing. Both connected to you. There's a file in my office a mile thick that points to you. When my partner picks up that information he's going to be taking a trip to your farm. You're screwing up, McAllister.'

'Keep talking, Flynn,' McAllister said. 'Ray's going to be a while.'

'Suit yourself,' I said. 'But when your file is handed over you'll be crawling with cops. They'll tear your little game to bits.'

McAllister hissed smoke behind me. 'So maybe we'll pay a visit to your office and borrow the file,' he said.

'You'll be too late. My partner will be there tonight.'

'That would scare me,' McAllister said, 'if I thought your partner was working the night shift. But I think your sidekick's at home with his feet up or his leg over. I think you're full of shit, Flynn.'

'You have my phone,' I said. 'Check the messages.'

'Why would I do that?'

'You'll see.'

Five yards away Ray Child quit his spade work to take a breather. The undergrowth was tough. He'd barely cleared a six-by-three area and taken the soil a couple of inches down. I wasn't complaining. He could take all night.

'Pull the trigger, Paul,' he said. 'We're not going to get any peace until Mr Snoopy is out of it. Why isn't he doing the spade-work?'

Wouldn't work. I dig slow.

But I knew that McAllister couldn't care less whether they dropped me in an hour or right now. Suggestions like Child's I could do without.

McAllister was silent behind me. The dancing of his flashlight told me that he'd pulled out my mobile and was pressing buttons. Curiosity and all that. He didn't believe there was anything to give him a problem but he couldn't resist a peek. There was only one message in my inbox and I knew by the continued silence that McAllister had found it.

'What's this?' he said.

'A message from my partner. He'll be heading back to the office anytime now. He'll pick up my note then stash your file somewhere safe.'

'Is there a problem?' Child asked.

'Maybe,' said McAllister. 'Looks like Snoopy's as good as his word. Okay Flynn, what's this text about?'

'Just like it says. That's my partner confirming that he got my message to call by at the office if I don't contact him by ten. He'll read my note pointing to your farm. There's a couple of them will be round there tonight. Maybe you can just shoot them all.'

'They can look all they like,' McAllister said. 'There's nothing to find there.'

'Sure,' I said. 'You had the girl at the cottage right here. But the farm was where I was headed tonight. If I go missing everything will point to you, McAllister. You're not going to put out that fire.'

'So you want to see us burn, Flynn?' Child pulled the spade out of the ground and came towards me. Just a few feet more and he'd be within McAllister's line of fire. When he swung the shovel I'd be ready.

'Wait,' said McAllister.

Child stopped.

'We'll go back to the house,' McAllister decided. 'I need to put a lid on this.'

'Let's bury him first,' Child said. 'Save listening to any more hot air.'

'No. I want you to get to their office before his partner. Take everything that matters, including Snoopy's note. We'll come back out here when I've had a good look at what they have.'

I breathed out quietly against the bark of the tree. I'd needed McAllister to buy that one. It was only a delay but it would give me time – and this time there'd be just the two of us. McAllister was a cold case but I could maybe work it.

Child looked like a kid who'd had his sweets stolen. He planted the spade and picked up his shotgun. McAllister aimed the torch back down the track.

'Walk,' he said.

I didn't need a second invitation.

We walked back down to the lane and went in through the cottage garden.

Child opened the house door and switched on the lights.

The parlour was old-fashioned but without charm. Cheap furniture and frayed carpets, nothing to say it was ever lived in. Just an untraceable rental. Somewhere for McAllister to keep his abductees.

An IKEA coffee table held an ash tray overflowing with cigarette butts, and a doorway to the back kitchen gave a view of unwashed cups and takeaway cartons. Someone had been staying here and someone else had been watching them. My guess was that Rebecca Townsend had spent the last ten days in the house. Maybe Tina Brown too.

'Give me your jacket,' McAllister said.

I turned and gave him a puzzled look. McAllister's eyes stayed uninterested but his gun twitched and Child started to move towards me. I didn't fancy another tap in the face so I took off the jacket and tossed it onto the sofa. McAllister waggled the Mossberg some more.

'Pockets.'

'The office keys are in my jacket,' I said. 'Or are you looking for fivers?'

The gun dipped to point at my feet. I turned out my pockets. There was nothing there. Ray Child rooted through my jacket. Came out with a Swiss knife, a dry-cleaning ticket I'd lost and a bunch of keys.

'These open up the office?' McAllister asked.

'Yes,' I said. 'Don't leave the lights on.'

His eyebrows raised.

'You're a very funny man, Mr Flynn,' he said. 'You should be on the telly. Probably pays more than snooping, and I hear it's better for your health.'

'I had a bad career advisor,' I said.

McAllister gestured to an armchair in the corner of the room.

'Make yourself comfy, Flynn,' he said. He handed the Merc's keys to Child.

'Put your foot down,' he said. 'In and out before Mr Snoopy's friend pokes his nose in at the office. If the guy does arrive while you're there, close him down.'

Child turned his ugly smile on me. 'Maybe we can put your whole firm out of business tonight, Flynn,' he said. 'If he turns up at the wrong time your private dick partner will wish he'd never read your text. Stayed safe in front of his telly.'

Shaughnessy never watched TV but Child didn't know it.

Neither had he read any text, but I didn't mention that either.

CHAPTER THIRTY-NINE

When Child had gone McAllister relaxed on the sofa with the gun across his lap where he could swing it up if need arose. I calculated how long Child would be gone. An hour into central London. Twenty minutes at the office. An hour back. We had two hours plus to kill.

'Let's see if my assumptions are right,' I said. 'You've just extorted half a mill' from the Slaters.'

McAllister lit a cigarette but wasn't talking. Most villains can't shut up. It's the criminal ego, the urge to air their special philosophy on life, as if talking their delusions through makes them true. Villains never see their own uselessness. They paper over the question of worth with a code of respect. If they are respected it must mean they're worthwhile. They never figure that it just means that everyone's scared of them.

McAllister wasn't the delusional type. He was the worse breed, the one driven by meanness rather than ego. McAllister just enjoyed doing bad things. It was the taking that was important. McAllister wouldn't have earned his bread legitimately if it could have pulled in ten times the dosh. Villains like McAllister didn't want your respect. They wanted the raw thing - fear.

To McAllister I was a fly in the ointment and he needed me out. The reason he wasn't talking to me was that he didn't give a damn.

'I'm guessing three quarters of a million,' I persisted. 'That's a good take-home for a few days work.'

McAllister watched smoke clouds eddying under the ceiling but I knew he was listening.

'We've got three families in our files,' I said. 'We've got Alpha Security and the blackmail thing, the ties to Tina Brown. And the trail is backed up in our online servers no matter what Child comes back with. He isn't going to wipe the slate clean in half an hour, Paul.'

McAllister sucked hard on the cigarette. Finally opened up.

'Who do you think I am, Flynn?' he said. He was still watching the ceiling. 'Some kind of amateur? Do you think your two-bit outfit frightens me?' He didn't look frightened. 'Let me explain something,' he said.

So even McAllister couldn't resist a little yackity. It was probably the boredom.

'I don't give a damn what's in your computers,' he said. 'I actually assume there's nothing there. Everything you've got will be squirrelled away in the paper file the hobgoblin's gone to fetch. There won't be enough left at your agency for the filth to even send me a birthday card.'

Hobgoblin! I wondered how Ray would like that one. Maybe I could work it into the conversation when Child got back, stir up a fight whilst I dived through the window.

'So what's the big deal?' I said. 'How come you and your goblin are waving your sticks at everyone?'

'You were rocking the boat, Flynn,' McAllister said. 'Becoming a dangerous bastard. Our business depends on discretion. Peace and quiet. When Ray gets back we'll take that walk into the woods and then I'll get my peace and quiet again.'

I thought about that.

'Let's see if I have it figured out,' I said. 'You stake out wealthy families. Not so rich that they have minders or the money to come after you, but rich enough to get their hands on upwards of a million inside a week or two. Then you fete the man of the house at a five-star hotel with a five-star hooker thrown in. That's the bit that stumped me at first. Was it just a phoney business deal to feel the guys out before you went for the kids? That didn't make sense. You already knew that the families were sitting ducks. I was intrigued that you booked the hotel suite for three nights when your guest was only staying one. The extra nights had to be to set things up. Cameras and things. So we're looking at a honeytrap blackmail. But this thing's supposed to be about taking the kids.'

I watched McAllister. He blew a long stream of smoke and watched it rise to the ceiling.

'Finally I got it,' I said. 'The thing with the hooker actually is blackmail. You set up a phoney business meeting that's not intended to come to anything, but you throw in a night on the town for your guest anyway, with your girl as an irresistible extra. If the guy falls into the trap then you've got your blackmail ammo. Only the blackmail's not for money. Sex-blackmail isn't going to bring in half a mill'. Kidnapping the kids brings in the money. The blackmail kicks in afterwards.'

McAllister was still watching the ceiling. I couldn't tell whether he was pleased that someone had worked out his caper or didn't give a damn. Guessed the latter. I went on anyway. I always talk when I'm nervous.

'The whole thing's about repeat business,' I said. 'The ideal kidnap and ransom scheme is one you can repeat - one that the cops never hear about. The thing never gets out because you've got the father by the balls. The family pays the ransom and the kid is sent home with the usual threats that you'll come looking for them if they blow the whistle. The threats are enough to make them think twice but not enough to keep them quiet for long. So that's where you enlist the help of the man of the house. You show him the movies of his weekend away and persuade him that it's his job to make sure his wife and kid clam up permanently. He's your Trojan horse, working for you inside the family. His wife is screaming for the cops but the husband stands his ground, persuades her that the cops won't be able to protect them. Persuades her that it's better to cut their losses. What he doesn't tell his wife is what he's really afraid of - those movies. The ones of him in bed with the villains' hooker. What's his wife going to say when she hears it was his bit of fun that gave the crooks the opportunity to target their children in the first place?'

I nodded a reluctant acknowledgement to McAllister's scheme. 'You've got the ideal caper,' I said. 'You've got the family while you're holding their child, then when you release the kid you get the husband to lock their front door. He makes sure that the thing never gets out.'

'For a two-bit private eye,' McAllister said, 'you're pretty smart, Flynn. The sooner we take that walk into the woods the better.'

'So how many have you done?' I said. 'How many repeats? Five? Ten? Or were you just getting started? I know the McCabe family is lined up. Were they next?'

'Not the McCabes,' McAllister said. 'They were our little failure. Tina had the guy drooling over his dinner jacket but the retentive bastard sent her packing at the last minute. You win some, you lose some,' he said. 'No dirty movies so no snatch. But we've got others lined up.'

'Was Tina Brown part of your scheme? Did she babysit the kids? Or was she only the bait? I'm still trying to figure why you buried her up there in the woods.'

McAllister looked at me. Raised the Mossberg and pointed it my way, kind of playfully.

'Ask her yourself,' he said. 'You'll soon be friends.'

'I'm saying she wasn't in on it,' I said. 'All she knew was that she was hired to supply a little corporate hospitality. You killed Tina because she found out.'

McAllister lit up another cigarette and lapsed into silence again. No longer interested.

'You had Tina's phone,' I deduced, 'and you picked up Sammy's message about Eagle Eye searching for her. I guess that spooked you. Enough to entice me to your farm.'

McAllister pursed his girlish lips and opened up again with a weary sigh. 'To be honest,' he said, 'sending you that text today was a long shot. That was the goblin's brainwave. I told him that not even you would be stupid enough to walk into a trap like that. I stand duly corrected.'

Not that it seemed to matter to him.

'How long did you think you could keep your scheme quiet?' I said. 'Once or twice I could buy. But when you keep going back, no matter how tight your operation is, there's going to be a crack sooner or later. Maybe a family that isn't intimidated. A wife who won't be kept quiet by her husband. A husband who's been caught before, doesn't see your dirty pictures as such a big threat.'

'You're wrong,' McAllister said. 'We do our homework. Our husbands are all kosher. Clean peckers, the lot of them – at least as far anyone knows, which is what counts. These are gentlemen of standing in the community. They all have very good reasons to avoid bad publicity. And our Tina could tempt a saint. She was truly wonderful at her art.' He shook his head in wonder. 'I've got pictures that would shock you.'

'Alpha Security organised that side of it,' I said. 'A full-service operation.'

McAllister talked to the ceiling again. 'Roker thinks we're just scamming the husbands for fifty thou'. The real game's just between me and Ray.'

He still hadn't told me why they'd buried Tina Brown.

'There's no foolproof caper,' I said. 'Sooner or later your racket is going to come unravelled.'

'Not the way we work,' McAllister said. 'We take very great care. The thing isn't going to come out. Ever.'

'Maybe it won't be the families,' I suggested. 'Maybe the thing will be brought down from the outside. You're looking at proof of that right now.'

'I'm looking at bad luck. Unlikely to recur. And now that the Slater girl is back and telling her mates that nothing happened do you think anyone will keep stirring?'

'Eagle Eye will keep stirring,' I promised, 'until you and the hobgoblin are hatching your schemes behind bars.'

'I tremble,' McAllister said. 'Truly I do.'

'Why keep going back?' I asked. 'You must have made a stash already. Whatever you say about the thing being tight you know it must crack sooner or later. Are you just greedy, Paul?'

McAllister thought that one through. He pursed his lips and gazed into space and for a while I thought he wasn't going to answer. But then he looked at me and gave me his conclusion: 'The fact is,' he said, 'I enjoy it. I like to see those families pee their pants. I like to see Daddy's face when we show him the pictures, when he realises that he's responsible for his kid being targeted.' He gestured around the room. 'I like it when the kids are here. Spoiled brats seeing the world in a new light. The Hanlon girl was a treat. She got it into her head that we were sex fiends, out to rape and murder her. She wet her pants on the bed upstairs. It wasn't difficult to get her to put on a convincing tone when she called her parents. It was wonderful stuff.'

I thought it through. Gave him my conclusion.

'McAllister,' I said, 'you're a piece of shit.'

He nodded in agreement. Didn't care.

I nattered on but McAllister just smoked and ignored me. Time dragged. It was getting cold in the parlour. Luckily I was used to crashing at Eagle Eye. Two and a half hours had gone by and I was beginning to wonder whether Child had perhaps got involved in an accident or had had a stroke, or maybe got religion and wasn't coming back. Wishful thinking. At twenty to eleven I heard the Merc pull up outside.

When Child came in he had the Slater card file. He hadn't needed to search. Picked it straight off my rolltop. It couldn't have taken him more than five seconds to spot it, five minutes to check that the file was the only thing he needed. I made a note to be less tidy in future. Whatever future there was.

Child went through to the kitchen to crack a beer then came and sat on the sofa arm whilst McAllister flicked through the paperwork – the telephone numbers, addresses and hotel bills. Not so much, really. Nothing that looked irreparable to him.

He closed the file and looked up.

'Is that it?' he said. 'You were going to bust us with this?'

'It's more than enough,' I said.

McAllister turned to Ray Child.

'Any trouble?'

Child sneered.

'None. Snoopy's partner stayed home. His lucky day.'

McAllister stood up.

'That's good,' he said. 'No mess at their place. Better that way.'

He gestured to me with the gun. The wavy stuff again. Up and down. Very casual. Like he was inviting the dog out for a piss before bed.

'Second time lucky,' he said. 'I think we can finalise things this time.' He looked at me. His eyebrows floated like cumulus clouds under his golden locks. 'Unless you've any other little ruses to slow things down.'

I was out of ruses.

'Good,' McAllister said. 'So let's take a walk. And one funny move and I'll pop you. You understand, Flynn?'

I understood. McAllister tilted his head towards the door.

'Go out, Ray,' he said. 'Cover us.'

Child looked at me. 'You're going to dig this time, Flynn,' he said. 'Exercise is good for you.' He laughed and headed through the door.

Everyone's a comedian when they've got a gun.

CHAPTER FORTY

Child went out first. McAllister followed behind me, out of reach and out of Child's line of fire in case I did something stupid.

I didn't think of anything stupid to do.

Once we were all outside Child pointed his flashlight at the ground and walked ahead of us to the gate. McAllister stayed two yards behind me, lighting our footsteps with his torch. Off we went. Back to the woods.

Heigh ho.

We didn't make it.

I'd got ten paces clear of the cottage when McAllister yelled fit to scare your granny's pants off. His flashlight dropped. I turned and saw him going down sideways as a silhouette pulled the shotgun out of his hands then stepped sideways out of the doorway's light. The gun snapped up, pointing at me. I hit the deck. Child turned by the gate but all he could see were shadows. A voice yelled at him to drop his weapon.

Child's answer was to loose off two shots like bombs going off. Shot fizzed over my head and smacked into the side of the cottage. The parlour window exploded. Child pumped the weapon to refill the chambers but he never pulled the triggers. The shadow rose from its crouch by the door and two booms shattered the night so close to my head that they nearly took my hair off. Child went backwards and down. By the doorway McAllister was rising up, ready to come back into the game, but whatever had hit him had hit hard. He moved too slowly. As he lurched in the Mossberg was lifted clear and its stock came down on the back of his neck with a force that nearly put him through the ground. He lay there face down, groaning. Out by the gate Child was face up and quiet.

I stood up, feeling to see which side my hair had parted. My ears were ringing like the bells at a vicarage orgy.

'Am I late for the show?'

Shaughnessy's voice was faint through the cacophony.

He walked past me to Child.

'Late?' I said. 'You nearly missed the finale.'

McAllister was trying to get up but his heart wasn't in it. I walked across and put my foot on his back. Pressed hard. It was unlikely that he had another weapon but there was no point taking chances.

Shaughnessy retrieved Child's flashlight and checked the body. Came back. The way he ignored Child's gun saved me a question.

'Looks like your pals were about to cut up rough,' Shaughnessy said.

'They told me we were just going for a walk,' I explained.

Shaughnessy smirked.

'They have a spot,' I said. 'Up in the woods.'

McAllister was still squirming under my foot and I was still pressing. My leg was beginning to cramp but I'm tough. The pressure held.

'Watch his jacket,' Shaughnessy said. 'Linen's hell when you crease it.'

I lifted my foot and stooped to take an arm. Shaughnessy stayed clear so that McAllister couldn't make a grab at him, but McAllister was not in a grabbing state. He managed some words but he let me haul him back into the cottage without resistance. Shaughnessy tossed me a pair of cuffs. Plastic. Strong as steel. The cuffs help occasionally with citizen's arrests. Our arrest technique was that I kicked his ankles out and Shaughnessy pressed on his head and he went down on his arse by the wall. I got his wrists in the cuffs and looped them around a central heating pipe. The pipe wouldn't stop a determined man, but I rooted around and cut the cable off a vacuum cleaner. Used it to bind his arms and ankles. Then I rooted again and snipped the TV cable, added more loops. Electric cabling has many uses. By the time I'd finished McAllister wasn't going anywhere, with or without the central heating.

Once he was trussed up I relieved him of my mobile phone whilst Shaughnessy dialled 999 and informed the operator we had a shooting incident. He had our location ready when the operator asked. The advantage of not riding in a car boot.

I satisfied myself that McAllister was trussed and weaponless. He'd kept quiet for a bit but as I finished he looked up.

'I'm going to kill you, Flynn,' he snarled.

I guess he'd forgotten that that was what he was trying to do in the first place. I considered pointing it out. Decided against it. By the time McAllister was free to do any revenge killing he'd have to chase me with his Zimmer frame. I'd have a Zimmer too, but mine would have racing treads.

'McAllister,' I said, 'do you know the first thing they're going to do to you in jail?'

He looked at me.

'They're going to cut your hair,' I said.

Petty, but it felt good.

We took a look around the cottage.

An upstairs bedroom had a metal bed with a sleeping bag on top.

The floor was littered with food wrappers. A chamberpot was pushed into the corner. Alongside the sleeping bag was a metal chain and two large padlocks. The chain would have been secured to the iron bedstead. The other end was probably around Rebecca's neck. Five or six plastic fasteners were scattered on the mattress. Ties for Rebecca's hands when they left her. We looked in the second bedroom. Empty. Nothing to show that Tina Brown had been babysitting, which tied in with what I now knew - Rebecca had been on her own. Child probably called once a day to feed and water her.

'How many have they had here?' Shaughnessy asked.

'Probably just Rebecca and the Hanlon girl,' I told him. 'But McAllister had long-term plans. My guess is he planned to run his scheme a couple of times a year. That's one to two million a year, tax-free. Not a bad earner.'

Shaughnessy pursed his lips. 'All revolving around the fact that the families keep quiet afterwards.'

'Repeat business,' I said. 'McAllister thought he could keep it going forever. Why are the smartest criminals always the stupidest?'

Shaughnessy shrugged. 'Did he say how they kept the families quiet?'

'It's what we figured,' I told him. 'Heavy threats backed up by photos of hubby misbehaving. Belt and braces. It almost worked.'

'Photos starring our girl Tina Brown.'

'Yes,' I said. 'But she wasn't in on the scheme. She just thought she was being hired to show business clients a good time. She knew nothing about the blackmail. Or the abduction.'

We went back downstairs.

'Do we know where Tina is?'

'Let's take a walk,' I said.

I checked McAllister again but the way I'd tied the knots he was going nowhere. I wasn't thrown out of the Boy Scouts for nothing.

We took the flashlights and went out through the garden, giving Child's body a wide berth. Crime scene contamination and all that.

We went back into the woods and I took Shaughnessy up the hill to the place where Child's spade was sticking out of the ground. I shone the light on the mound of earth beside it.

'Poor woman,' Shaughnessy said. 'What did she do to get in their way?'

'She found out,' I said. 'She was the thing McAllister is denying – the flaw in his perfect scheme.'

'He's denying that his scheme's gone bust?'

'He figures it's just bad luck,' I said. 'Maybe it was. First he had bad luck with Tina Brown then he had bad luck with us.'

'An unlucky kind of guy,' Shaughnessy said.

'McAllister thought he had the whole thing covered,' I said. 'Take the kid, take the money, then shackle the family by blackmailing the husband. A perfect tie-up. McAllister missed just the one flaw. He didn't keep Tina isolated. He wouldn't have made that mistake again.'

'The question is how did Tina find out?' said Shaughnessy.

'I need to talk to Larry Slater,' I said. 'The police will get it anyway but I want to hear it from the man himself. Maybe Larry will talk when he realises that he got Tina killed.'

We gazed down at the grave, barely visible in the torch light.

The half-dug hole next to it was harder to look at. Shaughnessy didn't ask and I didn't say.

CHAPTER FORTY-ONE

Blue lights strobed through the trees as we walked down. When we came out into the lane two East Sussex patrol cars and two vans were pulling up a hundred yards short of the cottage and an armed response squad was dispersing behind cover.

One of them yelled at us to identify ourselves. I yelled back that it was all over. The bad guys were out of action. The cops were not the trusting types. They brought me and Shaughnessy forward and patted us down under the muzzles of a dozen semi-automatics. Then they had us wait with our hands on a patrol car roof while four of them moved through the cottage garden and went inside the building. A couple of minutes later they gave the all clear. A guy introduced himself as the squad sergeant and told us to start talking.

We handed him our IDs. Gave him the gist of what had happened and told him about the body up in the woods. He wasn't interested in the woods. He was focussed on whether there was going to be any more shooting. I reassured him, asked what McAllister had said for himself.

'Nothing,' the sergeant said. 'He's clammed up.'

I grinned. 'The guy's waiting for his lawyer. Sign of a guilty conscience.'

They radioed in the details and called for support and once the cops had decided that the scene was safe they relaxed. Two of them stayed in the house with McAllister. They gave me and Shaughnessy the back seat of a car each. I didn't know if we were arrested or not so I guess that meant we weren't. It was nearly eleven thirty.

I pulled out my phone and saw three missed calls. One number. I dialled.

'Bel,' I said, 'I got caught up here.'

'Caught up?' There was an edge to her voice. We hadn't spoken in nearly forty-eight hours. And our night out was well and truly in the sink. Change of plans was nothing new to Arabel but I should have called before I rushed off to Kent. I apologised and told her that things had blown up fast. She'd see how much they'd blown up when she saw my face and my new wheels.

'Another fun night with the detectives,' Arabel said. 'Are you going to make it at all tonight?'

I looked at the uniforms milling around outside the car.

'No,' I said. 'I'll be tied up for a while.'

I promised I'd call her tomorrow. We'd set something up. I threw in a sweetener and told Arabel that Rebecca Townsend was safe.

Arabel's voice lifted. 'You got her, Flynn?'

'She's safe back home,' I said.

There was a pause. 'What about the bad guys?'

'We got the bad guys,' I said. 'We're just tidying things up.'

The news must have passed muster in Arabel's valid-excuse almanac because her voice softened. 'Be careful, babe. I don't need you to get hurt.'

I was touched. Wait till she saw the Citroen.

'It's all over,' I said. 'I won't get hurt.' I didn't mention my face.

I closed the line and cleared my text inbox whilst we waited. The single text there had served its purpose. The one saying that Shaughnessy was planning to call in at the office to check the Slater file. The one that took Ray Child back to London and bought me the reprieve.

Shaughnessy and I don't text each other. I'd sent the text to myself from Lucy's phone.

Neither were we the types to chase off to a remote farm where someone might be waiting to spring a trap. We always have backup. It's usually on scene, but tonight things had happened too fast and I took a risk I shouldn't have. I'd had a tug on the line that couldn't be ignored. I'd briefed Shaughnessy on where I was going and he agreed to wait for my call. If he didn't get it by eight p.m. he'd come to the farm. If there was nothing at the farm he'd go back and wait at the office until one of the bad guys showed up there.

The clever scheme didn't paper over the fact that I'd misjudged things. I'd expected trouble at the farm but I didn't expect to walk right into McAllister's gunsights. And if something went wrong I expected the action to stay at the farm, where Shaughnessy would gatecrash when I didn't call back. The phoney text ruse to send one of the bad guys chasing back to the office if I ended up in trouble looked more desperate the longer I sat in the patrol car. What if McAllister had decided to do the dirty deed first before checking out Eagle Eye's offices? I'd caught a break I didn't deserve when he decided he needed me alive in case of complications.

More headlights approached and suddenly the lane was crowded. Two plainclothes men appeared and were shown around the garden. They spent a while there and then came over to the cars. Asked us to step out. The man in charge introduced himself as DCS Skinner of the East Sussex police. His buddy was DS Parch. He asked to see our IDs again. Skinner was a stocky guy in his mid-fifties with a taut face halfway to fat. I recognised a lifestyle thing. His eyes were smart, though. He listened to a rerun of our story and then the two of them went back to take a look at the house. McAllister's conversational skills must not have improved because they were back out in ten minutes. Skinner was trying to figure which way to play this. We were going to be taken in. Private detectives don't go around shooting people no matter how the heat turns up. Skinner had a mess that only a good deal of paperwork could salve. He nodded towards the woods.

'Show me,' he said.

We picked up a couple of flashlights and set off back into the trees with two SOCOs carrying portable lighting. When we got to the spot Skinner took a gander, careful not to disturb things. It didn't take him long to recognise the mound of earth for what is was.

'You say this is a woman?' he said.

'Her name's Tina Brown. She was mixed up in this but we don't yet know exactly how. Apparently she became a liability to McAllister. He decided that she needed to be silenced.'

'Don't yet know?' Skinner was sharp. 'Are you two figuring on carrying on with this? Am I interrupting something here?'

'We just want to close a few loose ends.' I said.

Skinner looked at his sidekick then moved up to me and his eyes in the lights weren't friendly.

'Consider the case closed,' he said. 'If I believe your little tale you've done a nice job of digging out some nasty people. It would have been much nicer, of course, if the nasty people were all still alive. If there are any loose ends we'll be taking care of them now.'

'No problem,' I said. 'You'll get everything we have.'

'Technically,' he said, 'I need to arrest you both. You'll need to spend the night in our hospitality suite whilst we check out your story and decide how the shooting will be played.'

'No problem,' I said. 'You going to cuff us?'

'I'll think about it,' Skinner said. We walked back down to the cottage.

Skinner went through the arrest formality and sat us in the back of separate cars whilst he organised things outside. He didn't say anything more about cuffs. He went into the house and brought out McAllister. Hands cuffed. Must have said something wrong. McAllister was pushed into the back of another patrol car.

Skinner and his partner stooged around for an hour with the SOCOs. At one point Skinner pulled me and Shaughnessy out separately and had us go through the exact sequence of the shooting. Our descriptions seemed to tie in with his notes.

Skinner and his buddy finally put us in their backseat and we drove south in convoy with McAllister's squad car. Twenty minutes later we were in Brighton.

They took us up to the CID room. Skinner sat us in separate interrogation rooms but offered coffees before we went in. Shaughnessy asked for a glass of water. I asked for black, extra strong, plenty of sugar. McAllister was brought through and taken to another room. I didn't hear anything about coffee.

Skinner took my statement and asked me to sign it. Then he told me to sit tight whilst he had another chat with McAllister. Now that McAllister was arrested I guess there was a little more formality behind his refusals to talk. Skinner was in there fifteen minutes getting the *no comment* line. When he came back he grinned a weary grin.

'The bastard wants his lawyer,' he said. 'That's fine by me. We'll have him here first thing tomorrow. My real problem is how to play it with you two.'

'Check us out,' I said. 'There are people who will vouch for us.'

I gave him Karl Dewhurst's name. Karl was a commander in the Metropolitan Police. Skinner raised his eyebrows.

'You were in the Mets?'

'A while back.'

'So why the move to the private sector?'

'There were complications,' I said. 'The job no longer fit.'

Skinner watched me a moment then looked at his watch. 'So now some Metropolitan brass is going to jump out of bed at two o'clock in the morning to vouch for you?'

I grinned. The idea of Karl being pulled from his bed had a certain appeal. Karl and I went back. He would vouch for me all right. He'd just bitch about it for a couple of years afterwards.

Skinner looked at his buddy and made a decision. He walked across to his office to call the Mets and pick up Karl's number. I just hoped Karl was in reach of his phone. Five minutes later Skinner came out. He looked at me in a new way.

'It looks like you've still got admirers on high, Flynn,' he said. 'So how come the best detective inspector they ever had – quote, unquote – with high-up friends, is scratching around as a private investigator?'

'Not enough of the high-ups,' I said. 'They only spread so far.'

'A first-class detective doesn't need a truckload of friends to stay in the job,' Skinner said.

'Call it a character flaw,' I said.

'Commander Dewhurst tells me I should send you straight home to bed,' Skinner said. 'Probably wants me to make your Horlicks and tuck you in. Whereas the standard procedure for a couple of guys who've just shot a man is to keep them behind bars where we can keep an eye on them.' He looked at me. 'What should I do?'

'I don't know about my partner,' I said, 'but I find Horlicks a little sickly. The going home bit would work, though.'

Skinner nodded.

'We need to talk,' he said. 'I want to go right through this thing. Tomorrow.'

'Tell me when you want me in,' I said.

'First thing,' he declared.

'We'll be here,' I promised.

Skinner and his buddy were going to be tied up at the station for the rest of the night but they got us a lift in a patrol car. It dropped us back at the cottage. The garden was lit up with Kliegs but Ray Child's body was gone. A couple of SOCOs were tidying up and a uniformed man was unreeling crime tape across the entrance to the path. The main action had moved up into the woods. Lights flickered through the trees.

It was two thirty. I climbed back into the Citroen. Child had left the keys in the ignition and a wad of chewing gum on the dashboard. ValuDrive could keep the gum. Maybe they'd increase the rental. Shaughnessy's Yamaha was hidden in the trees further down. I gave him a lift and he hopped out as the engine stalled by his bike.

'Give my apologies to Jasmine,' I told him. 'I'm sorry I ruined her evening. You told her that this was an emergency, right?'

Shaughnessy shrugged. 'I only mentioned that your life was in danger.'

I looked at him. Sometimes a straight answer would be fine.

'Tell Jasmine we'll be seeing her,' I said. 'We'll have a day out.'

'I'll tell her,' Shaughnessy said. 'I'll tell her you're still alive, too.'

'Tell her it was you who saved my backside,' I suggested. 'You'll get brownie points.'

Shaughnessy smacked the top of the Citroen. I fired up the engine and started rolling before he could do it again.

'Yeah,' Shaughnessy called after me, 'I like that. I'll tell her I saved your skin – yet again, Eddie.'

But I knew he wouldn't.

Yet again.

CHAPTER FORTY-TWO

I hit the sack at four and stared at the ceiling for two hours. Whenever I dozed off it didn't take. I kept coming awake with images of trees and darkness.

At six I quit trying. I got up and pulled on my running gear and headed out into a still spring morning. I did three laps of the park, deadly slow, then added another to prove I still had willpower. Pushed up the pace until I was finally overtaking the first of the morning runners. When I got back to the Sun Gate I was gasping like a bulldog in a sauna. I kept up a jog for appearances but by the time I was inside the door and climbing the stairs the act was over. I barely made it to the top. I stood for twenty minutes under a lukewarm shower and let needles of water batter my head. My cheek had swelled up and the water stung.

I looked in the mirror and decided that the thing needed a couple of stitches. Made do with Savlon and a plaster. I called Shaughnessy then drank a half-litre of orange juice and headed out into bright sunshine.

The Citroen went through its start-up routine and limped away south against the flow of rush-hour traffic. I began to feel half human. Even the shit-heap's asthmatic progress was a little less depressing in the sun.

I was in Brighton by eight thirty. I found a café a block from the police station and gave Shaughnessy the location. Then I boosted my spirits and cholesterol with a full English. It was the first thing I'd eaten in twenty hours. The fry-up slid down as if bacon grease was the new super-lubricant. I was mopping up with the last slice of bread when Shaughnessy came in. He ordered fruit juice and watched me like a disapproving aunt. I called the police station and confirmed that Skinner was waiting, then we paid up and left.

A uniformed woman took us up to the CID room. As we pushed through the swing-doors I spotted a face through the half-open door of a holding room and stopped dead. On the far side of a metal table James Roker's expression betrayed the ugly mood of someone who's been hauled out of bed at the crack of dawn. I'd given Skinner the details of Alpha Security's involvement and I guess he'd read our file. Roker had a few tricky questions to answer. Skinner's buddy Parch was in the room with him. I stopped a moment at the door. Our policewoman escort tried to keep me moving but I resisted until Roker saw me. He gave me a look.

It was going to take more than looks.

'How's it going, Jimmy?' I said.

'Fuck you, Flynn.'

Some people you can never talk to.

'Have you told them how you set it up?' I said. 'Did you show them the dirty movies? Those guys with Tina?'

Roker raised a hand and gave me an emphatic bird.

Spirit.

I threw in something to dampen it.

'Have they told you that they've dug Tina up?' I was making an assumption but I was on safe ground. 'It's a murder rap now, Roker. I guess that's the chance you take when you work dirty jobs. My advice is go for Queen's Evidence.'

Parch had jumped up and was slamming the door before an all-out war got going. The last I saw was Roker giving me the bird again but I knew by the feeling he put into it that he understood his situation. As we walked away the door opened again and Parch skipped out of the room to escort us across to Skinner's office. He gave me a filthy look but said nothing.

Skinner kept us two hours, going over the details. Parch came in for part of it. He'd read our file whilst Skinner had been at the morgue viewing the body they'd brought out of the woods. The two had been on the job since they'd first arrived at the cottage last night.

Skinner confirmed that the body was Tina Brown's. I'd known it but it was still a blow. Somewhere along the way Tina had become our adopted client. I'd hoped to see her safe and preferably innocent, back home along with Rebecca Townsend. Life isn't like that. I was going to have to call Sammy.

We went through everything, end to end. I took them through Paul McAllister's scheme and the part Alpha Security had played. In the end, Skinner had everything they needed to go back and continue their chats with both McAllister and Roker. He sat back and puffed his cheeks.

'This could have gone on for a while,' he said. 'If you can keep the families quiet there's no reason a racket like this couldn't run indefinitely.'

'That's what McAllister thought,' Shaughnessy said. 'Another guy who thinks he's invented the perfect crime.'

'McAllister probably still thinks he was unlucky,' Skinner commented.

I nodded. 'He'd be right. You wouldn't expect some upstart college girl to blow the whistle on her friend's disappearance when the family are denying everything. And McAllister didn't expect the problem with

Tina Brown. So I guess he was unlucky. But sooner or later something similar would have happened, because McAllister wasn't going to stop until something did come apart. He didn't see that that was the real flaw in his scheme.'

'So how did it go wrong with Tina Brown?' Skinner asked.

'Larry Slater is the one who knows that,' I said.

Skinner nodded and flipped his notepad shut. He was scheduling a trip to see the Slaters later in the day once they'd cleared this end. They'd have Larry's story then.

Skinner finally turfed us out and we headed back to town. I was back at Chase Street just after midday.

As I parked the ZX on Gerry Lye's spot a little guy with a cord jacket and clipboard was prodding the bones of the Frogeye. The insurance company was quick off the mark. I identified myself as the owner.

'Bit of a mess,' the guy told me.

You can't fool these assessors.

'Yeah,' I said. 'A write-off. Unless you know a good paint shop.'

The guy looked at me po-faced. He was one of those people who only recognise humour when it comes from their own lips. 'I'll put in the report and then we'll see,' he told me.

'Sure,' I said, 'but I assume it will be a write-off.'

He stayed noncommittal. 'The company makes the decision,' he said. 'I just confirm the condition of the vehicle.'

I gave him aghast.

'Decision? You think they can resurrect this?'

'That's not for me to say, Mr Flynn.'

I looked at the guy. I'd had assessors before. They're usually working mechanics from the body shops. It looked like this insurance company had its own department dedicated to stupidity. *Stupid* was the only way you could categorise a guy being cagey about a heap of ashes. But what the hell did I care? If the insurance company wanted to try and resurrect the Frogeye they were welcome. The guy knew and I knew that the car was dead. I turned and walked away.

I had more important business.

The day had topped out at eighteen degrees. Spring was finally here. We drove up through Cricklewood and came out on the North Circular. I decided to brave the din of the Citroen's blowing exhaust and let cool air in but when I tried to wind the window down it seized after six inches. If I forced it further the mechanism would break and leave it permanently open. I wound it back up. Tried the fan in the hope that it might have cured itself. Got the same wash of warm air as yesterday.

We turned off the North Circular and drove along the fence that protected HP Logistics. The barrier was up, just like last time. Unlike last time I didn't make the courtesy stop and even the Citroen was fast enough to outrun the pensioner.

We parked outside the maintenance entrance and went up the stairs.

Godmotherzilla was still manning the defences. She looked up as we came in and I guess she must have recognised me because she came up from behind her counter as if she'd been stung in her main target area.

Trouble is, when you're big you're not fast. We were past her and into Harold Palmer's office before she could tear off even a couple of my limbs. She came huffing behind but I slammed the door and put my back to it and after a few seconds she got the message and backed off. We were in.

Palmer had jumped out of his own chair and was stood like a bull in the arena watching us with popping eyes. I noticed that his panoramic window had been replaced.

I gave him Sam Sneer and waited.

'What the hell is this?' Palmer said. 'I'm calling the cops!'

He reached for his phone.

'You'd better listen first,' I told him.

He paused.

'That was a mistake,' I said.

He gave me his own sneer. His was better. 'What the hell are you talking about? Get out of my office.'

I waited. Palmer waited too.

'You'd made your point,' I said, 'and I'd made mine. Better we'd just left it at that.'

'I still don't know what you're talking about, Flynn. Now get the hell out of here or I make the call.'

'I'm talking about knowing when to stop. I was out of your life. No threat to your little scheme to get your haulage contract.' I gave him a grin. 'A company called Fashion-Ex. We dug out their name.'

Palmer shook his head and came round to go chest to chest.

'Flynn, you're full of shit. HP's business is nothing to do with you. You declined our commission.'

'That's because I declined to work your illegal scheme,' I said. 'I walked away. It would have been better if you'd just left it at that.'

Palmer moved an inch forward. 'What are you saying?'

'I'm saying you shouldn't start fires you can't put out.'

Palmer couldn't hold back the sneer. 'So how's your toy car running?' he said. He was leaning forward now, trying to push me back. I stayed put.

'As you probably know,' I said, 'the car's not running very well at all.'

Palmer laughed. 'A pity. I hear it was a vintage.'

I stared into his eyes. 'That was a stupid thing to do, Harold.'

The laugh shifted to a smirk. 'I don't know what you're talking about. Are you accusing me of something, Flynn?'

'You had to have the last shot,' I said. 'But I guess it's the kind of man you are. Vindictive. The trouble is, that kind of thing can rebound.'

'Are you accusing me?'

'You burned my car out of spite because I wouldn't work your little scheme with Fashion-Ex. Yeah, I'm accusing you.'

'Prove it! Prove there was a scheme with Fashion-Ex.' His eyes closed up suddenly. 'Are you taping this?' he said. 'Is that it? Are you trying to incriminate me? Do you think I'm an idiot, Flynn?'

I shook my head. 'I'm not taping anything, Harold. This is just between us.'

'Then take this as just between us - you've got nothing that proves anything, Mr Met-Reject. Nothing about Fashion-Ex and nothing about your poxy little car.'

'Did you find someone else to steal your info?'

Palmer laughed again and stood back, shaking his head.

'You're a joke, Flynn. I'm not telling you anything. But yeah, we're ready with our bid. And yeah, we have all the information we need. With or without your help. There's always someone will do a job.'

I grinned. 'Yes,' I said. 'I guess there is.' The thought suddenly hit me that Alpha Security would have been the ideal firm for Palmer's dirty work.

I stayed on the main issue. 'You're in trouble if you don't get that contract, Palmer,' I said. 'You'll have a lot of units idle.'

'We're going to get the contract, Flynn. Believe me.'

'Unless your illegal spying game gets out.'

Palmer sneered. 'Get out of here, Flynn! If you let one whisper of "illegal" out onto the street I'll sue you for everything you have. How come it needs two of you to come threaten me?' He looked at my companion. 'You're a real talker, mate,' he said. 'The two of you make a good act.'

I turned to the guy at my side. 'Do you need to talk?' I said.

He looked at me. Shrugged his shoulders. 'No,' he said. 'I've heard enough.'

Palmer looked from one to the other of us. 'What is this?' he said. He looked back at the guy.

The guy handed Palmer a card. Palmer scanned it. And his expression changed.

The card wasn't Eagle Eye's. The name on it was Andrew O'Connor, Purchasing Director, and it bore the logo of Fashion-Ex. Andrew had heard all he needed. He didn't need to say anything. Not even *Save the postage on the bid*, which personally I would have thrown in. But Palmer's pop-eyed look told us that he understood that he would be wasting his stamps.

We left him to it and walked out.

Rhino glared at us from behind her counter. I gave her a cheery smile. She'd soon have something to glare about.

We got back into the Citroen and Andrew O'Connor blew out a whistle.

'We owe you, Mr Flynn,' he said. 'They were right about our contract policy. The second-lowest bidder. If they'd put in the rigged bid we would have swallowed it. We'd have had Palmer running our logistics for the next two years. Working with criminals we can do without.'

'Just a little tit for tat,' I said. 'We were going to keep our nose out, but Harold tipped the scales.'

O'Connor shook his head. 'Incredible. To think he burned your car. Wouldn't you think a firm like HP would be above that?'

'An organisation stoops to the level of its highest officers,' I said. 'In this case they had to stoop a long way.'

O'Connor smiled. 'How were you so sure it was Palmer who had your car torched?'

'It would never have occurred to me,' I said. 'We've had some far more likely suspects on our plate recently. It was just a face. In the wrong place.'

We were back at the gatehouse. The same old guy came out and pressed the button for the barrier with a scowl on his face. HP were a company of scowlers.

Behind the guy, through the glass of the security building, I saw the face I'd seen at the Podium two nights back, just before the Frogeye went up. Palmer had set his security man on me with a little out-of-hours assignment. The guy must have followed me that night and seen his chance to go for the Frogeye while I was at the club. When I recalled where I'd seen the Podium face I knew who'd burned the Frogeye. It had taken a day or two for the image to click, but eventually it did. The torching wasn't down to McAllister after all. The joke was that Harold Palmer had unwittingly turned up the heat on McAllister's operation. Probably it made no difference. Events have a momentum of their own, but I like to think that Palmer helped us move faster on McAllister.

As the barrier lifted, the guy behind the glass looked up and spotted me. I saluted and was returned a look of surprise. The guy hadn't expected to see me again. Knowing HP Logistics' shaky financial condition, he'd probably be scanning the job pages in a couple of weeks.

Maybe he could try for insurance assessor.

At three o'clock I was back in the office.

Shaughnessy was working on some stuff that had fallen behind. Lucy was out. I was at a loose end, lacking the file to close off the Rebecca Townsend job and not in the mood to go back to my company-exec telephone trawling.

I'd already called by at Gina Redding's and told her that her commission was closed. Explained that Eagle Eye hadn't been part of Rebecca's reappearance. Gina didn't care. What mattered was that the girl was okay and that Gina had done her duty. Without Eagle Eye she could have done nothing. The second thing she'd been pleased to hear was that Rebecca's abductors had been caught, though I don't know if "caught" quite covered Ray Child's predicament.

I'd angled my Herman Miller way back and was reclining in an indecisive daze behind my desk when Shaughnessy came through and flopped into a club chair.

'Are you going to talk to them, Eddie?' he asked.

I nodded. 'I want to close off the Tina Brown thing. I figure Larry will talk now.'

Shaughnessy looked sceptical. 'The track record isn't good,' he said.

'Slater already knows he's going to have to give everything to the police,' I said. 'He's the closest link to Tina Brown. He can't keep the thing quiet any more.'

We heard steps on the stairs. The outer door opened and Lucy came trotting through.

'Hey, you guys are heroes! You got the girl.'

'We didn't get the girl, Luce,' I pointed out. 'The Slaters paid the ransom and Rebecca was sent home. It was nothing to do with us.'

'But you got the villains,' she said. 'You've stopped this happening to anyone else.'

'That's true,' I said. 'It's not quite what Gina Redding was looking for, but she seemed happy.'

'Happy enough to pay the bill?' Lucy's eye was on the bottom line.

'She's happy enough,' I said.

'Great. So we can pay the water people. Maybe even me.'

'Sure,' I said. 'We'll pay you everything, Luce, maybe a bonus.' I was throwing money around today.

Maybe my insurance company would even throw some money my way and I could get some new wheels, save the rental that was draining into ValuDrive's pockets for the privilege of driving their shit-heap.

The phone rang in the outer office and Lucy went to take it. She came back in a hurry.

'It's Jean Slater,' she said.

Life never stops surprising you. Shaughnessy and I looked at each other.

I reset my Herman Miller and went out to take the call.

If I was expecting to hear grateful on the other end I was in for a surprise. I heard panic.

'Mr Flynn?' Jean Slater's voice was urgent. 'Something's happened. We need to see you.'

CHAPTER FORTY-THREE

The Citroen stalled twice before I got to the street but I coaxed it back to life and progressed on three and a half cylinders towards Swiss Cottage. I tried to jump the crawling traffic on the main road but whenever I put my foot down I hit a flat spot. The Citroen bucked and lost power and the slow traffic overtook me with horns blasting. Twenty five minutes of white-knuckle cursing got me to Hampstead.

The house door opened before I was out of the car. Tears streaked Jean Slater's face as she urged me in to where Larry was sat in the lounge. I looked at him. Yesterday's assertiveness was absent. Now Jean was the one making the play. She didn't wait for me to ask.

'Rebecca's gone,' she said.

She picked up a sheet of paper from the coffee table. It trembled in her hand as she handed it over. Larry stayed quiet on the sofa, his face a mixture of disapproval and confusion. Two sentences were scripted in red felt-tip across the paper:

Pretend I'm OK. That always works.

'We thought she was sleeping,' Jean said, 'but when I went into her room I found the note.'

'Have the police been to see you yet?' I asked.

She shook her head. 'They told us they would be here this afternoon or early evening.'

'Did they tell you what they wanted to talk about?'

Jean nodded wearily. She was still staring at the note in my hands. 'They know about Rebecca's abduction. They've caught the people responsible.'

I nodded. 'They've got the main guy. A man named McAllister.' I looked from the note to Larry Slater. The name still produced no reaction.

'What you told me yesterday about Rebecca being ill...' I said. 'We're not pretending anymore?' I was looking at Larry but Jean answered for him.

'We're not pretending anything anymore,' she said.

'What has Rebecca been doing since yesterday?'

'Nothing. She just stayed in her room.'

'Did she come out for meals?'

'She's hardly eaten since we got her back,' Jean said. 'She only came down for half an hour this morning because my sister called.'

Kathy Pope.

'Does your sister know what's been going on?'

Jean shook her head. 'She was here before we got the call from the police. We were still trying to keep it quiet. Kate noticed that Rebecca looked off-colour but we told her that she was recovering from flu.'

'What else did Rebecca do today? Did she mention going out?'

'No. She's just stayed in her room listening to her music. She wouldn't let me in to talk. She didn't eat lunch.'

'How has she reacted to what's happened?'

Jean looked away. 'I thought she was okay. She was emotional at first when they brought her back. She assumed we'd call the police right away. We had to explain how these people could still hurt us if we didn't stay quiet. Rebecca wanted us to tell the police anyway but Larry managed to dissuade her.'

'Rebecca talked to Sadie yesterday,' I said. 'Did she talk to anyone else?'

'She may have done. She had her phone. Now it's switched off.'

'Might she be with Sadie?'

'No. I've already called her. Gina Redding too. She's not with them.'

'When exactly did you last see her?'

Jean Slater tried to pull her thoughts together but her mind hit a dead end.

Larry Slater spoke for the first time, 'Jean went up at twelve. Rebecca spoke to her but wouldn't come out of her room. Then my wife went up about an hour later to break the news that the police had contacted us. That's when she found the note.'

So the girl had been gone three hours.

'Rebecca probably needs some time alone,' I said. 'She may be on her way to Sadie's right now.'

'The note doesn't sound like that,' Jean Slater said. 'I'm frightened to death she might do something foolish. If she was going to see Sadie she would have called her!'

'Has Rebecca ever tried to hurt herself?'

Jean shook her head. 'She's not that kind of girl. She's highly strung but she's sensible.'

Maybe sensible wasn't enough this time. Even the strongest person would find something lacking when they got home from their nightmare to face the Slaters' wall of denials. Before the police contacted them the Slaters had been fixated on hiding the abduction. Maybe for Rebecca being in the house was worse than being alone. My guess was that she'd gone off to take a breather. Anywhere but this house. She probably just needed time to catch up. I didn't know the girl or how badly she was hurting so it was just guesswork. Mostly though, I didn't know why Jean Slater had called me. This was nothing to do with what went before. Eagle Eye weren't in the social services business, just like I'd told Sadie Bannister right at the start. But Jean was looking at me with a desperation in her face that was hard to disregard.

'Is there any way you can find her?' she asked. 'I want her home.'

Needles in haystacks – Eagle Eye's speciality. One girl. The whole of London. Barely a hunch.

I looked at the misery in Jean Slater's face.

'I'll see what I can do,' I said.

The whole of London. One girl. The thing might daunt some. But sometimes you get lucky. My hunch panned out; I found Rebecca in twenty minutes.

I parked the Citroen in the Inner Circle of Regent's Park by the College and walked across the road. The café was just closing up but there were a few customers still inside. Rebecca had a table by the window under the trees. She was nursing a cappuccino that had gone cold a couple of hours ago. She looked up when I came across and her face pulled up a tired smile.

'Mr Flynn,' she said. There was no surprise in her voice. As if she'd taken it for granted that someone would find her. More likely it was just indifference. I sat down.

'How are you doing, Rebecca?'

She took her time, continued watching the world outside. She'd fixed herself up. Her hair had lost yesterday's dull stringiness. It was washed and flowing over her shoulders in a gleaming black river. Her face was what her mother's would have been two decades earlier, skin so clear it was almost translucent. But the unhappiness in her eyes was plain to see. What had happened in the last week had taken its toll.

The two of us watched the trees for a while.

There were a couple of grey squirrels darting around in the branches. I recalled a day trip from Yorkshire when I was a kid, feeding the same squirrels on an autumn afternoon in Hyde Park before heading back to King's Cross.

Different time, different world.

'Did Sadie really go hiring a private eye?'

Now I was the one lost in thoughts. When I pulled my attention back Rebecca was watching me. The clouds had drawn back for a moment. This was the one thing she could hang on to. A world where you could depend on crazy friends.

I hid my grimace in a smile. 'Your friend seemed to have picked up the idea that she could just walk into our office and have half a dozen heavies on your tail. Sadie's an interesting girl.'

The clouds stayed parted. 'Yeah,' Rebecca conceded, 'She's okay. Just a little nutty.'

Nutty! Finally I could give Lucy exact instructions. Keep the nuts out of my office.

'She was going to pay us out of her ninety-day account,' I said. 'I didn't ask how much she'd got in there.'

Rebecca's eyebrows arched as she dug for the information. 'Probably a bit over three hundred?' she told me.

Three hundred! So Sadie would have shafted us after all!

'Luckily,' I said, 'your friend Gina had a little more capital. And she went along with Sadie's idea that someone should find out what you were up to.'

'Yeah,' she said. 'At least someone cared.'

'Your family cared, Rebecca. I think they've been through hell.'

She said nothing.

'Did those people hurt you?'

She shook her head. 'They just chained me up. Left me to rot. One guy really scared me, though.'

Ray Child. Not someone you'd leave your kids with. My guess was that the only thing that had reined him in from harming his charges was that McAllister's scheme depended on the kids staying safe. It would be difficult to keep the families quiet if their children were brought home hurt or raped. The problem was that Rebecca hadn't known about the scheme. Having Ray Child as a jailer for ten days was not an experience any young girl would appreciate.

'Did they feed you okay?'

Now it was Rebecca's turn to grimace. 'Crap. Cold pizza. Sandwiches. Soft drinks. I got so I was nearly throwing up. They had soap and water but the water was cold. And I had to use one of those chamber pots. That was the worst thing. That and the way the guy kept looking at me. I wasn't sure if he was going to do more than just look.'

Ten days with some very unpleasant people. That's a hard thing to put behind you. But the hardest bit had probably been when Rebecca got home and was told to bottle it. That no one must know.

'That must suck,' I said. 'Your parents wanting to keep it a secret.'

Rebecca stayed quiet, staring at her coffee. Her voice was tiny when she spoke again.

'That's all they're interested in. Pretending the whole thing didn't happen. Larry insists that the men will hurt us unless we keep quiet. So I'm supposed to lie to Sadie and Gina and everyone else.'

She looked at me. 'I guess eventually they'll even convince themselves that it never happened. I told Larry no way I was keeping it quiet but my mother got in such a state I felt like I'd be hurting her if I let it out. That's what it comes down to, their own fears. Like they'd got a stolen car back. No scratches. No harm done. Don't call the insurance company. Keep the no-claims.'

The staff were cleaning up behind the bar. The last of the customers walked out. We were alone.

'It's as if what happened didn't matter,' Rebecca explained. 'When you came to the house yesterday we all just lied. Then the same thing when my aunt called this morning. She asked how I was and Larry started this whole thing about how I'd had the flu. We all had to pretend that nothing had happened. It's a little play we have to perform over and over. The story of how nothing happened to me.'

I saw a single tear expanding in the corner of her eye.

'It's all over, Rebecca,' I told her. 'That play won't be running. The secret is out.'

She looked at me.

'The men who took you have been caught. They'd abducted another girl before you and they were planning more. But it's over. There's no longer a threat to your family. No need to keep the secret.'

She said nothing. Tried to take in what I was saying. Then her eyes went back to the world outside. The tear rolled down her cheek and fell.

'Are they really caught?'

'Really. The police have arrested the men involved.'

'Was it you who caught them?'

'We were involved. It's police business now. They'll be calling at your house later and they'll need to talk to you all. They aren't interested in any lies.'

'But it was you who got them?'

We seemed to be stuck on this point.

'You can thank Sadie,' I said. 'She set us on the trail.'

The clouds drew back. The hint of a smile again, but there was still a shadow behind it.

'Will we really be safe? Maybe they can get back at us some time.'

I shook my head. Reached across and took her hand. 'Rebecca,' I said, 'your family are of no interest to these people any more. They only needed to threaten you so that they were free to abduct other kids. That's all changed. The men won't be abducting anyone else.'

'So they'll go to jail?'

I let go of her hand.

'One of them will,' I said. 'The big guy – the one who frightened you – had an accident last night. He didn't make it.'

She watched me.

'It's over, Rebecca,' I repeated.

We waited for a while longer. The light was fading. The staff were moving in on us armed with mops.

'How did you know I was here?' Rebecca asked.

I gave her my Sly Uncle. 'I'm a detective. I analysed your note.'

Her mouth opened wide enough to drive a train through.

'Bullshit!' she said.

These kids!

The woman wiping the table next to us gave us a look.

'There was nothing in my note,' Rebecca hissed. 'I was just angry. I wrote the first thing that came into my head and ran out of the back door. I didn't know where I was going myself.'

'That's what the note told me,' I said. 'That's how I knew where to come. You couldn't charge round to sob on Sadie's or Gina's shoulders because you thought the whole thing was still secret. Seeing them would have make things worse. You ran out with that secret bottled up inside you and nowhere to go.'

She was watching me like I was a mind-reader. One of the skills of the profession.

'I talked to an ex of yours last week,' I explained. Rebecca kept her face straight but her eyes were locked on mine. 'Marcus told me how you always came here to sit and watch the world. To think things through.'

Her eyes drifted. She smiled.

'He also told me to make sure you were safe. He seemed pretty emphatic on that.'

She looked back at me. Her lips stayed clamped.

'I guess,' I said, 'that this whole thing – getting kidnapped, held to ransom – was just the icing on the cake. From what I hear it's been a bad couple of months.'

'Yeah.' She sighed. 'It's been a shitty year so far.'

'I got the impression,' I remarked, 'that Marcus was having the same bad time. Maybe you should talk to him about it. Do you need his number?'

She laughed and rolled her eyes. 'You think I need a detective to give me my boyfriend's number?' she said. 'I'm not that stupid.'

The cafe woman finally pounced and cleared away Rebecca's mug, empty or not. Started wiping the clean table. I sensed a hint.

'Do you need a lift home?' I offered. 'I still want to talk to your father.'

'Yes,' she said. 'That would be great. But he's not my father.'

I said nothing.

We stood up and she turned to me. 'Sadie told me you had this really cute car.'

I gave her my Shit-Eater. Held it wide.

'That Sadie.'

CHAPTER FORTY-FOUR

Jean Slater raced out of the door and smothered Rebecca in a bear hug. You could see the weight come off her shoulders as the girl pushed her face into her neck and wept. No more secrets. When the two of them unclinched I followed them into the house.

Jean offered me a drink. I declined.

'I just need a word with Larry,' I said. 'Then I'm through.'

Jean gestured to the lounge as if she couldn't care less. She and Rebecca walked up the stairs together.

Larry Slater was sat where he'd been two hours earlier but now had the company of a half-empty bottle of scotch. He was easing his own burden in his own way.

'Better go steady,' I said. 'You'll need your wits when the CID arrives.'

He looked up at me.

'You're a persistent guy, Flynn. So where did you find her?'

'Where she often is,' I said. 'Alone.'

Slater watched me. 'I understand you chased these people down.'

'They chased us. It came to the same thing in the end.'

He reached forward and picked up his drink.

'I only wanted to protect Rebecca,' he said. 'Protect my family. The money was nothing. You can always make more.'

'Maybe protecting the family should have started the night you were offered a good time with Tina Brown.'

'Jesus,' Slater shook his head. 'How was I to know what they were up to?'

'You didn't have to know,' I told him. 'I spoke to another family. The guy was cast the same bait. Same place, same woman. He didn't bite. Their child didn't get taken. That guy didn't turn down a night with Tina because he knew anything you didn't, Larry.'

Slater cracked the drink back down onto the table and jabbed a finger.

'Are you preaching at me, Flynn?' he said. 'Because I don't need sermons right now.'

I shook my head. 'Events are the best preachers. You reap what you sow, and all that. And you already know that if you'd kept your hands off Tina Brown then your stepdaughter wouldn't have been put through this.'

'We'll make sure she's all right,' said Slater. 'We're not monsters. Whatever it takes, Rebecca will be okay.'

A somewhat vacuous assurance from a guy showing the unhealthy interest in his stepdaughter recorded in Rebecca's diary. But it was none of my business. Rebecca would handle things from now on in her own way.

'What about Tina?' I said. 'Will she be okay?'

Slater shook his head. 'I don't know what the hell's going on with

Tina.' He looked at me in challenge. 'You tell me. You seem to know it all.'

So the police hadn't mentioned it when they called. Larry still didn't know what we'd found in the woods.

'I'm still trying to square the last details,' I told him. 'The thing that sent McAllister's scheme off the rails.'

'I don't know myself,' said Slater. 'I still don't know how Tina is involved in this whole thing. She told me she knew nothing about Rebecca's abduction.'

'She didn't,' I said. 'Tina's involvement was innocent. As far as she knew she was just being paid to entertain McAllister's business contacts.'

'So she didn't know about the photos? The blackmail?'

'No. That's why she became a liability. When you told her that Rebecca had been taken she reacted without thinking. She ran straight to McAllister and demanded that he let her go.'

Slater sighed and sat forward, hands clasped.

'Fill me in,' I said. 'My guess is that it started that first night in Brighton. You liked what you tasted. Wanted more. Tina had strict orders – no follow-up contact – but you made her an offer she couldn't refuse.'

'She's a stunning woman,' Slater admitted. 'I was out of my mind. I persuaded her to see me again.'

'How many times?'

'Three. Once here in London. Twice back in Brighton.'

It tied in.

'It was the thing McAllister had to avoid,' I said. 'You got to know Tina. You found out who she was and where she lived.'

Slater nodded. 'I dropped her off at her place a couple of times,' he said. 'She was happy with me knowing.'

'Then one day the bomb explodes. Rebecca is missing and you get a call from the bad guys demanding money.'

'That big one with the shaved head came here,' Slater said. 'He actually came into the house. Right where you're standing. Jesus, he was a frightening bastard. You always know there's this underworld operating, but here it was right in my own living room.'

'And they gave you the deal - no police, not during and not after. Child showed you the stuff they'd collected to help the "after" bit.'

Slater's shoulders dropped. 'He laid it all out. If we wanted Rebecca back we kept the police out and paid the money. Then he told me that my job was to keep Jean and Rebecca quiet afterwards. He showed me the movie stills. The stupid thing is that the blackmail should have convinced me that they were serious about returning Rebecca. But I wasn't thinking straight. I saw us handing over the cash and Rebecca staying missing. I assumed Tina was in on it. She denied everything but I didn't believe her.' He grabbed the scotch and drained the glass, rubbed his palms over his face. 'I tried to persuade Tina to help me get Rebecca back. When she played innocent I kind of lost it with her. The next time I tried to call her she was gone.'

'Unfortunately,' I said, 'Tina was telling the truth. But my guess is that she didn't think it through after you confronted her. She just stormed in to see McAllister and threatened to blow the whistle.'

'You think she did that?' Slater said.

'That's why she disappeared,' I told him.

'Oh, shit.' Slater ran his hands through his hair. 'She hasn't answered her phone in a week. I could never catch her at her apartment.'

'Tina went to see McAllister right after you spoke to her. Twenty-four hours later McAllister had solved his problem.'

Slater stared at me. 'Sweet Jesus – surely they didn't...'

'The police identified the body this morning,' I said.

Slater put his head in his hands and shuddered. 'The bastards! And she knew nothing!'

'She knew nothing until you talked to her,' I corrected him. 'She and you were the flaw in McAllister's scheme. His plan depended on you knowing nothing about Tina – she was supposed to remain the anonymous girl in the blackmail pictures – and on Tina knowing nothing about anything. When you talked her into seeing you again you started a crack in the scheme that put Tina right into the firing line.'

Slater's head stayed down as he massaged his face. I left before he looked up.

As I got out of the house my phone rang. I picked up the call.

'Hey babe! You coming to get me?'

'Arabel! Sure I'm coming. Where are you?'

'Still at work.'

'I'll be there when you're out,' I said. 'What are we doing?'

I heard a laugh with an undertone. 'You owe me for last night, babe. I've told the girls you're taking me somewhere expensive.'

'You're looking for a special night?'

'Got it in one, Flynn.'

Something special! I looked at the Citroen and saw that the suspension had dropped further. The rotted exhaust was now dragging along the ground. The result of Child hammering it along that track last night. The thing was a zombie of the auto-world. Not quite dead but only capable of moving in lurches.

'What time are you out?'

'Seven thirty,' Arabel said.

'Come out of the main entrance,' I told her. 'Bring the girls with you. I'll drive by and sweep you away.'

There was a happy laugh from the other end.

'You're the best, babe,' Arabel said.

'Aye,' I said, 'ain't that the truth.'

I killed the line.

ACKNOWLEDGEMENTS

You're holding this book thanks to the vision of two organisations - New Writing North and Business Education Publishers. The people there saw an opening for a fresh imprint within the British crime writing scene dedicated to bringing new - and maybe different - writing to the market. Moth Publishing is the result of that vision and I was lucky enough to be selected as one of their first authors. For their determination to bring their venture to fruition, as well as for their faith in this book and their work to get it into the marketplace I'd like to thank Andrea Murphy of Moth Publishing and Claire Malcolm and Olivia Chapman of New Writing North, together with their production teams.

Writing the book was fun. Polishing it into a form where a reader might also enjoy it felt a little more like work. Considerable help in that task was given by Sarah Porter at Moth, whose ear for what is right and what is wrong has kept out flaws that might otherwise have spoiled things. Imperfections that remain are all mine, and my technique for dealing with these is to ask you to overlook them. If you did enjoy the book, scuff marks and all, maybe we'll meet again...